BROTHERS IN VALOR

Other Military Science Fiction by H. Paul Honsinger

THE MAN OF WAR TRILOGY

To Honor You Call Us

For Honor We Stand

Brothers in Valor

H. PAUL HONSINGER

BROTHERS IN VALOR

A NOVEL OF INTERSTELLAR WAR

The Man of War Trilogy: Book 3

This is a work of fiction. Names, characters, organizations, places, events, and incidents are either products of the author's imagination or are used fictitiously.

Published by 47North, Seattle
www.apub.com
Amazon, the Amazon logo, and 47North are trademarks of Amazon.com, Inc., or its affiliates.

ISBN-13: 9781477830000
ISBN-10: 1477830006

Cover art and illustration by Gene Mollica
Cover design by Ink'd Inc

Printed in the United States of America

To my beloved wife, Kathleen. You are the sine qua non—

of these books, of our family, of my happiness.

None would exist—none can exist without you.

You are the most generous, the most kind, the most wise,

and the most admirable person I know. You have my thanks,

and all my love, from the bottom of my heart . . . forever.

A NOTE FROM THE AUTHOR

For the benefit of lubbers, squeakers, and others unfamiliar with Union Space Navy terminology and slang, there is at the end of this volume a Glossary and Guide to Abbreviations, which defines many of the abbreviations, terms, and references used in these pages.

CHAPTER 1

02:27 Zulu Hours, 9 May 2315

"New contact! Mass detection at bearing three-five-seven mark zero-six-eight. Designating as Hotel eleven and classifying as a definite hostile." Lieutenant Kasparov's announcement from the Sensors Station somehow managed to sound both exhausted and on edge. "Insufficient data for range determination as of yet." He paused to listen to a few words spoken over his headset. "And, sir, this time they're making absolutely no effort at stealth." He paused for a beat. "Arrogant bastards."

"Very well." Lieutenant Commander Max Robichaux, Union Space Navy, captain of the *Khyber* class destroyer USS *Cumberland*, acknowledged the report but let the comment pass, not because it was appropriate—which it certainly was not—but because he heartily concurred. And judging by the quiet murmurs of agreement and occasional grumbled, sulfurous profanity Max could hear from some of the men around him at their stations in the *Cumberland*'s Combat Information Center (CIC), he wasn't the only one. The men had been at their General Quarters stations without a break for nearly seven hours and were a bit on the testy side.

"I suppose one more ship full of rat-faces won't make any difference," Executive Officer Eduardo DeCosta said to the compartment at large, hoping that he was doing a better job of convincing the men than he was of convincing himself. "But, Skipper," he continued at a volume calculated to reach only Max's ears, "if you ask me, it's a show of outright contempt. That Krag skipper is gloating that we're pinned down and don't constitute a threat to him."

Max shook his head, giving the Main Tactical Display yet another once-over. This wasn't his first rodeo. Or his tenth. "No, XO," Max said calmly and quietly, "coming in without stealth is a message, all right, but it's from the commander of this attack group, not that particular skipper, and the message is not one of contempt."

Max rose from his seat and casually took the step and a half necessary to bring him beside the XO's console. He leaned over as if to point out something on one of DeCosta's displays. "Not contempt, Ed. Intimidation. Look at it from their perspective. The Krag know what this ship can do. Even outnumbered and outgunned as we are, we can inflict a lot of damage. This Krag commander sure as hell doesn't want to tangle with humans as aggressive and determined as we were at the Battles of Pfelung and Rashid V B. So, before he faces us in battle, Commodore Squeaky intends to defeat us psychologically. Exhaust our courage. Destroy our morale. Beat us down. *Break* us. Once he does that, blowing us to flaming atoms will be a piece of cake. Or cheese."

DeCosta smiled weakly at Max's feeble joke, sat back in his seat, digested what he had just heard, and rubbed some of the grit out of his eyes. He was exhausted. Everyone was. He met his skipper's gaze, seeing the same mind-numbing fatigue he felt from being at General Quarters fifty-eight of the last sixty-three hours.

"Sir, it might just be working," said DeCosta.

Max had no reply but a barely visible nod. *It just might.*

Since he was standing, Max took the opportunity to look around CIC. The men's energy was flagging. Although he couldn't give them rest right now, Max could give them something that might restore them somewhat. He returned to his seat and used his console to order the galley to deliver sandwiches and candy bars to the men at their stations throughout the ship (everyone already had coffee and other drinks available). A bit of food and sugar would provide some energy for the hours ahead.

They were going to need it.

"Now getting a firm track on Hotel eleven," said Lieutenant Bartoli, the tactical officer, after a few minutes. "Range is just over 7 AU. Course is one-six-eight mark two-eight-five—and it's a pure lubber line. No constant helming, no zigzag, no effort at all to conceal his base course. I might say something about him being an arrogant bastard, but someone beat me to it. Anyway, he's on the deceleration leg of his trajectory, and he's right at the Standard G load for type. He's too far away to get any kind of visual, but based on spectrography of his drive emissions and our rough calculation of his mass, our preliminary classification is one of their heavier destroyers, probably *Dervish* class. It appears that he plans on joining the containment group. The other ships in the containment group, by the way, have also dropped any effort at stealth. We're picking up the full spectrum of EM, mass detection, and IR. No trouble tracking them now, sir." As soon as he stopped speaking, Bartoli looked down and made himself conspicuously busy at his console.

"Mr. Bartoli," Max said in a didactic tone after watching him for about half a minute, "haven't you forgotten something?"

"I don't think so, Skipper," he said.

Max simply looked at him impatiently, his head taking on a slight list to starboard.

"Sir, you can't mean that you want me to, um . . . ?"

"Yes, Mr. Bartoli, I *do* want you to, um . . ." Max said, his voice firm but not harsh. "A ship has joined the enemy formation. That's a major change in the tactical situation requiring that the tactical officer provide a summary for the benefit of everyone in CIC in order to maintain adequate situational awareness. It's not just regulations, but *immemorial naval tradition*." He spoke the last three words in the way an engineer would say "law of physics." "No matter how many times you have said most of it or how unpleasant it may be to say."

"Yes, sir," Bartoli said with resignation. "The *Cumberland* is moored to a 6.4 kilometer diameter Kuiper Belt Object orbiting 75.9 AU from Monroe-Tucker B, the K class primary of an uninhabited system in the Rubrulram sector. Hotels one, two, four, six, seven, eight, and nine, soon to be joined by eleven, make up an eight-vessel containment and search group surrounding us in three dimensions. The containment group consists of one *Barbell* class battlecruiser, one *Crusader* class light cruiser, and six destroyers of assorted classes. The group is now shifting from the Krag's standard seven-ship containment formation to their standard containment formation of eight. We're looking at a cube measuring just over 4 AU between the vertices, with us near the center—the Krag apparently know that we are somewhere near the middle of their enclosure and that we're drifting with the KBO's out here in a matching orbit, or maybe joined with one, but they don't know exactly where.

"The other three hostile ships in this system, Hotels three, five, and ten, are the interdiction group. They're all *Crocodile* class medium cruisers, and there's one of them at each of this system's jump points. So if we manage to escape the Krag Cube of Doom, we'd have to defeat a cruiser with roughly eight times our firepower in order to jump out. And if we can't jump, we can't get home because we don't have enough fuel left to get home on compression drive. That is, unless there's a Standard Hydrogen Corporation filling station out here that I don't know about.

"Oh, and I also have this cheerful news. We're picking up multiple coded data transmissions in the vicinity of the cruisers. Intel and Tactical Sections concur that the transmissions mean that, apparently, each cruiser has filled the area around the jump points with *Jackrabbit* or *Prairie Dog* class sensor drones, so there's going to be no sneaking up on them, even if we're stealthed. The exits are covered.

"On the good side, we are still hidden: trapped but not caught. The Stealth Section reports that all of their systems remain nominal. Thermal stealth functioning at peak effectiveness: the hull is being chilled to 48.3 degrees Kelvin, a perfect match for the temperature of the Kuiper Belt Object we're on. The Krag infrared detectors see only a black bump on this black iceberg floating in all this black space—*this isn't the ship you're looking for; move along.* All ship's systems, including life support, are at minimum thermal output mode to conserve heat-sink capacity, but even latched onto this snowball and dumping as much of our waste heat into it as we can without boiling off the volatiles and giving ourselves away, we're still storing up heat faster than we're dumping it. Our heat sink is at 94.2 percent capacity. Depending on how much stray enemy sensor output our stealth systems have to null or sequester, we've got somewhere between an hour and an hour and a half before we hit the maximum.

"We've been monitoring the Krag search pattern and doing some probability extrapolations. The most likely time until they detect us, plus or minus one standard deviation, is—what a coincidence!—roughly an hour to an hour and a half. Of course, we could catch a break, and it could be two and a half hours when they will have had time to scan every single grid square in the search area, or the Krag could get incredibly lucky and get a solid return off of us five minutes from now. But I'm pretty confident that we've got at least an hour and pretty certain that we've got no more than ninety minutes. It's a flip of the coin as to whether it will be heat-sink saturation or active detection by the Krag that gives us away, but it will be one or the other, no more than ninety minutes from now.

"Of course, once that happens, things get real predictable again. Having detected us, the Krag blow us to flaming atoms *with celerity*. All of those ships launch a full salvo, which means something between twenty-five and forty-two Ridgeback superluminal missiles, depending on whether the ships covering the jump points decide to get in on the action. The missiles will converge from all directions in a time-on-target coordinated attack that will be impossible to evade. Based on their previous missile attack profiles, speed settings, seeker acquisition intervals, and a few other variables, I estimate the time between detection and destruction to be eight minutes and forty-seven seconds, plus or minus twenty-two seconds. The only reason it's so long a time is that the Krag ships are still at pretty long missile range—about 3 AU—so even at superluminal velocities, it takes a while for the missiles to get here. Then it's all over."

Bartoli was working very hard to keep a distinct whipped, beaten, trampled tone out of his voice.

He did not entirely succeed.

"Thank you, Mr. Bartoli, for that oh-so-cheerful news," said Max. "You're a regular ray of sunshine."

"Any time, sir."

The dots representing the enemy ships slowly drifted toward their intended resting places. "Vessels in the containment group don't appear to be in any particular hurry to get where they're going," Bartoli observed. "None is running its main sublight drives at anything over 45 percent thrust. I reckon they know we're not going anywhere."

"Not for the moment, anyway," said Max.

The food arrived. Max and the men in CIC ate their assorted roast beef, ham, salami, and bologna sandwiches; munched potato chips; and consumed their Nebula Nougat, Heath, Milky Way, Mars, Almond Asteroid, and Snickers candy bars. The simple food filled their bellies and fueled their metabolisms, sustaining their bodies so that, if their hearts and minds were up to the task, these men could carry on the fight just a little bit longer. As they ate, the men grimly watched the ships of the containment group vessels reach the positions predicted by Bartoli, enclosing the humans in a giant cube, each side about 600 million kilometers long, with an enemy ship at each of the eight corners, each holding position roughly 500 million kilometers from the *Cumberland.*

Originally Max and his crew had the entire system in which to hide. Now they were hemmed into a space roughly equal to that enclosed by the orbit of Mars in the Sol System. To some that might have seemed like a lot of room, but in space combat it was the equivalent of an infantry company being trapped in a mountain valley. And the Krag weren't done yet. Not by a long shot.

The men knew it. Despite the banter Max could feel their tension ratcheting up to an even higher level as the new formation took shape. He didn't know what it was about that one additional ship, but there was something about being surrounded by *eight* ships that made a man feel much more hopeless than being surrounded by only seven.

Seven ships. Eight ships. Either way, it's pretty damn hopeless. Studying the tactical displays, evaluating the firepower and performance of the ships arrayed against him, and weighing the obviously considerable command abilities of the enemy admiral, Max thought that the odds against him and the *Cumberland* were at least 50,000 to 1.

As soon as this thought occurred to him, he mentally kicked himself for being pessimistic.

In fact, Max's estimate was wildly *optimistic.*

Unknown to the skipper and totally without anything remotely approaching official authorization, an up-and-coming able spacer second class named Nyombe in the Tactical Back Room had run the *Cumberland*'s predicament through the tactical scenario evaluation algorithm on the ship's computer. Known as T-SEA, the algorithm was a sophisticated computer routine that predicted battle outcomes with 95.78 percent accuracy. T-SEA had dutifully stated that the *Cumberland* faced a "highly unfavorable correlation of forces" and calculated that her odds of surviving the encounter were one in 981,966.

Rounded up to a more gossip-worthy "one in a million," this estimate circulated within two and a quarter minutes to every corner of the ship by means of the *Cumberland*'s breathtakingly efficient jungle telegraph, made so much speedier because the duties of many crew members required that they be tied into at least one of the ship's thirty-six voice communication channels or "loops" and were already exchanging information in real time with men in other parts of the ship.

Officially, of course, the crew members on the loops were supposed to limit their communications to official information directly related to the performance of their particular duties. Naval regulations clearly stated that skippers should punish severely all breaches of "loop discipline." In reality, conversation on the loops contained as much gossip as official information, and if a skipper started locking up everyone who breached loop discipline, he wouldn't have anyone left to man the ship.

Short, pithy, and deeply relevant to every man on board, the T-SEA calculation seemed almost genetically engineered to spread over the loops. As the news permeated the ship, so did a feeling of resolute fatalism: a sense that, although the *Cumberland* would fight bravely to the last, the 215 boys and men on board were, at that very moment, living out their final moments. And while like most men, they were apprehensive about coming face-to-face with the mysteries that lie beyond this life, the belief that the ship would soon meet its end also filled the crew with grim determination. If they were going to die, the crew was determined to die well and in the best traditions of the Union Space Navy. The *Cumberland* would go down with her guns blazing and her pennant flying. Her men would die with their boots on.

The skipper and the XO, however, heard none of this. Although Max and DeCosta could tie into any of the ship's loops at any time, they rarely did so. The men at Sensors, Tactical, Intel, and all the other stations that quite literally surrounded the CO and XO in CIC were plugged into the loops every second. And for Max and DeCosta, that was enough because, by listening to what the CIC crew said "over the airwaves," the skipper and the executive officer were "plugged in" to those officers and men and, through them, to the entire ship. The final connection wasn't over an electronic circuit. It was face-to-face, eye to eye, man to man. And in the confines of CIC, those men were close enough to each other to smell each other's sweat.

Ultimately, command and combat are not about the machines with which men fight. They are about the men doing the fighting.

News of the T-SEA estimate had not yet reached the Command Island because the men at the consoles in CIC had not passed on this bit of gossip. Every man in the navy knew that there were things that the skipper and the exec needed to know and things that they didn't. And this information, by tacit but unanimous agreement, clearly fell into the latter category.

"I suspect that this is everyone who is coming to the party," Max said to DeCosta, gesturing toward Hotel eleven. "And while I'm sure it's bound to be the most glittering Krag social affair of the season, I'd very much like to leave before things get too exciting. I'm open to any brilliant ideas you might have for making our exit. In fact, I'll even listen to any not-so-brilliant ones if you've got 'em."

DeCosta shook his head. He would have loved to be the hero by coming up with some genius-level maneuver that would save himself and his shipmates, but his magician's hat was as rabbit-free as Max's. "Well, sir, the only thing that is coming to mind right now is what Commodore Middleton said in his *Handbook for New Warship Commanders.* Remember the chapter titled 'Techniques for Evading an Enemy of Greatly Superior Force'?"

DeCosta's remark earned him Max's best "are you kidding" look. Asking Max whether he remembered something from Admiral Middleton's book was like asking a professor of Alphacen literature whether she could recite any verses from Sok Vong Than's *Lamentations for Angkor Wat*. Middleton, now a fleet admiral and widely admired as an authority on both tactics and leadership, had been Max's mentor for many years. Max idolized him, had practically memorized "Uncle Middy's" famous (but notoriously prolix) book, and could, in fact, recite that volume's famous "Swoop Down" chapter verbatim.

"*The 'Three M's' of evading an enemy of superior force,*" Max quoted, "*are Minutes*—meaning time—*Maneuvering room, and Misdirection.*" Max paused and regarded DeCosta grimly. "We're running very low on the first two."

"But, sir," DeCosta replied, smiling, "you always seem to have an inexhaustible supply of the third."

Misdirection. The third "M." My favorite.

Unfortunately, not only was the *Cumberland* nearly out of minutes and maneuvering room; the men's emotional reserves were also badly depleted, a situation that was not helped by the Krag's practice of firing a missile or two at any particularly promising set of target coordinates generated by their computers. A *thermonuclear* missile or two.

Glancing at the chrono, Max observed that the Krag should be firing again very soon. Just as Max opened his mouth to announce this observation, he saw Kasparov tense.

"Vampire! Vampire! Detection of seeker scans for enemy missiles, Ridgeback type, two sources, designating as Vampire nine and Vampire ten. Bearing one-seven-three mark two-four-two. Range 1.35 AU. Velocity is settling in at . . . 1.5 c."

Sometimes Max hated it when he was right. Especially when being right meant being shot at with highly advanced, superluminal, active multimodal sensor homing, antiship, fusion missiles.

Once Kasparov, the sensors officer, located and classified the contact, Bartoli, the tactical officer, took over responsibility for tracking it and predicting what it would do. Everyone in CIC knew that, at the range from which the missiles were fired, plotting their trajectory would require Bartoli and his team to receive and process the incoming seeker scans from the missiles for just under four seconds.

For four seconds, no one spoke. For four seconds, no one breathed. Those four seconds crawled through these men's awareness as four unbearable eternities stretched end to end, in which each man held in agonizing suspension his expectation of living beyond the end of the current watch.

"Bearing to Vampires changing rapidly," reported Mr. Bartoli, almost joyfully. Born in Mobile, Alabama, on Earth, Bartoli pronounced "Vampire," not with two syllables as "VAM pire," but with three, "VAM pye uh," but everyone was too relieved to notice. The rapid change in bearing meant that Vampire nine and Vampire ten would miss the ship by a large margin. The men of the *Cumberland* would not die.

They would not die, at least, in the next ten minutes.

"I've got enough data points to generate a rough track now," Bartoli said, the pitch of his voice nearly half an octave below where it had been a moment ago. "Closest approach is going to be in the neighborhood of 1.45 million kilometers. No chance their seeker heads will pick us up."

"Very well," Max said. *I've got to do* something. *Maybe there's time for a little misdirection after all . . . like hiding in plain sight.* "Gentlemen, when those warheads detonate at the end of their runs and the effects front reaches the enemy ships, their sensors will be scrambled for about three minutes. I intend to use that effect to cover a sprint right into the middle of the fireball from the nearest warhead. The rat-faces think that warhead explosion just proved we aren't in that particular grid square. And since they know for certain that we're not there, I know for certain that there is where we need to be." There were a few smiles at the odd phrasing, but everyone understood what the skipper meant. "Maneuvering, prepare to make a high-speed run to those coordinates. Stealth, let's get ready to buy ourselves a few more minutes of heat-sink capacity by radiating when the Krag can't detect it. Extend the radiator fins the instant the effects front reaches the enemy and keep them out until just before the fireball cools enough for the enemy to be able to get an IR detection."

Maneuvering and Stealth acknowledged Max's orders. Max scanned the faces of the men at their stations. The faces were still grim, but not as grim as they had been a few moments before. When he met their eyes, he understood that they knew what he knew: this series of maneuvers would not get the *Cumberland* out of the Krag search pattern—they would not get the ship to safety. But they would preserve it from immediate destruction, if only for a little while longer.

It would have to do.

"Probable Krag firing solution computed, Skipper," Bartoli said. "Feeding it to Maneuvering."

"Mr. LeBlanc, how much do you know about Kuiper Belt Objects?" Max inquired.

"I'm just a ship driver, sir, not a planetary scientist, so not much," he answered.

"Then you won't take it amiss if I point out to you that this snowball we're bellied up against isn't just made of water ice, but also frozen methane, ammonia, and other ices, some of which are pretty volatile. So, you might want to plot your breakaway maneuver so as to avoid hitting that thing out there with much in the way of thruster fire, because the heat could cause some of it to flash-vaporize and blow the whole body to smithereens, which—at the very least—would betray our position to the Krag. And, of course, getting out of the debris field might prove to be a more difficult navigation problem than we care to deal with today."

"Point taken, sir," LeBlanc said, smiling. "I'll give you a gentle separation."

"Excellent, Mr. LeBlanc. I knew I could count on you."

"Firing solution received," LeBlanc said a few seconds later. "Course computed."

The minutes passed as the Krag missiles followed their sinuous trajectories, twisting through space along corkscrew-like paths to give their seeker heads the greatest chance of scanning and locking onto a target. The men scarcely breathed, almost as though they were afraid that the Krag homing missiles could hear them.

After what felt like hours but was actually just over ten minutes, Kasparov snapped out, "Detonation! Detonation! Optical detection of thermonuclear explosions at predicted end of missile run. Given the distance and the lightspeed delay, warheads on Vampire nine and ten detonated approximately five seconds ago."

Kasparov rattled off the ranges, bearings, and measured explosive yields of the two explosions and started a countdown clock. Almost half an hour crawled by—the time it took for the electromagnetic radiation from the two 51.4-kiloton Krag thermonuclear warheads, traveling at the speed of light, to reach the eight Krag ships almost 3.5 AU from the center of the enclosure—as the CIC crew sat ready to act, like a loaded and cocked weapon set to fire at a touch to the trigger.

Max could almost hear the men sweat.

Finally the clock reached zero. The electromagnetic radiation from the Krag warhead explosions reached the Krag ships, blinding their sensitive detectors to the fainter emissions given off by a *Khyber* class Union destroyer running for its life.

Max pulled the trigger. "Go, LeBlanc, go."

In a heartbeat, CIC went from tense immobility into brisk, focused activity. Nelson extended the radiator fins, while Chief LeBlanc and the three men under his direction at the Maneuvering Stations expertly maneuvered the *Cumberland* away from the oversize iceberg that had concealed it and then steered the ship through a redline-the-drive-and-make-the-space-frame-groan acceleration/deceleration and course change maneuver that, two minutes and forty-seven seconds later, placed her in the middle of the dissipating fireball from one of the Krag warheads. Even after coming to rest in the center of the fireball, the *Cumberland* continued to radiate her stored heat for as long as she could do so without detection.

In four minutes and fifty-six seconds, it was over. The Krag sensors had recovered from the effects of the detonations, and the fireball into which the *Cumberland* dashed was now sufficiently reduced that the ship had to rely on its stealth systems to remain undetected. As quickly as she had sprung into motion, the *Cumberland* was at rest and nearly indistinguishable from the cold vastness in which she drifted: engines shut down, radiator fins retracted, attitude control thrusters deactivated, viewports shuttered, running lights extinguished, hull cryogenically chilled to just above absolute zero, her thermal energy sequestered in a massive heat sink, mass signature suppressed, EM emissions nil—"a hole in space." Fully stealthed, the ship was virtually invisible: as difficult to detect as any space vehicle ever constructed by humankind. *Cumberland* was a black schooner with black sails ghosting across a dark ocean on a moonless night. Unseen and unheard, she was a shadow of a shade.

"All right, people, let's settle down and watch carefully. Keep your eyes open for a pattern, a mistake, anything we can exploit," Max said.

"And what if they don't make a mistake?" asked DeCosta quietly.

"Then we'll have to make one for them," Max answered. *That didn't come out exactly right.* "You know what I mean."

DeCosta smiled. "Yes, sir. I do."

Max had bought some time, but only some. He'd shed some of the heat stored in the heat sink, freeing up about 15 percent of its capacity—capacity that would soon be consumed. He'd moved the ship into a grid square already eliminated in the search, but the talented Krag commander would spot the ruse before long. Max had delayed the inevitable moment when the Krag located the *Cumberland* by an hour or two at most.

"Bearing change on all contacts," Bartoli announced after a few minutes. "Looks like they're closing the range." Pause. "Confirmed. Range decreasing on all eight vessels in the containment group."

Twelve minutes passed. "Ships from the containment group are all taking up new positions," Bartoli announced. "Decelerating now. From their D/C curves, it looks like they are going to wind up at these points." Eight blinking red dots appeared in the tactical display. "Each point is roughly equidistant from our present position and about point three-seven AU closer than their previous stations. And the center of their formation is only point one-five AU from our present position, so their best guess as to where we are is much closer than before." After a few minutes, the white dots representing the actual positions of the ships in the containment group merged with the blinking red dots. Bartoli touched a key that extinguished the red dots.

"Containment group ships are now holding at their projected positions," Bartoli said redundantly. "They should resume multistatic scanning in the next five minutes or so. At the closer range, their scan intensity will be higher, so they will be able to eliminate each grid more quickly. Once I get a read on their scan rate, I'll come up with an estimated time of probable detection."

"Thank you, Mr. Bartoli," Max acknowledged. *I can hardly wait.*

"Tightening the noose." This statement, loud enough to be heard throughout CIC, came from the Commodore's Station, located on the Command Island to Max's left, a console equipped with an exceptionally comfortable chair but only a rudimentary set of controls and displays. It was uttered by Lieutenant Doctor Ibrahim (Bram) Sahin, the *Cumberland*'s Chief Medical Officer (CMO), whose nonmedical talents included proficiency as a naturalist, linguist, trader, and budding diplomat. The doctor's observations were often extremely useful and had, on at least one occasion, saved the ship, which explained why he was seated on the Command Island, when most CMOs weren't even allowed to enter CIC absent clear necessity, much less permitted to occupy the Commodore's Station at will. The doctor had come into CIC a few minutes before and was just now being handed a mug of coffee by a midshipman.

Notwithstanding Sahin's previous contributions to the *Cumberland*'s successes over the past few months, this last remark made Max wish to supplement the doctor's less than perfectly turned out uniform with a strip of duct tape over his mouth. It was just what the men in CIC didn't need to hear.

Even if it was true.

Max glared at Sahin and, in return, received an embarrassed shrug, which he acknowledged with an almost imperceptible nod: rebuke administered, apology offered, and apology accepted. Both men knew that Sahin had a bad habit of speaking the truth bluntly, especially at times when blunt truths were best left unspoken.

Like now. Over the past few weeks, the *Cumberland*'s crew had lived through enough drama to last a lifetime. There was, of course, the thrill of answering a Vaaach invitation for a rendezvous on 15 April beyond the edge of Known Space to receive a Krag surrender ultimatum for delivery to the Union. After that there would normally have been a rest period for officers and crew before having to return to the rendezvous point with the Union's response to the demand. Those days, however, were filled with feverish work as—under Admiral Hornmeyer's specific orders—the *Cumberland* received new and upgraded CIC consoles, which were installed in a new and more logical arrangement, a nifty new weapons system that the crew was calling the "Equalizer," and various other less visible but equally important upgrades.

That accomplished, the *Cumberland* had the dubious privilege of returning on 2 May to the same rendezvous point it visited on 15 April, there to deliver humanity's defiant answer of "NEVER," all the while not knowing what the answer was until they actually transmitted it. In fact, Max and just about everyone else on board (except for a few of the perpetually ebullient midshipmen like

Hewlett, Park, and Gilbertson) had believed the Union was going to agree to accept the Krag promise not to exterminate humankind in exchange for the Union's surrender.

After delivering the Union's unexpectedly defiant response, things went well. At first. With a powerful Vaaach vessel looking on, the Krag ship sent to receive the answer withdrew from the rendezvous and cracked on toward Krag space at more than 2000 c without so much as a peep. Once the Krag vessel was out of sensor range, the *Cumberland*—promised safe passage out of their space by the Vaaach—withdrew and headed for Union-controlled space. The journey was uneventful until the ship crossed out of Vaaach space.

That's when things went to hell.

When the *Cumberland* came out of its jump into the Garbo-Watkins A system, its first after leaving Vaaach space, two *Derrick* class destroyers were lying in wait with weapons zeroed on the jump point. The *Cumberland* escaped only because Max—obeying a hunch—had fired two Talon missiles just as the ship emerged from the jump. Because the ship's computers and sensors were still in restart mode after having been shut down for the jump, it was a "blind fire," with the missiles untargeted, their guidance systems set for a wide search pattern and their seeker heads programmed to identify and lock onto any vessel that didn't transmit a friendly Identification Friend or Foe (IFF).

Both missiles missed. Because the weapons were not aimed precisely on their targets, the enemy had four precious seconds to begin evasive action before the missiles locked onto them and ran their drives up to attack speed. Max did not regard the missiles as wasted ordnance, however. Occupied with saving their skins from imminent thermonuclear immolation, the Krag were too busy to carry out their attack on the *Cumberland,* which went into stealth mode and escaped.

The jump into the next system, ironically named Bonnevie by its inhabitants before the Krag killed them all, was uneventful. But while the ship was crossing the star system from jump in to jump out, a "rat pack" of four Krag destroyers arrived on compression drive, obviously on the hunt for the *Cumberland,* and staked out the jump point. Max used the *Cumberland*'s stealth to sneak up on one and take it out with a missile attack, launched an emulator drone to lure away two more on a wild-goose chase, and slipped past the fourth to make the jump, a process that took a total of twenty-one exhausting and nerve-racking hours.

That jump brought the *Cumberland* to a never-inhabited system known only by its Union Space Navy Galactic Survey number. While never home to any humans, on that day the system was hosting tourists in the form of three Krag *Crustacean* class cruisers that had jumped in a few hours ahead of the *Cumberland* and were making their way to the jump point that they knew she would use to take her one step closer to home. Max went stealthy, slipped into the drive trail of the hindmost cruiser, and followed the formation for fifteen grueling hours to the jump point. Once the Krag ships got there, they had just begun to arrange themselves into an interdiction formation and begun their active sensor scans of the likely approaches to the jump point when Max darted between them at high speed and jumped out before the Krag could get a good sensor fix, much less a weapons lock.

Which brought Max and the *Cumberland* here: Monroe-Tucker B, where—before the men could so much as exchange a few high fives and hit the head—they were set upon not by a rat pack, not three cruisers, but a full-fledged attack group under the command of a Krag whose fighting skill declared him to be at least the Krag equivalent of a commodore, if not a rear admiral. The Krag commander hadn't made a mistake yet and was using his forces with skill and assurance. This time the Krag had come with their A game.

The *Cumberland* was on her own. Too far from Union forces for reliable communications, she hadn't been able to get a message through to the fleet requesting assistance before Krag jamming had blocked all long-range signals.

Max caught the eye of Midshipman George R. Hewlett, assigned to CIC for this watch to render whatever assistance a nine-year-old boy could give, from fetching coffee to blowing off a Krag's head with the sawed-off M-92 shotgun he had slung over his shoulder. By tilting his head in the direction of the coffeepot, Max indicated that he needed the boy in his coffee-fetching rather than Krag-decapitating capacity. Max noticed that, as the young man carried over the steaming, black, fragrant brain fuel, his brows were furrowed, and his eyes kept straying to the tactical display.

Max knew that look. The born teacher inside Max could tell that Hewlett saw something that he didn't understand and that today—this very moment, in fact—was the perfect time for Hewlett to learn it. Every bone in Max's body wanted to seize that moment to further the midshipman's naval education.

Not the best time. With eight hostiles trying to generate a valid firing solution on his ship, Max could certainly find something of more obvious importance to do with his energy. If he was going to be dead in a matter of hours, why waste the time giving a tactical lesson to Midshipman Hewlett?

Why? Because we're not dead yet.

"Thank you, Mr. Hewlett," Max said. "Oh, Mr. Hewlett, take a look here, if you would." Max gestured to the tactical display. "Tell me what you see."

The almost impossibly fair-skinned boy, who needed only a dirty face and patched nineteenth-century clothes to be able to pass for Oliver Twist, blushed with the attention, his ears turning a distinct shade of pink. He gulped and turned his pale blue eyes to the Main Tactical Display, a shimmering column of light containing a three-dimensional plot of the *Cumberland* and the ships hunting her. "Well, sir, the blue dot is us. The eight red dots forming the corners of a cube around us are the Krag warships in the containment group. The display is projecting a transparent pink sphere around each Krag ship—that's the PDR—the Probable Detection Range for each ship. Even with our stealth systems engaged, we have to stay outside of those spheres, or the Krag will pick us up on their sensors . . . because *stealth makes us difficult to detect, not impossible*." Max smiled at the boy's accurate recitation of one of his own favorite space combat maxims.

Blushing even more deeply at his skipper's subtle but evident approval, Hewlett continued. "The yellow and orange areas are zones that the Krag have eliminated by high-intensity multistatic scanning or with their missiles."

"Okay, Hewlett, let me stop you for a minute. One of the things that slows down learning is people using memorized terms that they don't understand, and then telling themselves that they know what they are talking about. Tell me about multistatic scanning."

"Oh, sir, that's not hard at all," the boy said, smiling. "One thing that stealth technology does is to redirect active sensor pulses so that they are not reflected back toward the transmitter that sent them, like putting a mirror at a forty-five-degree angle when someone is shining a hand torch at it. Multistatic sensor deployments try to defeat that by sending the pulse from one location and trying to pick up a return from another. So, the Krag just have several ships coordinate their sensor scans: each ship sends on its own set of frequencies that all the others in different locations listen for. You saturate an area of space with enough sensor beams from enough directions on enough frequencies with enough ships listening in enough different locations, you'll pick up even the most heavily stealthed ship."

"Exactly right, Midshipman. Continue."

"Anyway, sir, the Krag think that they know we aren't in any of the orange or yellow parts. But we're right in the middle of that yellow zone right there, so we're safe for now."

"Very good, Hewlett." The boy was shaping up to be something of a budding genius—from all reports he fit in on a warship far better than he did in primary school back on Archopin. "You looked as though you had a question."

"Yes, sir. The PDR spheres don't touch each other. There are gaps between them."

"That's right, son."

"Then why don't we just scoot out through one of those gaps and make a run for it?"

"I was wondering the same thing," added Dr. Sahin.

Max shot Sahin his reproachful *I can't believe you don't know that* look, resulting in Sahin shooting Max his *I'm a doctor, not a sensor specialist* look. "Mr. Nelson, would you enlighten *the doctor* and the midshipman?"

"Gladly, sir. The Krag ships have generated a LeLo Hex."

"Which is?" asked Sahin.

"A Lehrer-Lobachevsky Hexahedron."

"*Which is?*" The doctor shook his head with frustration. "Why is getting useful information from the personnel on this vessel like pulling teeth? How many times do I have to ask a question before I get an answer that doesn't assume I've been continuously on warships since I was Hewlett's age?"

"I'm doing my best, sir, but it's more difficult than you might think," Nelson said patiently. Sahin tilted his head, inviting further explanation. "You see, I *have* been continuously on warships since I was Hewlett's age, and that means that since *I* was Hewlett's age, almost every person I've ever talked to has been *another* man who has been on warships since *he* was Hewlett's age. I don't have a lot of experience communicating with people who don't share that background."

Sahin spent a moment digesting what he had just heard, nodded slowly, and then exhaled loudly, as though by releasing the air he was holding in his lungs, he was letting go of months of pent-up frustration. "I understand, Mr. Nelson. And I thank you for that explanation. Please continue."

"Thank you, sir. Anyway, four ships that are in precisely the same plane in space and less than about 10 AU apart can produce a Lehrer-Lobachevsky Discontinuity. That's a microscopically thin, artificially generated disruption in the space-time continuum. It is so thin that any vessel can cross it easily with no harm, but as an object passes through the discontinuity, it generates a detectable flux of Cherenkov-Heaviside radiation where the field intersects its surface. Eight ships properly arranged can create six contiguous planes, known as a Lehrer-Lobachevsky Hexahedron, or Le-Lo Hex for short. Usually a Le-Lo Hex is a fairly close approximation of a cube. A ship that's inside one of these things can't leave without giving away its position when it crosses the discontinuity—you're giving them a good, solid datum point, you know? Then the bad guys illuminate that area with high-intensity multistatic sensor scans, and in thirty seconds or so, Mr. Rat-Face has a firing solution. So, inside the hex, we're pinned down, essentially negating our normal advantages in speed and stealth."

Hewlett turned to Max, his elfin face creased with almost teary concern. "But, sir, the third law of destroyer and frigate combat is: *A destroyer or frigate's primary strengths and, accordingly, its most significant advantages over most adversaries, are speed and stealth. If either or both of these attributes is compromised, the ship is in grave peril.* Sir, we've lost our only advantages over the enemy!"

Max smiled warmly. "Everything you've said in the last few minutes, Midshipman, has been correct. Except for that last sentence."

"Sir?"

"We've got one other advantage."

"What's that, sir?"

"Motivation. As far as the Krag are concerned, this battle is about whether they *get* the kill. For us it's about whether we *are* the kill. Survival is a more powerful motivator than duty or glory or hatred or the thrill of the hunt or whatever it is that drives the Krag." He placed his hand on the boy's shoulder and looked him in the eyes. "Do *you* want to live, Hewlett?"

"Abso-fucking-lutely!" Into the sudden dead silence that followed his breach of protocol, the boy almost whispered, "Sir. I mean, yes, sir. Very sorry, sir. But, yes, sir. I *do* want to live."

"So do I, son. Thank you, Mr. Hewlett. That will be all." The boy returned to his post.

Max sipped his coffee and stared at the tactical display, his practiced ear taking in and interpreting without conscious attention the chatter from the stations around CIC. Slowly he stood and walked around the display, hands behind his back, viewing it from every angle, again and again, unconscious of the eyes of the men following him (to the extent their duties allowed). These same men watched Max's face for any sign that he had found an escape from their mutual predicament. For nearly fifteen minutes, they watched him: taking a few steps, squinting at the positions of the ships and the progress of their search as projected in three-dimensional space, taking a few sips from the coffee mug he carried, alternately resting his right hand on the hilt of his boarding cutlass and on the grip of his M-62 10 mm sidearm, and then repeating the process with some variation in the order of the steps.

To one man after another, the same thought occurred: *Nothing's coming to him. He's out of ideas.* And they all knew what that meant.

Then, after his twenty-seventh orbit of the Main Tactical Display, Max stopped suddenly, drained his coffee mug, and waved it absently in Hewlett's general direction. The boy leaped to his feet and scampered over to take the mug from the skipper's hands. By the time Hewlett had gotten to the coffeepot, Max was at the CO's station rapidly pulling up data on his displays.

Max performed a few minutes of research and calculation, punctuated by occasional sips of coffee, still unaware that every nuance of expression that crossed his face was the subject of the most intense scrutiny by every man within line of sight. Another gesture at Hewlett with the mug. Another refill. Another few sips. Finally, at long last, a crooked smile slowly wrote itself across his face.

Knowing what the smile meant, the men who could see it smiled, too, and elbowed the men at their sides to be sure they saw it. And they passed the word on the loops: "the skipper has another trick up his sleeve," or "the Swamp Fox has got something cooking." Soon men in the farthest recesses of the ship were exchanging smiles and knowing nods. Maybe, *just maybe*, they would live to see another day.

Oblivious for now to the sudden change in mood throughout the ship, Max quickly swiveled his chair 120 degrees to his right so that he faced the Computers console.

"Mr. Bales."

"Yes, sir?"

"You do remember our little present from our friends the Vaaach, don't you?"

"Yes, sir." Bales did his best to keep from sounding hurt. He did not entirely succeed. On a recent escort mission, the *Cumberland* had damaged a Krag *Crayfish* class cruiser and chased it into Vaaach space, where she had found it engaged in a running battle with a badly outgunned and outmatched Vaaach scout vessel. Max had persuaded the young Vaaach pilot to participate with him in a typically Robichauvian deceptive maneuver, in which the two ships managed to destroy the Krag vessel. That outcome presented a dilemma to the senior Vaaach commander who showed up after the battle. The strict Vaaach rules of Hunter's Honor required them under the particular circumstances of that engagement to share the "meat" of the kill with Max. But as the *Cumberland* had vaporized the Krag vessel with a pair of thermonuclear weapons, the Vaaach found themselves without any physical meat to share. The Vaaach scout ship had, however, used that race's staggeringly advanced technology to copy all the data from the Krag computer core immediately upon encountering it; accordingly, the Vaaach were able to fulfill their obligation in the form of a Vaaach data storage device containing *all* of the data from the Krag cruiser's computer, accompanied by an apparently custom-fabricated and programmed Vaaach module allowing Union computers to interface with the storage device. It was, quite literally, the greatest intelligence haul of all time. Mr. Bales was more likely to forget his own name than forget having access to the Krag cruiser's database. "You bet, I remember."

"I thought you might," said Max. "When we had our little present from the Vaaach plugged in down in Captured Hardware, I know that you copied as much of the Krag data into your quarantined servers as you had room for in case the Vaaach device stopped working for some reason. I also know when he took the Vaaach data module with him, Admiral Hornmeyer told you he wanted your files purged for security reasons. But, Mr. Bales," Max continued innocently, "knowing how new you are to actual combat service, not to mention your career-long history of *creatively* interpreting orders from senior officers, I was wondering if in all the excitement, and with the stress of being in the presence of an actual, real live, holy and exalted vice admiral, especially one as *loud* as old 'Hit 'em Hard' Hornmeyer, some of that data might have, well, been *missed*, if you catch my meaning."

Christopher Bales, whose seemingly boundless brilliance about computer systems did not extend very far into the realm of human nature, spent a few seconds pondering why the skipper asked such an odd question in such a peculiar manner. Then he considered the question in light of Max's personality and began to play along. He stared at his boots in mock embarrassment. "Now that you mention it, sir, it *was* a rather confusing time, and I really didn't have a clear protocol to follow when it comes to having an alien data core plugged into my processors down there. So, sir, it is, I think, entirely *possible* that some . . . er . . . *mistakes* in that regard may have been made."

"Shameful, Mr. Bales, truly, *truly* shameful," Max scolded. "And is it *possible* that, in the gravely negligent performance of your duties, some of the Krag sensor protocol data may have—quite accidentally, mind you—escaped being purged?"

"Skipper, I'm quite embarrassed to report that I think it's conceivable that all of that data may still be stored somewhere in the quarantined servers."

"I see," Max said, smiling broadly. There was no way that the storage capacity of the computers in Captured Hardware would hold more than a twentieth of the Krag data. Leave it to Bales to know what would be useful and to keep copies. Max forced a serious expression. "I'm sure some sort of discipline will be forthcoming." *Eventually.* "And, while we're on the subject, I don't suppose that the same kind of thoroughly deplorable dereliction of duty extends to the files on the Krag point-defense systems?"

Bales adopted an aspect of even more exaggerated contrition. "You've got me there, sir. It's very possible that I missed those too.

Not only that, but the sloppiness of my department may go so far as to cover most of the data for their combat systems as well as engineering and navigation."

"You are an enormous embarrassment to the USS *Cumberland*, young man. I suppose, though, since we *do* have the data, we might as well put it to good use. So, until I get around to the matter of your punishment, which I assure you will be *quite appropriately severe*, I need you to make those files available to the Special Attack Tiger Team."

"I've never heard of that team, sir."

"That's because I haven't created it yet. Officer of the deck?"

"Here, sir," answered Sauvé from Countermeasures.

"Log this order. The Special Attack Tiger Team is hereby constituted. It consists of the XO, plus the department heads from Computers, Tactical, Countermeasures, Weapons, and Stealth. Gentlemen, summon your reliefs. I need a detailed operations plan in one hour. You can work in the Fighter Control Back Room. It's empty right now. XO, you know what I want?"

"A new variation on Cagle's Corner Cutout?"

"Exactly." *Either a stunningly lucky guess or a brilliant deduction.*

"But, sir," DeCosta said quietly, "you know . . ."

"Yes, XO, I know," Max replied just as quietly. "The book says that Cagle's Corner Cutout was a bust. Cagle's flagship, the *Impala*, destroyed. Cagle dead. Only three of the seventeen-ship attack group survived. But we've got one thing on our side that old 'Big Chief' Cagle didn't have back then."

"The data from the Krag computer core?"

"Exactly. Get back to me in an hour. We've got a few hours before the Krag figure out that we sneaked back into a spot they thought they cleared." He turned in the direction of the coffeepot and drinks chiller. "Oh, Hewlett?"

"Yes, sir?"

"Summon *your* relief. I'm attaching you to the Tiger Team as an aide. Anything they need, you get it for them. Any help they ask for, you give it. Got that?"

"Aye, aye, Captain." Hewlett knew that his skipper had assigned him to be a fetch-and-carry boy for a group of exhausted senior officers performing a highly technical task under enormous pressure who would have little or no patience for a wet-behind-the-ears hatch hanger. He could scarcely contain his glee.

CHAPTER 2

06:52 Zulu Hours, 9 May 2315

"All stations report ready to execute," DeCosta announced.
"Very well. We'll go at 08:00 hours," Max said." DeCosta turned to his console and entered a series of commands, setting 08:00 as the starting point for the complex and intricately timed series of actions designed to save the ship from certain annihilation. When Max saw that DeCosta was finished, he got up, crossed the step and a half or so that separated his station from the XO's, and laid his hand on the man's shoulder. "Outstanding job, XO," he said in a voice loud enough to be heard throughout the compartment.

"Thank you, sir," DeCosta replied, and then continued more quietly, "Sir, you know that it's as much your plan as ours. We got stuck, and you got us over the hump. What you came up with . . . well, sir, there's no way we could have gotten past those problems by ourselves." He contemplated what the *Cumberland* was about to attempt and shook his head in wonder. "It's an aggressive plan, sir—extremely aggressive, particularly given that our overall tactical objective isn't offensive, but only to escape and get home."

"Given the 'highly unfavorable correlation of forces,'" Max answered, "it's only as aggressive as it has to be." The men shared a smile. So much for the T-SEA run being kept secret from the skipper or the XO.

While every other man in CIC had his mind on the next few minutes and his part in the plan, Dr. Sahin had his mind on an adjective uttered a few seconds in the past. "*Aggressive*? If *you two*, of all people, are calling this plan *aggressive*," he said, coming to his feet and using the term like an epithet, "it must surely be a veritable symphony of inordinate risk-taking and wildly dangerous maneuvers. I thought that this scheme was formulated by the Tiger Team alone, but now that I hear that a certain gentleman of Cajun descent participated in the plan's formulation, I have little doubt that each movement of that symphony is now punctuated with strategically inserted music containing the kind of diagnosable, raving insanity with which I have become all too familiar since joining this ship."

The CO and XO looked at each other blandly. "I don't regard that as an insult," said Max. "How about you, XO?"

"Not even remotely, sir."

"Further," sniffed Sahin, continuing his almost obligatory rant oblivious to the unconcern with which his remarks were being received, "as insane as the upcoming performance is going to be and pursuant to what must be a formal shipboard policy mandating that the Chief Medical Officer be kept utterly in the dark at all times, I confidently predict that no one will provide me with a program of the evening's performance so that I can know whether I'm about to witness the tactical equivalent of Bach, Tchaikovsky, Ghar-Vhish 817, or Havenstrite."

DeCosta chuckled quietly. "Insane or not, Doctor, this plan is detailed enough that we had to put it all in writing. If you want to read it or follow along as we go, it's in the database anytime you want to look at it. In fact, here." He touched a screen a few times. "I just sent it to your console. The file is called 'Special Attack Tiger Team Escape and Evasion Plan.'"

"Excellent, Mr. DeCosta. I congratulate you on the imaginative title," Sahin replied. "It has that bland, bureaucratic ring so cherished by the navy. It is not nearly as off-putting as, say, 'Into the Jaws of Death, Into the Mouth of Hell, Will Charge the Valiant *Cumberland*.' I will certainly examine it. I can hardly wait to read the entry that says, 'At this point the heavily damaged USS *Cumberland* careens out of control, colliding with the Krag destroyer at 10 percent of lightspeed, reducing both vessels and their crews to high-energy elementary particles.' I'm certain that I will find it deeply entertaining." Several of the senior enlisted men, who had been suppressing laughter at the exchange, burst into open guffaws at this point, bringing Sahin to a sheepish, sputtering halt, at which point he sat down.

Max turned back to DeCosta. "The only thing that frustrates me is that no one could come up with a way to use Bales's idea about hacking the Krag REFSMMAT. I just can't see any way around the star imager correction utility."

"Neither could we, but we wanted you to have that particular screwdriver in your toolbox, even though we've never seen the screw it fits."

"Thanks."

Both men turned their attention to their consoles, reviewing the plan, checking the readiness of various systems, and exchanging short messages with men around the ship to confirm that they understood precisely what they were to do.

All the while trying to ignore that they were very likely to die while doing it.

The seconds slowly ground past on the chrono, each seemingly taking longer than the one before. Every several minutes or so, a grid "square" on the Main Tactical Display changed from the black of ordinary space to yellow or orange to indicate that the enemy had searched the area. Gradually, ominously, the yellow and orange were beginning to predominate over black. Men struggled to ignore the passing seconds, the disappearing black areas on the display, the dwindling count of their own breaths from that moment until the moment of the *Cumberland*'s desperate and—most likely—fatal attempt to break out of the Krag trap.

So low as to be audible only to him, Max could hear Bram humming something. Both men were fans of the nineteenth-century British operetta composers Gilbert and Sullivan, and Max recognized the tune as coming from one of their most famous offerings, *The Pirates of Penzance*. It took Max little effort to match lyrics to notes.

Go ye heroes, go to glory.
Though ye die in combat gory,
Ye shall live in song and story.
Go to immortality.
Go to death and go to slaughter.
Die, and every Cornish daughter
With her tears your grave shall water.
Go ye heroes, go and die!

Max fixed his friend with an icy stare. "Not funny," he said in a low voice.

"I intended no humor," Sahin replied.

Not knowing whether to be furious or merely annoyed, Max returned his gaze to the tactical display. All around him the young skipper could feel the level of tension in the compartment ratcheting higher and higher with every heartbeat. Just as he was trying to think of a way to relieve the pressure, he heard the vault door–like CIC hatch cycle and glanced over his left shoulder to see who was coming in. No one. At least no one tall enough for his head to be visible above the Firefighting and Emergency Control Stations, colloquially known as the "Firehouse," located directly between the Command Island in the center of CIC and the hatch, behind the island and to its left. Max was about to open a voice channel to one of the marine sentries posted outside to ask why they opened the hatch, when he saw the reason. Clouseau, the rounder-by-the-day ship's cat, came nonchalantly into view, ambled across the compartment, and—notwithstanding his considerable girth—leaped easily into the seat at the Commodore's Station beside the doctor. By tradition, ships' cats had the run of the vessel (except for dangerous spaces where they might be injured), and when the cat had pawed the CIC hatch, one of the marines had—in perfect accord with naval custom—let him in. Clouseau promptly curled up with his head resting on the doctor's leg, purring loudly enough to be heard by at least a quarter of the men in the compartment, a model of feline tranquility. The doctor absently stroked the animal's glossy, jet-black fur.

Clouseau's entrance instantly lowered the tension level. According to spacers—a notoriously superstitious lot, for whom cats were the center of a whole branch of voluminous lore—Clouseau was solid gold, 200 proof, certified, bona fide, Kentucky-fried good luck. Even the smallest hatch hanger knew that because they had nine lives, cats were lucky, and their luck necessarily rubbed off on any ship on which they traveled. After all, a cat can't be lucky if its ship gets blown to flaming atoms, right? Clouseau was luckier still, however, because he was solid black—black like space, black like warships were painted—which, the men told each other, was the luckiest kind of cat to have (setting aside, for the moment, tailless cats, which were luckier still, a fact seldom mentioned on the *Cumberland*). The jewel in Clouseau's crown of good fortune, though, was that he had joined the ship of his own accord by running onto the destroyer across a docking tube joining it to a freighter carrying Krag cargo. The *Cumberland* must be a lucky ship because this supremely lucky creature had chosen it as his new home. Then, when it became widely known on board that the freighter from which the cat had fled had been destroyed, probably by enemy action, Clouseau's status as an icon of good luck was secure.

Therefore, the fortunate feline's appearance in CIC just as the ship was about to engage the enemy could, in the minds of the crew, be viewed as nothing other than an exceptionally favorable omen.

Of course, as an experienced combat officer, Max was completely immune to that kind of unscientific hooey.

Well, maybe not *completely* immune.

The ship's chrono turned over to 07:58. Two minutes. While the spirits in CIC had lifted somewhat, Max sensed that pessimism still pervaded the ship. *Damn that T-SEA estimate and the data bus it rode in on.* He knew that if these men went into combat with that attitude, they would certainly die, the Krag having already beaten them in spirit.

Like hell.

"Mr. Chin. Give me MC1."

"MC1, aye." The light on Max's console came on, indicating that his voice was being transmitted throughout the ship over the number one main voice circuit.

"Men, this is the skipper. You know what we're about to do. You know what is expected of you. You know what the odds are and what happens if we fail. So, then, why am I speaking to you?"

He took a long, slow breath. "Because I have two things to say. First—I want to remind you what you're fighting for: not the great cause that the whole of the Union has been fighting for these past thirty-four years, but what you and I are fighting for right now, today. Men, we've fought together before: to save the Pfelung, to save Rashid, even to save the Union, and that's a noble thing. As navy men we're bred to fight and sacrifice for others. Because of that and because you think that today you are fighting to save yourselves, some of you may feel that what you do today is less important than what you did before. I understand that, but it's bullshit. Listen carefully. You are not fighting for yourself. You are fighting for everyone on this ship: every man, every officer, the cooks and the medics, everyone down to the smallest hatch hanger. It's not one life you are fighting for; it's your 214 shipmates. That's a cause worth the best you have to give, and as noble as anything for which you or any man has ever fought or will fight in the future. Shipmates are family, and fighting to save your family is the noblest fight there is.

"Second, I want to talk about the odds. You've all heard about our computer's prediction. And there's a lot of people who would feel pity for us in our current situation. But let me tell you something. There's not a computer ever made that can measure the heart of a man. There's not a computer ever made that can measure human courage, tenacity, and defiance. And I know for damn sure that there's not a computer ever made that can measure the fighting spirit of this ship! The odds? Guess what! I don't give a flying fusion fuck what the goddamn odds are, and neither should you. I know you. I know this ship. I've led you into battle. I've seen you fight and win when the odds said it couldn't be done. And I know for an indisputable fucking fact that if there is anyone who deserves pity today, it's the Krag. They're sitting out there laughing because they think they've treed a fox.

"Well, shipmates, we're going to have the last laugh because what they've really done is cornered a lion! And the Krag aren't ready to tangle with a lion. When the story of this day goes into the history books—and I assure you that it will—they're not going to be talking about the odds. They're not going to be talking about the goddamn T-SEA. What they're going to be talking about—what the Union will always remember and what the Krag will never forget—will be the glorious victory won today by the officers and men of the USS *Cumberland*!"

Max looked around to find that he had unconsciously risen to his feet. Almost every face in CIC was turned to him. The men's faces shone with courage and defiance. Chin opened some voice circuits—the ones connecting the sound pickups in the parts of the ship that had the most men working in them—to the speakers in CIC, allowing Max and everyone else in the compartment to hear the men shouting, "Victory! Victory! Victory!"

That did the trick.

The chrono rolled over to 08:00. It was time. Max spoke into the open circuit: "Phase One: *Execute*."

Unlike the Age of Sail, there was no series of orders snapped out by the skipper to be repeated and carried out throughout the ship—nothing to bring to mind the age-old seafaring calls of "set the mizzen topgallants," "ready about," and "hard a lee." Instead, the orders were already given, stored in the ship's computer and displayed in detail as needed on each man's console or implemented directly by the computer itself according to a timetable automatically synchronized and corrected to remain in step with actual events. It all started without another word being spoken. And it all started, as it did more often than not on any warship, at Maneuvering.

Chief LeBlanc gave the word to Able Spacer Fleishman at Drives. The young man engaged the main sublight drive, nudging the *Cumberland* from a standstill (or, at least, station keeping relative to the Krag formation) into gradually accelerating motion, with the men at Yaw and Pitch steering it through a series of bizarre, often reversing, corkscrew-like maneuvers plotted for them by the computer as they went. The course looked insane, but there was method in the *Cumberland*'s madness.

The Krag active sensors functioned by emitting a tight beam, like a powerful but narrowly focused searchlight, that swept the search area. Because a predictable sweep pattern would enable an enemy to avoid detection by avoiding the beam, the beam's path was "pseudorandom," that is, designed to be difficult to predict and containing no discernable pattern, but precisely aimed according to instructions stored in the Krag computer to intersect and synchronize with the beams emitted by other ships in selected areas of the search grid to carry out a coordinated, multistatic sensor sweep. Armed with the sensor protocols from the captured data core, the *Cumberland*'s computer could now recognize which of the several hundred standardized patterns each ship was using, predict where the Krag ship would scan next, and compute a path around the scans, at least for a while.

At the same time, Mr. Nelson and the Stealth Section under his command made equally skillful use of the captured Krag data. Narrow-beam sensor scans weren't the only arrow in the Krag's sensor quiver. The enemy also had systems, less sensitive but much harder to dodge, that projected wide cones of energy blanketing large swaths of the search area. These pulses also followed pseudorandom time, frequency, phase, amplitude, and polarization patterns governed by the Krag computers. Armed with the detailed specifications for those patterns, Nelson could set the ship's own stealth and emulation emitters to emit pulses precisely timed to coincide with those of the Krag sensors, canceling out the enemy scans, preventing them from being reflected back or sufficiently weakening them so that the returns were below the enemy's detection threshold.

The men not directly involved in these activities watched tensely as the ship evaded the enemy scans, all the while drawing closer and closer to the Krag destroyer. Every man understood clearly the furious activity that kept the enemy unaware of the *Cumberland*'s approach and the increasing risk of detection and rapid destruction as she drew nearer to her target.

Every man, that is, but one. Dr. Sahin spoke with his usual obliviousness into the edgy near-silence. "With all these baffling and inexplicable course changes, it is difficult to tell, but aren't we getting closer to the Probable Detection Range for that destroyer . . . what are we calling it . . . ah, yes, 'Hotel two'?"

"We are," Max replied.

"Are you sure that's a good idea?"

"Quite sure."

"As long as you are sure," Sahin answered, not entirely convinced. "But we're not going to get close enough to be detected, correct?"

"We *are* going to be detected. Absolutely. No question about it."

"But," he sputtered, "isn't that a bad idea? And don't tell me that I can read the plan from my console. I can display the whole thing right in front of me, but it's so full of your confounded tactical, topological, space geometrical, systems operational, computer cryptological, military situational mumbo jumbo that the only thing I can get out of it is likely to be a manifestation of your worn-out 'three *B*s of evading an enemy' and 'warfare is deception' bromides."

"That's 'three *M*s,'" Max corrected icily. Sahin cringed at the sound of his friend's voice. One did not misquote Fleet Admiral Charles Lake Middleton around Max Robichaux.

"Forgive me," Bram said quickly. Max nodded his acceptance. Sahin continued, "In any event, at your repeated and, I might add, repetitious-far-beyond-the-point-of-being-annoying insistence, I have devoted extensive hours to the study of the tactical primer in the ship's database. Those same hours, I might add, could have been spent far more productively on tasks more directly correlated with success in my primary area of responsibility on board this vessel, which, I remind you, is the health of its crew, not the obliteration of its enemies. At any rate, according to my admittedly limited understanding of such things, when we get within the destroyer's Probable Detection Range, is it not true that the ship in question will be able to compute a firing solution, and not only will it shoot at us, it will share the solution to the other seven ships?"

"Yes," Max answered blandly, "that's exactly right. Your studies are paying off."

"This is one case where I would rather suffer in ignorance." The pitch of his voice started to rise as he started to get wound up. "And isn't it also true that, since those murderous rodents are now armed with that truly, truly wicked new faster-than-light, long-range Ridgeback missile of theirs, *every one* of those ships will open fire on us, even though they are many millions of kilometers away? All eight of them! Meaning that we will be dodging superluminal missiles fired by eight ships and not just one!"

"Actually," Max answered even more blandly, "that's not quite true."

"Really?" Sahin sounded a bit relieved.

"Really, Doctor. You left out the three ships guarding the jump points. There's a better-than-even chance that they will want to get in on the kill by firing their missiles at us too. So, it could be up to eleven ships firing on us at the same time."

"Oh. *Eleven*. Thank you for that relevant and oh-so-comforting correction. And am I further correct in my understanding that the enemy has fired one of those damn new high-threshold Egg Scramblers, the kind that disrupts metaspace only at the higher quanta so that their superluminal missiles will function but we can't outrun their missiles with our compression drive?"

"That's right."

"So, at least from my simplistic tactical perspective, you might forgive me for saying that this plan of yours looks to be a wonderfully superlative way to set us on the short road to jinnah. Correct?"

"Correct on both counts," Max said.

"Both counts?" Sahin croaked, the blood draining from his face.

"Both counts. Correct, I forgive you for saying so, and correct, it *looks* like the short road to heaven. Don't worry. It's not. I assure you, my friend, I have no plans to stand before the pearly gates today and account for my actions in this life. *Notre cher amis, les nique à rats* out there, on the other hand," he gestured toward the enemy ships displayed in the tactical projection, "at least most of them, should be having to explain themselves to *Sainte-Pierre* very shortly."

"Skipper, our range to Hotel two is just under two million kilometers. It's starting to get a little tight," announced Chief LeBlanc. Because the sensor beams emitted by the destroyer designated as Hotel two radiated outward from that vessel like the spokes of a wheel, the space between the beams became ever narrower as the *Cumberland* closed the range. Soon the beams would be so close together that even the splendid ship handling of the men under LeBlanc's direction could not keep the ship from being caught by a high-intensity scan at what was now very close range. In that event no stealth technology possessed by the Union could thwart detection.

"Very well, and well done, Mr. LeBlanc. Maneuvering, maintain stealthy approach. All stations prepare to execute Phase Two. Mr. Kasparov, notify me as soon as we're scanned with anything strong enough to generate a detectable return." Thanks to the Krag data, Mr. Kasparov now knew to a very high level of precision what that threshold was.

"Aye, sir. You'll know that very second."

"Mr. Kasparov."

"Yes, sir?"

"Better make it that *half* second."

"Understood. Half second, it is."

After abating somewhat in the face of the banter between Max and Bram, the tension in CIC had snapped back to its previously high level and was rising. Max could hear it in the tone of the watch standers' voices as they spoke to each other and to their back rooms. He could see it in the nervous shuffling of their feet, their anxious squirming in their seats, and the covert wiping of sweaty palms on the legs of their uniforms. He could smell its acrid scent in the air.

He couldn't blame them. Max had been in command of the *Cumberland* only since 21 January. Before then, since its commissioning the ship had been under the command of the inept—perhaps even mentally ill—Commander Allen K. Oscar, and although he had done everything short of abusing the crew with the cat-o'-nine-tails to ensure that every surface and fitting on the ship had gleamed from being cleaned within a millimeter of its life, the crew had experienced nothing but humiliation in fleet exercises and defeat in battle. Certainly since the change in command, this crew had met the enemy several times under Captain Robichaux and had been victorious on each occasion, but—as Max liked to say—they had gotten only a few forkfuls of good food to dispel the taste of years of slop.

And now, once again, they were going into battle together.

"We were just painted, Skipper," announced Kasparov. "High-frequency tachyon radar, synthetic aperture, five-centimeter band.

Signal strength is 136 Dusangs per square meter. That's at least five times the Krag detection threshold."

Max came to his feet without any conscious decision to do so. "Phase Two: *Execute*."

As with Phase One, the script was already written. The actors merely had to follow their cues and carry out their parts. Mr. Nelson disengaged most of the ship's stealth systems and extended the thermal radiator fins, allowing the *Cumberland*'s electronic and thermal signatures to make her presence plainly visible to Krag sensors. At that same moment, Mr. Sauvé at Countermeasures activated a program—quickly but meticulously written by himself and Mr. Levy at Weapons—that loaded an unusual response code into the ship's IFF transponder. Meanwhile, the men around CIC quickly and efficiently armed weapons, engaged deflectors, enabled point-defense systems, ran the main sublight drive to Emergency, and pointed the ship's bow right at Hotel two. In a few seconds, the *Cumberland* was accelerating hard on a collision course with the enemy destroyer.

Once the humans were visible to enemy sensors, both the Krag and every man on the *Cumberland* knew that the orthodox tactical solution in this situation was what Union tacticians called ELEVES (pronounced "elves"), an acronym for ELude, EVade, and EScape. Essentially, ELEVES meant that when confronted by a vessel or vessels of superior force, the destroyer should use its speed and stealth to elude and evade the enemy, all while biding its time until the Krag made a mistake that allowed it to escape and get away for good.

Given, however, that conventional tactics applied to this situation would result in the eventual but certain destruction of the *Cumberland* and the valiant, but futile, death of its crew, Max had other ideas. The *Cumberland* wasn't eluding. The *Cumberland* wasn't evading. The *Cumberland* wasn't escaping.

Alone, outnumbered eight to one and facing at least a twenty-five to one disadvantage in firepower, the USS *Cumberland* was *attacking.*

"Hotel two is reacting as anticipated." Bartoli narrated the action, much as would a sports announcer—a sports announcer who would die if the home team lost, which tended to lend a certain excitement to the commentary. "She's engaging deflectors, enabling point-defense systems, energizing the missile-targeting scanners, and reorienting to unmask her missile tubes and most powerful pulse-cannon batteries. She is not, repeat not, under acceleration at this time. She should have a firing solution in about thirty seconds. The other ships are maintaining their relative positions in the formation."

Generating a firing solution required thirty seconds because doing so not only required that the Krag know the location of their target, but also that they compute the humans' course and speed. One aims missiles, not at where the target is now, but at where it will be when the missiles arrive.

"Thank you, Mr. Bartoli," said Max.

"Why isn't the Krag ship moving?" asked Sahin. "I seem to recall your telling me once, 'mobility is the essence of naval warfare,' or something like that—one of your typical military aphorisms that has the benefit of being both quotably pithy and entirely uninformative."

"Her skipper doesn't think he needs to move," Max responded. "All he's looking to do is get a firing solution and blow us to flaming atoms ASAP, without any fancy footwork. That new Ridgeback missile of theirs gives them such an enormous range advantage that he plans to just sit there, launch, and watch us die—he thinks he's got nothing to worry about."

"Does he?" Sahin asked.

Clouseau picked that moment to emit a loud, rumbling purr, after which he rolled over and draped himself over the doctor's leg like an impossibly rotund yet almost perfectly limp black fox stole, the very picture of feline relaxation.

Max simply looked at the cat and smiled.

"We are well within Hotel two's weapons range. He should have a firing solution in the next few seconds," Bartoli announced, unable to eliminate a certain subtle but definite "oh shit" tone from his voice. "At that time Hotel two will still be more than half a million kills beyond our maximum weapons range."

"Very well. *Steady, boys, steady.*" Max quoted the age-old naval song. It actually helped.

"Missile launch detection," Bartoli sang out. "Two seeker heads, Ridgeback type, designating as Vampire eleven and Vampire twelve. Bearing zero-four-seven mark two-one-two. Speed zero point two c. My opinion is that the missiles are set for reduced velocity to allow more time for target acquisition. Estimating run time at this speed at thirty-five seconds." Pause. Three beats. "Bearing to Vampires is constant. Seekers have locked on and gone to terminal acquisition mode. Missiles are now accelerating to defeat countermeasures. Revised projected impact: fifteen seconds."

The doctor made a choked sound. "Aren't you going to evade?"

"Nope. Friendly ships don't evade."

"But we're not . . ."

"Vampires now sending IFF interrogation." Pause. "Response transmitted." Although the crew of the Krag *ship* knew the *Cumberland* was an enemy vessel and didn't bother to confirm that with an Identification Friend or Foe signal, the *missiles*, on the other hand, were equipped with an IFF system to prevent accidental attacks on other Krag vessels. The Krag were supremely confident that the Union could never duplicate their complex and constantly shifting IFF codes.

But with the aid of the captured data, the *Cumberland* was able to transmit a valid response to the missiles' IFF signal. Because their target properly identified itself as a friendly ship, the missiles broke off their attack, veered off onto harmless trajectories, shut down their seeker heads, nulled their drives, and safed their warheads.

The two Ridgeback missiles stayed that way for exactly 4.1557 seconds while their onboard computers accessed a deeply secret routine buried in the innermost interstices of their programming, compared the instructions they found there with the IFF response received from the *Cumberland*, and calculated an appropriate action.

Hotel two's commander, no fool by any stretch of the imagination, recognized that the humans had somehow spoofed the missiles' IFF transponders. No matter. He would use his superior firepower to close whisker tips to whisker tips with the humans and pound their last-of-the-litter vessel to a pile of seed hulls. Just as he had given the order and begun to anticipate the upcoming glorious pulse-cannon duel, his tactical officer told him that the two missiles had reactivated their seeker heads.

How peculiar.

Searching for an explanation for this unexpected development, he quickly pulled up the IFF response transmitted by the human vessel and had the computer find which vessel had that code assigned to it. When that information appeared, the commander's ears stood up, and his tail bent suddenly and sharply to the right, instinctive signs of extreme alarm. Effective leader that he was, however, the commander quickly mastered his emotions, relaxed his ears, and restored his tail to its proper orientation. He didn't know what the missiles would do with the information they had just received, but he feared the worst.

According to the message, now flashing an alarming shade of blue at the lower left of the commander's master display, the *Cumberland* had not just identified itself as a run-of-the-mill Krag warship. Rather, she had identified herself to the missiles as the Personal Yacht and Royal Space Barge of Her Magnificent and Imperious Luminescence, the Dowager Matriarch and Birth Mother of the High Hegemon. In other words, the IFF return signal told the missiles that the Krag Queen Mother was on board.

With a history of political and dynastic assassination that made the Borgias look like the Von Trapp Family Singers, the Krag were not only treacherous, but scrupulously vengeful. The Krag language didn't even have a word for "loyalty." Accordingly, all Krag missiles had programming hardwired directly into the deep recesses of their processor architecture, specifically designed to exact vengeance against any vessel or installation that dared to fire a weapon against a member of the Hegemon's family line. In accordance with that programming, after just over four seconds' computation to verify their instructions, confirm the correctness of the IFF signal, recheck the identity of the launching ship, determine that they were not launched by accident, and check for the presence of an overriding instruction from the Hegemon himself, the missiles pivoted, locked on their seekers, ran their drives up to maximum, easily blew past countermeasures and defensive systems designed for subluminal Union missiles, and blotted Hotel two from space in a flare of fusing hydrogen.

"Hotel two destroyed!" Bartoli announced with the mandatory obviousness associated with his post.

"The three nearest Lehrer-Lobachevsky planes are also gone," came the follow-up announcement from Kasparov. With Hotel two now a rapidly dissipating cloud of disassociated atoms, three faces of the Krag detection enclosure winked out of existence. The door to escape was now open.

"Phase Three: *Execute*," said Max.

The *Cumberland* slightly altered its course so that it went straight into the rapidly dissipating fireball that had just engulfed the Krag ship, now attenuated enough that it did not overwhelm the deflectors but still the locus of enough heat, hard radiation, and electromagnetic energy to screen the destroyer from enemy sensors. Upon reaching a set of predetermined coordinates, Maneuvering executed a radical course change.

"On new course two-three-five mark zero-two-one," announced LeBlanc. "Speed zero point one-five c."

"All stealth modes reengaged," said Nelson.

"There are a lot of people who would say that we should have kept going right through that vertex and made a run for it," DeCosta said confidentially.

"True, and that was my first impulse," Max replied. "But they've got cruisers at all the jump points. That means before we could jump out, we'd have to engage and defeat a ship of greatly superior firepower. While we were doing that, the remaining ships from this battle group would catch up with us. And with one of them being a *Barbell* class battlecruiser with easily a dozen times our firepower, maybe more, that would not be a winnable fight. No, XO, we've got to whittle down the odds some before we can try to jump out of here."

"There are also a lot of people who would say that heading right back into the enclosure we just blew up a destroyer to escape from is . . . um . . . well . . . *unorthodox*, sir."

"It's what you Tiger Team guys came up with, XO. And it's also not what the rat-faces are expecting." He raised his voice so that it could be heard throughout CIC. "Tactical, I need a report on activity of the enemy vessels."

"Sir," Bartoli responded, "they've taken the bait. Vessels have adopted pursuit courses, apparently based on the assumption that we continued our previous course of approximately zero-five-zero mark two-one-zero. I'm projecting our assumed course in blue. Projected enemy courses are coming up on the tactical display now in orange." Orange arrows appeared, showing the current courses of each of the red dots, all angled to intercept the blue line.

"Very well. And what's the *Barbell* up to?"

"That would be Hotel six." He entered a command on his console, and the red dot that had been in the upper left corner of the cube started to blink. "He's fallen into the same course as the others, but he's on a slower acceleration profile, following the standard Krag pattern where the command ship of any formation of four or more ships hangs back to coordinate rather than participate in the battle unless needed."

"Outstanding. That will open up some range between him and the other ships, exactly as we expected. Maneuvering, continue to adhere to the battle plan."

"ETA at the intercept point is eight minutes and nineteen seconds," said LeBlanc. The *Cumberland* altered course and speed so that it would soon emerge from the fireball and insert itself in the space between the formation of Krag ships sent to intercept it and the battlecruiser following them to coordinate their attack.

Max regarded the Countermeasures console, almost straight ahead of him. He could see that Sauvé was frantically busy there, as were three other people from his back room, as well as Bales, whose relief was at the Computers Station while he assisted Sauvé. Max could do nothing to help these men. Either these specialists would solve the problem before them, or everyone onboard the *Cumberland* would die less than eight minutes from now. Their task had to be completed between the instant a few moments ago, when the *Cumberland* got within range of certain short-range transceivers on board the enemy battlecruiser, and when the battlecruiser armed its weapons to fire on the humans. Staring at the men wouldn't help, so Max pulled up a set of status displays on his console and checked the readiness of weapons, engines, and other systems for what was to come. He did his best to immerse himself in that review, checking for anything that his still undertrained and largely unseasoned crew might have missed. He caught a few minor mistakes that he corrected with a few carefully chosen words over the voice loops. Just as his concentration was starting to fray under the friction inflicted by the ever-increasing tension, he heard a strange popping noise.

Max looked up, and he saw the men at Countermeasures slapping each other on the backs and, in some cases, somewhat lower. "We did it, sir," Sauvé said. "Command transmitted and acknowledged."

"Outstanding, gentlemen. Simply outstanding. Officer of the Deck, log my order for an extra spirits ration for every man presently standing at the Countermeasures console, now in the Countermeasures Back Room, or in the Computers Back Room, effective the next time we are on Condition Blue or lower."

"Aye, aye, *sir*!" answered Sauvé, both the Officer of the Deck and the most conspicuous beneficiary of the order. Mr. Sauvé was rather fond of a particular golden-colored spirit known as *tequila*.

Max looked at his coffee mug and noticed that Hewlett had refilled it unnoticed. Max met the boy's eyes, pointed at the mug, and nodded his thanks. Hewlett mouthed, "Anything else, sir?"

Max shook his head gently.

"Intercepting Hotel six's course . . . now," announced LeBlanc. "Altering course to approach Hotel six head-on."

Dr. Sahin's head snapped around at that announcement. "Head-on? You're attacking that huge battlecruiser head-on? We won't last a minute!"

"Doctor," Max said, "we'll last considerably longer than that." He turned to the Stealth Console. "Mr. Nelson, I think it's time for you to unleash your inner thespian."

"Aye, sir," he answered, actually grinning with enthusiasm rather than grimacing in fear as most of the CIC crew were doing not too long ago. Destroying that first ship had been tonic for everyone's spirits. "The show begins now." He keyed in a command that started a sequence of events designed for viewing and consumption by Hotel six's command crew.

First, the *Cumberland*'s emulation emitters gave off a burst of electromagnetic energy of the kind associated with a catastrophic computer core shutdown. Then came a cascade of other emissions, simulating the failure of numerous other systems throughout the ship, followed by a burst of incoherent gravitons and the venting of hydrogen plasma, indicative of an emergency decompression of the ship's fusion reactor. Another emission mimicked the ship switching over to its auxiliary Rickover-type fission reactor to supply its basic power needs. When that was done, the emitters began to transmit a gamut of signals by which the *Cumberland* essentially emulated itself in a crippled condition, while its stealth systems kept the true condition of the ship hidden from view.

At a nod from Nelson, LeBlanc signaled Fleishman, his man on Drives, to cut the power to the main sublight drive, allowing the ship to coast.

"There, sir," Nelson said. "As far as the Krag are concerned, we're practically dead in the water. Mobility limited to maneuvering thrusters only, weapons off-line, point-defense and deflectors dead, main computer cooked, vessel subsisting on auxiliary power."

"Outstanding. Tactical, what's Hotel six up to?"

"Skipper, he's reducing speed," said Bartoli. "Deceleration profile shows he'll stop about 425,000 kills off our bow."

"Outstanding."

"Picking up active scans, Oscar and Victor band," said Kasparov. "Nothing too powerful. He's not probing us. My estimate is that he's refining his firing solution."

"Hotel six is now station-keeping 424,853 kilometers off our bow," said Bartoli. "I'm expecting her to fire her missiles momentarily."

"Very well," said Max. "Everybody hold what you've got."

Not the most orthodox order, but everyone understood it.

"Romeo band target acquisition tachyon radar. Locking on . . . they have a lock. Hotel six should commence missile firing in less than five seconds."

"Thank you, Mr. Bartoli."

"Max," Dr. Sahin said in a strangled voice, "aren't you going to *do something*?"

"No, Bram," he answered. "We already did it."

"Hotel six is opening missile doors on all *fourteen* forward missile tubes. He is apparently preparing to fire a *fourteen-missile salvo*," Bartoli said. Then as an aside, "They must really, really want us dead." Pause. About two seconds. "Warheads armed. Missile tubes are energized. Missile drives powering up. He's ready to fire in all respects. Explosion! Explosion! Explosion! Again! Again! Still more! All fourteen missile tubes have ruptured with missiles still in their tubes. Sir, I'm reading several, no, make that *dozens*, of bulkhead breaches. At least forty, maybe more. Secondary explosions throughout the ship. There's some more! Hull breach! Multiple hull breaches! Her fusion reactor just shut down; she's on her fission auxiliary now. Another set of secondary explosions. I think she just lost most or all of her maneuvering thrusters too."

"Whatever did you do to them?" Sahin asked.

"Mr. Sauvé," said Max, "why don't you do the honors?"

"We tricked the missiles into firing their drives at full power in the launch tubes," Sauvé explained. "Krag computer security on the ship is just too good—just about everything that could be used for any kind of sabotage requires a biometric authentication from inside the ship, you see—so we couldn't spoof any of the key systems. But we were able to deceive the missiles into thinking that they were being fired from the pylons of a fighter, where they're programmed to run their drives up to full thrust immediately, instead of from a ship's launch tubes, where they are programmed to wait until they're clear of the ship."

"How much thrust is that?" Sahin asked.

"Something like 40,000,000 Newtons."

"Astonishing. Humankind went to the moon with less. It's a wonder the ship survived at all."

"The Krag build them very, very strong," DeCosta interjected.

Max turned to the tactical officer. "Current status on Hotel six, Mr. Bartoli?"

"Heavy internal damage throughout the forward quarter of the ship. She's not going anywhere for at least ten or fifteen minutes, sir. Her main reactor is definitely off-line. We don't know the exact restart time for the fusion reaction on this class. It's possible that she is damaged beyond capability for restart. All forward missile tubes out of commission indefinitely. No pulse-cannon until she has the fusion reactor online to supply plasma. Maneuvering thrusters are out because the explosions blew the hydrazine tanks. There are several fires: secondary combustion started by missile drive plasma, as well as primary from the hydrazine. Other missile tubes appear to be operational, but she can't turn to unmask them, so she can't fire on us for now. Her comms and computers all seem to work, plus life support, artificial grav, and most other systems, including deflectors and blast-suppression fields. She's also leaking nitrogen tetroxide from some of her hull breaches, which leads me to believe that some of those tanks are blown too. Not only is that stuff hypergolic with the hydrazine, which is why they have it onboard in the first place, it's extremely toxic, so they may have several compartments that are now a toxic atmosphere hazard."

"Why don't we blast it to pieces, then?" asked Dr. Sahin.

"You heard the man," said Max. "He's still got deflectors and blast suppression. Not to mention a three-meter-thick armored hull. We would have to fire every missile we have just to inflict some real damage. No, we have better plans for our friend."

Chin spoke up. "Sir, intercepting comm traffic between Hotel six and the other Krag ships. Getting a good decrypt. He says he's heavily damaged and drifting. He's transmitting our position and ordering them to close the range and to fire their missiles—coordinated fire, time on target, as soon as possible." He stopped and listened to his back room for a moment. "And he's instructing them to manually disable the IFF modules on every missile they fire. He's ordering Hotel seven to do the fire-control calculations, time the launches, and provide to the other ships the parameters to program the missiles for a flank attack to be sure that, from the perspective of the missile-seeker heads, there is a safe angular separation between their ship and us." Pause. "Hotel seven acknowledges." Pause. "Hotel seven is telling the other ships to stand by for firing instructions." Pause. "Transmitting firing instructions. I'm relaying the decrypt on those to CO, XO, and all combat consoles."

"Very good, Mr. Chin."

"Hotels one, three, four, five, seven, and eight are all changing course," announced Bartoli. "Settling in on new courses—constant bearing decreasing range. Not in any hurry, though. They're all accelerating at the standard for their various classes."

"They're planning to let their missiles do the work," said Max.

"An excellent tactic," said DeCosta, smiling.

"I highly recommend it," answered Max.

"Hotels one, three, four, five, seven, and eight all firing," said Bartoli. Short pause. "And they're not kidding, either. Total number of incoming missiles . . . thirty. Repeat, three zero incoming

Vampires." He read off the bearings to each group of missiles, one for each attacking enemy ship. "Missiles are dialed in at different velocities. Speeds are synchronized for a time-on-target arrival. ETA, one minute, forty-three seconds. Bearings changing slowly on all missiles—they appear to be programmed to fly to a waypoint on our port beam, where they will turn and go to terminal attack mode; that way when they are making their final runs, the missiles' seeker heads will see at least a forty-degree separation between Hotel six and us to prevent them from targeting their own ship. They appear to be on course."

"But I thought the enemy believed we were essentially helpless," Bram said.

"As far as we can tell, they do," Max responded.

"Then wouldn't thirty missiles represent a commitment of ordnance greatly in excess of that necessary to bring about our destruction? I'm sure you naval types have a suitably testosterone-laden term for that sort of thing."

"Overkill. We call it *overkill*. And actually, if we were as crippled as we have let on, *four* missiles would be overkill. Thirty would be insane, screaming, maniacal, blood-guzzling obsession. Which seems to be Krag SOP for dealing with the *Cumberland* since we delivered the *NEVER* message." He glanced at the tactical display and then at the chrono, after which he said to the compartment at large, "Things are about to get a little hairy, gentlemen. Mr. LeBlanc, are you and your men ready for some skin-of-your-teeth maneuvering?"

"Sir," LeBlanc said as a warm grin spread across his friendly features, "if you've got the balls to order it, we've got the skill to fly it."

"Well said, Mr. LeBlanc," Max said, smiling. "*Very* well said."

A few tense seconds ticked by. No one spoke as they watched the tiny, twinkling motes in the tactical display representing the missiles converge on the point at which they would turn to attack the *Cumberland*. No one, except perhaps for Mr. Bartoli, whose job it was—and Mr. Levy, who could not help himself—to calculate how many deadly megatons those motes signified.

Bartoli broke the spell. "Vampires have reached the waypoint and are going subluminal, average bearing two-five-two mark one-one-seven, range 545,060 kilometers." Pause. "Vampires now turning toward us and preparing to go into terminal attack mode. In five seconds. Four. Three. Two. One. NOW."

"Missile targeting scanner detections, bearings consistent with Vampires," said Kasparov.

"Phase *FOUR*: *Execute*," said Max, adrenalin making his voice louder than he intended.

LeBlanc patted Fleishman on the shoulder. The Drives man shoved the controller all the way to the stop and then turned a ring around the controller stalk, illuminating a purple light in Engineering. As a result the *Cumberland*'s drive went to Emergency, and Chief Engineer Brown—responding to the light—disabled the safeties and governors on the main sublight drive, enhancing *Cumberland*'s already extraordinary acceleration. The ship sprang forward, like a cheetah darting out from behind a clump of grass in pursuit of a particularly tasty gazelle, straight at the crippled Krag battlecruiser.

Not only were the Krag caught flat-footed by this unexpected development, but so were their missiles, which had been programmed on the assumption that the *Cumberland* was dead in space. Determining that nothing in their targeting instructions for this particular launch covered this eventuality, they reverted to their default targeting and intercept mode: they pointed their seeker heads right at the *Cumberland*, even as it rapidly approached the crippled battlecruiser, and accelerated to follow.

Meanwhile, Nelson abruptly ceased his now-irrelevant sophisticated theatrics. He shut down the emulation emitters, ending the *Cumberland*'s masquerade as a heavily damaged vessel. Further, since the redlined main sublight drive's exhaust was bright enough to be seen by the Mark One Eyeball for at least a million kilometers in every direction, he abandoned all efforts at stealth, even to the degree of extending all of the ship's thermal radiator fins, bleeding heat from the heavily stressed heat sink bright red into space.

Now plainly visible to every conceivable sensor and violating half a dozen regulations regarding safe combat maneuvers (an oxymoron if there ever was one), *Cumberland* closed on the battlecruiser, first on a collision course and then veering off at the last microsecond to hug the contours of the giant ship's hull, at times coming within a meter and a half of its metal skin. The more experienced crew members could feel the almost imperceptible bumps and jolts through their feet as the ship collided with and clipped off various small antennae, emitters, sensor masts, and other nonstructural objects protruding from the Krag vessel's hull.

In a blur of relative motion, the gigantic Krag battlecruiser seemed to flash past the rapidly accelerating *Cumberland* in less than a second, the destroyer traversing the battlecruiser's defensive firing arcs too fast for its degraded antiship point-defense systems to be able to lock on. There was only the tooth-rattling *WHAM! WHAM!* as two point-defense rail-gun rounds slammed into the aft hull as the smaller ship pulled away, the high-tech bullets robbed of most of their punch by the *Cumberland*'s rapid acceleration along the projectiles' line of travel. In an instant she was astern of the giant ship, running as fast as her legs could carry her.

As the *Cumberland* had dashed out of their initial firing solution, the thirty missiles fired by the remaining ships of the containment group had turned radically to keep their fleeing target centered in their seeker heads' field of view and pursued it in a roughly cylindrical pack, closing from the destroyer's seven o'clock position. Unfortunately for the battlecruiser, as soon as the destroyer got within 9.427 meters of the larger ship and came between it and the missiles, the missiles' sensors lacked the resolution to distinguish the *Cumberland* and the battlecruiser as two separate targets, a fact now known to the *Cumberland*'s crew by virtue of the captured data. Accordingly, the weapons' targeting logic concluded that the huge object in front of them was a single very large and very attractive enemy target and altered their course to strike that object dead center, completely losing their lock on the *Cumberland*.

Ordinarily the missiles' IFF systems would have identified the battlecruiser as a friendly vessel and aborted their attack. But because the *Cumberland* had earlier used the IFF system against its makers, the Krag attack group commander onboard the battlecruiser—exactly as the Tiger Team predicted—had ordered that the weapons' IFF systems be disabled. The Krag warships, he assured them, need only make certain of their targets before firing, and fire from a position ensuring an adequate angular separation between the battlecruiser and the destroyer.

The battlecruiser didn't stand a chance. The Krag command crew scarcely had time to be first shocked and then terrified that the supposedly crippled destroyer had sprung into motion with the missiles in its wake before all thirty superluminal thermonuclear weapons delivered their warheads within microseconds of each other. They exploded as one, instantly consuming the enormous and powerful Krag vessel—and with it, the attack group commander—in an irregular, roiling cataclysm of brilliant, swirling plasma.

With six Krag ships still out there—six Krag ships to which the doomed battlecruiser had just sent the *Cumberland*'s exact location as of only a few moments before—there was no time for jubilation (save for the occasional "Yes!" and a dozen or so fist pumps around CIC). As the battlecruiser's funeral pyre slowly dimmed behind them, Max called out, "Phase Five: *EXECUTE*!"

Under LeBlanc's guidance, the three men at Maneuvering steered the ship through a maneuver known as a "flapjack," in which the ship flipped itself over bow for stern. Fleishman at Drives reduced the engine setting from Emergency to Flank, the still-powerful thrust of the main sublight engines pushing against the ship's forward momentum, gradually slowing it, then pushing it back in the direction from which it came. Within a few moments, LeBlanc had Fleishman rapidly reduce the thrust, and under his expert direction, the *Cumberland* glided back into the center of the still-dissipating fireball created by the battlecruiser's destruction, which had screened the course reversal maneuver from the other Krag ships and which now helped shield them from enemy sensors. The thirty warheads created a zone of space more than 2000 kilometers in diameter, full of plasma and powerful electromagnetic disruption that, even as the immense nuclear fireball cooled and dissipated, would be opaque to most sensor scans for more than half an hour.

Following the minutely developed plan formulated by the Special Attack Tiger Team, Kasparov signaled the men in his back room to launch two highly stealthy Mark XLVIII sensor drones, which popped out on opposite sides of the fireball to provide the destroyer with sensor information unobstructed by superheated plasma, electromagnetic fields, and bomb residue.

"All deflectors at maximum," announced Shimomura from Deflector Control. Even as it spread and cooled, the fireball left by the detonation of thirty thermonuclear warheads was still a dangerous place.

"Very well," answered Max.

Two minutes passed. "Beginning to get sensor returns from the drones," said Kasparov. "Target motion analysis in progress."

"Mr. Nelson, how much longer can we safely radiate?" Max asked.

"The fireball is attenuating and cooling rapidly, sir. To be on the safe side, I would like to retract the radiator fins in about a minute and a half," the Stealth officer replied.

"Very well, Mr. Nelson. Retract at your discretion." Max reflexively checked the heat sink status, which his console was programmed to display at all times. It showed that the ship's heat storage capacity had gone from 98 percent of maximum to 18 percent. By the time Nelson retracted the fins, it would be 15 or 16 percent. Max would have liked to get it down to 2 percent or so, but it would have to do.

"TMA coming in now," said Kasparov. "Enemy vessel positions plotted in the tactical display." He then rattled off the bearings and ranges to all six targets as the red dots representing the computer's best calculation of their positions appeared in the 3D tactical display and on the 2D tactical overview displays on several consoles around the compartment.

"Hotels one, three, five, seven, and eight are arrayed in a ring or pentagon and will pass our position with the fireball remnant in the center of the ring," Bartoli said, offering the tactical assessment. "They are actively scanning the area beyond the fireball along our former course, apparently assuming we are still on the run. Hotel four is hanging back outside of the formation, approximately 27,000 kilometers. Based on standard Krag tactical doctrine, that would make Hotel four the new apparent attack group leader. Just as a reminder, Hotel four is a *Crusader* class light cruiser. He is on a course tangential to the fireball—he'll just graze the outside edge."

Max regarded the six red dots slowly moving toward the blue "you are here" dot. "Mr. Kasparov, can you refine the distance from Hotel four to the nearest Krag ship in the formation. I want it to the kilometer if you can get it."

"I believe so, sir," he answered. "I just need to instruct the probes to upload their high-frequency tachyo-photon interferometer data at high resolution. I've been getting a low-res take because I didn't think we needed the higher level of precision yet."

"Very well," said Max. "And when you get it, I'm betting it's going to turn out to be 27,253 kilometers."

"Retracting radiator fins," Nelson announced.

"Very well," responded Max.

About thirty seconds passed. "Skipper," Kasparov said, "you're right. Exactly 27,253 kilometers."

Max looked at DeCosta and raised an inquiring eyebrow.

The XO nodded. "A nice round number in Krag units, sir."

"So, at least we know something about the new combat group commander," said Max.

"We do?" DeCosta asked.

"Sure we do, XO. Have you ever seen me position this ship a nice round number of units away from anything? When you studied their campaigns, did you ever see Hornmeyer or Litvinoff or Middleton or Barber or Lo do it?" The XO shook his head. "Damn straight you didn't. And you never will, unless it's part of some deeply complex head game. But unlike the wickedly competent fellow on that battlecruiser we just killed, his successor out there is failing to take the same kind of pains to avoid being predictable. In all likelihood, not only is he prone to formulaic thinking, but he's probably also lazy. We are going to take advantage of that.

"Mr. Bartoli, get with Mr. Nelson. I want a joint opinion from the Tactical and Stealth Sections as to the point in the fireball zone that is closest to the path of Hotel four that will still provide adequate concealment from his sensors. Weapons, load Ravens in tubes one and two." As the Stealth console was directly behind the Tactical one, this particular bit of coordination didn't prove difficult. Less than a minute later, Bartoli had transferred the coordinates, and Mr. LeBlanc was guiding the *Cumberland* into position, just over a thousand kilometers inside the edge of the fireball area.

"Gentlemen," Max said to CIC at large, "my intention is to take Hotel four with a Raven, waypoint bow attack. Minimum range. I'll hold tube two in reserve in case the first missile misses or malfunctions. When that warhead detonates, we will attack the remainder of the Krag formation with the Equalizer. Attack pattern Sierra-5. As soon as all weapons are discharged, begin standard reload cycle and make for the Bravo jump point at maximum stealthy speed. You think you can manage those weapons orders, Mr. Levy?"

"With pleasure, sir," he said. The man was practically salivating as he repeated the order and went to work. A few seconds later, he said, "Skipper, the timings on these weapons firings are very critical. I recommend auto-fire mode on both the Raven and the Equalizer."

"I concur in your recommendation, Mr. Levy." Then, in an official tone, "Officer of the Deck, this is a Nuclear Weapons Automatic Firing Order. Commanding Officer authorizes weapons free and automatic launch on the following nuclear launch systems: 1. Raven missile loaded in tube one, targeted on Krag ship identified as Hotel four; 2. HSRLMS, all loaded ordnance, targeted on remainder of Krag formation."

"Nuclear Weapons free and automatic launch, Raven in tube one and HSRLMS, acknowledged and logged," said Sauvé. "Executive Officer?"

"Executive Officer concurs," said DeCosta. While the firing and detonation of nuclear weapons had become almost routine in the course of the more than thirty-year war with the Krag, allowing those weapons to be fired by automatic systems without a human being's finger on the button had not. Accordingly, an order to do so required the concurrence of the Executive Officer.

"Officer of the Deck acknowledges and logs Commanding Officer's order and Executive Officer's concurrence," Sauvé said. "Weapons officer may proceed to program automatic launch."

"Weapons officer acknowledges. Programming as ordered. Estimated time until execution: four minutes, nineteen seconds." Levy input the instructions and checked them. Seven times.

Maybe eight.

A growing expression of alarm formed on the doctor's face, while his body language became increasingly agitated. After a few minutes, he could contain himself no longer. "Max," he said, a certain shrillness creeping into his voice, "does all of this talk about *automatic launch* mean that the computer is going to launch a bunch of fusion missiles on its own?"

"Why, yes," Max replied, with all the worry he might express when telling the bartender that he didn't want any ice in his bourbon.

"Isn't that a bad idea? You saw the CineVid we all watched together on Movie Night when we were outbound to the rendezvous—the one with Damien Matthew and Julie Angeleoni? The computer decided that it didn't like being given orders by humans and used the nuclear weapons under its control to blackmail the human race into letting it rule them. What was the name?"

"*Colossus: The Fordman Project*," said Levy. "But, sir, the ship's computer is not self-aware. It has no likes or dislikes; it simply follows our instructions."

"But when I talk to it, it sounds emotional," Sahin said. "When I tell it I'm having a problem with a system, it sounds regretful; when I log a happy event, it sounds happy for me; and so on.

When it asks questions in response to my orders, it sounds interested. It reacts like a self-aware being."

"That's right, Doctor," Bales, the head of the Computers Section, piped up. "It *acts* sentient. The computer has sophisticated heuristic software designed to emulate emotion, to determine the proper tone to take based on your tone of voice, content analysis of what you say or log, parsing of your word choices and tone of voice, and so on. It is a very powerful, nonthinking machine, containing brilliantly designed software carefully crafted to replicate the semblance of human emotion. Doing so makes it easier for people to interact with the computer, tell it what's going on, and give it truthful log entries. It's a lot easier to log some huge mistake you made running some system if you feel like you're telling your troubles to a trusted friend than if you're just making a recording to be stored by a soulless machine."

Sahin looked to Max for confirmation; he nodded. "I suppose that makes sense. Aren't there disadvantages to giving the computer control of the weapons?"

"Absolutely," said Levy. "It deprives me of the satisfaction of pressing the button that nukes those sorry rat bastards."

Sahin pursed his lips disapprovingly. "I consider it unseemly and impious to take joy in the death, no matter how necessary and justified, of fellow thinking creatures who—"

"Krag vessels are reducing velocity to 0.05 c," Bartoli interrupted. "No change in course. Their main formation will pass our position in two minutes and fourteen seconds."

"The enemy is engaging in very intense active scanning of the space along our former course," Kasparov added. "Their scans appear to be optimized to pick up a stealthed ship and to detect a drive trail."

Max turned to DeCosta. "XO, what do you think they're up to?"

"Sir, my opinion is that they are reducing speed to increase the efficacy of their sensors. We've managed to fool them a few times, and they're getting wary. From where and how they're scanning, it looks as though their main worry is that we will go stealthy and lie right in their path. Which, by the way, would be a pretty stupid thing for us to do. No matter how highly stealthed we were, five ships engaged in a coordinated scan of the same area would pick us up before they were within range of our missiles. They'd take us out with that damned new Ridgeback missile before we'd ever get a chance to shoot."

"It *would* be pretty dumb," agreed Max. "You'll learn, however, that all but the top 20 or 30 percent of Krag commanders have no problem believing that our next move is going to be something incredibly stupid because their propaganda says that we're stupid. But, yes, I agree. That is what it looks like they're doing. What's the impact on what we are planning to do?"

"None, really. Unless they start trying to scan inside the warhead blast zone from the inside, which they aren't showing any inclination to do."

"They are very unlikely to try that," Max said. "Their navy has a standing order to stay out of these zones until they've dissipated to the point at which a ship can enter them safely with deflectors at 10 percent—that way they can experience a 90 percent deflector failure and not suffer any damage. Their commander is engaging in projection—assuming that everyone else thinks and operates the way he does. It's a good way to get yourself killed."

"A principle," DeCosta said, "that you are about to demonstrate."

"True," Max replied, "but I don't expect *Monsieur le Krag* out there to live long enough to make use of what we are about to teach him."

"Auto fire has initiated a countdown," Levy interjected. "Tube one will auto fire in five seconds. Four. Three. Two. One. Firing."

"Phase Six: *EXECUTE*," Max said.

The five remaining enemy destroyers passed the widest point of the fireball, arranged in a ring around its circumference, with Hotel four, the enemy cruiser and now the command ship for the formation, following. The Raven missile, auto-fired by the *Cumberland*, headed toward the edge of the fireball at its lowest speed setting, emerging only 1255 kilometers behind Hotel eleven, deep inside that vessel's deflector wake and drive exhaust. There, the missile turned hard toward Mr. Levy's estimate of the oncoming Krag light cruiser's position, activated its seeker head, acquired the target, ran its drive up to maximum, and steered itself straight at the cruiser's bow.

Behind a screen of five destroyers and with the humans predicted to be somewhere ahead of the screen, running for their lives, the cruiser was not ready for a missile, so much so that not only were its missile defenses not activated but the sensors best suited to missile detection were on standby. As a result the crew of the cruiser had less than a half second's warning. The Raven easily penetrated the dormant Krag defensive systems and detonated its 1.5-megaton fusion warhead. The cruiser simply ceased to exist, its ionized atoms merging with those from the warhead and missile in a blinding globe of incandescent death.

Meanwhile, no one in CIC had time to enjoy the spectacle of Hotel four's funeral pyre. Oblivious, for now, to the cruiser's fiery demise, the five enemy destroyers passed the fireball and continued to follow their estimate of the *Cumberland*'s course. Even before the *Cumberland*'s warhead blew, Max's call to execute Phase Six triggered Fleishman to run the sublight drive up to full and the other men at Maneuvering to steer the ship to pop out of the fireball directly behind the enemy formation. As soon as the ship was in the clear, the fire-control computers correlated tracking information received from the ship's sensors with what they had been receiving from the stealthed probes and began to grind out firing solutions for the five Krag destroyers.

It took a full eleven seconds for the explosion's light and radiation to reach the Krag formation and for their sensors and associated computers to process the explosion, come to the surprising and more computationally difficult (and, therefore, slower) determination that it was a Union warhead, calculate that the cruiser had been attacked and destroyed, and compute the area from which the weapon that destroyed the cruiser had likely been fired. After ten of those eleven seconds had lapsed, Mr. Levy called out, "Firing solution computed. Targeting data routed to the Equalizer. Weapon drives and warheads arming. Arming sequence complete. Warhead safeties disengaging. Safeties disengaged." Pause. "Equalizer is ready to receive targeting data. Equalizer has accepted targeting data. Translating into individual weapon guidance commands . . . Data translated. Guidance commands loaded. Auto fire has initiated countdown. Firing in three seconds. Two. One. Firing."

The crew felt ten quick jolts over a period of less than two seconds as the high-speed rotary missile launch system, installed under the ship's "chin" during her last refit and which the crew called the Equalizer, rotated its ten missile-holding cylinders past an abbreviated launch tube, each cylinder firing its missile as it came into alignment with the launch tube, operating much like a revolver. The process resulted in the launching of ten of the new Kestrel mini antiship missiles.

"Missiles away," Levy called out. He paused for a second to examine his display. "Missiles are hot, straight, and normal. Executing pairing maneuver now. Maneuver complete—each Krag destroyer now has two missiles on intercept." Pause. "Missile crews are reporting by lights that they are reloading the Equalizer. Estimated time to completion: twenty-three minutes."

Max briefly shook his head. Twenty-three minutes was a lifetime in combat, but that was the nature of the weapon. The rotating drum that housed the missile cylinders was mounted outside the ship. Only the cylinder that aligned with the firing tube could be reached from the missile room. Accordingly, the ten cylinders had to be reloaded one at a time, a process that took even the most skilled crews nearly fifteen minutes. Between the newness of the weapon to the ship and the generally lower level of competence of the missile crews, the operation took just over twenty minutes on the *Cumberland*.

Max turned to his tactical officer, who should have been updating him on what the enemy vessels were doing. Instead, Bartoli appeared to be transfixed by what he was seeing on his displays. "Mr. Bartoli," said Max, "how about letting the rest of us in on what you find so fascinating."

"Sorry, sir," he said, with genuine remorse. "Krag vessels are decelerating, so it looks as though they have figured out we destroyed their cruiser. They are still directing active sensors along their former course. Except for one: Hotel eight. He's broken formation and is accelerating at a right angle to the rest of them and away from the fireball at course two-three-three mark zero-nine-five." Pause. "The rest turning now, probably to close on the cruiser's last position. Pause. Missiles just went to terminal homing, except for the ones targeted on Hotel eight. They never acquired a lock and are now in search mode . . . they're going to miss. Okay, the other targets all went evasive, drives redlined. Missiles are setting up for pincer attacks from amidships. HIT! HIT! TWO MORE! Direct hits on all four ships. Four solid kills. Nothing left but debris."

"But . . . but . . ." the doctor stammered, "but how did those little missiles destroy those destroyers? I thought they were so tough that it was hard for a normal-size missile to take them out."

"New binary warhead design: neutron flux from a small enhanced radiation warhead pushes the deflector's gravitons out of the way, making a hole in the deflectors for the main warhead to get through and blast the enemy ship. We borrowed the design from the Pfelung. Ask Levy to explain it in detail when we have time, Bram," Max said. "He'd love to tell you all about it."

"I cannot begin to tell you how eager I am for that conversation," Sahin said.

"All remaining enemy targets destroyed, sir, with the exception of Hotel eight," said Bartoli. He gave the range and bearing. "We're passing through the field of debris and radiation created by our missile explosions, and when we emerge, it will still be screening us from him, at least for the next few minutes before dissipation of the fusion plasma and the angle change allow his sensor beams to penetrate."

"Very well," said Max.

DeCosta leaned toward Max. "But, Skipper, isn't there a chance that he'll deduce our location and what we're doing anyway?"

"More than a chance, XO. I'd rate it is a virtual certainty. This guy was smart enough to see through our play back there—remember how he dashed in one direction when the other ships went in another, and how he wound up far enough outside of our firing solution that the missiles could not acquire him? I have no doubt that he'll see the most straightforward concealment and evasion play here. He'll come off his sprint, figure out what we just did to his buddies, and guess that we're using the debris field to screen ourselves while we run for the jump point. He knows that's what I'm doing because it's exactly what he would do. Unless we want to double back, he's got to know that we are headed for the Bravo jump point, not the Alfa or the Charlie, because only the Bravo takes us in the direction of the Union forces. We can't run at high speed if we want to stay stealthy, so if he's smart, he just goes to Flank or Emergency, joins up with his buddy guarding the jump point, and he'll have us outgunned two to one when we get there. That engagement would last about two minutes, and then we would all get to have reunions with our dead ancestors."

"What if we don't sneak to the jump point, but sprint instead? Can we get there fast enough to have time to defeat the cruiser at the jump point and be lying in wait for the destroyer when he gets there?" asked DeCosta.

"Let's find out," Max said. He turned to Bartoli and repeated DeCosta's idea.

"Not likely, Skipper," answered the tactical officer after only a few seconds' consideration. "Setting aside for the moment the issue of whether we could defeat the cruiser given that—with our drive at Emergency—we're not exactly going to be sneaking up on him, we're not significantly faster than Hotel eight. Intel is a little fuzzy on the top speed of the *Dervish* class, since they're so new, but we know that they are definitely in the same speed class as we are. If we beat him to the jump point, it won't be by much."

DeCosta was watching Max when Bartoli was speaking. He could see that nothing Bartoli said was a surprise to Max; the skipper had elicited the information for the benefit of his still very green XO.

The explanation also bought Max a little time. The crew was expecting him to give the orders that would extricate the ship from its current predicament, and Max had no such orders to give. He had expected to get all five of the Krag destroyers with the Kestrel mini-missiles fired from the Equilizer, after which he had planned to sneak up on the cruiser and hit it at close range from behind, with a time-on-target attack consisting of a full salvo from the Equalizer and two Ravens. But, with a *Dervish* class destroyer very likely to find his trail any minute, there would be no sneaking.

He turned to his console and regarded the tactical overview display. He changed the scale and rotated the view to help him create a three-dimensional mental picture of the *Cumberland*, the star Monroe-Tucker B at the center of the system (typically referred to as *the primary*), and the jump point. The primary was just over 30 AU away and about 19 AU off the straight line between the *Cumberland* and the jump point. He pulled up a few data screens, including some seldom-used information from the scientific and historical databases, and reviewed them quickly.

One moment he had no idea what he was going to do, and then suddenly, he saw it. Max knew that there was one way, and only one, that would get his ship and his crew out of this system alive.

Almost imperceptibly he shook his head. *It's highly unorthodox.* No one had ever tried it in a warship. And because it involved contact with a hazard that spacers were taught from their first days as a squeaker to give a wide berth, it would be viscerally terrifying to the men, and truth be told, more than a little daunting for Max as well. He took a breath and set his jaw.

Damn the torpedoes.

"Maneuvering, main sublight drive to FLANK, but keep us below .80 c so we don't have to deal with too many relativistic effects. Shape course for this system's primary. Continue to keep the debris field between us and Hotel eight as much as possible, but make sure to point the drive right at him every now and then so that he can detect us anyway. Make it look like it's unintentional. I want him to get a good clear detection and to follow us without it looking like we are trying to get him to follow us." LeBlanc acknowledged the order, and within a few seconds, Max heard the ship responding. He pulled up a NAV display that told him that the ship would reach the primary's outer atmosphere in just over eight hours. At sublight speeds, even interplanetary distances were immense.

Having made the decision to do what he was going to do and having implemented it, Max found himself both strangely relaxed and filled with a sudden exhilaration.

DeCosta leaned toward him, trying to conceal his mystified expression. "Skipper? May I ask . . . ?"

Max's comm panel beeped. He didn't need to look at the source ID to know who it was. "Just a minute, XO. The British are finding their upper lip to be in need of stiffening." He keyed the circuit. "Hello, Wernher. What a surprise to hear from you at this juncture! How may I be of assistance?"

The *Cumberland*'s Chief Engineer, Lieutenant Vaughn J. Brown, whom Max insisted on referring to as "Wernher" because of the accidental similarity of his first and last name—Vaughn Brown—to the surname of the great German/American rocket engineer Wernher *von Braun*, sounded as though he was having some difficulty maintaining his customary British reserve. "Captain! Sir! I looked at the course projection. With all due respect, you *can't* be thinking of doing what I think you're thinking of doing."

"Well, Wernher, I *think* that if you're talking about the tactic you and I discussed in my quarters three nights ago, then, yes, that's exactly what I'm thinking."

"But, sir! Our discussion of that issue was preceded by our having imbibed substantial quantities of that insidious whiskey you Yanks distill in Kentucky. Even then, it seemed a crazy idea."

"Wernher, one word of advice. Never call someone from Kentucky a *Yank*. I'll explain it to you later. As for the idea, of course it's crazy. But, Wernher, we're going to be in serious trouble if the only ideas we consider are the sane ones. Remember what Commodore Middleton used to say: *the general consensus of considered tactical opinion is that it is better to be crazy than dead.*

Besides, I think that this ship has already been saved by my crazy ideas at least two or three times. "

"Actually, Skipper, depending on what you call 'crazy,' it's somewhere between six and ten by my count," DeCosta chimed in.

"Twelve by my reckoning," said Brown, "if we include today's events."

"True," DeCosta admitted. "I hadn't tallied up the past few hours. There are at least two seriously crazy ones in there, for sure."

"Gentlemen," interrupted Max, "this is an exercise in engineering and tactics, not accounting. When you told me that it could be done, Wernher, was it the bourbon talking, or was it your engineering expertise?"

"A little of both, I venture," said the engineer. "Actually, sir, I checked it thoroughly and had a few of my lads go over it as well, and it all checks out. *Theoretically.*"

"It looks like Hotel eight has spotted us. He's coming about in a very high delta-v maneuver," Bartoli interrupted, and then listened briefly to his back room. "All right. He's now on course two-four-four mark zero-five-three and is accelerating hard. I can't tell at this range whether it's Flank or Emergency for him, but he's definitely in a hurry. And, yes, it's within an arc second of a perfect intercept course. I'm sure he'll refine it shortly."

"Either he's detected us, or he's deduced what we're doing," DeCosta said.

"He's a smart one, XO. And remember, that cross-range maneuver he pulled when we were nuking his buddies is only so-so for retreat but great for setting up a missile attack, so chances are, he's pretty aggressive, too," Max said. "Tactical, is he overtaking us?"

"Affirmative, sir," Bartoli said. "Just barely. When we reach the primary, he'll still be a few minutes behind us. But by the time he gets in range, he won't be able to shoot at us very well. We'll be so close to the primary that its radiation and solar wind effects will be too strong for a missile-seeker head to track. Pulse-cannon isn't worth squat there, either. The star's magnetic flux tends to rupture the plasma containment field unexpectedly. Sometimes immediately upon firing."

"That'll ruin your whole day," muttered Levy from Weapons.

"So, to hit us," Bartoli continued, sharing a smile with Levy, "he'll have to close within about fifteen hundred kilometers and fire his missiles from a generated bearing in non-homing mode—like firing a torpedo from an old diesel-electric submarine in one of the first world wars."

"So, back to the matter at hand, Wernher," said Max. "I'm going to need you to pull this off for me in . . . ," he consulted the NAV display, "eight hours and two minutes. Can you do it?"

"Well, sir, Professor Nekton did it about eighty years ago. Of course, he had a specialized research vessel, with specially configured deflectors and hull optimized for heat rejection. On the other hand, he stayed inside for several hours, whereas you're talking about only about a few tenths of a second, so our task is considerably easier."

"Nekton?" Sahin broke in, incredulous. "Auguste P. Nekton, the astrophysicist?"

"That's the man," Max said warily.

DeCosta reached for his console to query the database. The doctor made an impatient waving gesture in the direction of the console, as though he were a waiter shooing a fly away from a diner's soup, presumably his way of informing the XO that the query was unnecessary. Sahin stood up, walked over to the XO's station, and grasped DeCosta's forearm urgently. "Lieutenant, Nekton was one of the leading astrophysicists of the mid-twenty-third century. He was a fabulously brilliant man, but he was widely referred to as 'Nutcase Nekton' because he took his research ship *inside* a star and nearly immolated his whole crew. They barely escaped with their lives." He turned to Max, genuinely frightened.

"You're not thinking of taking *this* ship inside *that* star, are you?" The doctor's voice had a distinctly accusatory tone as he pointed forward in the general direction of the system's primary, which the *Cumberland* was now approaching at over half the speed of light and accelerating.

"Sir," Max prompted, his voice a pond of very cold water coated with a thin crust of ice, "you're not thinking of taking this ship inside that star, are you, sir?" Very softly he added, "We're not in my quarters, Doctor."

"Sir. My apologies, Captain," Sahin said, loud enough to be heard by everyone in the compartment.

"Apology accepted, Doctor," Max said at the same volume.

"It's just a shocking idea," Sahin said quietly.

"It really is," murmured DeCosta. "It never occurred to me that we could survive in there."

"It's actually not so shocking when you break it down intellectually, Doctor, XO. I'm always looking for new ways to hide from, evade, or sneak up on the enemy, so I've been toying with this idea for months. What got Nekton into trouble was that he let himself get too close to the core: superdense plasma at ten or fifteen million degrees Kelvin—we're not getting anywhere near it. We wouldn't last a microsecond. This star is about a million and a half kilometers across, and I mean to slice across at a shallow angle, a chord less than 100,000 kilometers long, never going below the upper layers of the convective zone. The temperature there is in the neighborhood of 6000 degrees Kelvin. A thermonuke warhead is 10,000 degrees, and the shields are made to withstand that, at least briefly. At that depth the internal pressure is about one six-thousandth of sea level air pressure. The hull won't know the difference between that pressure and a vacuum. Given that we'll be through in about four-tenths of a second, those conditions won't prove too much for us."

"But, Captain, why?" Brown asked over the still-open comm circuit. "What good does it do us to go through that star? Hotel eight will just follow us through or go around."

"He'll follow us in, and that's just what we want him to do." Max smiled. A predatory expression. "XO, remember that technique Bales came up with for spoofing the Krag nav system?"

"Sure, Skipper," said the XO. "But we just couldn't manage to come up with a way to use it in combat."

"I just came up with one."

■

"We'll encounter the photosphere of the primary in just over a minute, Skipper," Bartoli said. "Hotel eight is one minute and twenty-eight seconds behind us now, and will be one minute and twenty-six seconds behind us when we reach the outer boundary of the photosphere."

"Very well," Max said. "Mr. Bales, have you finished wrapping the little gift for our friends?"

"It's ready to go, sir," he answered. "Complete with a nice pink bow."

"I can always count on you to make things festive, Mr. Bales." Max keyed the comm circuit to Engineering. "Wernher, you ready to keep us from getting cooked?"

"Aye, Skipper. Computer simulations indicate that we won't get more than lightly browned. Deflectors are tuned for maximum thermal rejection and to keep the stellar plasma off of us. We may lose some of the sensor and comm arrays on the hull, but supposedly we'll make it. *In theory.*"

"Thank you, Wernher." *Weasel words noted, Wernher.* He closed the circuit, sat back, and tried to look relaxed. The seconds passed. Glacially. Max tried and failed to ignore his damp palms.

The reddish-yellow inferno that was the star Monroe-Tucker B grew steadily larger on the monitors until it filled them and the star's burning surface was visible. Max had to will himself not to stare at it. At this range this system's primary was not the featureless disk that Max was accustomed to seeing, but a seething, roiling, turbulent mass of living thermonuclear fire irregularly ejecting vast planet-size geysers of its glowing plasma essence into the dead blackness of space. The star seemed capable of ingesting and destroying whole worlds, much less the insignificant, mostly hollow, metal box that was the USS *Cumberland.* According to the instruments, the star was radiating huge amounts of energy, such as heat, light, gamma rays, and radio waves. To Max's eyes, however, it seemed to radiate nothing but pure, undiluted danger.

"Five seconds," said Bartoli with the verbal equivalent of a cringe. "Four. Three. Two. One. *Now.*" Almost before men in CIC had time to frame in their minds the idea that they were actually traveling through the interior of a star, Bartoli said, "We're clear."

Every man let out the breath he didn't know he was holding.

"Executing sickle maneuver," LeBlanc announced.

"Launching surveillance probe," Kasparov announced.

The *Cumberland* launched a stealthy surveillance probe to watch the area of the star from which it had just emerged as it carried out a sickle maneuver—a high G nearly ninety-degree turn leading into a curved sickle-shaped trajectory that followed the curvature of the star.

"Maneuver complete. Now following the limb of the star 544 kilometers above the photosphere. Braking thrusters are at EMERGENCY," LeBlanc called out after a few seconds. Having lost most of her velocity in making the turn, the *Cumberland* quickly slowed to orbital velocity for that altitude above the star. "Nulling braking thrusters. On attitude control thrusters only."

"Very well," said Max, ignoring the increasing number of red and yellow caution and warning notifications appearing on his console. The *Cumberland* wasn't built to do this, and she was starting to complain. There would be a price to pay. Later.

"We should be in line of sight with Hotel eight in about five seconds," said Bartoli. No matter how hard they tried, just about everyone in CIC counted down in his head. "Contact. It's Hotel eight. Still on former course and speed. He's twenty-three seconds from the photosphere."

A second later Bales said, "Package transmitted."

"Very well," said Max.

"No change in target's course or speed. There's no sign that he's aware we're here or that we did anything. He'll be entering the photosphere in six seconds." Bartoli dispensed with a countdown, as everyone seemed to either have his eye on Hotel eight's position or one of the chronos displaying a countdown. "Hotel eight has entered the star."

Max, Bram, DeCosta, and just about everyone else in CIC who didn't have something urgent requiring his undivided attention had their eyes on Bartoli. The tactical officer studied his screens and shook his head. "Surveillance probe is detecting no sign of Hotel eight, sir. It doesn't look as though she came out the other side."

Max slowly smiled. "She didn't. And she won't. She's gone, and we didn't even have to expend any ordnance to do it."

Max hit a key on his console. "Wernher, damage report."

"Just a tic, sir," the noticeably irritated voice replied. "It's not as though my brain is hardwired to the ship's systems. I have to call up the displays and actually *read* them, you know, instead of just punching the comm button and asking other people what's happening." The circuit hung open for a few seconds. "Sir, there are a few things I'll want to inspect personally, but here's my preliminary report. We lost just about everything that protruded more than a meter from the hull—comms masts, point-defense turrets, and some of the more oddball sensor arrays. We have replacements for everything in stores except we'll be two point-defense turrets short. We lost all twelve, and we've only ten spares. Otherwise, everything seems nominal. I would rate our combat capability as 94 percent of nominal."

"Thank you, Wernher." Max closed the circuit.

Max turned to the Sensors Officer. "Mr. Kasparov, you're the closest thing to an astrophysicist on board. What altitude would we want if we desired to reduce the strain on the deflectors and cooling systems but remain undetected by the Krag ships in the system?"

Kasparov considered the question for a moment and pulled up a few displays on his console. "Something between 50,000 and 80,000 kilometers should do the trick, sir."

"Thank you. Maneuvering, adjust our orbit to 58,297 kilometers. Burn your thrusters after that only as necessary to maintain that orbit against the friction of the corona. Now, gentlemen, we have one last problem: getting past the ship at the jump point."

Ever since it had become apparent that Hotel eight was destroyed, Dr. Sahin had been suppressing what was obviously extreme curiosity and frustration. When he could restrain himself no longer, he blurted out, "Is no one going to tell me what happened to that ship? Or do I have to wait to find out in the year 2347 when Admiral Max Robichaux, Union Space Navy (Retired), publishes his memoirs?" He turned to Max. "Presumably your editor will cause the book to be written in plain Standard rather than in arcane naval jargon and polysyllabic aerospace gobbledygook. Or at least, require that you provide a glossary."

"Well, Doctor, it's simple," Max replied, working very hard not to laugh, which would only make Bram angrier. "He burned up inside the star."

"Why did he burn up when we did not?"

"Because we stayed in the upper photosphere, and he went straight toward the core, although I doubt that he made it that far." The statement did nothing to cure Sahin's perplexity. Max made eye contact with Bales and gave him a go-ahead gesture.

"Doctor, space navigation is dependent upon measuring distance, direction, and speed relative to a fixed point in space. We use the center of our galaxy—it's not *really* fixed, but we tell the computer that it is. The term for that point, going back to Jurassic Space, is REFerence to Stable Member MATrix, or REFSMMAT. We found that one of the few functions on the Krag computer not protected by a biometric lockout was an almost-never-used routine for changing the REFSMMAT. We guess it wasn't locked out because no one ever uses it and because the computer checks its navigation against what its star scanners are seeing several times a second. Anyway, just before the Krag ship went into the photosphere, we sent a command to wait half a second and then change the REFSMMAT. The computer couldn't correct the error with star scans because it couldn't see the stars from inside the primary. So, following its instructions to stay on the same course, the computer veered radically because we had moved the point from which that course was measured. The ship turned straight toward the star's center. At the speed they were going, they were vaporized before they knew what hit them."

"I understand," the doctor said, turning to Max. "Killing them in that manner was a necessity, but it is a shame that they did not have even a moment to prepare themselves for the journey into the next life."

"I suppose," Max said without much conviction. Mentally he had already moved on to the next tactical problem. "Mr. Kasparov, is there any possibility that our friends guarding the jump points know what just happened?"

"Not a chance, Skipper," he answered. "Those jump points are more than 30 AU from the primary. That far away they can't read anything this deep in the corona. They probably couldn't pick up a thermonuclear warhead detonation at that distance, much less something happening inside the star."

"Outstanding," Max responded.

"How are we going to do it this time, Skipper?" DeCosta asked, eagerness in his eyes. "What's the plan for taking that cruiser at the jump point?"

"We don't," Max replied.

"We don't?" His disappointment was evident.

"No. We don't. We use the captured Krag codes and comms protocols to identify ourselves as Hotel eight, tell the cruisers that we just bested the blaspheming humans in battle, and advise them that we are lingering near the primary to repair some battle damage. We wait for them to leave, and then we just quietly slip away."

"But, sir," asked DeCosta, "don't you want to get that cruiser? Wouldn't that be a nice trophy to hang on your wall?"

"It would. But," Max said, shaking his head gently, "don't forget, our objective right now is to return to the fleet so that this ship can be sent on further missions. Destruction of that cruiser isn't in our orders. It's one thing to take on ships of superior force when necessary to save the ship. It's quite another to do so once the ship has already been saved. Besides, Lady Luck has been very, very generous with us, so let's not ask any more of her today." He sighed heavily. The adrenalin was wearing off. "I intend to convince the enemy that we're dead and then leave."

Max noticed a look of disappointment on DeCosta's face. "I know that look, XO. You're wired like me—you're aggressive. Your first instinct is to go after the enemy and keep going until every Krag within your reach is dead. But if a commander wants his ship to survive, he has to know when to go looking for trouble and when to avoid it. So, for now, we're going to avoid trouble.

"But don't be too disappointed. If I know Admiral Hornmeyer, our next orders are likely to send us looking for trouble in a very big way."

CHAPTER 3

22:59 Zulu Hours, 10 May 2315

The *Cumberland* never made it back to the fleet, but not in the way that Max was worried about. Immediately upon reestablishing comms with the task force, she received orders to rendezvous at the edge of Union-held space with the tender USS *Bartlett Roth Gurtler* for replenishment of her fuel, ordnance, and consumables, as well as repair of the minor damage she sustained at Monroe-Tucker B.

She also received, delivered directly into Max's hands from the hands of the tender's captain, new orders. Very unusual orders. In two parts. The first part was a standard set of operational orders printed on the standard form and sealed in the standard envelope, ordering the *Cumberland* to impose EMCON (EMissions CONtrol: no outgoing messages, no electronic transmissions of any kind), travel to an unremarkable set of coordinates in deep space, and upon arrival, access the second part of its orders. That second part was stored on a triple-encoded, time-locked data chip designed to erase completely and irretrievably every bit of data if anyone attempted to access its contents before the programmed date and time: 23:00 Zulu Hours, 10 May 2315.

In one minute.

The *Cumberland* was at the ordered coordinates. Max's regular Kitchen Cabinet was assembled in the Wardroom to review the orders. He knew that those assembled were allowed to see what was on the chip because, if it had been classified *Captain's Eyes Only*, the chip's plastic case would have been orange. This one was blue, meaning it was merely *Top Secret*. Around the Wardroom table, in addition to Max, were: Executive Officer Lieutenant Eduardo M. DeCosta, Chief Medical Officer Dr. Ibrahim Sahin, Marine Detachment Commander Major Gustav Kraft, and Chief Engineer Lieutenant "Wernher" Vaughn Brown. And one addition, Chief Petty Officer Heinz Wendt.

After the stewards had served coffee and sweet rolls, then been excused from the compartment, Max brought the meeting to order. "Good evening, gentlemen. Before we start, I want to congratulate the COB on his promotion to Command Master Chief Petty Officer."

There was a general approving murmur of "Hear, hear" and rapping of knuckles on the table. Every officer present raised his coffee mug in salute. Master Chief Petty Officer Heinz Wendt, the senior noncommissioned officer on board, referred to as the Chief of the Boat or COB (pronounced "cob") was both highly regarded and well liked by virtually all the officers and crew. At age fifty-four, he was also, with the exception of a few "ancient mariners" in the galley, the oldest man on the ship.

"I understand that the wingding the other chiefs put on for you last night was one for the books," Max added. The chief could only smile. The less said about *that* celebration, the better. "I am also pleased to welcome the COB to this meeting and to future meetings of this type. As more than one of the officers here has tactfully pointed out, under long-standing naval custom, Chief

Wendt has always belonged at these meetings. You all know, I am usually a great respecter of naval custom. In this case, however, I made the mistake of following the example of one of my former commanders who, I have just learned, had a long-standing personal disagreement with the COB on his ship. My mistake, Chief, not a deliberate snub. I hope you won't take it personally."

"Of course not, Skipper," Wendt replied reasonably. Naturally the exclusion had rankled. Had it gone on much longer, it was entirely possible he would have resented it. But there was no point of making an issue of it now. "I'm just glad I'm here today and hope I can make a contribution."

"Outstanding," said Max. If the grizzled old chief had decided to hold a grudge, the belated invitation to the Kitchen Cabinet meetings would have been worse than no invitation at all. Max knew, however, that Wendt was nothing if not professional. He was going to do what was best for the ship and his men. Which was as it should be.

Max watched the chrono on the Wardroom table computer terminal tick down to 23:00 hours. After letting fifteen more seconds go by, more out of a semisuperstitious desire to avoid blanking the chip by accident than anything else, he inserted the chip into the terminal's reader and keyed it to show the orders on the compartment's display wall. An area of a bulkhead that had been an ordinary military gray turned flat black and then displayed text.

They all read together:

21:29 ZULU 9 MAY 2315
TOP SECRET
URGENT: FOR IMMEDIATE IMPLEMENTATION
FROM: HORNMEYER, L. G. VADM USN, CDR TF TD
TO: ROBICHAUX, MAXIME T., LCDR USN,
CDR USS CUMBERLAND

1. PROCEED AT BEST PRUDENT SPEED TO ANGELOS VI C. THERE YOU WILL RENDEZVOUS WITH FLEET TENDER USS NICOLAS APPERT, TRF 0034, LCDR SIGMUND ANDERSSEN URSF, COMMANDING.

2. USS NICOLAS APPERT IS HEREBY ATTACHED TO YOUR VESSEL FOR THE PERIOD DESCRIBED BELOW.

3. UNDER YOUR OVERALL COMMAND, USS CUMBERLAND, DPA 0004, AND THE AFOREMENTIONED TENDER ARE TO:

A. AVOIDING ALL CONTACT WITH THE ENEMY AND EMPLOYING CAPTURED IFF CODES PROVIDED HEREWITH, COVERTLY ENTER KRAG-HELD SPACE AT THE POINT OF YOUR CHOOSING.

B. PROCEED TO COORDINATES LISTED IN ATTACHMENT HERETO, THERE TO RENDEZVOUS WITH JOINT OPERATIONAL GROUP HOTEL PAPA AT 01:30 ZULU 14 MAY 2315. IF JOG IS NOT AT RENDEZVOUS AT THE STATED TIME, YOU ARE DIRECTED TO LOITER IN VICINITY OF RENDEZVOUS COORDINATES FOR FIFTEEN (15) HOURS. IF JOG DOES NOT ARRIVE BEFORE THIS TIME EXPIRES, EXECUTE THE INDIVIDUAL VESSEL OBJECTIVE DESCRIBED IN PARAGRAPH 5 ET SEQ. HEREIN. DO NOT, REPEAT DO NOT, ATTEMPT TO ATTACK GROUP OBJECTIVE ON YOUR OWN. I MEAN IT, ROBICHAUX. IF THE KRAG DON'T KILL YOU, I WILL. SLOWLY.

C. RENDEZVOUS OF CUMBERLAND AND NICHOLAS APPERT WITH JOG HOTEL PAPA CREATES NEW JOG DESIGNATED AS HOTEL INDIA.

4. ORDERS FOR JOG HOTEL INDIA ARE AS FOLLOWS:

A. ONCE JOG HOTEL INDIA IS FORMED YOU ARE TO ASSUME CHARGE AND COMMAND THEREOF WITH

ALL THE HURRAH HURRAH HAPPY HORSESHIT APPERTAINING THERETO AND FOR THE SAME LET THIS BE YOUR WARRANT.

B. THE JOG UNDER YOUR COMMAND IS TO ATTACK AND, IF POSSIBLE, DESTROY CRITICAL KRAG FUELING AND LOGISTICS FACILITY BELIEVED TO BE LOCATED IN THE EHMKE 17-MARBLOCK D-CHAMBERS 343-HYNDMAN A PASSAGE. ESTIMATED COORDINATES AND INTEL REGARDING THIS FACILITY ARE PROVIDED IN THE ATTACHMENT.

5. UPON COMPLETION OF THIS OBJECTIVE, FAILURE OF AN ATTEMPT TO COMPLETE THE OBJECTIVE, OR YOUR DETERMINATION THAT THE OBJECTIVE CANNOT BE ACHIEVED WITH THE FORCES UNDER YOUR COMMAND WITHOUT UNREASONABLE RISK, CUMBERLAND IS TO BE DETACHED FROM THE JOG, WITH NICHOLAS APPERT TO REMAIN WITH JOG. JOG WILL PURSUE UNDISCLOSED OBJECTIVE(S) UNDER PRIOR COMMAND.

6. BEFORE PARTING COMPANY FROM JOG, CUMBERLAND WILL REFUEL AND REPLENISH STORES/ CONSUMABLES FROM NICHOLAS APPERT TO MAXIMUM EXTENT POSSIBLE UNDER THE CIRCUMSTANCES IN PREPARATION FOR EXTENDED DETACHED SERVICE.

7. ORDERS FOR CUMBERLAND AFTER PARTING COMPANY FROM TASK FORCE ARE AS FOLLOWS:

A. NORFOLK N2 CLAIMS TO HAVE OBTAINED ITINERARY FOR PERIOD 17 MAY THROUGH 19 JUNE 2315 FOR LEGENDARY KRAG COMMANDER CODENAME ADMIRAL BIRCH [WE'RE NAMING THEM AFTER KINDS OF WOOD NOW—I SUPPOSE THAT'S BETTER THAN MINERALS OR FISH LIKE WE'VE DONE

IN THE PAST]. ACCORDING TO NORFOLK, BIRCH WILL BE TRAVELING IN TRIBUNE CLASS VIP TRANSPORT IN COMPANY WITH ONE OF THEIR FAST FLEET TANKERS, ALL WITH LIGHT ESCORT. ITINERARY IS CONTAINED IN ATTACHMENT HERETO.

B. INTERCEPT BIRCH'S TRANSPORT AND KILL THE ADMIRAL.

8. LCDR ANDERSSEN WILL BRIEF YOU REGARDING ADDITIONAL INTEL NECESSARY TO MISSION COMPLETION.

9. YOU HAVE MADE IT KNOWN THAT YOU AND YOUR CREW ARE "LOOKING FOR ACTION." WELL, YOUNG MAN, HERE IT IS.

10. KICK ASS AND GODSPEED.

When Max and DeCosta came to the part about going looking for action, their eyes met. Max gave the XO his best "I told you so" smile.

There was dead silence in the Wardroom as everyone digested the orders. Max noticed that, as Wendt reread the orders, he was shaking his head, slowly and almost imperceptibly. Max keyed the comm panel.

"Maneuvering. LeBlanc here."

"Chief LeBlanc, this is the skipper. Plot a best prudent-speed course and velocity profile to Angelos VI C. Who's Officer of the Deck right now?"

"Hobbs, sir."

"Hobbs. Good. He knows his navigation. Let Hobbs look at it, and if he says it's okay, then go ahead and implement it. Any problem, contact me immediately."

"Aye, sir."

LeBlanc repeated the order back to Max, who then broke the circuit. Max turned his attention to Wendt. "All right, Chief, let's have it."

"It's that obvious, Skipper?" replied Chief Wendt.

"It is to me. Or didn't you know that mind-reading abilities came with the skipper's job?"

"I thought that was only a story that Mother Goose tells to scare the squeakers," the old chief said, smiling. "Sir, don't get me wrong. I think that these are great orders. We'll have a chance to make everyone forget that '*Cumberland* Gap' bullshit for good. It's the big picture I'm worried about."

"What about it?" Max grew serious as everyone in the Wardroom could feel the ship come to a new course and increase its speed, hurrying toward the rendezvous. When a noncommissioned officer of Wendt's experience was worried, Max worried along with him.

"Skipper, as you know, I served under Admiral Hornmeyer for more than ten years, starting out when he was Lieutenant Commander 'Bighorn' Hornmeyer, master and commander of a beat-up old destroyer named the *Harfleur*, and then when he commanded frigates, cruisers, battlecruisers, battleships, and various attack groups."

In response to the unspoken questions from the officers, he added, "I've always had a flair for structural damage control—figuring out ways to patch holes in the hull and the gaps in the space frame's interior supports so the ship will hold together after she's been pounded. The old man got himself into a lot of bad scrapes back when he was a warship commander, so he always liked to have me along. Then I was injured at the Battle of Reid 39, spent several months in the hospital, and when I was returned to duty got assigned to the *Cumberland*."

Having satisfied the others on this point, Wendt continued. "Anyway, Hornmeyer is a born gambler. He's smart. He's *lucky*. He's got balls the size of gas giant planets. And he plays to win. Hell, he may be the best gambler in Known Space. He's certainly the best gambler I've ever seen. If you ever want to make some money, go to a racetrack with him and bet just like he does. Anyway, one of his favorite sayings is an old horse-racing maxim: *when the track's muddy, bet on the long shot.* And Skipper, with all due respect, you are a long shot, in spades. Think about it: a twenty-eight-year-old Lieutenant Commander with less than four months in the Big Chair sent after what I'm betting is a major logistics node in what, if I remember right, is one of the main transit corridors through that area, all behind enemy lines. Follow that up with an Operation *Vengeance*—Kill Yamamoto-type mission against one of the Krag's top admirals. So I'm wondering . . ."

"Why Hornmeyer believes the track is muddy," Max finished.

"Exactly," said Wendt. "What's going on that makes a gambler like Hornmeyer willing to bet so heavily on the dark horse?"

"Maybe there's a major enemy offensive under way, and he needs us to kill the rat-face who's taking over command of it and to throw a spanner into the gears of their logistics," suggested Brown.

DeCosta shook his head. "Sounds reasonable, but there's been no significant change in the enemy's tempo of operations. We get regular battle reports from all the combat groups, and today is not much different from yesterday, and this week is little different from last week. If Mr. Rat-Face is up to something, it hasn't worked its way up to the FEBA yet."

"That's *Forward Edge of Battle Area*," Brown whispered to the doctor, who was seated next to him.

Sahin graciously nodded his thanks, even though he was well aware what that particular acronym meant. He had, in fact, known since the day before yesterday.

"But," DeCosta went on, "as far out as we are, all we're getting right now is the major combat bulletins via metaspace plaintext. We aren't getting the detailed Intel reports, much less the raw data backing them up. We'd have a better idea if we had access to that information."

"Don't the orders say that we're to be briefed by this Anderssen fellow on all of these things?" asked Dr. Sahin.

"They do," said Max. "But that doesn't exactly fill me with warm, happy comfort. I don't want to wait that long. I want time for *my* Intel Section and *my* Tactical Section to sift through the data with an eye toward what it all means to *us*. On top of that, there's something in the wording of these orders that's giving me heartburn. I haven't had time to dissect the words yet, but I don't like it. Furthermore, I don't want my understanding of tactical background information essential for the operations of an attack group under my command to be dependent upon an intelligence briefing delivered by a reserve officer whom I have never met and never even heard of. Not to mention that this intel data—probably highly processed data at that—consists of whatever the naval bureaucracy has decided I need to know instead of what *I* have decided we want to know. We're going to be a long way behind enemy lines, and data that may look trivial to some weenie wearing an ice cream suit and conning a mahogany desk back in Norfolk could be critical to us when we're two or three dozen light-years deep in Krag-controlled space. I want *couchon de lait*, not SPAM, and I want to pick whether what I'm putting on my plate is ribs, loin, or shoulder."

"*Couchon de lait*?" whispered Wendt to the doctor.

"A sort of Cajun kalua pig," he answered, suppressing his revulsion as an observant Muslim at the thought of being in the presence of a pig roasted whole.

Overhearing but ignoring this exchange, Max opened a voice circuit, pulling the circuit number from memory.

"CIC Navigation, Chief Silva here."

"Silva, this is the skipper. Does our course take us close to any NAVCOMMNET relays?"

"Just a moment, sir." He entered the query into his display. Max could have entered the same query from the Wardroom general-purpose terminal, but the Navigation console in CIC was designed for finding and displaying this kind of data, so it made sense for Max to ask the navigation officer. "Affirmative, Skipper. We're going to have to jump through seven systems to get to the rendezvous, and there's a relay—Number 7888—in the second one. It's nowhere near our track between the two jump points, though. Not counting time actually spent at the relay, rendezvousing with it will add one hour and fifty-seven minutes to our ETA."

"Very well. Thank you, Mr. Silva."

He broke the circuit and punched up the CO's station.

"CIC, Hobbs here."

"Hobbs, prepare for a change in navigation orders."

"Ready, Skipper. Do you want me to log an order to deviate from course to the rendezvous with the tender to rendezvous with NAVCOMMNET Relay 7888 so that we may . . . complete a *highly critical database update*?" Hobbs had obviously heard Max's exchange with Silva.

"Yes, Mr. Hobbs, that's exactly what I'd like you to do. Keep that up, and before long BUPERS will make you someone's XO."

Hobbs recited the order back to the skipper. "One moment, sir." The circuit hung open for about half a minute. Max could hear Hobbs issuing orders in the background. "Order logged. ETA at the relay is in five hours and nineteen minutes. And as for the XO berth, I wouldn't mind that a bit, sir, especially on your first cruiser command."

"I'll keep you in mind. Skipper out." He closed the circuit. "Hobbs is on the ball tonight."

"Even the brownnosing is first-rate," said DeCosta with a chuckle.

Max nodded as he pulled up a crew directory on the Wardroom terminal and found the name he was looking for. "You gentlemen might want to cover your ears for this," he said. Max opened another circuit and leaned toward the audio pickup until his lips almost touched the grille. "BALES!" he nearly shouted. "ENSIGN CHRISTOPHER BALES! BALES, WAKE UP!"

"Whaaa? Hoozat?" came the sleepy mumble a few seconds later.

"BALES!" Max continued in a voice loud enough that Bales could probably hear him in his quarters without benefit of the comm system. "This is the SKIPPER! Shake the cobwebs out from between your ears, get your comatose ass out of bed, and come to attention! MOVE IT!" Pause. About a quarter minute. "I said GET YOUR ASS OUT OF BED, Bales. Are you standing? Are you at attention? Talk to me, Bales!"

There was a rustle of bedding and a few bumps and curses. It sounded like Bales got tangled in his bedding and fell to the deck. More thumps, then silence.

"Ensign Bales, report your status!" said Max in a more human tone.

"Ensign Christopher Eugene Bales at attention in my quarters, sir." His diction was approaching normal, and he sounded somewhat coherent.

"Are you ready to understand and obey orders now, Ensign?"

"Affirmative, sir," he said, still a bit thickly.

"Good. Then I need your happy ass in the Wardroom ASAP. You got that?"

"My happy ass. Wardroom. Alfa, sierra, alfa, papa. Got it, Skipper."

Max closed the circuit and noticed the puzzled looks from some of his officers. Others who knew Bales better were striving mightily to suppress smiles. "Bales is a very, *very* heavy sleeper," Max explained to the puzzled. "If you don't get him standing and responding to you, he'll just go back to sleep and never remember that you were talking to him. He actually pays a midshipman to wake him up for every watch. The poor little farts usually wind up having to pour cold water in his ear or poke him with their dirks."

Three minutes later Bales came through the hatch. "Sorry to cut into your rack time, Bales," said Max. "Grab yourself some coffee and have a seat." The young ensign grabbed a one-liter soda cup from the sideboard, filled it halfway with ice from the dispenser, tossed in some sweetener, and filled the rest with coffee. He stirred it briskly, melting the ice, downed the lukewarm contents of the mug in three long pulls, then poured himself a mug full of hot coffee, added sweetener, and sat down. No one batted an eye—in order to get a good dose of coffee into their bellies in the shortest possible time, navy men had been following a similar procedure for centuries.

"Bales, we're going to rendezvous with NAVCOMMNET Relay 7888 just over five hours from now. Naturally we're going to establish a laserlink, tie into the data stream, and do a standard database update, but . . ."

As he had been making his coffee, Bales had been reading the orders still up on the display wall. "But you'd like to know what's *really* going on. What's behind those orders."

"Exactly," said Max. "At minimum I want the Flag Intelligence Brief and the supporting documentation. If possible I want the raw takes from the sensor outposts looking into Krag territory at the likely crossing points, the SIGINT intercepts, the unprocessed reports from patrols along the FEBA, that sort of thing. Get with

Levy, and he can give you a detailed list of the data it would be useful to have. Do you think you can get me some of this stuff?"

"Well, sir, as you know, the toughest nut to crack is accessing the system in the first place, and we're authorized to do that." When no one at the table agreed with his statement, Bales thought for a moment. "Oh, I get it. We perform the database update under our own identity, but if we gain unauthorized access to these other databases—the ones where we aren't allowed to go—under our own ID, the hack will be traced to us, and we all get to spend the rest of our lives on Europa chipping ice off the centrifuges. All right, then. With your permission, sir, I can get into the system under one or more false IDs. I have half a dozen that I've *borrowed* from other computers along the way. Once in, I'm pretty sure I can get at least some of what you want."

"How would you ever manage to do that?" Dr. Sahin's voice was a mixture of skepticism and annoyance. "I have considerable computer skills and used to amuse myself by wandering into areas of the Travis Station system to which I did not have authorized access, but every time I got on NAVNET and tried to go outside of the public areas, I always found myself locked out immediately."

Bales smiled indulgently. "Doctor, with respect, I'm a little more than a casual hacker. Unauthorized access has been a part of my job for most of my naval career. In this case, I've *found* several key access codes while exploring systems that I'm not precisely supposed to have been exploring. How much I can get is going to depend on how quickly the system figures out it's being hacked and shuts me out."

"Mr. Bales," asked Dr. Sahin, "how did a commissioned officer in the Union Space Navy get so good at obtaining unauthorized access to computer networks?"

Max and Kraft both looked away, their faces a study in innocence.

"Well, Doctor, that's how I came to be *in* the navy in the first place. When I was a kid, I was a hard-core simhead. The navy caught me downloading official warship combat-simulation software. What the hell did I know? As far as I was concerned, they were just especially realistic games. Anyway, they conscripted me under the Supplemental Service Manpower Augmentation Act of 2302. I had a choice of shipping out as a midshipman or designing firewalls for Union computer networks from a workstation on a penal asteroid. You can see what choice I made. I wound up doing, um, *special jobs* for Admiral Hornmeyer before he assigned me here."

"I surmise that the less one says about the *special jobs*, the better," said the doctor. Bales nodded. "Then I have a few more questions for Mr. Bales, if I may."

Max nodded for him to proceed.

"You have obtained access to every database on this ship, including the ones that you are not allowed to enter, isn't that right?" He watched carefully as Bales formulated his answer. "Never mind answering. Your face and your delay in answering tell me everything I need to know. You have. That concerns me greatly."

"Not *every* database," Bales said. "Now, don't get me wrong. I *could* get into any database I wanted, but I don't want to go into all of them. I don't go snooping around for the fun of it. I go only into the databases that have information I need—it's just that the people who assign database access clearances have one idea about what information I need, and I have another. So I've accessed at least the upper-level directories of all of the technical and engineering files, intel, operations, comms, nav, internal systems, and so on. I've never even accessed the directories of—much less read—anyone's personal files, the captain's logs and notes, internal emails, and absolutely none of the medical records. There's no reason for me to. I mean, what do I care about whether Able Spacer Second Class So-and-So picked up a case of crotch rot on Khan-Achel III B?"

"Do you swear on your honor as a Union officer that you have not accessed confidential patient records, my medical logs, or any of my personal files, and that you will make no attempt to do so in the future?" asked Dr. Sahin with almost priestly seriousness.

"I do," Bales responded in kind.

"Excellent, Mr. Bales. Then I shall not be forced to kill you," the doctor said with every appearance of utter sincerity. A few of the men around the table chuckled, but neither Max nor Kraft displayed the slightest trace of levity. "So, is it fair to say that, when Admiral Hornmeyer assigned you to this vessel, it was probably not *despite* your proclivities for electronic trespassing but *because* of them?"

"Yes, Doctor, I think that's fair."

"Good." Sahin turned to Max. "I was concerned about the propriety of this proposed course of action. Now, however, I am entirely comfortable with it." In response to questioning looks from around the table, Sahin went on, addressing his remarks to the group at large. "We won't be doing anything that the admiral does not wish us to do. Follow my reasoning, gentlemen. One: assume for a moment that Admiral Hornmeyer wants us to have information for which the captain is not cleared. Two: we know that the admiral can't give us the information directly because, as we have all been reminded *ad nauseam* by a seemingly unending series of communiqués from Norfolk, the IG has been cracking down on instances in which individuals who have clearance for certain data disclose that data to other officers and shipmates who are not so cleared. The admiral knows that if the IG audits his secure communications—something the rumors say happens frequently, even to admirals—he could find himself in serious difficulties. I hear that even Admiral Litvinoff fears the Inspector General."

"God himself fears the Inspector General," Max quipped, earning scattered laughter from around the table and a disapproving glare from Sahin for his impiety.

"So, three: the admiral writes a set of orders that leaves us wondering what he has up his sleeve and that contains language of equivocation." The doctor stood, walked over to the display wall, and pointed at the relevant language in the orders as he discussed them. "Words of equivocation such as 'Norfolk N2 claims' and 'according to Norfolk.' Clearly, gentlemen, the admiral is disclaiming responsibility for the conclusions that follow these words, hardly something he would do if he wished to inspire confidence in the accuracy of the intelligence on which these orders are based. Captain, if you had not come up with the idea of supplementing your intelligence with independent sources, I would have recommended that you do so based on this language alone.

"Four: then he contrives things so that we receive our intelligence briefing from an officer whom the captain does not entirely trust. Five: he knows that, as a result of the foregoing, Captain Robichaux will wish to supplement the official information. And last of all, six: the admiral has, in the person of the redoubtable Mr. Bales, already provided to the captain the means to obtain that information without the IG ever being the wiser." He turned to Bales. "Young man, do not be surprised if you discover that the admiral has compiled everything we need in one easily accessed location, waiting for your unauthorized access."

"Like where?" said Bales.

The doctor sniffed. "I'm quite certain that I have no idea. You know the admiral and NAVNET far better than I do. Remember, young man, *the admiral knows you.* So I suggest you put yourself in his shoes and determine where in the network he would hide intelligence files that he wanted you and only you to find."

"All right, then, Bales, consider it an order from Vice Admiral Louis G. Hornmeyer himself," Max said. "Get with Mr. Bhattacharyya and have his section give you their intel wish list—you might have to go looking for what we need. The admiral may not have been as helpful as our good doctor suspects, although I have to admit that it does sound like him. Then help Mr. Chin set up the necessary comm protocols. Anything you need to get the job done that he can't supply, you come straight to me or to Mr. DeCosta here. Got that?"

"Yes, sir, I do."

"Thank you, Mr. Bales, you're dismissed." Max waited until Bales had closed the hatch before speaking again. "This doesn't sit well with me. I feel as though the admiral is manipulating me, pushing my buttons, so to speak."

"Sir," Wendt said, "with respect, I don't see it that way at all. You've read between the lines of your orders before, right?"

"I believe I have, yes," Max answered, having done considerably more to some of his orders than just read between the lines.

"So, the admiral is letting you know what he wants you to do and is making sure you get your hands on information you need, all without so much as a blip showing on the IG's sensors. It's not manipulation, Skipper. It's communication. It's subtle, but it's still communication. Look at it this way: you and one of the greatest military minds in Known Space are on the same page."

"Thank you, COB," Max said. "I suppose that's the way I need to look at it. Admiral Hornmeyer has found a way to give us some rather unorthodox orders, and we're going to follow them because, as you all know, we are a ship that *scrupulously* obeys *all* orders from duly constituted command authority." Those assembled had sufficient respect for their commanding officer that they managed to hide their smirks at that statement. Oblivious to the great efforts being expended on his behalf, Max forged on.

"So, gentlemen, all we have to do is hack into the most secure computer network in Known Space, steal the intel we need from our own people, penetrate the most heavily defended battlefront in the history of space warfare alongside a ship so enormous that shuttlepods keep trying to land *on* it instead of dock *with* it, slip deep into the enemy's rear area, conduct aggressive combat operations light-years away from any hope of reinforcement or resupply, and slip through that same battlefront in the other direction, all without getting blown to flaming atoms by the enemy or by our own forces."

"That's it?" said DeCosta. "And here I was, hoping for something challenging."

"Maybe next time, XO," Max said. "Keep your hopes up. There's always next time."

■

"Admiral Hornmeyer was very, very helpful," Ensign Bhattacharyya said, somewhat nervously, to the ship's department heads assembled in the Wardroom. "There was a *special disciplinary file* on Ensign Bales containing what purported to be a complete list of all of his infractions against naval regulations. Some of which made for very entertaining reading, by the way. For example, there's the time when a woman dumped him, and Bales executed a hack that made her name and picture come up when anyone in eleven whole star systems did a computer search containing the word bi—"

"Mr. Bhattacharyya, I don't think that the adventures of Ensign Bales are a fit subject for this meeting," Max cut in. "Mr. Bales is not the only person at this table who has a less-than-perfect disciplinary record, if you catch my meaning." He glowered meaningfully at Bhattacharyya.

"Yes, sir." Bhattacharyya gulped, a certain incident involving a sidecar powercycle, two Pomeranians, and three ladies of the evening coming to mind. "Um, anyway, the list referred to fifty attachments. The first forty-one of the attachments are exactly what the cover document says they are: source documents relating to the, um, *activities* of Ensign Bales. The other nine, however, looked like gibberish, even after we applied standard decryption techniques. So, naturally, Rochefort from Crypto and I assumed that we were dealing with a dual-layer encryption."

"Naturally," the doctor said, rolling his eyes. "After all, *what* could be more obvious?"

"Exactly," Bhattacharyya continued. It was, after all, obvious to *him*. "We worked from the proposition that the admiral was communicating with Bales in particular, so we focused on encrypts that Bales and the admiral would associate with each other. We pretty quickly determined that the first level was *Tundra*, a flag-level encrypt that none of us are supposed to be able to read but that the admiral knows Bales cracked six months ago *just because he was bored* from spending a week in the brig. The second is in *Flurry*, which is an old encrypt that the admiral used to use to communicate with Bales when he was working on his *special jobs*."

"But that doesn't do you much good if you don't know the cipher keys," Max noted.

"Just like the encrypts, we assumed the cipher keys were words that the admiral knew were of significance to Bales. The *Tundra* key turned out to be Gwalchmai."

"Gwalchmai?" six or seven people asked at once.

"My mother's maiden name," said Bales. "It's Old Welsh."

Bhattacharyya continued, "And the one for *Flurry* was *Tawny*."

There were a few salacious snickers around the table. "Tawny" was the name of the promiscuous female protagonist in a series of sexually explicit trid vids of enduring popularity among naval crews, including *A Little Tawny Is Good for Morale, Tawny: Permission to Come Aboard,* and most famously, *Everyone Stands at Attention for Tawny.*

"It's not what you guys think," Bales hastened to add, the hurt evident in his voice. "Tawny isn't some girl in a smutty vid. She was my dog when I was growing up. A Chow Chow mix. A really good dog. Followed me everywhere. Totally loyal to me. Only friend I ever had before joining the navy. She did her best to keep me safe." He added in a low voice, "No one else did."

Bram felt a twinge of sympathy. He had seen the ensign's bone scans, showing countless healed fractures from his childhood. An abusive upbringing may not have been an excuse for the man's military and legal infractions, but it did help explain them.

Max had never seen the bone scans and had not heard about the young man's abusive childhood from the doctor or from anyone else. But he learned all he needed to know about the ensign's childhood from the way he said those few sentences. Max met the young man's eyes. "Never forget, Ensign, that you are surrounded by loyal shipmates now. Anyone or anything that raises a hand to you will have to answer to them. And me." When Bales slowly nodded his understanding, Max said, "The bottom line is that we can read the files. What did the admiral give us?"

"Just about everything we could ask for," said Bhattacharyya. "It took a while to wade through it all, and I needed Mr. DeCosta and Mr. Bartoli to interpret all of the tactical information. The XO has the brief on what we found."

DeCosta leaned forward. "Now I want to emphasize that the admiral made sure the information we got was vague as to the exact time and place or places, in case we were captured I suppose, but the bottom line is pretty clear." He paused for emphasis. "Sometime in the next fourteen to twenty-five days, the Union is going to launch a major counteroffensive—the biggest one of the war. It will occur in both theaters of operations simultaneously: both Admiral Hornmeyer and Admiral Middleton will attack in their respective sectors with their primary task forces. I'm guessing that this is why we haven't seen much of the new *Churchill* class Super Dreadnaughts and the new ships coming out of all the other yards in combat—they're being saved for this.

"Now, we know from the captured data core that for the last few months the Krag have been expecting some kind of counteroffensive from us, which is probably why they pushed so hard to end their war against the Thark when they did. They've been rushing their ships as fast as they can from the Thark front to staging areas short distances behind the FEBA to meet our expected attack.

"But our intel suggests that the infusion of new forces at this battlefront is stretching the Krag logistics infrastructure to the limit. It's a journey of more than two thousand light-years, and the ships arrive out of fuel and in need of serious maintenance. Which is why they have set up a series of new logistics nodes: deep-space bases along their traffic routes with fuel dumps, supply caches, repair facilities, and a fleet of tugs to get all of it loaded and unloaded. The node that Admiral Hornmeyer wants the JOG to hit is one of the largest and is located along one of the most important lines of communication. If we can deprive the Krag of their new logistics nodes, we deprive them of much of their ability to use the newly transferred forces. But that isn't nearly the most interesting part of what the admiral gave us."

"It must be pretty hot to be more interesting than what you've just told us," Max said, leaning forward with interest.

"I guarantee you, it is," DeCosta said. "The label on this file says that it's for the skipper and his senior officer group, which is us, I think." He went to the Wardroom's computer terminal, pulled up a file menu, keyed for access, and hit DISPLAY.

The display area of the Wardroom wall went from gray to black to the standard Union Space Navy visual recording test pattern, followed by a security warning screen stating that what followed was TOP SECRET, that disclosure would result in severe penalties, that violations of security protocols were investigated by the Inspector General's office and prosecuted by the Judge Advocate General's office to the fullest extent of military law, and so on. After displaying this message for far longer than necessary, the display showed a head-and-shoulder shot of a strongly built, bulldog of a man just on the far side of middle age, with iron-gray hair in a severe crew cut, square jaw, craggy features, a high forehead, and piercing gray eyes. He wore the uniform of a Union Space Navy vice admiral, with enough fruit salad to feed a hundred vegans at a weeklong all-you-can-eat buffet.

"It's old Hit 'em Hard Hornmeyer himself," Bhattacharyya said reverently. The admiral was practically an Olympian deity to the young officer.

An ironic smile flickered across Hornmeyer's features for a moment, to be replaced by his customary severe scowl. "Robichaux, gentlemen, if you're seeing this recording, that means you figured out the subtext I hid in your latest orders. Not bad. Don't smile, Robichaux, I know it wasn't you. My money is on Chief Wendt or Doctor Sahin or maybe that kid Batty. There's a reason I surround you with all that brainpower—you need it in the worst way.

"I made this recording because I have a few words for you about your mission that are either observations that I can't pass along through official channels or that are classified far, far above your security clearances. In fact, I have been specifically ordered—by a fleet admiral, no less—not to divulge some of this to you, Robichaux. I'm disobeying that order because I believe it is outside of that admiral's authority to issue it. Bottom line: Norfolk doesn't think you need to know. I do. So, I win, and the penguins lose."

"Pause," the doctor said emphatically. The computer paused the recording. He looked at Max. "I know what a penguin is, but I think I'm not understanding what a penguin is in this context."

"Well, Doctor," Max replied, "it's a derisive term that warship personnel have for headquarters officers. A penguin is a bird, in formal attire, that doesn't fly, just like these guys wear dress uniforms and don't go into space."

"Ah," Sahin replied. "I love naval insults. Extremely clever and colorful."

Max nodded to DeCosta, who hit the PLAY key. Computer execution of voice commands uttered by a crew of more than two hundred, with all their varying voices and accents, was problematic at best. Max and DeCosta both preferred manual controls whenever feasible. The admiral resumed speaking.

"All right. Now that Robichaux has explained to Dr. Sahin what a *penguin* is, we can get down to business." Several heads around the table shook slowly in amazement. "The first objective is fairly straightforward. The only thing you need to know that's not in the attached materials or your orders is that I am totally fucking serious about you, Robichaux, being in command of that Joint Operations Group for the attack. Not that plodder Hajjar. Don't get me wrong; I've got nothing against Commander Hajjar. Good officer. Brave as a lion. Borderline brilliant ship handling. But no dash, no ability to think out of the box. And he's ambitious, so he'll want to take things over. It will be a fine line: knocking him down hard enough that he won't challenge you further but not so hard as to damage his ego and reduce his combat effectiveness.

You're a subtle tactician, but in dealing with people you're a blunt tool—like a goddamn sledgehammer. Robichaux, sometimes you need to be a laser microtome. You've got a few days to learn. I suggest you apply yourself.

"But that mission's not your biggest problem. Not by a long shot. It'll be a tough nut to crack, but between your craziness and the firepower I'm putting under your command, I'm pretty sure you're going to be able to pull it off. It's this raid to take out Admiral Birch that's the solid gold, fusion-powered, RSVP/Invitation Only clusterfuck. Actually, it's more than a clusterfuck, Robichaux; I'm thinking that, more likely than not, it's a trap.

"The penguins don't see it, but my N2 has concluded that there is probably a Krag mole in Norfolk, probably in the office of the Chief of Naval Operations or an office closely associated with it. There have been several of the navy's most effective small rated ships, destroyers and frigates mainly, under the command of some of our most promising young officers disappear under circumstances that make me more than a little suspicious. I truly cannot share those operational details with you without seriously compromising security, but you can trust me on this. If you saw what their orders were and looked at the data we got from those ships before they went missing, you'd have some serious goddamn suspicions about what happened to them and about this Admiral Birch thing.

"It just smells bad to me—like it's designed to look attractive to us. I mean, every snotty-nosed hatch hanger in the fleet learns about how the United States forces took out that brilliant bastard Yamamoto. This mission looks a little too much like that one to suit my tastes. And the intel that put us onto the idea was too clear, too easy, too devoid of the contraindications and ambiguities that always seem to come with even the best intel. But we've got some corroboration from an independent source that makes it look better. On the other hand, about a third of my staff thinks that the raw data from this *independent source* is bogus: that it's being manufactured somewhere along the data reporting chain."

The admiral took a deep breath and let it out. He seemed tired and his usual hard-charging "hold 'em by the nose and kick 'em in the ass" enthusiasm more muted. "Robichaux, if I were a betting man," he smiled slightly at the thought, "and you know that I am, I would bet that this target is some kind of trap to kill you and destroy your ship. On the other hand, if we have a chance to knock off the real Admiral Birch, we've got to take it. That bastard is good. Very, very good. If he's in command in this theater at the critical moment, our chances of success in what we have planned go down measurably.

"Robichaux, there's no denying that you are a huge pain in the ass. But you've been a significant asset to me over these past few months. All things being equal, I'd rather not have your crawfish head-sucking, gumbo-eating ass blown to flaming atoms. So, here's what I'll do for you. I'm modifying your orders, and I'll put it in my official log that I sent the modification to you via a tachyon Morse signal, of which there will somehow be no record. Sloppiness down in the comms department and all that. From now on, your orders for the Admiral Birch mission are to proceed on your sole discretion. If anything smells fishy to you, if the hairs on the back of your neck stand up, if anything raises a red flag that something is not right, you bug out of there and return to the nearest Union outpost.

"In this job I have to live every day with sacrificing good ships and good men, but I will *not* throw them away." He clenched his jaw. "I will never throw them away. Never. And neither will you. If you sense a trap, not only do you have my permission to get out of there, you are ordered to do so. Get back to our side of the lines, and we'll kick some Krag ass another day, I promise you. That's all I have to say. If anyone ever asks, I'll deny ever sending this to you, and you will deny ever receiving it. Godspeed, kick ass, bring yourself, your ship, and your men home so you can help me win this lousy war. Hornmeyer out."

The display went black.

The admiral's departure, even if he was present only by electronic proxy, left a vacuum in the compartment into which no one seemed willing to step. In order to follow the admiral, one had to be either brave or foolhardy.

"Coming from Admiral Hornmeyer, that message was a veritable fountain of maudlin sentimentality. I wonder if, on the day he recorded this, he was suffering from some kind of dissociative psychosis or perhaps a serious physical illness," Dr. Sahin said.

Damn, that man says some strange shit sometimes. God bless him.

"That's an interesting bit of news," Max said. "I can't say that I like it one bit. But if things start to go sour, the admiral gives us the choice of getting out of the situation, which I really appreciate. That's pretty far down the road, though. We've got a short-term objective that has to be our focus first, and where we fit in is pretty straightforward and of enormous importance," Max said. "The Union is about to make a major push, and the Krag have assembled a significant reserve to meet it. That reserve, however, needs to be reprovisioned, and we're being sent in to destroy one of the key assets they plan to use to do that. If we and the other ships with similar missions succeed, the Union will probably win its greatest victory in the entire conflict."

"And," the doctor said quietly, "if not?"

"It could cost us the war."

CHAPTER 4

06:04 Zulu Hours, 12 May 2315

"Ten seconds," announced Stevenson from Jump Control. The *Cumberland* was jumping into the Angelos system to rendezvous with her tender, the *Nicholas Appert*, an enormous ship—though very fast for its size—that was part deuterium tanker, part supply warehouse, part cargo carrier, and part arsenal. "Nine. Eight. Seven. Six. Five. Four. Three. Two. One. Jumping." The *Cumberland*'s jump engines punched through the boundary that separated the ordinary universe of protons and neutrons, gravity and electromagnetism, strong and weak nuclear forces, matter and antimatter, humans and Krag, from the bizarre, little-understood universe of n-space—a realm no larger than a single geometric point and yet somehow vast enough under its own incomprehensible physics to be in contact with every point in our own universe and to encompass however many ships might happen to be crossing through it at any given moment in time. After spending only a Planck interval in n-space, the ship reappeared 9.4 light-years from where she started, emerging in a flash of Cherenkov-Heaviside radiation at the Bravo jump point in the Angelos system.

"Jump complete," Stevenson said blandly. "Systems restoration in progress." Most humans endured the transition between spacial regimes with few difficulties. Some people experienced a brief flare of nausea. Others became dizzy, got headaches, felt tingling in their extremities, or even had premonitions or mystical visions. For the *Cumberland*'s skipper, going through a jump generally gave rise to food cravings that varied wildly from jump to jump. Sometimes he wanted a chicken salad sandwich. Sometimes it was seafood gumbo. Sometimes it was barbecued ribs. Sometimes it was boudin. Today it was alligator tail sauce piquante. Max smiled.

I think the galley is fresh out of alligator.

Many ship's systems, however, were far more vulnerable. The transition into and out of n-space would spin the metaspacial field polarization in the Faster-than-Light (FTL) processors essential to all of those systems, seriously damaging, if not destroying, the delicate processor matrix. Virtually every major system in a warship had to be shut down when it jumped, leaving it without sensors, external comms, navigation, computers, and sublight and compression drives—nearly every other system except lights, clocks, auxiliary power, and life support. A ship's crew restored her to functionality one step at a time, in a process that typically required about five minutes and was marked by routine reports as system after system was brought back on line and began to do its job. On this occasion, the reports were routine, until one minute and eleven seconds after the jump when the PRTY SGNL (Priority Signal) lamp illuminated on Chin's console, prompting him to press the adjacent DSPY (Display) key. He gasped loudly enough to be heard throughout CIC and sang out, his volume too high by half, "Sir, metaspacial data transmission from the *Nicholas Appert* on the ALL CALL channel. She sends *WHISKEY FOXTROT*."

WHISKEY FOXTROT—the two letter "flag signal" that meant: *This vessel under attack by superior force. Destruction imminent unless relieved.* Only ALFA ZULU, the equivalent of *MAYDAY*, was more urgent.

On his feet without any conscious decision to stand, Max ordered, "General quarters, ship to ship." The alarms started, and the voice of Tufeld at Alerts began to echo throughout the ship, calling the men to their battle stations. Max could see and hear the watch standers in CIC reconfiguring systems to their combat settings, tying their displays into the data channels they would need to grapple with the enemy, even changing the physical properties of the compartment itself by activating CIC's independent sources of power and life support so that the consoles and the men who served them could continue to function if those primary systems were disrupted. The men worked quickly and excitedly but with no evidence of panic.

Max observed all of this in the way an orchestra conductor takes in the first few notes of a symphony and can tell whether the musicians are in tune and on the beat. Max liked what he heard. "Maximum stealth, all systems, all modes," he called out over the buzz of voices. "Maneuvering, get us in motion. Best sublight speed to the rendezvous point." He leaned over and keyed the circuit to Engineering. "Wernher. I need everything you can give me on the main sublight, as soon as you can give it to me. And I'll probably need to make an intrasystem run on the compression drive, as well."

"You've got it." A brief exchange could be heard between Lieutenant Brown and some of his men in the background. The fusion reactor and its massive cooling pumps started to sing a succession of ever-higher notes that told Max what he needed to hear even before the engineer resumed speaking. "Main sublight is approaching 100 percent of rated maximum right now. I'll have her at 112 percent in thirty seconds. Compression drive will be ready for an in-system run in just over two minutes. What's up?"

"The tender is sending *WHISKEY FOXTROT*."

"Bugger all! Why didn't she run, sir? She's faster on compression drive than just about anything the Krag have."

"They probably surprised her and hit her with an Egg Scrambler. We won't know until after we pull her ass out of the fire."

"Aye, sir."

Max closed the circuit and turned to Kasparov. "Sensors?"

"I'm afraid I can't tell you much yet, Skipper. The processors for all my sensors are still rebooting, so I don't have any reads from passive EM, Grav, Neutrino, and other particle-based detectors. We've got some low-tech working for us, though. Goldman is second-desking Harbaugh in the back room and came up with the idea of tying one of the high-resolution imagers into the long-focus Cassegrain astronomical telescope. We can image enough to put together a rough idea what's going on. Between their non-reflective hull coatings and the range, we can't image the Krag ships, of course, but we are seeing flashes that we interpret as Krag pulse-cannon hitting the tender's deflectors just over 750,000 kilometers from the rendezvous point. The old chiefs back there are telling me, based on eyeballing the images—none of the analytics are available yet—the rate of fire and the apparent color temperature of the pulse-cannon blasts are consistent with an attack force of two Krag ships, probably a cruiser and a destroyer. We won't know more until we get more of our systems working or we get closer."

"Then we need to get closer," Max said.

"Plus," Bartoli chimed in, "we need to remember that the rendezvous point is 3.7 AU away. That's about thirty light-minutes . . ."

"So until we get FTL sensors on line, our knowledge of what's happening out there is half an hour old," Max finished. "A lot can happen in half an hour." He thought for a few seconds. "XO, time our run on the compression drive so that we arrive at the earliest possible second after all our systems are returned to full function. And tell Wernher that I want *him* to manage the timing of when we drop to sublight—about 150,000 kilometers from the battle. The timing is going to have to be unusually precise because we're not going to be playing it safe by making the run at 10 c like we've been doing."

"We're not?" Dr. Sahin, in his usual perch at the Commodore's Station, asked with no small amount of trepidation.

"Nope. Every second counts. We're going to do this one at 50 c, or as close as Wernher can get us."

More than a few heads turned at that last statement.

"Isn't that dangerous?" Many minds had formed the question, but naval custom and protocol meant that only the doctor could speak the words.

"Yes, Doctor, it is, but I have a feeling that everything we do for the next few hours is going to be dangerous, so this maneuver isn't going to be anything special. XO, you have your orders."

"Aye, sir, 50 c," DeCosta acknowledged with a gulp. The executive officer knew from Max's tone that he was in no mood for further discussion of the wisdom of crossing interplanetary distances at fifty times the speed of light, even though doing so greatly increased the risk of overshooting or undershooting the *Cumberland*'s destination by millions of kilometers, possibly delaying arrival at the battle and giving an enemy possessed of advanced sensors and superior firepower more time to detect the destroyer and blot it out of existence with a well-placed nuke. Or five.

And there was always the risk of compression shear, which would shred the ship down to the subatomic level in a spectacularly brilliant explosion producing X-rays, gamma rays, and a cloud of incandescent subatomic particles zooming away from each other at 99.9999 percent of the speed of light, leaving behind a lovely astronomical object visible from a dozen or so nearby systems.

And now, class, if you would all slew your telescopes plus 49 arc seconds in declination, you will be able to see the beautiful Cumberland Nebula!

Several short conferences with Stevenson and Brown later, DeCosta set a countdown for the *Cumberland* to engage her compression drive calculated so that she would arrive at the battle with her weapons, sensors, and other systems on line and ready to fight. He informed Max of the timing—the destroyer would go superluminal five minutes and fifty-seven seconds after she emerged from the jump that had brought her to the Angelos system. "XO, you're telling me that the ship will be fully ready to fight less than six minutes after a jump?"

"Aye, aye, Skipper. That's exactly what I'm telling you."

"Well, XO, the next time you see the ship's training officer, you might let him know that he's done a damn fine job and that he deserves the captain's thanks."

"I'll pass that along, Skipper," DeCosta replied, deadpan.

On the *Cumberland*, as on most smaller destroyers, the executive officer doubled as the training officer.

"XO, you may take the ship superluminal when ready."

"Going superluminal on my command, aye," DeCosta acknowledged. "Deflector Control, forward deflectors to FULL, lateral and rear to CRUISE."

The man at that station acknowledged the order.

"Maneuvering, null the main sublight drive," DeCosta ordered confidently. "Main sublight drive to STANDBY. Maneuvering thrusters to STANDBY."

LeBlanc acknowledged these orders and had the three men under his direction at the Maneuvering Stations execute them. When the status lights had winked into the appropriate configuration, he announced: "Main sublight nulled and at STANDBY. Ship is coasting. Maneuvering thrusters are at STANDBY. Attitude control is by inertial systems only."

"Prepare to engage compression drive on my mark. Set c factor for five-zero-point-zero. Compression shutdown to be commanded from Engineering."

"Aye, sir," answered LeBlanc. "Engaging compression drive on your mark. C factor set for five-zero-point-zero. Green light from engineering—compression drive is ready for superluminal propulsion at your command. Engineering confirms by voice that compression shutdown will be commanded by Lieutenant Brown from the MECC."

Brown, in the Master Engineering Control Center, would personally shut down the compression drive and return the ship from physics as governed by the laws that Pawar and Karpinski discovered in the twenty-second century to that governed by those discovered by Newton in the seventeenth and Einstein in the twentieth.

"Engage on my mark. Five, four, three, two, one, *engage.*"

"Engaging," LeBlanc announced. "Compression field forming. Field is going propulsive. Speed is zero point five. Zero point nine." Every eardrum on the ship recoiled from the piercing agony of "Einstein's Wail," the bloodcurdling, tooth-splintering shriek produced as the ship cracked through "Einstein's Wall" and exceeded the speed of light as measured from the viewpoint of an observer outside the zone of compressed space. "Ship is now superluminal. Speed is one point eight. Three. Five. Nine. Eighteen. Twenty-nine. Thirty-five. Forty-four. Field is now reaching equilibrium. Equilibrium achieved. Compression field is now propulsive and stable at fifty-one point two c." Everyone in CIC held his breath, straining to hear or feel the slightest irregularity in the ship's progress that might herald a compression instability. Although it felt like hours, less than forty seconds passed before LeBlanc said, "Compression shutdown commanded from Engineering. Ship is now subluminal." Then, in an amazed tone, "Bull's-eye, Skipper. Our current position is only 1974 kilometers away from the target coordinates."

Not bad. Especially for a ship traveling 15 million kilometers per second. "Maneuvering, null our rates, then go to station keeping. Sensors, Tactical, I need to know what's going on, and I need to know it two minutes ago," Max said. "Gentlemen, my intention is to ascertain the tactical situation before engaging. We've got a friendly ship out there, and we can't afford to go in with guns blazing."

Kasparov and Bartoli rapidly coordinated the data coming in from their respective systems and back rooms. It took less than half a minute before Bartoli started to rattle off the information. "There are three ships engaged in a running battle off our bow, bearing three-three-seven mark one-five-five, range 151,252 kilometers, speed of advance less than 10,000 meters per second: one Union tender and two Krag warships: a cruiser and a destroyer. The Krag appear to have the upper hand. There is also a debris field at three-two-nine mark one-six-one, range 152,830 kilometers, that appears to be the remnants of a Union destroyer, *Alfred Thayer Mahan* class, likely the USS *Vauban*. I'm assuming that *Vauban* was the tender's escort. Radial velocity of the debris and size of the debris field are consistent with *Vauban*'s destruction by a fusion weapon approximately fifty minutes ago. The engaged vessels are as follows. One Union *Clarence Birdseye* class tender, designated as Charlie 1, and identified by her transponder as the USS *Nicholas Appert*. Her heading is zero-two-zero mark one-eight-seven, and she's barely making any headway—speed is only 9345 meters per second. One Krag destroyer, *Demerit* class, designated as Hotel one, and one Krag medium cruiser, *Crusader* class, designated as Hotel two. Both enemy vessels are circling Charlie 1 and hitting it with plasma cannon fire."

"What kind of shape is the tender in?" Max asked.

"Not good, sir. She appears to have sustained at least moderate damage. Her main sublight drive appears to be inoperable, and she is on maneuvering thrusters only—that's why the group is making such slow headway. Deflectors are down to 60 percent average, but coverage is spotty—we believe deflector strength to be below 20 percent amidships. She appears also to have suffered significant EMP and moderate blast damage, but I'm not showing any hull breaches at this time and the ship is still under active control. But it won't be more than ten minutes before her shields are down to nothing. Sir, I don't get it. With her shields down to 20 percent amidships, why don't the Krag just hit her with a big nuke and be done with it?"

"The rat-faces don't want to vaporize her; they want to board her and take her cargo. Remember, the Krag shortage of fuel and supplies is the reason we're in this area to begin with."

"Skipper," Bartoli broke in, "Charlie 1 . . . he just fired a missile at Hotel two." Three seconds passed. "Hit! A good, solid hit near the bow sensor array!" His excitement melted two seconds later. "Little or no effect, sir."

"Fucking Goshawk," Ensign Levy could be heard to mutter from the Weapons console.

"Mr. Levy?" Max said. His voice held mild reproof and genuine interest in equal measures.

"Sir," said Levy, somewhat embarrassed, as though he hadn't intended to say the remark out loud, "sorry about the 'fucking' part. The tender fired an ASM-768 Mark III Goshawk missile.

NAVWEAP needs to fit those logistics ships out with a more effective missile type. The Goshawk's dinky little ten-kiloton unitary warhead just isn't big enough. It's like a kid throwing pebbles at ground cars as they drive past on the highway. Against the current crop of Krag first-line warships, it just doesn't do *chara*, if you'll pardon my Hebrew."

"If *chara* means the same thing as *merde*, you're right, Levy, it doesn't," Max allowed grimly.

"Sir," Bartoli said, "we've got enough data for a reasonably good damage assessment on Hotels one and two, and it's looking now as though neither has suffered any meaningful damage—both are at 95 percent efficiency, probably higher. That doesn't leave us with any way to engage both enemy ships with conventional tactics and win. We could probably destroy Hotel two with a surprise missile attack, especially with the Equalizer, but attacking Hotel one at the same time as Hotel two risks destroying the tender. Hotel one is just too close to the tender, and her deflectors are too depleted. And if we don't kill both ships simultaneously, we'd be in a fair fight with a *Demerit* class destroyer, which is practically a light cruiser in terms of firepower. We lose that one every time, even if we could safely engage her when she is this close to the tender, which we can't. I can't see any way for us to engage these two ships without significant risk of destroying ourselves and the tender. As your tactical officer, it's my duty to inform you that the rules of engagement for this situation say that we are more valuable to the overall conduct of the war than the tender. Accordingly, we are required to consider the tender . . . uh . . . expendable under these conditions. The rules say that we're supposed to make good our escape, secure another tender from the fleet, and start over."

Max's jaw muscles rippled, and his fists clenched. In an instant, though, with what appeared to be a supreme exertion of his will, he became composed, even serene, and took a slow, even breath.

"Lieutenant, your job as tactical officer is to tell me what the rules of engagement have to say on this subject, and I appreciate that. Sincerely. On the other hand, my job as commanding officer of this vessel is to say that the rules of engagement . . . *can go fuck themselves.* The tender is a navy vessel, and that makes every man aboard her our brother. I'm not going to turn tail and leave my brothers to die." Then, in a whisper, "Not again."

Brave words. Now how in the hell *am I going to do that?*

Max quickly scanned the eyes of the men in CIC. Although he saw some fear, these men were ready to follow him into battle rather than leave their brothers in the hands of the Krag. His eyes locked with those of his weapons officer, the brilliant nineteen-year-old Menachem Levy. *Nothing but determination there. He'd use the jawbone of an ass if that's what it took. Well, Levy, that makes two of us. I'd like to unleash some biblical wrath-of-God stuff on those Krag bastards.* Suddenly Max smiled.

"Mr. Levy, throwing rocks at the passing ground cars is useless, right?"

"Um, yes . . ." the young man answered uncertainly.

"But what if you could hit those cars with rocks hurled at the speed of a bullet? You think that might do something?"

"Sir?"

"Stand by. Get ready to deploy a weapon you've never worked with before. If there is no way to win with conventional tactics, we're just going to have to invent some unconventional ones. Mr. Kasparov, can you give me an active scan of the *Vauban*'s debris field without giving our position away to the Krag?"

"Affirmative, sir. We've got a good angle. Not much chance they'll pick it up, especially if I keep the power low."

"Then do it. Find me something big and heavy and solid in there that we can latch onto."

"Yes, sir," he responded, trying to keep his incomprehension from showing.

Kasparov spoke to his back room and got the scan going.

"Skipper," Chin interjected.

"Yes?"

"Shouldn't we let the *Nicholas Appert* know we're here? She might fight harder if she knew help was on the way."

Chin always wanted to talk to whatever Union ship was in the vicinity. *I guess it goes with the job.* "Chin, are you telling me that if they know we are here, those men on the tender are going to fight harder than they would just from the prospect of being boarded by Krag, killed—or tortured and killed—and then having their bodies hacked to pieces and tossed into space? Is that what you are saying, Mr. Chin?"

"I guess not, sir."

"I don't think we have to worry about the fighting spirit of the men of the USS *Nicholas Appert,*" Max said gently. "Besides, we can't take the risk right now, Chin. We derive an enormous tactical advantage from the Krag not knowing that there is another Union ship in the vicinity. Don't worry, the folks on the tender are going to notice the cavalry coming over the hill before too long."

"Sir," Kasparov said, "I've got the ventral hemisphere of the destroyer's CIC pressure bulkhead. It's ten point four meters in diameter, nineteen centimeters thick, and made of solid Michiganium. Mass is 13,530 kilograms." Michiganium, first produced at the University of Michigan Engineering College in 2117, was an alloy of depleted uranium, titanium, chromium, some exotic trace elements, and a healthy dose of plain old iron, all combined into an incredibly tough molecular matrix by quantum orbital manipulation technology. Nearly as hard as diamond, denser than gold, and virtually impervious to ionizing radiation,

Michiganium was the ultimate armor for the parts of Union warships that most needed protecting.

"That will do quite nicely," said Max. "Maneuvering, ahead one quarter. Put the ventral hemisphere—let's call it *the boulder* to make things easy—five hundred meters off our five o'clock."

LeBlanc acknowledged the order. Max could feel the questioning stares of his CIC crew. *They'll understand it soon enough.* "Mr. Levy, I seem to recall that one of your ancient countrymen once slew a giant with a stone thrown from a slingshot."

"That's what the *Nevi'im* says, sir."

"You think you can duplicate the feat in space with a 13,530-kilogram CIC pressure bulkhead hemisphere?"

The young man smiled broadly as understanding dawned on him. "Watch me."

Less than five minutes later, having come around in a wide arc, the *Cumberland* was creeping toward Hotel two on maneuvering thrusters, approaching the Krag vessel from its six o'clock position, with all systems set for maximum stealth. This was not an orthodox battle maneuver. Not even slightly. There was, of course, nothing odd about creeping up behind one's adversary, but it wasn't every day that a destroyer came up on the enemy's six using its grappling field to tow a 13,530-kilogram, solid Michiganium CIC pressure hull hemisphere from a recently nuked Union warship.

The novelty of the maneuver wasn't lost on Dr. Ibrahim Sahin, occupying his accustomed place at the Commodore's Station with the ship's cat, Clouseau. The black tomcat was in one of his many accustomed places in CIC, this time lying in the seat of the Commodore's station beside the doctor, resting his head upside down on Sahin's leg, sprawled in the boneless repose of which only felines are capable. Sahin spoke to his skipper at a volume calculated to keep his remarks between the two of them. "Max,

I've read the *Manual of Standard Union Battle Maneuvers* and descriptions of all the destroyer battles you listed for me to read, but I don't think I've ever seen this particular maneuver."

"I'm sure you haven't. As far as I know, it's never been done before," Max responded.

"I seem to recall hearing from you some kind of maxim to the effect that one should never be the person to do something for the first time."

Max shook his head. "That was one of Commodore Middleton's Rules of Bureaucratic Behavior. This is combat, not bureaucracy. Entirely different set of rules. In combat, doing the unexpected is the second-best way to survive."

"What, pray tell, is the best?"

"Running away."

"Oh.

"At least," said Max, "you know in advance what we are going to do this time. Does that make any difference to you?"

"Less than I would have suspected. Even though I have a rudimentary understanding of our proposed course of action, I understand so few of the details by which we seek to effectuate this objective that I still feel singularly uninformed. I don't even understand so basic a fact as what happens if we aren't able to accomplish the objectives we have set for ourselves in a timely fashion."

"Oh, that's easy. If we screw up, and we're lucky, we'll be able to run away, and the Krag will take the tender.

"And if we're not lucky?"

"We get blown to hell in about three minutes." Max could see Bartoli slowly shaking his head. Apparently, the tactical officer's hearing was better than Max and Bram had counted on. Max met Bartoli's gaze, and the tactical officer held up two fingers. "That's *two* minutes."

Bram took a slow breath and squared his shoulders. He was not a fearful man, not by any means, but he had not been in warship service long enough for facing possible death to have become routine. Routine or not, facing death was part of his job, and Doctor Ibrahim Sahin always did his job, whether it involved supporting his friend and captain here in CIC or taking care of his patients in the Casualty Station. He would do his job today, too, without flinching. Much.

Max reverted to his "CIC voice." "Tactical, any change in enemy dispositions?"

"None, sir," Bartoli replied. "Hotel two is still standing off about 27,000 meters from the tender, pummeling it fore and aft with pulse-cannon blasts. Hotel one is at close range—2,700 meters or so—hitting her with concentrated blasts amidships to wear down the deflectors in that area. Hotel one is still looking as though she intends to board. No sign that either is aware of our presence."

"Outstanding." Max hit a key on his console.

"Kraft here."

"Major Kraft, are you ready?"

"*Ja vohl!* Ready to bring the war to the enemy, *SIR*!" Kraft sounded as though he were ready to swing from the yardarms onto the enemy deck with a knife in his teeth.

"Outstanding. CIC out." Max punched the circuit closed. "Chin, do you have that message prepared? Blue-on-blue casualties make me cranky."

"The barnacle is prepared and loaded for launch, sir."

"Very well."

Everything was in place, and all the *Cumberland* and its adrenalin-marinated crew could do for the moment was hold themselves in readiness for just the right moment. Ever observant, Dr. Sahin noticed the tiny beads of sweat that glistened on the upper lips and foreheads of many of the CIC watch standers, notwithstanding the compartment's closely regulated temperature of 22.2 degrees Celsius. He glanced to his right at his friend Max Robichaux, the young man on whose shoulders the weight of more than two hundred human lives rested every minute of every day. Although Max's face was composed, his hands were clutching the arms of the chair at the CO's station so hard that his fingertips were white and the tendons were standing out on the backs of his hands. But the skipper's head was held high, and his eyes were fixed firmly ahead.

The commander and crew of the USS *Cumberland* felt fear. Fear of defeat. Fear of failure. Fear of death.

And they defied it.

The wait wasn't long. Less than two minutes after the *Cumberland* was in place, Bartoli sang out, "There she goes, sir. Hotel one is making his move to dock."

It was important for Max to wait for this moment to make his move because, when Hotel one closed with the *Nicholas Appert* to dock, the tender blocked its view of Hotel two, meaning that Hotel one's commander would have no direct view of Hotel two's destruction and would (Max hoped) have no idea that there was another Union ship in the vicinity.

"All right, men," said Max, "Let's slay the giant. *Go!*"

LeBlanc patted Fleishman on the shoulder and said, "Go, son, go."

Fleishman pushed the main sublight drive controller from NULL to FLANK. With a glare of fusing deuterium and towing the "boulder" 5000 meters behind it, *Cumberland* leaped into motion straight toward Hotel two.

"Fire the barnacle," Max said at the moment the main sublight drive controller began to move under Fleishman's hand. Chin flipped up a protective cover and pressed the button underneath, causing a cylinder about the same diameter as a grapefruit and half a meter long to issue from a dedicated tube on the *Cumberland*'s belly. It swiftly crossed the distance separating the destroyer from the tender, used its compact sensor package to locate one of the tender's dozens of receptacles for external comms umbilicals, and fired its tiny thrusters to aim itself so that it slammed into the umbilical's armored cover. The barnacle transmitted a digital signal, causing the cover to retract, after which it extruded a tiny fiber optic filament, tied itself into the comm receptacle, and transmitted a short message. Because the barnacle was hard-wired to the *Nicholas Appert*, it was totally immune from detection and interception by the Krag. Shepherded by the appropriate access codes, the barnacle's message immediately found its way through the tender's comms network to her commander.

Meanwhile, the *Cumberland* was bearing down on Hotel two, having accelerated to roughly 10 percent of the speed of light. Only five-hundredths of a second before colliding with the enemy ship, in an automatically executed move programmed by LeBlanc and Levy into the Maneuvering computer, the *Cumberland* veered off and released the grappling field at a carefully calculated point in the course change, slinging the pressure bulkhead hemisphere directly toward the enemy cruiser. The Krag vessel, which had detected the attacking destroyer only 2.67 seconds earlier, had no time to evade. The only defensive measure it could take was to route additional power to its rear deflectors.

Unfortunately for the Krag, deflectors designed to turn aside three-ton missiles built mostly of lightweight materials were useless against a thirteen-ton-plus, superdense pressure hull, particularly when that thirteen-ton-plus pressure hull is traveling at about 10 percent of the speed of light. Ensign Levy's expertly slung boulder pierced the Krag deflectors' layers of polarized gravitons like a rifle bullet through balsa wood and struck the enemy destroyer about thirteen meters left and four meters below dead center. The bulkhead's enormous kinetic energy (half of its mass times the square of its velocity: more than 5 x 10^{16} joules—the rough equivalent of a *500-megaton* thermonuclear explosion) vaporized the Krag cruiser in less than five-hundredths of a second.

Thus, the late USS *Vauban,* or at least, a piece of her, had her revenge upon the Krag.

Screened from the event by the enormous bulk of the tender, the commander of Hotel one knew only from the explosion and the cessation of Hotel two's transponder signal that his sister ship had been destroyed. Because he believed no Union vessels other than the tender were in the vicinity, he attributed the vessel's destruction to a lucky shot from the tender, or the supreme bad luck of being struck by high-speed debris from the defunct USS *Vauban*, the latter theory being not very far from the truth.

Just as the glare from the explosion started to fade, LeBlanc announced, "Executing next maneuver."

"Outstanding shot, Mr. Levy!" Max proclaimed. "We might have to start calling you 'David.'"

"It's sure easier to pronounce than 'Menachem,'" Bartoli added, his Alabama accent doing things to the name that Levy's parents never imagined when they bestowed it upon him.

Behind the cover of the tender, the *Cumberland* wheeled around, dumped velocity, and pulled up alongside the larger vessel bow to stern, so that the main starboard docking ports on each ship aligned. With a few deft maneuvering thruster pulses, the two ports kissed gently and then engaged with a firm *THUMP.*

"Hard dock with the *Nicholas Appert*," LeBlanc said.

Max looked at his comms officer. "Hard-line comms with the tender established," Chin said. "They signal that the Krag have not yet boarded. The midships deflectors will keep them off for five minutes, maybe ten."

"Very well." Now that the first enemy ship was history, Max needed to destroy the second. But the *Cumberland*'s weapons and deflectors were simply not strong enough to go toe-to-toe with Hotel one, a *Demerit* class destroyer with an array of weaponry equivalent to that carried by many light cruisers. Max needed his marines to tilt the scales back in his favor.

Max opened a comm channel that piped his voice onto the Salute Deck. "Marines! You are GO!"

"Aye, aye, sir," Kraft responded with enthusiasm.

But do the Marines feel the same way as their commander? Just as Max formed that question, the audio transducer on his console practically exploded with sound as the marines that filled the Salute Deck thundered, "SEMPER FI! DO OR DIE!"

Good answer.

At that moment, the hatches that joined the two ships opened. With Zamora and Ulmer, the two largest and most aggressive of the marines in the lead, the *Cumberland*'s twelve-man marine detachment stormed onto the deck of the *Nicholas Appert*. Following them closely were one special-skills naval officer and twenty-four "honorary marines," navy men chosen for their size, skill with weapons, toughness, and killer instincts. Major Kraft himself trained them intensively during breaks in their regular naval duties and called them at need to fill out the marines' ranks to make up a full platoon of hard-charging, remorseless, blood-up-to-their-elbows Krag killers.

Meeting them was a small but intense-looking lieutenant wearing a space combat uniform along with a combat helmet and blast visor. He was carrying a Model 2309 submachine gun, a wicked little weapon with an insanely large magazine that held 250 rounds of 9 millimeter ammunition. Known as the "sandblaster" because of its resemblance to the business end of that particular piece of industrial equipment, it was designed to be used in close quarters with the enemy. The little man looked eager to strip the paint from some rat-faces.

Kraft and the lieutenant exchanged salutes. Under the exigencies of the situation, the customary salutes to the flag were omitted. "Welcome aboard, Major. I'm Lt. Maynard, the XO," he said. He didn't wait for Kraft to introduce himself. The messages from the *Cumberland* told him whom to expect, and with his ship under attack, Maynard—businesslike under even the most relaxed of circumstances—wasn't in the mood for chit-chat. "We've done just what you asked. Follow me." Maynard led the contingent across the waist of the ship to a narrow L-shaped space, one leg of which was about twelve meters long and the other about eight. The marines spread themselves out down the legs of the "L," with Kraft and Maynard at the angle, flanked by Zamora and Ulmer. Maynard activated a padcomp that was stuck on the wall with a few blobs of adhesive putty. "This will tell you when the guests have arrived." Then he handed Kraft a small munitions trigger known as a "pickle," because it was about the size of a reasonably sized kosher dill and dull green in color. "And this will let you greet them properly."

Kraft looked down both legs of the "L" and saw that he could dispense with his planned order for his men to get ready. Each marine, actual and honorary, was on one knee, weapon at the ready, helmet cinched in place, blast visor down, war face on. Maynard was standing, braced against his weapon's anticipated recoil. Kraft turned to the lieutenant and said quietly, "Maynard, that's a good way to get your head blown off. Generally speaking, you want to be doing what all these marines are doing."

Maynard nodded and went down on one knee, emulating as closely as possible the posture of Ulmer to his immediate left, cinched his helmet, and lowered his blast visor. Satisfied that his men were ready to meet the enemy, Kraft kneeled. A breathless minute passed. Two. Another. Then they all heard the unmistakable WHUMP of a combat docking, followed by the BLAM of the hatch being blown.

Focused on the padcomp, Kraft could see the shattered remnants of the hatch fly into the tender's Port Salute Deck and ricochet off the bulkheads before coming to rest. Half a second later, the padcomp's screen flashed white, and the deck shook from several flash-bang grenades tossed into the compartment by the Krag to stun and dazzle any defenders who might be in the compartment. The padcomp image cleared from the flash-bangs just in time to display forty or so Krag, weapons at the ready, swarming into the compartment, their confusion at meeting no opposition evident in their body language. None of them noticed the fifteen or so innocuous-looking rectangular boxes mounted about chest-high on the bulkheads. Painted to match the surfaces on which they were mounted, the boxes looked like so many other of the boxes, bulges, pipes, and other fixtures that littered every wall and overhead in a warship. One of the invaders, apparently their leader, started toward what appeared to be a hatch in one of the compartment's bulkheads.

At that moment Kraft grasped the end of his pickle. He flipped the hinged top end up to expose a small red button, which he depressed with his thumb. All fifteen of those innocuous boxes concealed Claymore mines—their simple but effective design little changed over the centuries—containing plastic explosive charges that filled the room with tens of thousands of buckshot-size high-velocity steel pellets. Twenty-three of the forty Krag fell immediately to the deck, killed or grievously wounded by the hail of steel shot or the concussion from the explosions. The rest, shielded by their comrades, unscathed or only slightly wounded, swung their weapons looking for foes to kill but were still partly blinded by the flash.

Kraft stood. "Now, marines!" The marines had been hiding behind false bulkheads erected inside the Salute Deck and paralleling the compartment's forward and port walls, so that the Krag had stormed into a normal-looking, if slightly smaller-than-expected, compartment. At Kraft's command, the marines stood in unison and rotated the large latches located on the back of each bulkhead, withdrawing the locking pins that secured them to the deck, to the overhead, and to each other. The heavy, blast-resistant panels fell into the compartment, revealing the marines. Some of the panels fell on Krag, crushing them. Many Krag, however, dimly saw the threat with their half-blinded vision and managed to back out of harm's way.

Not for long.

As soon as the bulkheads hit the deck, the marines howled a ferocious "OORAH," deafening in the compartment's close quarters. The roar of M-88 battle rifles was punctuated by the blasts of M-72 shotguns as the men, whose "L" formation allowed them to fire without fear of inflicting friendly-fire casualties, mowed down the Krag in a lethal cross fire. Only a few of the Krag even managed to get off a shot, none of which had any effect. In less than five seconds, only the humans were on their feet. All the Krag were on the deck, dead or rapidly dying.

Time stopped for a few seconds as the men regarded the compartment, its air filled with powder smoke, the bulkheads scarred by weapons fire, its floor covered with Krag and the slippery gore of their loud and violent demise. For many this was their first time meeting the Krag nose to snout. The quick and stunningly violent victory took a few seconds to process.

Kraft, experienced commander that he was, gave his men those seconds, but no more. There were nearly three hundred Krag on the other side of the now-unguarded hatch, and they would not long be idle. "First detail," he roared in his best battlefield voice, "FIRING LINE!" Six men hustled forward and took prone positions on the deck, covering the hatch with their weapons. The remaining men stood with their backs to the wall on either side of the hatch, out of sight from the interior of the Krag ship.

True to rigid but generally effective Krag tactical doctrine, the absence of a "PROGRESS ACCEPTABLE" signal from the boarders prompted a "hand" of five Krag marines from a nearby protected guard station to run to the hatch to check the status of the boarders and protect the ship from being counterboarded. They stormed through the hatch, where the first detail mowed them down with a single, short volley, each man firing a three-shot burst from his M-88. Their bodies had not yet hit the deck before Kraft yelled, "DODGER! BATES!"

Lance Corporal Pyotr Vastislav Bomorovsky, known incongruously as the Artful Dodger or just Dodger, the nickname traditionally awarded to the marine who specialized in defeating locks, alarms, access panels, and security systems, stood. He was immediately joined by Private First Class Sodnomzondui Batbayar, who was almost never addressed by the name given to him by his Mongolian parents on the Asiatic steppes, but as Charlie Bates, the time-hallowed nickname for the man who assisted the Artful Dodger. The pair was immediately surrounded by a protective phalanx of six marine riflemen. Once so enclosed, Dodger and Bates ran onto the deck of the Krag ship and found the hatch's control and locking mechanism.

The failure of the recently deceased Krag boarders to transmit their "PROGRESS ACCEPTABLE" signal, combined with the failure of the even more recently deceased recon squad's failure to transmit a "NO BOARDING THREAT" signal triggered a countdown in the hatch mechanism. The marines knew that, unless they defeated the mechanism or entered a fail-safe code within the next fifty seconds or so, the Krag hatch would close and fusion-weld itself shut as a defense against counterboarding.

When they reached the hatch control mechanism, Dodger ripped the cover off with a tool Bates handed him. Before the cover hit the deck, Bates had slapped a pair of wire cutters into Dodger's hand. Dodger artfully cut three wires, then pulled four more from their connections. Bates then produced from a chest pocket several sets of wires with alligator clips on each end. Taking these wires from Bates as he needed them, Dodger connected the four loose wires to each other in a crossing pattern and then attached other alligator clip wires in a complex fashion to the terminals from which they had been ripped. Once that was accomplished, Bates pulled out a wire stripper and put it in Dodger's hand. Dodger used it to strip the ends of two of the three wires he had cut, using alligator clips to ground them to the bulkhead. As soon as the last clip made contact with the bulkhead, a light over the hatch control mechanism changed from blue-green to yellow-orange. The hatch was hot-wired open and the fail-safe defeated.

"Hatch secured," Dodger announced. At that moment six Krag appeared at the end of the corridor about twenty meters away, dropped to their knees, and started shooting at Dodger, Bates, and their protectors. These appeared to be ordinary Krag spacers rather than marines, as their weapons fire was enthusiastic but not particularly accurate. The marines returned fire with their customary lethal efficacy, felling all of the Krag with a single burst, but not before one marine caught a Krag round. All the marines were wearing body armor, but this bullet found its way into the marine's unprotected mouth and out the back of his neck, severing his spinal column. Even if he had been lying on Dr. Sahin's operating table when he received the wound, there would have been no saving him, and his combat-hardened comrades knew it.

Marine Private First Class Heile Tekeda had laid down his arms permanently.

Two marines dragged Tekeda's body back through the hatch, covering the seven feet that separated the place where he fell from the deck of the *Cumberland* in less than five seconds, doing their part to see that what was left of their comrade did not meet the end they planned for the Krag ship. There were two three-man naval fire teams setting up heavy weapons on the Salute Deck to defend the hatch against any counterboarding effort by the Krag. One of those men used his percom to request that orderlies come from the Casualty Station to remove the body.

Kraft, with Zamora and Ulmer beside him, strode confidently through the hatch, with the rest of the marines on their tail. By prior arrangement they separated cleanly and quickly into three groups, standing in quiet readiness. "All right, marines," Kraft said, his voice even. Professional. He didn't differentiate between the actual marines and the honorary ones. Today, fighting side by side under his command, they were *all* marines. "You're in enemy territory, so stay sharp, watch your backs, watch your buddies, and keep a full magazine in your weapon at all times. Let's get it done and get back home."

CHAPTER 5

07:11 Zulu Hours, 12 May 2315

Kraft's three teams, to which he had given the prosaic names of Team 1, Team 2, and Team 3, jogged off in three different directions. Team 1, consisting of eight men under the command of Gunnery Sergeant P. P. "Pissed Off" O'Carroll and accompanied by Lieutenant Maynard, had an assignment that was considered both the most important and the least hazardous of the three. They filed out of the staging area in which the Krag main hatch was situated into a corridor. With weapons at the ready, they jogged for about ten meters before they came to a corridor that went off to the left. They took it and came to an access ladder, which they took one man at a time, most of the men waiting just inside the branch corridor, with two men looking around the corners down the main corridor using nearly invisible fiber-optic peep scopes. One Krag spacer came down the long corridor on what appeared from his demeanor to be some routine errand. When he got within three meters of the marines, PFC Stanley "Bug Eye" Barrow calmly stepped into the corridor and shot it twice in the chest and once in the head with a silenced pistol. Barrow was one of the two men in each team equipped with the 10 millimeter Nordic Naval Arms Model 2212 silenced sidearm for just this eventuality.

Team 1 used the access ladder to descend five decks, where the marines emerged in another subsidiary corridor, which they followed to where it joined the main corridor. They could almost have been on a Union vessel—the same air, corridors, and access ladders of roughly the same dimensions. Even the controls and fixtures, which looked unfamiliar and were labeled in an unreadable language, still looked as though they might have been made for humans. Not even the—to the human eye—odd meadow green and butterscotch yellow color scheme could dispel the certainty that this ship was made for creatures whose ancestors came from Earth and who shared common genetic heritage with humankind. One could almost imagine the planet that spawned them both weeping that her children were killing each other in such great numbers.

After using the peep scopes to determine that the main corridor was clear of Krag, the marines turned right and jogged for about fifteen meters before coming to a locked hatch about two meters wide consisting of two panels that slid out of the wall and met in the center—the kind that the Krag used for compartments containing bulky equipment. Behind the hatch was the Krag Environmental Systems Control Room. Again Dodger and Bates went to work, popping off the control mechanism's cover, deftly snipping and ripping and connecting the alien wires with their alien color code of brown, butterscotch, green, tan, and rust instead of the familiar bright red, blue, green, yellow, and orange. After about a minute and a half, Dodger announced, "Almost done. When I attach this clip, the door will open in about six seconds."

While the Dodger had been practicing his art, O'Carroll had been arraying his men: three men kneeling, two men prone between them, and one man standing behind the kneelers, his feet in the spaces between the spread legs of the prone shooters. The sergeant had already ordered the men to fix bayonets. Each weapon was now tipped with 171.4 millimeters of razor-sharp, cold steel. O'Carroll stood to the side of the door with two anti-personnel grenades in his left hand, two flash-bang grenades hanging ready from loops on his tunic. His right hand held his silenced sidearm.

The sergeant verified that his shooters were ready—weapons in firing position, visors in place, bayonets fixed—holstered his sidearm, and nodded to Dodger, who connected the clip, nodded back to O'Carroll, and reached for his weapon. There was no room for Dodger and Bates to fit in and fire through the hatch, so they turned around and faced the corridor, protecting his buddies' backs, joining Maynard, who had been performing that function with his submachine gun. In 6.22 seconds, the hatch slid silently into the bulkhead, presenting Team 1 with a large compartment full of complex equipment and about a dozen Krag at work, a few of whom turned to see which of their shipmates was entering. With a yell of "FRAG OUT!" O'Carroll tossed in his grenades, while his men opened fire. All but three of the surprised Krag went down in the first five seconds as marines poured in rifle and shotgun fire. Then, with a deafening "OORAH!" the marines charged into the compartment: first the kneelers, then the man who was standing behind them, then those who were prone, and finally those who had been protecting the shooters' backs.

Three Krag had survived the initial shock attack. Two, stunned and disoriented by the grenades, tried to stagger their way to safety. O'Carroll took care of one with his sidearm, two quick, neat shots through the back. Able Spacer First Class Minh was just as quick but not nearly as neat when he brought down the other Krag with a well-aimed shotgun blast to the side of the head, sending the alien's brains in a red, gelatinous spray that coated four environmental systems status displays.

No one noticed the third Krag. As the humans were storming the compartment, it had crawled to a floor-mounted weapons locker, drew a submachine gun, chambered a round, and leaped to its feet. Popping up unexpectedly from behind the console with a high-rate-of-fire 8.1759 millimeter submachine gun, the Krag technician expected to catch the humans by surprise and, with a clear field of fire covering almost the entire compartment, cut them down like grain under a scythe, thereby earning a warrior's name for himself.

It didn't happen that way.

Lt. O. N. Maynard, shot and moderately disabled by a Krag pulling a similar trick two years before, had resolved that nothing of the kind would happen again on his watch. To that end he was standing on a Krag toolbox, weapon on his hip, covering the consoles near the rear of the compartment behind which the marines had not yet cleared. When the Krag stood up to shoot, Maynard beat it to the punch with a tightly grouped ten-round burst to the chest. The ratlike alien fell to the deck like a sack of potatoes, landing behind the same console that had concealed it only seconds before.

The echo of Maynard's shots had hardly died before Dodger announced that he had closed and secured the hatch. The marines responsible for searching the compartment's perimeter and possible hiding places announced that the room was clear. This finding was punctuated by a few pistol shots—*coups de grace* for wounded Krag.

Now the men got to the work that they were there to accomplish. Four men went around the room pulling the covers off of consoles and equipment boxes. Having exposed the equipment's Kragish innards, these same men donned heavy gloves and hoods, pulled large squeeze bottles out of their backpacks, and squirted the contents of the bottles into and over the exposed equipment.

"Damn," Dodger said, "that shit smells terrible. I've never been briefed on that stuff."

"Damn straight, it smells bad," answered McGinty from under his hood. "But what it does to the Krag is worse than it smells. It flows into all the nooks and crannies, and what it doesn't short out, it corrodes. Then it turns into rock-hard plastic that catches fire or explodes if you try to chip it out. Turns all this equipment into junk. The Krag will have to unhook it and toss it all out the air lock."

Dodger picked up one of the empty containers and read the label out loud: "*Electronics Operability Impairment and Materièl Denial Compound 27*. Don't tell me that's what you actually call the stuff."

"'Course not," McGinty answered. "We call it *goop*."

While the Krag destroyer's environmental equipment was being subjected to a coordinated goop attack, the rest of the ship was about to be subjected to an attack that was, arguably, even more diabolical. Two of the remaining men were pulling cylindrical packages out of their packs, opening them, removing their contents, and setting them on the deck. When they were done, they had what looked vaguely like thirty-six dull black twenty-five-centimeter-long centipedes, their bodies articulated into ten segments, each spouting two tiny legs. The units carried an array of small but wicked-looking tools lying flat along their "backs" and at their "tails." When they were all laid out on the deck, Lance Corporal Bondarenko popped open his percom and entered a few keystrokes. A tiny yellow light flashed on each centipede. A few more keystrokes. Each executed a test sequence by standing, extending each pair of legs in order from front to back, retracting its legs and rolling into a ball, and then returning to its original position. One could almost imagine them saluting.

"Gunney," Bondarenko said to O'Carroll, "all thirty-six units are ready for deployment."

"Then what are you waiting for, dumbass," O'Carroll replied, his enormous smile in contrast to his voice and his language, "a medal? Get the little fuckers deployed already. This is naval/marine boarding action, not some kind of half-assed kindergarten field trip!"

"Aye, Gunney."

The marines had chosen to break into that particular compartment because it had an access port for the ship's main ventilation duct and for the primary maintenance access crawlway. Dodger had cracked the security locks on both and had them standing open. Bondarenko grabbed one armload of the just-activated units and unceremoniously dumped them in one opening, then grabbed another armload and in similar fashion dumped those units in the other. He hit a single key on his percom, and the distinctly shudder-inducing devices scurried away on their tiny sound-silencing polymer legs. Suddenly Bondarenko laughed out loud. *Payback's a bitch.*

In this case payback *was* going to be a six-ton, barnacle-covered, cast-iron bitch. Stacked up against what Bondarenko had just loosed on the Krag, the biblical plagues visited upon the Egyptians would look like trifling inconveniences. Today the Krag would make the first acquaintance of the Articulated Ambulatory Autonomous Warship Sabotage Drone, Model 2314, Mark I, better known as the "Gremlin." Gremlins were every spacer's nightmare brought to metallic, undulating life: elusive, semi-intelligent robots that dispersed themselves throughout an enemy warship by crawling or slithering through air ducts, access crawlways, cable conduits, pipe routes, ceiling spaces, and in a pinch, walking upside down over the enemy's head along the ceilings. Once spread out, they cut wires, bored holes in pipes and tanks (preferably ones containing toxic, flammable, or explosive materials), tripped circuit breakers, closed or opened valves and then welded them there, opened air locks, and even cut off bits of metal from hatch coamings and fixtures and then insinuated the sharp slivers into delicate gearboxes, bearings, and other critical mechanisms. They cross-wired control circuits, sawed through actuator rods, drained lubricant reservoirs, welded nozzles shut, and set off emergency alarms. The first thing that they were programmed to destroy was the ship's internal sensors, depriving the enemy of the ability to track them. Equipped with a power supply that would keep it running for nearly a month, each Gremlin would continue its mischief and destruction until it was caught or ran out of power (in which case it would explode with enough force to blow a Krag's head clean off). A batch of Gremlins could turn a warship into a useless hulk in hours. In this case the bucketful of Gremlins raising their unique brand of maintenance mayhem would hamstring the Krag warship, making it possible for the much less formidable *Cumberland* to defeat it in battle.

His team's job done, Gunnery Sergeant O'Carroll gathered his men, had Dodger open the hatch, and led the team back to the *Cumberland*.

As the gunney and his men were unleashing the Gremlins to prey upon the vulnerable interstices of the Krag destroyer, Major Kraft was leading a group of a dozen to do a different kind of mischief. Naval planners had theorized that a full-strength Krag warship crew that didn't have too many other crises might be able to detect and defeat, or at least contain, a Gremlin infestation in its early stages. Kraft and his men were on board to ensure that the Krag crew did not long remain at full strength or without too many crises. Their target was the Krag crew members who would be best able to fight the Gremlins: the engineers.

Accordingly, they made their way to the Main Engineering Equipment Room. The men jogged down a corridor, turning into an alcove for an access ladder. Finding it clear, they began to climb down three decks, posting a man in the alcove on each deck as the group climbed past it. One Krag had the misfortune to turn into the alcove on the second deck and was dispatched with a knife to the throat. The Krag's death was silent but bloody, the knife severing the carotid and unleashing a fountain of blood the color and smell of which could not be distinguished from that of a human.

Upon reaching the third deck, the men jogged down a corridor for about five meters, took a right turn, jogged another twelve meters, and then took a left. Suddenly a repeating and highly discordant screech assaulted their ears. "Krag alarm," Kraft announced. "Sounds like an owl going after its dinner. One of the Gremlins must have wrecked something important." A few meters after the left turn, they came to a large hatch similar to the one leading to the environmental control compartment that was at that moment hosting O'Carroll and his men. Although Kraft had with him a man possessing skills similar to, but of a lesser order than, Dodger's, there was no point in subtlety now. He turned to another man whose vocabulary didn't even contain the word "subtle."

"Sockem! Charges!"

Able Spacer Third Class Claudio "Sockem" Saccomanni, who discovered his true calling as a demolition man after becoming one of Kraft's honorary marines, was more than happy to oblige. He placed four small breaching charges, one at each corner of the hatch, and laid six lines of high-explosive det cord: four lines making a square with the charges at the corners and two crossing the square with an *X*. To Kraft the arrangement looked oddly like a hand-marked election ballot. He smiled at the observation, knowing that the marines were about to vote this particular hatch out of office.

Kraft holstered his sidearm and drew his boarding cutlass, a signal for the other men to do the same. Main Engineering is not a good place for bullets—not unless you want to puncture something that is best left unpunctured, releasing toxins or radioactive materials or blowing up the ship with Union personnel still on board. Meanwhile, Sockem armed the charges' integral detonators, flipped open his percom, and touched the screen a few times. The percom found the coded transmissions from the detonators, locked onto their frequencies, configured itself to blow them simultaneously, and asked Saccomanni to press a key confirming that was what he wanted to do. He keyed the confirmation, causing the unit to display a *PRESS HERE TO DETONATE* key. "Charges set and ready to blow, Major," he said zestfully.

"Ready, men," Kraft said to the men who were already flattening themselves along the near bulkhead. While they were positioning themselves, he withdrew a small rectangular patch, about four centimeters on a side, ripped off an adhesive backing, and stuck it to the bulkhead near the door. The same color as the bulkhead, the patch was nearly invisible. When Kraft saw that the men were in position, he nodded sharply. "Okay, Sockem, blow it."

"FIRE IN THE HOLE!" Saccomanni yelled and hit the key. With a sharp *BLANG*, the explosives turned the hatch into so much shrapnel. The four men nearest the hatch each threw in two flash-bang grenades. As soon as the grenades blew, the marines poured into the compartment with a deafening "OORAH!"

They were met by fifteen Krag engineers armed and ready to receive them. Not surprised by the attack in the least, they had taken cover behind a row of systems status consoles that ran across the compartment about a third of the way between the hatch and the back bulkhead. The consoles had provided substantial protection from the flash-bangs; accordingly, the defenders were only mildly stunned and not blinded at all. The marines had scarcely stepped into the room before the Krag had popped up from behind the consoles and began a spirited defense, firing handguns and service rifles.

Because the marines were near the hatch, an area deliberately kept free of explosive or radioactive materials, the Krag were—for now—free to use firearms, while the humans were not. In war the playing field was almost never level.

Fortunately for the marines, the Krag weapons fire was not particularly effective because the flash-bangs shook up the engineering specialists—not particularly good shots in the first place—just enough to make it difficult to aim their weapons. The marines' body armor protected them from most shots lucky enough to find a target. Most, but not all. Krag gunfire killed two marines instantly, one with a shot through the face and another with a "magic bullet" that entered his body through his right armpit, was deflected by the head of his humerus, and arced through his chest cavity, the hydrostatic shock of the bullet's passage through the tissue making a ruin of his heart and right lung. A few of the Krag remembered their training about Union body armor and shot to incapacitate rather than kill, bringing three other marines down with hits to the legs.

Heedless of these casualties, the marines came on, half of them once again taking up the "OORAH!" yell, and the other half making fierce barking sounds to give voice to the nearly four-hundred-year-old nickname "devil dogs." In an instant they covered the distance between the hatch and the row of meter-and-a-half-tall consoles that had provided cover for the Krag engineers, climbed to the barrier's top, and jumped down into the thick of their enemy like Tommys, Doughboys, or Poilus leaping into the Jerries' trenches in World War I.

Kraft claimed the first kill. Holding his cutlass in two hands as he jumped down, he used his combined inertia and upper-body strength to split open a Krag skull. A slice consisting of just over 40 percent of the Krag's head fell to the deck at Kraft's feet, while the rest of the Krag's body fell backward, away from the human who ended its life. That Krag's fall left open a path to one standing just to its left, who was using its rifle to block and parry the cutlass thrusts of Neumann, an ordinary spacer first class from Alphacen. Kraft unceremoniously plunged his cutlass into the middle of its back, straight into the aorta.

Nodding his thanks Neumann turned to the Krag behind him, who was grappling with Lance Corporal Wong. Man and Krag each had an arm around the other's waist, trying to throw his or its opponent to the deck, each hoping to pull out a fighting knife and cut the other's throat. Neumann swung his cutlass at the Krag's leg, cutting it off just below the knee. As the alien loosed its grip on Wong and fell, Neumann finished it with a quick, powerful stroke to the neck, cutting it almost halfway through, sending the Krag to the deck in a shower of its own blood.

Behind Kraft, one of the Krag who had been using a pistol at the outset of the battle had cast caution to the wind and was firing it at the humans, ignoring the risk of boiling or poisoning or irradiating everyone in the compartment if his shot went awry. In the melee, it was having a hard time hitting anything that was not protected by a helmet or body armor, but the threat was very real. Saccomanni turned toward the sound of the shots, only to be hit by two rounds to his helmet for the trouble. The carbon fiber composite helmet turned the bullets, but the twin impacts left him hearing bells and seeing stars, momentarily taking him out of the fight. Just as the Krag extended its arm to take aim at another human, Marine Private Ostergaard eliminated the problem by slicing off the Krag's shooting arm at the elbow with a particularly wicked edged weapon known prosaically as the Model 2305 Battle Ax. Maintaining the momentum of his weapon in a great, overhead loop, Ostergaard swept the ax around to take off the Krag's head just as the severed arm hit the deck.

Looking like an enormous Viking and driven by a battle lust little different from that which sometimes moved his distant Danish ancestors when they were the terrors of Europe, the enormous Scandinavian waded with a deafening but inarticulate roar into the clump of five remaining Krag, who were bunching together to make a last stand. With a few deft strokes, Ostergaard mowed them down.

Kraft surveyed his diminished command. Not counting himself, he had seven effectives remaining, six of whom were covering the blown hatch from various positions of concealment around the compartment. If the Krag showed up, they would have a warm greeting.

The other five men were down, two dead and three injured. All three of the injured were unconscious from shock and blood loss. Because they were several decks away from the hatch leading out of the Krag ship, there was no practical way to evacuate the wounded to the *Nicholas Appert*. The mission rules specifically covered this situation. The major met the eyes of Private West, the assigned field medic for this mission, who was kneeling near the wounded, and nodded grimly. West pulled a pressure syringe from his kit, loaded an ampule, turned the dial at the syringe's base to set the dosage, and moved to administer the first injection. Kraft gently took West's wrist, shook his head, and held out his hand for the syringe.

"This duty falls to me," Kraft said quietly. West handed the syringe to the major, who pressed it against each of the three men's necks. Three quick hisses. Three hearts stopped. Gently, reverently, he removed the ID tags from around the necks of each of the five dead men and put them in his pocket, his face a grim mask, while another man took their ammunition, handguns, and some miscellaneous equipment. He then reached into each man's pockets, pulled out an orange painted round from each, loaded them into the dead men's rifles, and pulled the triggers. The "Phelps Cartridge" shattered the chamber and lodged a steel plug in the barrel, rendering the weapon useless without some fairly complicated gunsmithing. If the Krag vessel survived, there would be nothing left with these men that the enemy could use.

Kraft stood and made the "prepare to move out" hand signal, a circling motion with his right index finger over his head—no sense yelling orders to be heard out in the corridor. The men came out of their concealed positions and lined themselves up against the bulkhead on either side of the hatch. Kraft popped open his percom and input a short code. The wrist device linked up with the patch he had stuck on the corridor bulkhead earlier—a camouflaged ultrawide-angle visual scanner providing a view of the corridor, about twenty meters in either direction from the hatch.

Good thing he checked. There were ten or so Krag crouched behind a portable blast screen, with flash visors down, so that if the humans tried to soften them up with flash-bangs or fragmentation grenades, the only effect would be to warn the ambushing aliens that the humans were about to come out. He snapped his percom closed and turned to his men. Kraft made the standard hand signal for "Krag," wiggling his fingers in front of his upper lip to indicate whiskers and then gestured toward where they were located with an extended hand and forearm in a slow chopping motion. He then pumped his fist twice, each pump representing five Krag—they tended to do just about everything in multiples of five.

He then pointed to Able Spacer Third Class Hannum and patted the back of his left hand with the palm of his right. Hannum nodded sharply in response to the standard hand signal, handed his rifle to the man standing next to him, unshouldered his pack, and pulled out a tube, about half a meter long and about ten centimeters in diameter, closed at one end and open at the other, with the opening surrounded by a ring obviously designed to make a gastight seal with some flat surface. Reaching back into the pack, he pulled out two handles that he slipped into opposite sides of the tube and a cylinder just a few millimeters shorter than the tube that resembled nothing more than a grayish summer sausage, one end of which was squared off while the other had a small nozzle, a ring-shaped dial, and a locking pin.

After donning a set of aluminized gloves and hood that made him look like a half-dressed firefighter, Hannum turned the dial at the base of the sausage, setting it for his estimate of the thickness of the bulkhead in front of him, six centimeters, pulled out the locking pin, and dropped the device into the larger cylinder. Then, grasping it by the handles, he held the cylinder over his head with the opening toward the wall. He pushed the opening as tightly as he could against the wall, his legs straining to make as tight a seal between the tube and the wall as possible.

Since removing the safety pin, Hannum had been counting at a deliberate pace: "One, I'm navy, two, I'm navy, three, I'm navy . . . " Upon reaching "ten, I'm navy," he whispered hoarsely, "FIRE IN THE HOLE!"

Just when Hannum would have reached "twelve, I'm navy," things started happening inside the innocuous-looking little summer sausage. First, a shaped breaching charge blew a neat hole clean through the bulkhead into the corridor right over the heads of the crouching Krag. Three-hundredths of a second later, a small solid rocket motor at the rear of the sausage ignited for less than a tenth of a second—really more of a slow explosive than a conventional rocket—just long enough to push it out of the tube, through the still-smoking hole in the bulkhead, and into the corridor, where a small explosive charge inside the device detonated.

The charge itself wasn't powerful enough to harm anyone, and its purpose was not to do so. Rather, the small but precisely engineered explosive liquefied the grayish, gelatinous material that constituted the bulk of the sausage and shattered the hard plastic shell that enclosed it, turning the gelatin to a thick mist of tiny droplets, which, when dispersed, formed a fuel–air mixture filling the corridor for about eight meters in both directions. Just another two-hundredths of a second later, when mist and air were mixed in the proper proportions, a tiny detonator gave off an even tinier spark.

What ensued, however, was anything but tiny. A sixteen-meter section of the corridor exploded like a bomb, its force magnified by virtue of being confined in two directions by the corridor's bulkheads. The Krag in the corridor—quite literally inside the explosion—were dead before they hit the deck, the force of the blast reducing their internal organs to lukewarm, purplish-red soup.

These Krag were among the first to encounter another new Union weapons system, the Mist Ordnance Explosive Air Munition, or MOEAM, an acronym which, in the few weeks since the weapon was issued, the men had come to pronounce as "mom." In this case, at least, it appeared that MOEAM had cleaned house.

Because the hatch to the corridor was open, Kraft and his men felt the force of the blast as a hard slam to their guts. Were it not for the active sound-filtering earbuds protecting their eardrums, their ears would have been ringing for days. Instead, when Kraft whispered, "Get ready," the marines heard it perfectly, put a full magazine in their weapons, and checked their equipment.

As his men were carrying out his order, Kraft flipped open his percom and pressed a soft key. The sound of small-arms fire came over the unit's miniature transducer. "McMillan, report."

"McMillan's dead, Major. Krag grenade dropped down an access tube."

Kraft recognized the voice of the group's second-in-command, Master Sergeant Oldsen Urquhart. "What's your status, Urquhart?"

"An enemy force, estimated to be between squad and platoon strength, is between us and the objective. Another group that appears to outnumber us about two to one has cut off our escape. We . . ." A nearby explosion, likely a Krag grenade, interrupted him. "Mission success unlikely. We'll take a lot of rat-faces with us, but I expect this unit to be a total loss."

"Not if I can help it," Kraft said. "Create a defensive perimeter and hold your position, Urquhart. Help is on the way. Kraft out." Kraft hit a few keys on his percom, one of which caused it to ping the master sergeant's percom, triggering it to respond by transmitting the precise location of Urquhart's unit to be displayed on Kraft's device. He stepped back from the bulkhead and looked at his men. "Marines, our brothers in the third team are cut off from their objective and from escape. We're going to fight our way through to them and jointly complete the mission. Follow me." The marines strode out the hatch, turned right, and jogged down the corridor. Flanked by Zamora and Ulmer and with his sidearm in hand, Kraft led the marines at a trot by the shortest route to their comrades. Despite the danger, it never occurred to Kraft that he should be anywhere but in the forefront of his men.

In the Union Space Marine Corps, leaders lead.

Kraft, who had done his homework on the layout of Krag ships, led his men with no wrong turns. They encountered very few Krag, which they promptly shot, but heard a great variety of alarms and occasionally encountered flickering ceiling lights, varying artificial gravity, and in a few instances, even heard distant, muffled explosions—the Gremlins' work was really starting to tell. Having descended to the lowest deck, they heard shooting and an occasional explosion ahead of them as they pushed aft. Finally, they came to a dogleg in the corridor: two ninety-degree turns, one to the right and one to the left, one of many breaking up most of the longer corridors in the Krag ship, designed to prevent an enemy from being able to rake the entire passageway with weapons fire.

Kraft consulted his percom to compare the position of his group with the position being reported by the transponder in Urquhart's percom. He turned to his men and made a vertical chopping motion in the direction of the end of the corridor around the second turn, meaning, "The enemy is there." He then met the eyes of PFC Bradford "Pockets" Pickett, so named because he had customized his marine boarding and surface combat uniform to feature, as Zamora liked to say, "slightly more than three hundred pockets." The major made a gesture that looked like he was pantomiming an insect crawling up his forearm. Pickett nodded his understanding, reached into a pocket located just above his navel, and produced an object about as long as his thumb and resembling a large ant except that its color exactly matched the ceiling of the Krag corridor. He withdrew a slender locking pin in the ant's tail and pressed a few keys on his percom. The ant went through a series of test movements and blinked a tiny green light. After another glance at his percom to check that the ant was transmitting, Pickett turned the insect-like device so that its legs were facing up and tossed it to the ceiling, where it clung hanging upside down.

Obeying its simple but effective programming, the ant began to crawl along the ceiling down the corridor toward the enemy. While two men kept their "heads on a swivel" looking out for any approaching Krag, the others popped open their percoms, watching the image transmitted by the tiny "recon ant." In less than three minutes, the insect-like drone had made its way past the end of the corridor, through the open hatch two meters into the hangar deck, and was on its way back to the largest concentration of Krag, where it would stop and provide continuous imagery.

Those images made clear what had happened. Urquhart's men had blown the hatch to the hangar deck to find their way blocked by a dozen or so members of the Hegemonic Naval Combat Corps—essentially Krag marines. Unable to take the hangar deck immediately and concerned about being attacked from behind, they had detached one of the armored bulkheads that had formed one side of the corridor and set it up on its side as a barricade, preventing any Krag attacking them from the rear from having a straight shot at them down the corridor. A group of thirty-four armed Krag spacers had then attempted to relieve the Combat Corps troops in the hangar deck and had been held off by Urquhart's marines. Knowing a good idea when they saw it, the Krag had protected their own rear by an expedient identical to that adopted by the marines, except that they had pulled down two bulkheads. Accordingly, around the second corner of the dogleg, Kraft and his men faced several meters of corridor, a line of two armored bulkheads, thirty-four armed Krag spacers, another armored bulkhead, Urquhart's marines, an open hatch, and roughly twelve hardened Krag Combat Corps troops on the other side of that hatch, defending the hangar deck.

The weapons fire of the two forces on either side of the open hatch created a kill zone on each side, beginning with the hatch and spreading in an ever-widening angle representing the respective shooters' line of sight. Any marine who entered the Krag field of fire died, as evidenced by the mute but eloquent testimony of Lance Corporal "Jumping" Tsang Jinping, who was lying squarely in the center of the deadly zone in a slowly spreading pool of his own blood, his open but unseeing eyes aimed directly at the recon ant's tiny lens, silently reproaching his brothers for coming too late to save him. The kill zone created by the humans was equally deadly—two Krag lay dead on the far side of the hatch, carried away on the silent wings of the Night Owl, their culture's answer to the Angel of Death.

The Krag had taken refuge in the two triangular dead zones, one either side of the hatch, where the marines' bullets could not reach. The defenders made sure that they were far enough back that, shielded by makeshift barricades made of toolboxes and spare parts crates, they were protected from the occasional grenade that the marines lobbed in just to keep things interesting. The marines had also divided into two groups, on either side of the kill zone, flattened against the bulkhead opposite the hatch.

Kraft quickly determined what he and his men had to do. First, they had to eliminate the numerically superior force of Krag spacers, whose rear was protected by a two-meter-tall armored barricade with a Krag on each wing watching his comrades' backs, separating his force from Urquhart's marines. Then, once united, the marines needed to take the Krag hangar deck from a squad of what appeared to be battle-hardened Krag marines. MOEAM was no help with either because, in the case of the spacers in the corridor, the barricades stopped nearly a meter short of the ceiling, meaning that the weapon's shock wave would severely injure, if not kill, everyone in the corridor, Krag and human alike. And in the case of the Krag on the hangar deck, the blast might rupture the fuel tanks in that compartment, starting a fire capable of destroying the reason for taking the hangar deck in the first place and perhaps even threatening the entire ship before Kraft and his men could make their escape.

Kraft gave a brief, rueful shake of the head, wanting to take back all those times as a young man that he had wished for more challenges in his life. He glanced back at the image being transmitted by the recon ant and smiled coldly. The Krag spacers behind the barricade, likely a scratch force of technicians and maintenance personnel judging from the color of the metallic yarn woven into their tunics, had posted both their sentinels together near the center of the barrier, where they could see any attackers coming at them down the corridor but out of sight of their comrades. They should have placed one spacer where he could see down the corridor, and the other near one wing of the barricade, where he could see the first spacer and where the other spacers could see him, a placement that would have prevented what Kraft was about to do.

With a quick series of hand signals, Kraft communicated his plan to his men. While they made their preparations, Kraft handed his Model 2212 silenced pistol to Corporal Sergey Ivonovich Kozak. "The Cossak," as he was known, was the best handgun marksman in the group, meaning that he was an exceptional shot, indeed. The Cossak checked to ensure a round was in the chamber, dropped the magazine into his hand, moved the first cartridge in the stack back and forth slightly with this thumb to be sure that it would feed easily—something that all of his handgun instructors had told him was unnecessary but that he always did anyway—and slid the mag back in place.

He nodded to Kraft. Kraft nodded in return.

What happened next was almost bland. Forgoing the leap, roll, and come-up-shooting-type gymnastics one sees in trid vids, the Cossack simply raised his weapon, stepped into the corridor, and—before the Krag guards could react—shot them both cleanly through the head. The muffled cough of the silenced shots and the thump of the bodies hitting the deck were inaudible to the Krag on the other side of the barricade over the sound of the skirmish around the hangar deck door.

The instant the Cossack fired the second shot, his comrades were in the corridor crossing the sixteen meters to the barrier in quick but silent steps. Upon reaching the barricade, four of the marines pulled the pins on the grenades they had been holding in their hands and tossed them over. Five seconds and a cacophony of terrified squeaks and chitters later, the grenades detonated in near unison, and the Krag fell silent. The marines rushed around the barricade and verified that the Krag were really most sincerely dead.

"Chesty Puller," Kraft said over the farther barricade in a stage whisper, the recognition sign being the name of a legendary marine of the past, this one from the United States.

"Blondie Hanson," replied Urquhart with the countersign, naming another marine legend, this one from Great Britain. One could never be too careful. Krag could not mimic human voices, but they had machines that could.

Kraft's men joined Urquhart's on either side of the hatch. On orders from Kraft, Pickett ordered the recon ant back down the corridor, around the dogleg, and another twelve meters farther to where it joined with another corridor, to give the marines warning of any Krag coming up on them from behind. Pickett was then given the sole duty of watching the screen on his percom for the enemy.

That detail taken care of, Kraft turned his attention to Urquhart. "Sergeant, what's your status?"

"Not bad now that you got those rat-faces off our backs. Too bad we used all our grenades against the Krag in the hangar deck before that second bunch arrived, or we might have been able to take care of them ourselves. What you see here is all that's left: eight Marines plus me and this runt here," Urquhart said. At the word "runt," he gestured toward a man in naval uniform who was much smaller than the marines. "We're each down to about ninety rounds of ammunition, except for the two shotgun guys, who are down to about something like two dozen each. We've exhausted our special munitions getting to this point and blowing this hatch.

Those Krag marines were supposed to be defending CIC, not the hangar deck. I'm guessing that they were being loaded in that assault shuttle for another attempt to board the tender right when we got here. Just our luck."

"You're probably right," said Kraft. Every now and then, a marine would lean around the hatch frame and fire a few rounds into the hangar deck, causing the Krag to shoot back. While doing so spent precious ammunition, it also kept the Krag bunched together and backed into their corners, rather than creeping toward the hatch. It was what the book said to do under these conditions. "You've done well, Urquhart."

"Thanks, Major, but I'm worried that it all might be for nothing. If we can't get into that hangar deck . . ." He sighed.

Kraft and Urquhart looked at each other. Urquhart's group had the task of stealing an assault shuttle from the Krag hangar deck because the skipper had said that he needed a Krag assault shuttle as part of his plan B to get Admiral Birch. Given how often plan A had failed in this war and given the importance of taking out the legendary Krag leader, both men understood that a lot more was riding on the success of this mission objective than just being able to get off the enemy ship without having to fight their way past a bunch of Krag.

"Major," said the master sergeant, "I've been staring at this situation for a while now, and I just don't see any way other than brute force—put a lot of marines through that hatch and bombard the Krag in those corners with a salvo of pulse grenades."

"We'll be in an overlapping field of fire from both Krag groups," Kraft said, shaking his head. "They'll cut us to pieces so fast we might not be able to get the grenades off. A lot of men will die for nothing."

Kraft racked his brain for another solution. None of the standard tactics worked in this situation, or at least, none of them would work without killing most of his men. The problem called for some major out-of-the-box thinking, and Kraft was anything but an out-of-the-box major. He was much more comfortable inside the box. He *liked* the box.

Maybe hearing someone else talk would jar something loose. "Talk to me, Urquhart."

"Hell if I know what to do, sir. If only there was some way of firing pulse grenades into each of those groups without exposing so many men," Urquhart mused. "BUWEAPS needs to give us some kind of remote-controlled flying drone grenade that we can guide into spaces like that."

"Good idea, Urquhart. Put it in a memo when we get back to the *Cumberland.* Something like that would be very help . . ." he trailed off in thought. "Then again, *vielleicht*, they already have," Kraft said softly. He opened his percom and replayed the images taken by the recon ant inside the hangar deck, scrutinizing the angles. After a few moments, he smiled. "Urquhart, do you play pool?"

"No, sir. When I go in for a pint or two of bitters, I'm more of a darts man."

Kraft looked at the men he had with him in the Krag corridor, trying to remember what he knew about their lives off duty. It took only a few seconds before his eyes lit on Zamora and Ulmer, whom he knew had been playing pool every chance they got since they were old enough to see the top of the table. Less than a minute later, thirty seconds of which consisted of Kraft explaining what he wanted, Kraft had his plan ready for implementation.

Zamora and Ulmer stood on either side of the hatch with their backs to the bulkhead. A "sub-gun man," that is, a man armed with a Model 2309 9 millimeter submachine gun, was lying next to each of them on his stomach with another man holding his feet. When Kraft pumped his fist, the foot holders shoved the sub-gun men, heads pointing toward the center of the door, past the lip of the hatch just far enough onto the hangar deck so that each could sweep the Krag in the corner in front of him with his weapon. As soon as the muzzles of their weapons could bear on their targets, the men hosed each of the "dead zones" with 9 millimeter bullets. The Krag immediately took cover behind their makeshift barriers, so there were few casualties.

Casualties were not the objective. What *was* the objective was to make the Krag do exactly what they did: get behind cover. From there the enemy couldn't shoot at Zamora and Ulmer who, two seconds after the sub-gun men started firing, stepped through the hatch and took aim at the thruster blast deflectors—thick metal plates roughly three meters tall, four meters long, and twenty centimeters thick, standing roughly two meters apart in a long row—that protected personnel and materiel near the forward bulkhead of the hangar deck from thruster exhaust. Each man had previously flicked the FIRE SELECT switch on his M-88 pulse rifle to the GREN setting and now aimed at the bulkhead—Zamora to his right and Ulmer to his left—or, more accurately, a point on the bulkhead selected with eyes honed in tens of thousands of pool games played in hundreds of bars on dozens of worlds. Within half a second of each other, Zamora and Ulmer pulled their triggers.

This act caused each weapon's under-barrel coaxial launcher to fire a 35 millimeter MMD ("Make My Day") pulse grenade. Dialed into its lowest thrust setting, each grenade's compact rocket motor propelled it across the hangar deck and into the blast deflector. With their armor-penetrating shaped charges deactivated, the grenades bounced off the deflectors at the same angle at which they struck, continued to the far bulkhead, bounced again, and with their inertia depleted by the double bank shot, landed in the two groups of Krag, where they exploded.

Ulmer's grenade landed in the center of his target group, killing all but two Krag spacers who were too badly injured to be any threat. Because the grenades were roughly cylindrical, not spherical, Zamora's had randomly taken a bad bounce and landed near the edge of the group he targeted. As a result, several of the Krag in that group were stunned rather than killed by the explosion. They were clawing for their weapons and struggling to stand just as the marines stormed onto the hangar deck, yelling "OOOOORAAAAAH" as they mowed down every Krag that had managed to get on its feet.

The echo of the marines' shots had not died when Kraft pointed to five marines and swept his right index finger in an arc across the deck in front of him, then jabbed his finger at two more marines and pointed at the groups of Krag. While the five quickly took up prone firing positions on the deck covering the hatch, protecting their buddies' rear, the two finished off any surviving Krag. The other marines took up positions behind the impromptu Krag barricades, putting the hatch in their cross fire. Meanwhile, the "runt" to whom Urquhart had referred earlier jogged up to an assault shuttle, the largest vessel on the hangar deck. He produced a small yellow box, pressed the device's only button, and slapped it on top of the vessel's hatch-locking mechanism. A red light came on. After about ten seconds, the light changed to orange, and then yellow. It remained yellow for nearly a minute, and then turned green. With a warning yowl that sounded distinctly catlike, the hatch opened. Two shots rang out from inside the shuttle. The small man quickly stepped to his left out of the line of fire, tossed in a flash-bang, which went off with a muffled thump, drew his pistol, peered into the hatch, and fired two careful shots. Pistol in hand, he climbed into the shuttle and, two seconds later, shouted "CLEAR!"

Kraft boomed, "MARINES! LOAD UP!"

Which they did, in well-drilled fashion. First, the marines to the left of the hatch stood, jogged in a loose formation to the shuttle, and boarded. As soon as the first two were in the shuttle, the procession halted long enough for the pair to toss the Krag pilot's body out through the hatch onto the hangar deck, where it landed like a sack of wet clay. The rest of the group filed in quickly. A few seconds before the last man had boarded, the group on the right stood and followed suit. When those men were on board, the prone marines facing the hatch stood in unison and boarded, followed by Zamora and Ulmer, who had deployed to cover their rear, then Sergeant Urquhart, and finally, Major Kraft. The sergeant and the major had each covered the hatch with a submachine gun while their men were vulnerable.

As soon as Kraft was inside the shuttle, he barked, "Button her up and take us home, Mori."

Ensign Mori, the *Cumberland*'s best small craft pilot and the only man in the vessel who wasn't an actual or honorary marine, hit the control that closed the hatch and continued the shuttle's start-up sequence begun by the now-dead Krag pilot. While he worked his way through the memorized checklist with remarkable speed, considering that he was working with an instrument panel whose every control and display was labeled in an alien language, spacers Watt and Hu removed an access panel near Mori's right knee, plugging their own tablet-size control panel into a modular access jack inside. The mini-panel, quasi reverse-engineered from Krag ships over the years and with grudging assistance from the rare broken Krag prisoner who decided to make his life easier by collaborating with his captors, tied into the assault shuttle's hangar deck door remote-control system.

Watt and Hu worked the tiny panel speedily but methodically. After less than a minute, blue lights started flashing on the hangar deck, and a squeaking-chittering-clicking announcement came over the compartment's PA system, its brain-dead, canned, "this is a recording" character obvious even across the cavernous divide between the species. Kraft guessed that the announcement was a warning that the space doors were about to open.

Good guess. In a few seconds, the twin curved doors began to part, creating a gale of escaping air. The artificial hurricane picked up anything not firmly affixed to the deck, including the Krag bodies, and carried them out into space, where the alien corpses tumbled limply like rag dolls caught in a windstorm. By the time the doors were fully open, the gale was replaced by something approaching a moderate breeze, caused by air from the rest of the ship entering the hangar deck through the blown hatch. It showed no sign of stopping, as one might expect, most likely because the Gremlins had already sown their special chaos among the systems that otherwise would automatically be closing hatches and sealing vents to stop the ship from bleeding atmosphere into space.

By the time the hangar deck doors were half open, Mori had gotten the engines on the shuttle started. After a twenty-second run-up, he disengaged the magnetic lock that held the compact vessel firmly to the deck, lifted about a meter into the compartment's rarefied air, and engaged the main drive. As a parting gift to the Krag for their hospitality, Mori made sure to firewall the throttle and focus the thruster exhaust to obliterate just about everything on the hangar deck, blast the main bulkhead between it and the rest of the destroyer into oblivion, and melt the space door mechanism so that the doors would never close again.

When the shuttle shot out of the hangar deck into open space, no one heaved a sigh of relief. They weren't out of the woods yet. Not even close.

As soon as it got a few hundred meters from the destroyer, the shuttle came under fire from the larger ship's point-defense systems, which as of yet did not appear to be suffering any ill effects from the

Gremlin infestation. Mori responded with a series of evasive maneuvers so radical that, even with inertial compensators at maximum, the G forces shoved every man's stomach into the upper reaches of his left sinus cavity. Notwithstanding these wild gyrations, a few rail-gun projectiles slammed into but did not penetrate the shuttle's armored outer hull (it was, after all, an *assault* shuttle). While the rail-gun projectiles didn't concern Mori, the Krag destroyer's missiles and their fusion warheads most emphatically did. The shuttle was too small to be equipped with deflectors, and against a direct hit by a thermonuclear weapon, the most robust armor designed by man or Krag would serve only to delay the demise of the vessel's occupants by a microsecond or two.

Just as the shuttle's threat receiver indicated that the Krag destroyer's missile-targeting scanners were about to lock onto the shuttle, Mori executed a hairpin turn of such violence that it threatened to turn the men's brains into tapioca pudding, making straight for the *Cumberland*'s now-open hangar deck, accelerating in unpredictable spurts to throw off the Krag targeting solution. At the last possible moment, he executed a flapjack, braked the shuttle with the main thrusters, rolled it to align its landing skids with the deck, and set it down gently in the designated landing area with scarcely a bump.

The marines, who had been keeping their emotions in tight check until that moment, cut loose—slapping each other on the back, whooping, and shaking hands, all the while scrupulously ignoring Mori, who was starting to feel snubbed.

As Mori ran through postlanding "shut down and safe" sequence, Kraft turned to him and said coldly, "Get that hatch open ASAP and wait for me at the bottom of the ramp. I need to talk to you about something."

Oh, shit. That can't be good. "Open the hatch and wait for you. Aye, sir."

When the shuttle's systems were shut down and Mori's instruments showed that the hangar deck was repressurized, the young pilot opened the hatch and gloomily watched the marines disembarking. He thought he had performed well and had done a creditable bit of flying, but obviously, Kraft didn't agree.

Kraft was the last marine off the shuttle, and as soon as he got to the bottom of the ramp, Mori unstrapped himself, stood, and went to the hatch. To his surprise, as he went down the ramp, Mori could see that the marines were still on the hangar deck, in two lines with enough space between them for a man to walk, stretching from the bottom of the ramp almost to the hatch leading to the rest of the ship. They seemed unfriendly, and he would have to walk between the lines to get off the hangar deck. Mori regarded the marines unhappily.

"What the hell are you scowling at, flyboy?" Kraft barked in an uncharacteristically gruff voice.

"Well, sir, I thought I did a pretty good job back there, but I get the feeling that you guys don't think so and that I'm about to get my butt chewed," Mori said, somewhat defensively, when he got to the bottom of the ramp.

Kraft shook his head disgustedly. "Ensign, it's not like your contribution to this mission was particularly significant. Goddamn it, son, *these* men are the hard-charging, ass-kicking warriors who won the battle." He gestured toward the two ranks of marines. "*These* men are the heroes of the day. You were nothing more than the pissant bus driver for the trip home, and a fucking short trip it was, too. I can't believe you expect a bunch of marines to get worked up because, for less than two minutes of flying time, some shrimpy little navy puke managed to competently perform the duties for which the navy trained him for years at enormous expense. Is THAT what you were expecting, Ensign?"

"I suppose not, sir."

"You're goddamn right. You know what else, Mori?"

"What's that, Major?"

"Save yourself a goddamn fortune, son, and *never, ever* play poker for serious money. Don't you recognize someone doing an Admiral Hornmeyer act when you see it?" The major smiled broadly and slapped the much smaller pilot on the back. It was only then that Mori noticed that several of the marines were nearly purple from stifling laughter, and most of the rest were striving to plaster stern marine war faces over their grins. "Young man, I've been in more than two dozen combat landings and extractions, and never in my life have I seen flying like that, especially under enemy fire *and flying an alien vehicle*. You've chewed hot lead with us and pulled our asses out of the fire. From now on, Mori, you are my first choice to fly my marines into or out of combat. I'm going to cut an order authorizing you to wear an honorary marine patch. Go by the ship's store, pick one up, and sew it on your uniform. From today until the day you die, son, you're one of us."

Kraft led Mori between the two lines of marines to the hatch, with the marines shouting, "MORI, MORI, MORI," and slapping him on the back as he passed. Mori hadn't felt so proud since the day he earned his wings.

CHAPTER 6

08:16 Zulu Hours, 12 May 2315

"The hangar deck reports that the marines are disembarking from the assault shuttle," DeCosta said. This detail was so important that the chief collecting information there was under strict orders from the skipper to report it directly to the XO. "The shuttle appears to have sustained only superficial damage from enemy fire. Major Kraft will have the casualty list for you in a few minutes."

Max didn't ask how many men made it back. The instant the shuttle set down on the hangar deck, its mass had been measured and the number of men on board computed. Max knew how many had died. He just didn't know the names yet.

"Very well." Max was exceptionally relieved to have the men back on board. He was also very, very pleased to have possession of the Krag assault shuttle. Not only was the craft essential to Max's plan B for killing Admiral Birch; there were uncounted ways Max could think of to use the vehicle to make mischief for the Krag. Just contemplating the first three or four made him smile wolfishly.

"Skipper, receiving hardwired voice comms from the *Nicholas Appert*," Chin announced. A comm interface in the docking mechanism provided intercept-proof hardwired communications between any two docked ships, so long as their port architecture and comms protocols were compatible, a given in the case of Union naval vessels. "Captain Anderssen sends his compliments, thanks you for the damage-control teams we sent over, and reports that the docking hatch blown by the Krag has been sealed with a static deck plate. Full outer hull and compartment airtight integrity are restored."

"Outstanding. Reply to Captain Anderssen with my compliments and pass along the following orders: He is to notify us the moment the Krag grappling field fails—we will undock from him as soon as that happens. Our damage-control teams are to stay on board the tender for now—we'll retrieve them later. Once we've taken up a position about 50,000 kilometers off his beam, we will signal CLEAR TO MANEUVER by laser semaphore. At that time he is to undock from the Krag ship, execute a standard breakaway maneuver, and accelerate at best speed toward this system's Charlie jump point. If he should happen to reach it before us, he is not, repeat NOT, to jump, but to go to station keeping, monitor the situation, and await further instructions. If the *Cumberland* becomes a casualty, he is to jump through the Charlie jump point, report our destruction to Admiral Hornmeyer, and return to base. In no event is he to attempt any rescue or defense of this vessel. Make sure he understands that last part."

Chin acknowledged the order and began speaking over his headset with his counterpart on the tender. Max caught the eye of the CIC midshipman and pointed to his coffee mug.

While Gilbertson, who had just relieved Hewlett, was performing the holy act of preparing the skipper's sacred coffee in the manner of a priest of Apollo preparing a temple sacrifice, Dr. Sahin entered CIC and took his accustomed seat at Max's left. He had come to CIC as soon as it was clear that there were no injuries for him to treat. He wanted coffee, but knew better than to ask while Gilbertson was performing his ritual devotions. And of course, he dared not walk over and pour his own. Long-sanctified naval custom dictated that ships' surgeons never pour their own coffee while the vessel is under way—perhaps to prevent hot-coffee-spill injuries to their hands.

There had been barely enough time for Gilbertson to get Max a fresh cup of coffee and for the skipper to take his first sip before Chin suddenly pressed a key on his console and cocked his head slightly to the left. Knowing what that meant, Max was already giving the communications officer his full attention when he began speaking.

"Skipper, the *Nicholas Appert* has got most of its sensors back online. Their sensors/tactical officer reports that the Krag grappling field just failed. His opinion is that this is a genuine systems failure, and there are what appear to be numerous other systems failures on board the enemy vessel—I'm posting them on the Enemy Status Display."

"Thank you, Mr. Chin. Alert the tender that we are undocking at this time," said Max. "XO, undock us from the tender."

This order and what followed illustrated starkly how different the reality of naval service was from the way it was portrayed in fiction. In every popular trid-vid drama about the Great Krag War, the steely-eyed, jut-jawed, rippling pectoraled, doe-eyed-lass-in-every-port skipper personally directed every maneuver of the gleaming warship and every action of its razor-sharp crew, issuing endless, minutely specific orders governing the smallest detail of even the most routine matters. By contrast, on the *Cumberland*, Max routinely delegated control of important but routine maneuvers to young officers, from DeCosta all the way down to the greenest ensign. The navy recognized and Max knew from his own experience that officers simply can't learn in a simulator how to do what any one of them might have to do at any moment—take the con in an emergency or command the ship on his own. When a man makes a mistake in the simulator, he can hit RESET and correct on the next run. On a real ship, men have to live with their mistakes, if they are lucky enough to live through them.

"Aye, sir, undock the ship." DeCosta knew this procedure by heart. Nevertheless, he pulled the checklist up on his console. Undocking was such a critical maneuver with so much potential for so many kinds of horrific disasters that regulations required the officer conducting the operation not only to follow in the most rigorous fashion a checklist from Norfolk, but also for that officer to check off on a computer screen that he has completed each step in turn before he can proceed to the next. Those same regulations required that the Officer of the Deck (or another officer if the OOD was the one doing the undocking)—in this case Mr. Levy—follow the checklist from his own station and call a stop to the procedure if any step were to be skipped or completed unsatisfactorily.

"SYSO, confirm that all inner and outer hatches are closed and safed."

Chief Beaumont, the man at the System Operations console, flicked a few switches, stared fixedly for a few seconds at a bank of lights, and scrolled through several real-time visuals of hatches around the ship. "All inner and outer hatches confirmed closed and safed by auto-annunciation, by lights, and by visual feed."

"Very well," responded the XO. "Confirm that all conduits, lines, and vents are closed and shuttered."

"Closed and shuttered, sir. All conduits, lines, and vents confirmed as closed by pressure testing. Auto-annunciation and visual feeds show them as shuttered. I have a straight board."

"Very well. Confirm that there are no lines to the other vessel."

Beaumont flicked a switch, spoke quietly into his headset, and listened to the reply. "Voice confirmation from the line handlers. Based on the traverse board and visual inspection, line-handling crew reports that there are no lines to the other vessel."

"Acknowledged. Maneuvering, inertial attitude control to ready."

LeBlanc turned a rotary selector switch on his console from STANDBY to READY, and the system's status light went from red to amber. He checked an RPM readout that showed that the system was spun up. "Inertial attitude control system shows ready, sir."

"Very well. SYSO, retract the docking clamps."

Beaumont touched a key. A faint *screech-thump* communicated itself through the hull as the clamps slid out of their matching slots on the other ship and locked into their retracted configuration. Beaumont's docking clamp indicator light for that hatch progressed from red for CONTACT/LOCKED to yellow for CONTACT/UNLOCKED to green for RETRACTED. He checked a video feed that confirmed visually that the *Cumberland* was no longer physically joined to the *Nicholas Appert*. "Docking clamps retracted."

"Understood. Weapons, null the grappling field."

Levy hit the key near which his finger had been hovering. Half a second later, an indicator light changed from blue for ENGAGED to green for READY. "Grappling field nulled."

LeBlanc's displays indicated that the *Cumberland* was drifting slightly relative to the tender. "My instruments show that we are free of external restraints, sir."

"Very well. Maneuvering, engage inertial attitude control. Maintain current attitude on all axes." LeBlanc acknowledged the order and turned the selector to ENGAGED. A second later the status light changed from amber for READY to green for

ENGAGED, meaning that the computer was now directing the inertial system's rapidly spinning flywheels in response to changes in the ship's attitude as detected by the inertial measuring units and as commanded by the maneuvering controls.

"Inertial attitude control engaged." Pause. About two seconds later, LeBlanc scrutinized his displays. "System is responding and providing three-axis attitude control. Ship is stable."

"Very well," said DeCosta. "Bring the fine trim maneuvering thrusters online."

LeBlanc pressed the key that activated that system. "Fine trim maneuvering thrusters online."

"Sir," said DeCosta to Max, "we are undocked from the tender and are ready to maneuver at your order."

"Well done, XO." During the procedure Max had apparently been scrutinizing several engineering status displays, while his mind was actually devoted to careful monitoring of DeCosta's handling of the undocking maneuver. The young XO *had* done well. "Maneuvering, gently pull us away from the tender and take us straight away from her on her x-axis. Take up station keeping 61,443 meters off her beam, taking care to keep the tender between us and the Krag vessel at all times. I don't want Mr. Whiskers to see us yet."

"Aye, sir," LeBlanc responded, "gentle separation—no scorching of the tender—61,443 meters in relative X." First by controlling the relevant systems directly from his console, and then with expertly crafted orders to the men at the Yaw, Roll, and Drives consoles, LeBlanc directed the fine trim maneuvering thrusters, then the standard maneuvering thrusters, and finally the main sublight drive to position the *Cumberland* 61,443 meters off the *Nicholas Appert*'s beam.

"Station-keeping at the designated location, Skipper," LeBlanc announced.

"Very well." Max turned to Levy. "Gentlemen, my intention is to engage and destroy Hotel one using the POWER RUN maneuver. Discussion?" Silence. "Questions?" More silence. "All sections, configure your systems appropriately and give the XO a green light when ready."

While the CIC personnel were executing that last order, Bram turned to Max. "Power run maneuver? I've not heard of that one. Are we going to deplete the enemy's energy reserves and then retreat?"

Max shook his head almost imperceptibly. The stunning juxtaposition of the glittering peaks of his friend's brilliance with the black chasms of his ignorance never ceased to amaze. "No. It's a battle maneuver that works just like the power run play in American football." Bram regarded him with an expression of total incomprehension. "*Power run*. You know, the play where the quarterback hands off to the tailback while the fullback and one of the offensive guards run blocks into basically the same point in the defensive line. Then the tailback reads the blocks, exploits the opening, and . . ." The doctor's eyes had taken on a certain glazed appearance. "Never mind. I forgot that you don't know anything about the game."

"And I don't care to," Bram replied with a hint of superiority. "From what I've seen, it seems to be comprised of nothing but two moderately sized groups of very large men grunting and straining and colliding with one another at high speed. I don't see the point."

"You wouldn't," Max said. "Of all the professional team sports, that's the one that is most like war."

"All the more reason . . ."

"Skipper," DeCosta interrupted the doctor, "all sections report ready."

"Very well," said Max. "Weapons, status on missile tubes one and two."

"Sir, tubes one and two are loaded with Talons, launch coils on standby, missile doors closed," Levy rattled off eagerly. "Status of both missiles: drives are enabled, warhead safeties are released. Warheads are not armed. Targets are not designated at this time."

"Very well. Designating target for both missiles as Krag destroyer off our bow. Attack pattern is POWER RUN. Variant: DISCOVERED CHECK. Set both tubes for minimum launch speed. And to make absolutely, positively, totally, for damn sure that the missiles will not under any circumstances hit the tender, instruct both seeker heads to ignore any target with a mass in excess of 65,000 tons. Set both warheads for maximum yield."

Levy acknowledged the orders, punched in the commands, and then began working on some apparently intricate task at his console.

"Oh, Levy?"

"Sir?"

"I want you—and I mean *you, personally*—to verify sequencing instructions on those missiles. Don't rely on the ship's computer to address the weapons' sequencer. I want you to tie your console directly into the missile sequencers and check the control codes yourself. Do it twice, and let me know when you're finished. The trajectory of those missiles will be very close to the *Nicholas Appert*, and I want to take every conceivable precaution to make certain that the missiles ignore her. Admiral Hornmeyer might take umbrage if we accidentally nuke his brand-spanking-new tender."

"Not to mention that some of our own people are still aboard her, if I am not mistaken," said Sahin.

"True," Max said blandly. "There is that."

Bram leaned toward Max to rebuke him for his callous attitude toward the lives of his shipmates—until the look on the skipper's face told him that Max was speaking in jest.

"Already on it, Skipper," Levy responded, ignoring the byplay. "I don't think I can afford to have the admiral deduct the cost of a new tender out of my paycheck. I'm reading the machine code on the first missile's sequencer right now."

"Good man, Levy. Way to stay on top of things. Remember me when you make admiral." Max was only half joking—it was not out of the question that a young officer as sharp as Levy might someday hoist his flag.

"You'll be my favorite battleship commander, sir," Levy said, smiling—not at the thought of being an admiral himself, an idea that he found extremely intimidating given his own limited experience, but at the chaos and devastation he imagined Battleship Captain Max Robichaux would inflict upon the enemy.

After about two minutes of furious activity at his console, Levy announced, "Missile programming complete. I personally checked flight and target acquisition sequencing at the machine code level by direct processor access."

"Very well," Max said. "And good job, Levy. Mr. Chin, signal the tender by laser semaphore, CLEAR TO MANEUVER."

"CLEAR TO MANEUVER, aye, sir." Chin hit the key on his console that executed the programmed coded light sequence from the *Cumberland*'s ten-watt signal laser. About five seconds later, as could be seen from several displays around CIC, the tender's signal laser blinked three times.

"Tender acknowledges, sir."

"Very well. Weapons, this is a nuclear weapons arming order. Abbreviated firing procedure. Make missile tubes one and two ready for firing in all respects."

"Aye, sir, abbreviated firing procedure. Nuclear weapons arming order acknowledged. Making tube one and tube two ready for firing in all respects." Five seconds later, "Missile tubes one and two: outer doors confirmed open and tubes visually confirmed as clear, launch coils at READY, missile drives energized, warheads armed and set for maximum yield, seeker heads activated."

"Very well."

"Maneuvering thruster activity from the tender, sir," said Bartoli from Tactical. "She appears to be executing her breakaway maneuver from Hotel one." A few seconds later, "Breakaway complete. She's engaging her main sublight drive." Pause. "Starting to pull away from the enemy ship." Pause. "She's clear—we have a direct line of sight to Hotel one. No sign of the enemy's having spotted us through the tender's drive exhaust."

"Thank you, Mr. Bartoli," said Max. "This is a nuclear weapons firing order. Weapons, fire tubes one and two. Reload both tubes with Talons."

"Nuclear weapons firing order acknowledged. Firing one and two." Levy hit the two FIRE buttons half a second apart. The men in CIC felt the launches as two hard, thudding jolts through the deck plates. "Tubes one and two fired." After a second, "Both missiles running hot, straight, and normal." Following the detailed attack profile painstakingly input and checked by Mr. Levy, the pair of weapons traveled in line ahead formation, half a second apart, at their slowest, most stealthy speed, straight for the plume of searingly hot and nearly sensor-opaque plasma being expelled from the tender's main sublight drive. The missiles made for a point in the exhaust about 2500 meters aft of the tender, where the tender's drive plume was hot and bright enough to ensure that the enemy would not detect the weapons but not so hot that they would be destroyed during their brief passage. Once through, the first missile acquired the enemy ship and turned toward it, with the second missile, still a half second behind it, hard on its tail.

Even though the enemy destroyer did not detect the first missile until it had cleared the tender's drive plume, that brief warning was still long enough for the Krag vessel's most nimble point-defense systems to engage the missile. A particle-beam weapon rapidly slewed itself into alignment and transmitted a low-power aiming pulse to generate a lock. Once the pulse bounced back from the target, the weapon automatically began its two-microsecond-long firing sequence, which would culminate in unleashing a particle beam that would turn the missile into a ball of incandescent vapor. Only two microseconds.

One point four microseconds too slow.

The Talon's sensor/computer suite detected the aiming pulse, recognized it as a harbinger of its own destruction, and detonated the weapon, unleashing 150 kilotons of thermonuclear hell only 1813 meters away from the Krag vessel.

For which the destroyer was ready. The sophisticated electronic intelligence directing the enemy vessel's defense systems anticipated the warhead's premature detonation by temporarily increasing or "surging" the ship's deflector output in the affected area, turning aside the weapon's destructive force almost effortlessly and leaving the ship undamaged.

Undamaged, but not unaffected. For .62 seconds the intense flood of light and radiation from the explosion blinded Krag sensors to any target approaching from that bearing. Because the second missile was on the same attack vector and only .498 seconds behind the first, no point-defense systems were able to detect and engage it. Further, the blast's neutron flux pushed away most other subatomic particles in its vicinity, including the polarized gravitons with which the deflectors performed their function, briefly but significantly weakening the enemy's deflectors for more than a hundred meters in every direction from the epicenter of the explosion. As a result the second missile was able to penetrate within 214 meters of the destroyer before the deflectors arrested its forward motion, triggering the warhead.

A 150-kiloton thermonuclear explosion at a range of 214 meters would vaporize most targets, or at least, reduce them to a large field of baseball-size debris. But a Krag *Demerit* class destroyer was not most targets. Even at such an intimate range and even with the deflectors compromised, the vessel's two-meter-thick armor—made of the Krag equivalent of Michiganium—in conjunction with its blast-suppression systems, were able to prevent the vessel's destruction or even a breach of its thick, super-dense hull.

Max, however, had never intended that the two Talon missiles destroy or even meaningfully damage the enemy ship. The missiles and their warheads were the fullback and the offensive guard for this play, not the ball carrier. Like Tom Harmon, Walter Payton, Jerome Bettis, or Alnilam Woyongo bursting through the gap in the defensive line left by their blockers, the *Cumberland* exploited the sensor blind spot and the gaping hole left in the enemy destroyer's deflectors by the two thermonuclear blasts to charge within 2000 meters of the destroyer without being engaged by its point-defense systems or blocked by its deflectors.

Ordinarily, at this range, the *Demerit*'s highly capable close-range antiship defenses, based around the infamously wicked Doberman missile, would have made short work of a lightly built destroyer like the *Cumberland*. But as Max knew by virtue of the tender's report on the Krag ship's systems failures, the Dobermans remained kenneled in their launch tubes because the Gremlins deployed earlier by the *Cumberland*'s marines had cut all the power lines to the dedicated processor used to aim the missiles. The system's backup mode, which used the destroyer's primary sensor arrays to acquire the missiles' targets, failed to function because the Gremlins had cut all the data lines that carried targeting information from the primary sensors to the Dobermans' launch system.

Even with sensor blind spots and damage from the Gremlins, the Krag commander was aware of the Union ship located only the space-combat equivalent of a biscuit toss off his beam—at 2000 meters it could scarcely be missed. Aware of his peril, he desperately fought to open up the range between his ship and the Union vessel. When he tried to engage the main sublight drive, he learned that the insidious Union sabotage robots had cut all the data linkages between the Command Nest and the drive systems. He was able, with difficulty, to establish a voice link with Engineering, only to be informed that the fusion reactor was off-line because the Gremlins had gotten to the computer that regulated the reactor's plasma-containment field. So he ordered his running officer to engage the maneuvering thrusters, only a third of which responded to the firing command, thereby nudging the massive ship into sluggish motion, pushing it forward and yawing it away from the destroyer. He also ordered that the ship be rolled, to rotate the weakened deflectors away from the enemy on his flank.

Far too slowly.

"Weapons officer, this is a nuclear weapons firing order, terminal firing sequence," Max snapped out.

"Ready," Levy responded instantly, practically salivating.

"Maneuvering, don't wait for my order. Execute your EEM as soon as we fire."

"Aye, aye, Skipper," Chief LeBlanc replied. "Prepared to haul ass."

"Very well," Max said, suppressing a smile. "Terminal firing sequence . . . FIRE."

"Firing." Levy hit the key that executed the terminal firing sequence of the POWER RUN attack profile: two Talon missiles launched at minimum speed, fired .19 seconds apart, targeted at exactly the same point on the enemy vessel's hull. The launch impulses of the two weapons were separated by just enough time for the crew to distinguish them as two distinct jolts, like the sensation when the front and then the back tires of a fast-moving ground car run over a flaw in the pavement. While the men in CIC could still feel the second jolt through the soles of their feet, LeBlanc hit a key on his console and nearly shouted, "EEM: Executing!"

The tap of Chief LeBlanc's finger to the touch screen on his console directly commanded execution of the preprogrammed EEM (Escape and Evasion Maneuver), bypassing the men at the Yaw, Roll, and Drives consoles. The *Cumberland* peeled away from the enemy vessel and firewalled the main sublight drive to open up the range between the two vessels as rapidly as possible.

Because the missiles were fired from such close range, no point-defense systems had time to detect and engage them. Unscathed, both of the weapons easily pierced the *Demerit*'s now greatly attenuated deflectors. The first missile detonated within a meter of the enemy's hull, its variable-yield warhead set for its five-kiloton minimum to prevent damage to the second missile, a phenomenon known as the "fratricide effect." Gremlin damage and the point-blank range launch worked together to prevent the destroyer's blast-suppression systems from responding fully to the explosion, allowing the warhead to tear open a 5.3-meter-wide breach in the enemy ship's hull.

Plenty wide enough for the second missile. Its high-precision guidance system, designed to seek out weaknesses in the enemy's defenses, easily found the opening and steered the weapon through the hull breach *into* the Krag vessel, where, after crashing through several internal bulkheads with the aid of its armored nose cone, it came to rest inside one of the ship's cargo holds. Protected from explosive decompression by an automated system that slid an emergency bulkhead plate over the breach, five Krag cargo handlers experienced actually seeing the missile for 1.144 seconds—just long enough for them to be aware that they were in proximity to a thermonuclear warhead just a heartbeat away from exploding. To their credit, they merely bowed their heads in reverent submission, confident that they would soon be standing before their Creator-God.

They did not have long to wait. *This* weapon was set for the 150-kiloton maximum and went off as soon as its onboard sensors confirmed that the warhead had come to rest inside the Krag vessel. Its effects played out vividly on dozens of monitors scattered throughout the *Cumberland*. First, all the viewports on the Krag ship lit up with a blinding glare. After an instant all of the ship's external hatches blew out almost simultaneously, so that they—along with the hull breach opened by the first missile—poured forth blindingly white fusion plasma, like demonic mouths vomiting the very fires of hell. This infernal apparition lasted for less than a half-second, the time required for the turbulent nuclear inferno inside the ship to consume the enemy's nearly indestructible hull, leaving nothing but the fireball itself, a short-lived miniature star, intensely bright at first, that died slowly in the cold, infinite night.

CHAPTER 7

17:02 Zulu Hours, 12 May 2315

"Captain Robichaux, you and your *unge kamerater* are very polite, for which I thank you," Captain Sigmund Anderssen said amiably. "But it does not require an Eckmanian Deceptionist to know that very little in my intelligence briefing was a surprise to you." Another man might be put out by having his very capably delivered briefing go to waste, but rancor, after all, was not generally a part of Anderssen's disposition. Furthermore, what little irritation that may have afflicted him yielded swiftly to the widely acknowledged soothing powers of Wortham-Briggs Four Planet Coffee. Furthermore, it would be a churlish man indeed who was anything less than perfectly genial after Max's display of tactical brilliance and an expenditure of precious blood had saved him, his ship, and his crew. "But then again, it wasn't news to *me* that most of the briefing wasn't news to *you*. The admiral privately hinted to me that you might have received some intel from . . . let's call them *unsanctioned sources*."

Captain Anderssen and his XO, Lieutenant O. N. Maynard (whom everyone called "Owen" rather than the authentically

Anglo-Norman "Osbert Nuvel" with which his philologist parents had saddled him to go with his authentically Anglo-Norman surname), were in the *Cumberland*'s Wardroom with Max and the destroyer's Kitchen Cabinet. The formal intelligence briefing by Anderssen had ended minutes before, and the men were sitting around the table drinking coffee, the rich, earthy aroma of which filled the compartment.

"Positively ripping coffee," Maynard remarked.

"I thought you tender boys had plenty of everything," said Chief Wendt.

"I suppose that's true most of the time," Maynard allowed. "And we've always got plenty of coffee, but—as you know—there's coffee and there's *coffee*. Ours tastes like it's been in a tin since about the time of the Ning-Braha Expedition." Maynard pronounced "about" as "aboot," which, when combined with his saying "tin" instead of "can" and his use of "ripping" as an adjective, gave away that he was either from Canada or from one of the worlds settled largely by the industrious and pioneer-spirited people from that country. At least he hadn't yet called the Krag "hosers" or asked for a plate of poutine, whatever that was.

Anderssen set his mug down. "Even though my thunder," the word came out "dunder" in the Scandinavian way, "has been stolen with regard to the intelligence situation, I do think I have some other news for you, Captain Robichaux."

"Max. I *do* wish you'd do me the honor of calling me Max." This was not the first time Max had made such a request.

"All right, then, Max," Anderssen allowed. "But only if you call me Sig."

"It would be my pleasure, Sig, on the condition that you tell me what your other news is."

Anderssen smiled and nodded his assent. "Our cargo manifest." The tender captain produced a data chip from a uniform pocket and slid it across the Wardroom table to Max, who popped it into the reader and entered a few commands into the nearby terminal. A list of what the *Nicholas Appert* carried in its capacious holds appeared on the display wall.

Max scrolled down through the more or less predictable list of fuel, spare parts, foodstuff, lubricants, medical supplies, replacement tools, office supplies, uniform buttons, dental floss, paint, replacement hull plating, structural members, nuts, bolts, fasteners, plasma welding equipment, spare consoles, calibration gear, pressurized hostile surface survival shelters, and toilet brushes (or as they were listed on the manifest, "sanitizing implements—head bowl, long-handled), encountering nothing unusual or unexpected.

Then he came to the section for weapons and munitions. "Condor missiles? *Seven* Condor missiles? I've never even *seen* a Condor, much less had *seven* issued to me."

"I've never had one in my hold, either. The admiral let me know that, just in case you encountered an elephant and were of a mind to kill it, he wanted you to have an elephant gun," Anderssen said, smiling. Condors were very new, very expensive, and very scarce. The large, fast, but decidedly un-nimble weapon was designed for use against high-value, non-evading targets, such as large space installations or hardened ground facilities. It was capable of breaking through heavy shielding with an eight-megaton, high-neutron penetrator munition and then destroying even very large or very tough enemy assets with a *sixty-two*-megaton variable blast geometry thermonuclear main warhead. Condors were the largest missiles that could be fired from the *Cumberland*'s launch tubes and could obliterate a command bunker dug two thousand meters underground on a planet, split open a two-kilometer-diameter nickel-iron asteroid to destroy the early-warning outpost inside, or vaporize an orbital base with its various elements dispersed over a twelve-kilometer radius. The warhead was bigger even than the fifty-megaton Tsar Bomba, the largest nuclear warhead ever detonated on Earth.

"I might just develop a taste for elephant hunting at that." Max scrolled a bit farther down. "Mines! Proximity, delay, and auto-homing! Hundreds of them!" Grinning like an eight-year-old boy in a candy store, he scrolled farther yet. "Demolition and sabotage equipment. Assortment number three. Two complete sets. That's just . . . just . . ." Max was speechless with delight.

"Outstanding, sir?" Brown finished.

"That covers it, Wernher. Out*stand*ing," Max said, oblivious to the *Cumberland* men's poorly concealed smiles. "Given the right opportunity, we can do some very . . . interesting . . . things with that stuff."

"The admiral told me that these items might inspire your unique brand of tactical creativity," Anderssen said.

"He knows me only too well," Max replied, the wheels already turning. "This mission is starting to look even more intriguing than I thought it was going to be."

The group then fell into a general discussion of these weapons systems: their capabilities, their rarity, how they were better (or in some cases, worse) than their predecessors, what defenses the Krag might use against them, how they had been used and misused by various commanders, and what havoc the *Cumberland*'s miniature task force might inflict with them upon the enemy.

Midshipman Gilbertson popped his head into the Wardroom. "Pardon me, Skipper," he said. "Are you gentlemen ready for dinner?"

Max glanced at the chrono on the bulkhead and turned to Anderssen. "It's straight up 18:00 hours, Sig. You gentlemen *are* staying for dinner, aren't you?"

The tender captain's expression changed in a heartbeat from an affable smile to a mask of bland neutrality, hastily electroplated onto a base metal of mild panic. Anderssen's sudden and intense anxiety was no display of cowardice on his part, but the reaction of any sane man with intact taste buds. Typically, naval cuisine had very little to recommend it, and even among such undistinguished company, the food on most destroyers was conspicuous for its foulness.

Notwithstanding Anderssen's best efforts to conceal his feelings, Max correctly read his reaction and added quickly, "Not to worry, Captain—we're not having mystery meat, thrashed potatoes, and desecrated vegetables. My mess is run by Cajuns, and you *know* what that means. On top of that, Rashidian Prince Khalid, the older brother of King Khalil, is a friend of the ship. Every time we are in or near the Rashid System, he sees to it that we are provisioned quite handsomely. That's where the coffee you're drinking comes from. The prince personally selects and buys the coffee from four different planets—ruinously expensive, you know—and he then blends and roasts it himself.

"Serving on the *Cumberland* is hard duty in many ways, but we do get to eat pretty well. We're having surf and turf. I selected the menu personally: shrimp cocktail, lobster bisque, your choice of porterhouse or rib-eye steak grilled to your order, baked potato, green beans, fresh bread, of course, and your choice of strawberry pie or apple cobbler for dessert, topped, if you so desire, with your choice of whipped cream or ice cream."

The almost visibly salivating tender captain swiftly said, "So long as there are no *exploding ham sandwiches* on the menu, we will be *delighted* to stay for dinner."

During the general laughter, Max, DeCosta, and Brown looked at each other in wordless, shared amazement. Several weeks before, on a secret diplomatic mission with Sahin in the

Rashid System, Max had urgently called for the *Cumberland* to join him while the ship was receiving resupply, repair, and refit docked to the tender USS *Newport News*. The tender skipper had refused to release his vessel's docking clamps and withdraw its boarding tube until the operation, one personally ordered by Admiral Hornmeyer, was complete. DeCosta and Brown had "persuaded" him to allow the destroyer to depart immediately by placing what appeared to be small charges of plasti-blast with remote detonators in strategic locations, as though to blow the clamps and the tube. When the *Newport News* returned to base, its captain filed with the Judge Advocate General's (JAG's) office a request to court-martial the officers responsible, at which point DeCosta and Brown produced computer-verified hand-scanner data showing that the packages were not explosive at all, but were ham sandwiches (ham on white bread with spicy mustard and kosher pickle slices—just the way Max liked them—a combination now known on board as an "exploding ham sandwich") wrapped in plastic with small antennae attached.

The JAG lawyers declined to file charges. The relevant regulation prohibited "the employment or utilization of any substance, device, object, or instrumentality of any composition or description whatsoever in a manner calculated or likely to cause any damage, however slight, to naval, Union, or civilian property, or to bring about death or injury to any person or sentient being." As the ham sandwiches were not "calculated or likely" to injure persons or property, the *Cumberland* officers received nothing harsher than a halfhearted ass chewing from Admiral Hornmeyer, who admired the ingenuity of the ploy so much that he couldn't work himself up to his usual level of ferocity.

With no ham sandwiches, "exploding" or otherwise, on the table, hosts and guests alike closed with and engaged their designated culinary targets with the élan traditionally exhibited by navy men in close order battle. Against such a determined and sustained attack, their supremely edible foes didn't stand a chance. Only the pauses between the courses Max imposed to stimulate conversation kept all the food from disappearing in less time than it takes to sing all four verses of "The Spacer's Hymn."

Captain Anderssen was pleasantly surprised to see that someone had cut his meat into bite-size pieces and then pushed the pieces back together into the semblance of an uncut steak so carefully that this act of courtesy could be discerned only upon close examination. Although he had the use of only one arm and had lost both of his legs as well, he was able to eat his perfectly grilled medium-rare rib eye without having to ask for assistance from anyone else at the table.

Both visitors proved to be delightful dinner companions, particularly Anderssen, who, at sixty-six years of age, was by far the oldest man at the table. Not only was he the oldest, but—as a former full captain by rank in the regular navy, veteran of many years on combat vessels, and the highly decorated commander of various destroyers, frigates, and light cruisers in several creditable actions in three wars—he had the most combat experience by a full order of magnitude. Only grievous war wounds had taken him out of combat and relegated him to serving as a reserve lieutenant commander in the Big Chair of a tender in the Union Naval Service Command. Unlike most space-faring men (but not unlike Max), he rarely described his own exploits except when requested or when necessary for some military purpose, and even then only in the driest tactical jargon.

Nevertheless, he entertained his listeners with a series of elaborate space tales that progressed as the evening went on from the mildly unbelievable to the breathtakingly improbable. Many of the stories revolved around the misadventures of the likable but lazy and boastful "Ensign Richard Longman Pickwit," who Max was convinced was a composite of several real ensigns or, more than likely, an entirely fictitious individual.

The cumulative implausibility of the storytelling was aided, no doubt, by the generous supply of beverages offered. At the beginning of the dinner, Max had seen that every man, with the exception of Doctor Sahin who was an observant Muslim, had a glass of wine and a mug of beer in front of him. While Anderssen and Maynard consumed the wine with some enthusiasm, they quaffed the beer with particular gusto. The midshipmen serving as stewards had refilled the visiting officers' mugs several times.

"Is this your ship's beer?" Maynard asked after draining his fifth mug. Or maybe it was his sixth.

"It is," Max replied, proudly.

Unlike many naval terms, "ship's beer" was exactly what it sounded like: beer brewed on board the ship. Depending upon the talent of the brewers, there were vast differences in quality from ship to ship. Some ship's beer was of surpassing excellence and could pass for the best crafted by the most skilled brewmeisters in Munich on Earth or Shiner-Braunfels on Texia. The beer from certain other vessels, alas, was of extraordinary wretchedness and could easily be mistaken for rancid yak piss. The average was somewhere just above "adequate."

Maynard took another appreciative pull at his mug. "And how long has your man been brewing?"

"Just a few months," Max replied.

Maynard set his mug down in open-jawed astonishment. "Just a few months? I'm amazed. You know, I'm something of a connoisseur of these things, and I was sure that this brew came from a gray-haired old chief who had been hopping the wort since he was a squeaker. Now, I'm not saying it's the best I've had. But it *is* the best I've had in a while. Our crew is too small to brew our own." He refilled his mug, took a few swallows, and released a sigh of pleasure. "Your man must be talented. What did your galley chief do to cull this man out of the common herd? Test his ability to judge the quality of barley by its smell? Check for brewmeisters in his family tree?"

"Oh, no. None of that. The story told around the ship," Max said, giving his head a subtle tilt to indicate that he was not vouching for the veracity of the tale but that he thought it made for a good story, "is that my chief of culinary services ran his finger down a list of new transferees to his department, took one look at the man's name, and said, 'Aha, that's my man. His very name inspires confidence.' The man had never brewed a single barrel before. Yet the beer started out just on the good side of fair and has been getting better ever since."

"And the man's name?" asked Maynard.

Max let the question hang for a few seconds, timing the delivery of his punch line like a nightclub comedian. "Schlitz. Bodo 'Bud' Schlitz." As both brand names, though centuries-old, had survived humankind's migration into the galaxy and were familiar throughout the Union, Anderssen and Maynard laughed loudly, knowing that they would retell the story, and that many who heard it from them would retell it, and so on.

"So," inquired Maynard, once he caught his breath, "what do the men call it: *Bud* or *Schlitz*?"

"Neither," answered Max. "As soon as the beer started getting really good, they christened it *The Cumberland Tap*."

Maynard suppressed a look of horror, but Anderssen nodded slowly, a knowing smile on his face. "Excellent," the older skipper said. "Truly excellent. Most crews would do everything they could to forget that old insulting nickname. Mine certainly would. But not your men. From the rooftops they shout it." He pointed to the image of a cleft in a range of green mountains depicted on the ship's emblem patch sewn to Max's right sleeve. "There it is—the Cumberland Gap—right there in plain sight on every man's uniform. I recognize it because I've been to the Appalachian Mountains on Earth and seen the real thing. And there," his finger traced a long curving arc following the ground, going through the gap, turning to point almost straight up toward a cluster of stars, and ending in a tiny image of the destroyer, "they show themselves leaving the Cumberland Gap behind them and soaring up toward the stars. Your men have a streak of defiance in them—perhaps that's what men are like when they bounce back from being under the command of a chocolate caramel nut cluster like Allen K. Oscar. I wouldn't want men with that attitude on garrison duty or manning a refueling depot, but for a destroyer crew, it is a good spirit to have—iron in their backbone to hold them up when other men might bend and break. Men like that can look the devil in the face and spit in his eye. I never learned Latin, though. What does this motto, *Per laboram ad victoriam,* mean?"

"Through hardship to victory," Max answered.

"A good motto for us all," Maynard said, thumping his fist on the table with approbation. He raised his right hand, extended his index finger, and made a slow, circular motion—the signal throughout the human-settled galaxy for drink refills all around the table. Once every mug or glass was filled, Anderssen hoisted his mug in a toast. "Drink it to the bottom, men! To what lies at the end of our hardships: to victory!"

"Victory!" said the rest. They hoisted their drinks and drained them to the bottom.

"Beats the hell out of the motto from my first ship," Maynard said, a bit too loudly, as the stewards poured more beer and wine.

"Which was?" asked Wendt."

"*Uva uvam vivendo varia fit.*" Having, as a squeaker, committed the dictum to uncritical, unanalyzed memory, along with how to operate a lifepod and the right way to salute, he gave the words a sonorous, hieratic rendering. "It's got some sort of off-the-bulkhead meaning like 'over time, different kinds of grapes will grow together.' I'm guessing that, in a real vineyard, different kinds of vines actually grow together into a single plant, or something like that, but I know a lot more about deuterium pumps and cargo-loading procedures than grapevines."

Dr. Sahin leaned forward, his face taking on what Max had come to call his friend's "excited professor" look. "That is indeed what takes place," he said. "Grapevines of different varieties can fuse or merge, particularly if both vines are injured and the exposed vascular cambium of one plant comes into protracted contact with that of the other. In fact, it is surmised that the practice of grafting plants may have developed from observation of this phenomenon in nature, which is not uncommon." He paused. "But the usual glazing over of eyes, bored expressions, and fidgeting with coffee mugs tells me that you gentlemen have learned all you care to know about the exposed vascular cambium of grapevines. So I will give lie to the captain's repeated statement that I never know when to shut up when I am talking about botany or zoology by . . . as we say, shutting up." He looked pointedly at Max. "In the idiom of your ancestors, *c'est tout*." He fell silent.

During the ensuing good-natured laughter, Max looked at his friend's broadly smiling face. Notwithstanding the danger, the long hours, and the hard work, service on the *Cumberland* had been good to Dr. Ibrahim Sahin. There were few signs of the intensely sad, lonely, frustrated man Max had met on 20 January. The premature lines in his forehead and around his mouth had eased. The bags under his eyes were gone. His coloring had gone from greenish gray to a healthy brownish olive, befitting his mixed Turkish, Arabian, and European heritage. Even his formerly rumpled, soiled, and mismatched uniforms were now, if not perfect, then clean, unwrinkled, and (mostly) in compliance with regulations.

He smiled easily and laughed often. Sahin had not forgotten the deaths of his parents, siblings, and virtually everyone with whom he had served on Travis Station, but the losses were no longer fresh, ragged wounds. On the USS *Cumberland,* Dr. Sahin had found friends, companionship, patients who benefited greatly from his skills, and duties that suited his talents. Max knew that now his friend felt needed. His life had purpose.

All men—all humans—need that. They need it like they need air.

Max smiled, his heart warmed by that unique form of contentment that comes from the knowledge that a good friend or loved one is happy. Bram caught the expression and smiled in return, inclining his head slightly. A great gift acknowledged; thanks expressed and accepted.

Anderssen went on, oblivious to this silent conversation. "I don't know about the vascular cambium, but in terms of naval leadership, that motto about the vines is really quite profound," Anderssen said. "It's a metaphor for how a crew, though comprised of many different kinds of men from many different worlds, melds to form a unified whole."

While Max and Bram were nodding their understanding, Maynard said, "Far, far too subtle for me," thumping his now-empty mug down on the table a bit too loudly. "I like my mottos simple. *Fortune favors the bold. Don't give up the ship. Death before dishonor.* That sort of thing. Something you can tell the guys on the lower decks without having to explain it to them."

"I suppose there is something that can be said for that point of view," Max allowed. Maynard was a guest, after all.

The stewards came in to collect the plates, leaving behind any pitchers, mugs, and glasses that still contained ardent beverages, just in case the diners weren't finished drinking. They served coffee. Talk resumed when they were done.

By unspoken agreement their discussion turned to the mission. "The only thing that I don't like about the part of the mission in which our ships operate together is the ingress phase," Anderssen opined. "*Cumberland* is stealthy enough that, absent a stroke of some very bad luck, she can slip in undetected. Sneaking my ship in, on the other hand, would be like trying to sneak an elephant onto the ice rink in the middle of a hockey game. So, we've been furnished with a set of transponder codes from the Krag data core the Vaaach gave us. They're supposed to spoof the Krag into thinking that the *Nicholas Appert* is the USS *Peter Durand*, a tender from the same class captured by the Krag a few months ago. The paper-pushing penguins in Plans and Dispositions think that, if we offer up the right code, the Krag—whom you and I know to be the most paranoid species in Known Space—are just going to smile, bow, and wave us from the FEBA into their space without being inspected or challenged. I don't know about you, Max, but I've been in this man's navy since Litvinoff and Hornmeyer and Middleton were eating applesauce and playing with little toy spaceships, and I've never known anything to work that easily."

A short laugh had escaped from DeCosta near the end of Anderssen's remarks. Max regarded him with something less than total approval. "What's so funny, XO?"

"Oh, I was just imagining a miniature Louis Hornmeyer in short pants playing with brightly colored plastic toy spaceships and yelling in a high-pitched voice at the tiny, little imaginary captains inside them that they need to get off their little fucking plastic asses and execute his orders *with celerity*."

The other men at the table tried not to laugh. They really did. But the image of a boyhood version of their theater commander giving orders to a mock battle fleet using his trademark phrase was simply too funny.

"I'm not just talking about Murphy's Law, either," Anderssen continued once the mirth had dissipated. "We got our hands on that data core at the end of March. Now, here we are in mid-May. We haven't used that data much, but we have used it more than once to catch the Krag with their breeches around their knees. By now their whiskers must be twitching enough that some kind of precautions must have been taken by now. Even if they suspect nothing, we know that they change transponder codes at random intervals. If they haven't changed those codes already, they're going to do so soon. And not just the transponder codes, but passwords, encryption protocols, call signs, blinker recognition signals, the arrangement of mines in their minefields, and everything else that can be changed to make that captured data as useless as they can make it. Now, that's not to say that the data won't be useful to us. Hell, just knowing their method for jumping more than one ship at a time is worth a king's ransom, not to mention having the plans and specifications for all their military hardware, weapons, and installations, but they are for sure going to change the locks to the front door, and—in my view—they've already done it more likely than not."

"I don't doubt for one second that the life expectancy of this little secret is pretty short, Sig," Max said. "I just think we've got another two to four weeks before the Krag can wrap their brains around the magnitude of what we have.

"I feel that I have a certain latitude with regard to the methods by which I accomplish the objectives set forth in my orders. So, if anyone knows any other way to get past the two layers of sensor drones, the early-warning sensor stations, and the patrol ships that the Krag have in place to stop Union ships from doing what we are about to attempt to do, I'm certainly willing to consider it in place of relying on the captured transponder codes." He let five long seconds of silence pass, during which he looked at Anderssen, whose face conveyed his misgivings about the proposed course of action but also his lack of any viable alternative. "Very well, then."

"I thank you, Max, gentlemen, for a most delightful dinner," Anderssen said, exercising his traditional prerogative as the elder of the two skippers to end the gathering. "We should have *Cumberland* refueled and resupplied within the next eight to ten hours. Then we will be ready to go pay a visit to Mr. Krag."

"You are very welcome, Sig, Mr. Maynard." Max gave the formal reply required by naval custom. "We'll set out for Krag space as soon as those operations are complete."

Anderssen and Maynard shook hands with all of their hosts and bid them good night. Using his joystick-like hand control, Anderssen backed his Autochair away from the table and headed for the hatch. While seated at the table, he looked like any other man who ate while keeping his left hand in his lap. But without the table in the way, it was obvious that Anderssen's left arm was an inert mass of burned, scarred tissue, that much of his lower torso was simply gone, and that he had no legs at all. From the chest down, his body was encased in an intricate assembly of tubing, pumps, and support systems that kept him alive. Max watched the Autochair deploy a set of treads that allowed it to climb over the hatch coaming and carry Anderssen out of the Wardroom into the corridor, where the treads retracted and the Autochair went back to riding on wheels.

Once their guests were out of sight down the corridor, the contingent from the *Cumberland* slowly left the compartment, except for Max and Bram. The doctor had given Max a look that indicated that he wished the skipper to linger. Both pretended that they wanted to spend a few more moments drinking coffee.

When he was sure they were alone, Bram spoke. "Max, I'm outraged. Totally outraged."

"At what?"

"The total callousness of the navy and the damnable unfeeling human calculating machines who run it, who keep returning men grievously injured, both physically and psychologically, to space duty." Bram vented, and not for the first time. "That man," he said, pointing toward the hatch from which Anderssen had just made his exit, "has no business running around in deep space. How does he manage his CIC, for stars' sake? Does that contraption he drives around in bolt to the deck at his console?"

"Yes, it does."

"Medically speaking, a man wounded so horribly needs to be in a long-term care facility or at home being cared for by his family under full-time supervision of a practical nurse, not in the CIC of a starship. What happened to him?"

"He was on Sengupta-Patel IV about two years ago, the first time the Krag invaded it."

"First time?"

"They invaded twice. The first time, the marines, navy personnel stationed at the training center located there, planetary militia, and armed citizens defeated the invasion. The rat-faces came back four months later with a much larger force and took the planet."

"That's all very interesting." He paused and shook his head. "Actually, no, it is not. I haven't the slightest interest in the military history of Sengupta-Patel IV. What I wanted to know was precisely how he sustained the injury. The damage to that man's body certainly wasn't inflicted with an assault rifle."

"Plasma torch. Anderssen was an Olympic-class marksman. He had personally shot two dozen or so Krag officers at long range, and he was climbing a ladder to get to the top of a distillation column at a chemical plant to use it as a sniper position. The

Krag climbing after him on the same ladder hit him with a plasma torch. Fortunately, he hadn't climbed very high yet."

"A traumatic event, to be sure. Which brings to mind the further issue of his mental and emotional state. Two years is not nearly long enough for an emotional recovery from so horrific an event. A man who has literally had the lower half of his body incinerated has endured a traumatic experience of such magnitude that I find it inconceivable that he could function in any kind of command capacity. He should be receiving intensive multimodal therapy: individual counseling sessions, group therapy, progressive desensitization, guided hypnovisualization, psychodrama, Sigur-Grimsal-Venissat recitative neurolinguistics—everything in the psychotherapy toolbox. Yet I'm quite confident he's getting nothing of the sort. Tell me, does he even have a qualified physician over there to look after his medical needs, which, I imagine, are quite considerable?"

"He does. Quite a good one, I understand. A fellow by the name of Delbosque, Dr. James Kelly Delbosque."

"Why was the good Dr. James Kelly Delbosque not at the table with us this evening? I would have enjoyed meeting another physician."

"It's not my doing," Max said defensively. "I specifically included him in the invitation. Captain Anderssen informed me, though, that Delbosque is a particularly blunt, undiplomatic, and painfully direct man, prone to blurt out whatever comes to his mind and somewhat deficient in social skills. He further said that, in the interest of intership amity, it might be best if the doctor were introduced to us under more controlled circumstances. Quite naturally I told the captain that Dr. Delbosque would be welcome—notwithstanding his bluntness—and that, in fact, he might find a kindred spirit on board, but I wasn't able to change Anderssen's mind."

"When you say *kindred spirit*, I'm certain that I have no idea to whom you are referring," said Sahin, with just a trace of a smile leaking out from under his mask of mock indignation, "unless, of course, it is yourself. I am, after all, an accredited diplomat and the very soul of subtlety, whereas your bluntness and lack of decorum are renowned in two dozen star systems." He stood. "Nevertheless, with your permission, I am of a mind to meet this Dr. Delbosque immediately."

Max nodded his assent, and the doctor strode from the compartment with a spring in his step, leaving Max alone with the three midshipmen who had started to clear the table. He noticed that the young men had managed to get most of the plates and utensils but had not yet touched the glasses, mugs, and pitchers, many of which still contained wine, beer, and liquor. He also noticed the midshipmen occasionally stealing glances at him, as if to gauge how soon he would leave. It was the oldest midshipman trick in the very thick book of midshipman tricks (a book that Max not only knew very well but to which he had added several of the more interesting chapters), and Max was certainly not going to fall for it.

"Kurtz," he said to one of the midshipmen, "bring me three of those water glasses from the sideboard. And Chang," he said to another, "draw half a pitcher of beer from the tap. Now, you three young gentlemen take a seat at the table." Kurtz, Chang, and Rodriguez took a seat. They were all from the second or third youngest group of midshipmen. Each had been on the ship for about a year, and they were nine or ten years old.

Max poured about 150 milliliters—maybe ten or twelve good swallows for their small mouths and throats—of beer into each of the three glasses and gave one to each mid. "Now," he said, "drink that down." They did so with evident relish. This was not their first taste of beer. "Good. Now, lads, given your age and size, you've had all the strong drink that it is prudent for you to have today." The young men's disappointment at this statement was evident. Max had given them only enough beer to get them very, very slightly tipsy; they had been expecting to scavenge enough alcohol from the leavings at the table to get roaring drunk.

"All the rest goes down the Wardroom Galley drain into the recycling tanks instead of down your young hatches. Do we have an understanding, gentlemen? Do I have your word of honor as midshipmen and as members of the crew of the USS *Cumberland*?"

"Yes, sir," the three said, with an undertone of reluctance. Maybe not so much of an *under*tone.

"Outstanding," Max said, ignoring the undertone. "Remember, gentlemen, a navy man's word is his bond. It is as sacred as any oath or promise in Known Space. If you break it, your reputation and—very likely—your career are gone for good. So, now that I have your word, I feel safe in leaving this room. And remember," he said with just a trace of menace, "if you *ever* break your word to me, on even the smallest matter, you are going to wish you had never been born." He rose. "Good evening, gentlemen."

"Good evening, sir," the three mids replied, somewhat abashed.

Max left them to finish clearing the table.

CHAPTER 8

22:45 Zulu Hours, 13 May 2315

"No contacts," Kasparov announced, as he (or someone at his station) had announced every fifteen minutes—exactly—for the last fifteen hours and forty-five minutes.

"Very well," Max responded as he (or someone else at his station) had responded every fifteen minutes—exactly—for the last fifteen hours and forty-five minutes. Despite the repetition, neither man's voice held even the most infinitesimal hint of boredom.

For the last fifteen hours and forty-five minutes, the *Cumberland,* alongside the *Nicholas Appert,* had been crossing the roughly two light-years of space that separated the space unambiguously controlled by the Union and its newly acquired, quasi-allied "Associated Powers" from the space unambiguously controlled by the enemy. While under the dominion of neither human nor Krag, the zone being traversed by the *Cumberland* was by no means devoid of hazards. Any Union force attempting a crossing faced aggressive enemy patrols, extensive minefields, stealthed sensor buoys, even stealthier kamikaze drones, and the occasional hidden *Fishbait* or *Fruitbat* class fighter mini-base. Any Krag coming from the opposite direction would encounter similar perils.

The Admiralty's precise but typically bureaucratic and bloodless name for this area was the Zone of Indeterminate Control. There was even a set of standing special orders governing vessels operating in the zone: Rules of Engagement "S." The vessel commanders who guarded and patrolled the zone cut through all those syllables and generally referred to the area by the word for the letter "S" in the navy's phonetic alphabet, calling it "the Sierra."

But ordinary spacers had a way of coming up with names for things that had both less precision and more real meaning than the official ones. For the zone, they adopted a name derived from a term first coined (in Middle English) around the year 1320 by the people of London for the location of the frequent hangings imposed by the brutal justice of the day: *nonesmanneslond*. The term evolved over the centuries, and people, usually soldiers, applied it in many different contexts; but it was during the First World War that the name truly took hold.

No-Man's-Land.

In places such as Sectors Z-114, Z-403, Z-410, Z-415, Z-424, and Z-509, the fleets were at that very moment clashing as one or the other side attempted to force a crossing. But over more than 99 percent of their border, human and Krag stared at each other across two light-years of generally quiet space, neither knowing when and where the other might attack.

Max had chosen to take the *Cumberland* and the *Nicholas Appert* across No-Man's-Land in Sector Z-948, which was not only quiet at that time, but over which human and Krag had never fought. Indeed, because the Union and Krag star systems adjacent to Sector Z-948 were of little strategic value, neither side expected the other to attempt a crossing there and, accordingly, devoted few resources to guarding it. Few resources, that is, in comparison to those lavished on those sectors where strategists deemed an attack to be more likely. The two skippers, with the help of officers from both ships, had used intel gathered by Union patrols, as well as the captured Krag data, to plot and then follow a course that avoided the relatively few known obstacles in that part of the Sierra.

That was the easy part.

Destroyer and tender were traveling on compression drive in line abreast formation 1248 kilometers apart at the relatively sedate speed of 1039 c, which had brought them across most of No-Man's-Land to a point less than three hours away from Krag space. As far as Max and Anderssen knew, their ships had not yet appeared on Krag sensors. But as both captains and all the men on board both ships were keenly aware, the danger of detection and subsequent attack increased with each AU they crossed.

"Tactical," Max said to Bartoli, "show me the Krag sensor coverage and deployments in this sector."

"Aye, sir." Bartoli had been expecting this request and tapped a blinking square on his console. The *Cumberland*'s CIC had three holographic tactical displays, all on the front half of the Command Island: the main, about a meter and a half in diameter and right in front of the skipper, and two secondaries, eighty centimeters across, one on each side of the main. The starboard secondary, in front of the XO, went to flat gray, indicating that it was being switched over to receive new data.

"Here is Sector Z-948," Bartoli said. A greenish cube appeared in the lambent column. "And here," another touch to the screen, "is the near half of the abutting sector of Krag space." A red block fading out on the far edge appeared adjacent to the cube. "And here," another touch, "are the three long-range early-warning stations providing overlapping sensor coverage of this sector." Three white dots winked into existence, forming an equilateral triangle just inside the red rectangle and parallel to the boundary between the two sectors. The triangle was off-center to the left and low about a third of the way to the sector boundary in each direction—Krag and Union sectors weren't the same size and didn't align with one another. "These are the last-known locations of the fighter squadrons detailed to this sector." Eight red dots appeared, scattered through Krag space near the border with the Sierra. "And here are the projected locations of the cruiser/frigate groups assigned to back up the fighters." Four orange dots joined the red ones. "In addition, Intel suspects that there is at least one enemy fighter base concealed in this part of the Sierra, relying on the early-warning stations for sensor coverage. Intel also conjectures, without much in the way of hard evidence to back it up, that there is a battle group consisting of a battlecruiser, four cruisers, and an unknown number of frigates and destroyers assigned as a strategic reserve about ten light-years back dedicated to respond to any major incursion into this or any of the neighboring sectors. And don't miss the blue dot, sir. That's our present location."

Max didn't miss the dot. It was only a finger's width from the display's color change marking where Krag-controlled space began.

"Mr. Bhattacharyya, can you pin down the location of that fighter base or that strategic reserve force?"

"I'm afraid not, Skipper," the Intel officer replied. "The very *existence* of the strategic reserve force is conjectural, so its location is speculation based on conjecture. We haven't picked up any ship-to-ship comms that we can attribute to the force, none of our signal intercepts localize to any of the places the Krag are likely to put it, and there don't seem to be any especially favorable places for such a force to hide. Accordingly, any estimate of where it is would be pure guesswork on my part." Bhattacharyya said "guesswork" the way a Roman Catholic Cardinal would say "mortal sin."

"As far as the fighter base," he continued, "if there's one out there, the enemy has been playing his cards close to his vest, if

Krag have cards and vests. They've maintained total EMCON—we haven't picked up a single localizable signal. None of our patrols in the Sierra have any sensor contact consistent with enemy fighters, other than roving fighters on regular patrols, nor anything that even smells like a fighter base." Max thought he heard *something* in the way that last sentence sounded.

Hearing that sort of "something" is in the skipper's job description.

"Mr. Bhattacharyya," Max prompted, "was there something else?"

"Well, sir," he said with obvious reluctance, "this might sound a bit odd given my widely known aversion to speculation, but I think I have a pretty good idea where the Krag fighter base is located. Or, at least, where I'd put one if I were a Krag admiral."

"Really?" Many skippers would have loaded that word with several metric tons of sarcasm, particularly given Mr. Bhattacharyya's comparatively low rank and seniority. Max's tone, however, conveyed only genuine interest. "And where might that be?"

"Alderson I. Here." He touched one of his flat screens, causing a purple dot to appear in the tactical display just over a centimeter away from the blue dot representing the *Cumberland*. "When this area was under Union control, Alderson I was home to a moderately large mining colony. The planet is basically a nickel-iron rock—what's left from a protoplanet collision that stripped away the crust and mantle. It's tidally locked, with one side permanently facing its sun and one side permanently in the dark. The colony was on the dark side. Anything on the sun side would be cooked in a few seconds.

"Right now, though, the planet would be perfect for hiding a fighter base. One," he counted on his fingers, "sensors would have a hard time distinguishing metal spacecraft and support equipment from a metallic planetary surface. Two, sensors will have an even harder time distinguishing ships and base from the refined metal mining equipment and support structures left behind when the miners bugged out. Three, sensors won't work all that well anywhere near the planet because of all the radiation and magnetic effects you get when trying to scan a planet that's just 0.27 AU from a class B star. None of that bothers the fighters, though, because they're shielded by the planet—eighteen hundred kilometers of nickel-iron. They don't need sensors that we could pick up because the fighters will launch and get their initial intercept vector from the early-warning stations. It's exactly where I'd hide a fighter base."

Max noticed that Bartoli was smiling. "Something to add, Mr. Bartoli?"

"Only that I like the way Batty thinks." Bartoli called the ensign by his newly earned nickname. Under perverse naval logic, giving the man a nickname connoting craziness expressed the collective judgment of Ensign Bhattacharyya's comrades that his predictions and estimates were exceptionally reliable. In the navy if your shuttle pilot is known as "Gonna Crash" Nash or your navigator as "Wrong Way" McVay, you know you're in good hands. "If Mr. Bhattacharyya ever gets tired of his Ouija board, tarot cards, and tea leaves, I'm sure we could find a berth for him in the Tactical section."

"I appreciate the offer, Lieutenant, but I prefer something more intellectually challenging than looking out a viewport and shouting, *Hey, look, there's three Krag warships off the port bow, and I think they're hostile*," Bhattacharyya said, acknowledging the compliment with a smile while returning good-natured insult for good-natured insult in the time-honored naval manner.

"Well, Mr. Bhattacharyya, we're well past the Alderson system now, and we'll be sure to give it a wide berth on our return leg," Max said.

The scattered chuckles at the well-played banter between Bartoli and Bhattacharyya did little to dispel the growing tension in CIC. No matter how busy each man kept himself at his station, it was impossible to ignore the knowledge that each second not only brought the two ships just over 300,000,000 kilometers closer to Krag space, but also carried them 300,000,000 kilometers deeper into the sensor coverage generated by the Krag early-warning stations. At the forefront of every man's mind was the knowledge that, if the Krag identified them as Union vessels, they would almost certainly die shortly thereafter.

It wasn't long before CIC was much quieter than normal. There was still the background chatter of officers speaking over the loops to their back rooms, people in CIC exchanging information with each other, and sections making their periodic reports to the XO, but the exchanges were short and the voices muted. The banter was gone: the men said what duty required, not one word more. And almost as though the Krag could hear them across the vacuum of space, the more superstitious men also kept their voices very low. Time crawled forward in quiet agony.

"This is unbearable!" the doctor suddenly exclaimed in a voice far too loud for the currently muted sound level in CIC. "I don't know how you people stand this." Several men looked at him in abject horror. There were things that navy men endured but of which they never spoke.

"Doctor," Max said evenly, "do you need to return to the Casualty Station?"

For a moment, Sahin pondered the question and the implicit order that it contained, sighed, and then responded with quiet resignation, "No, sir. I don't believe that I do."

"Very well." Max met his friend's eyes, measuring the man's stress level. He judged it to be very high but still manageable. "You're welcome to remain in CIC." Max held Bram's eyes for two full seconds after he finished speaking, reinforcing his earlier implicit order. *But if you can't keep it together, you need to leave.*

Sahin nodded.

Max looked around at the men at their stations. While these men had seen a lot of action in the last few months, most of them weren't veterans by any stretch of the imagination. As much stress as Dr. Sahin was under, the men were under more because they had a clearer idea of what was happening and what could go wrong. Not to mention that they bore the stress of performing difficult, often highly technical, duties while being subjected to the anguish of waiting to be detected. But they were all managing. Some of them, though, looked as though they were near their limit: pale, sweaty, fidgeting. Dry tongues occasionally emerged from dry mouths to lick dry lips—a parchedness that no coffee or juice could ever quench.

But there *was* a treatment that Max could administer. "COMMs, give me MC1."

"MC1, aye," Chin responded.

"Men, this is the skipper," Max said in a studiously relaxed tone. "Hang in there. It won't be long now before we know whether we continue sneaking or commence running. Whatever happens, you can take comfort in knowing you've got a good ship and outstanding shipmates quite capable of handling it. That is all." He nodded to Chin, who broke the circuit, avoiding the *THUNK* that would reverberate through the ship when Max cut the feed from the button on his own console.

Max had *told* the men that things were going to be all right. Now he needed to *show* them. He caught the eyes of the midshipman posted to CIC—Vizulis for this watch—and pointed to his coffee mug, causing the boy to begin the process of providing the skipper with a refill. Max's fixed stare at DeCosta's mug, combined with a raised eyebrow and a subtle nod, induced the

XO to do the same. Max studied the young midshipman, who had been milking cows on his family's farm in Latvia on Earth just thirteen months ago. The young man was pale, taking shallow and rapid breaths, and his hands were shaking slightly. Yet he served the coffee, prepared the way he knew each of the officers liked it, without error and without spilling a drop. It was a seemingly inconsequential duty, but it was the duty assigned to him. And though he was afraid, he did it.

Max thanked the boy with a nod.

Max and DeCosta made an elaborate show of sipping their coffee, perusing the displays on their respective consoles, and keeping an apparently anxiety-free weather eye on everything in CIC. The always-observant Dr. Sahin noticed these behaviors and had little difficulty discerning the underlying reasoning. He, too, requested that Vizulis refill his coffee, and made a show of sipping the brew while studying a set of Pfelung surgical manuals.

This display of nonchalance had the desired effect of calming the men, even though few were fooled into thinking that the skipper, XO, and CMO were actually relaxed under the present circumstances. The officers on the Command Island *looked* calm and collected. Today, at least, that was enough.

Another twelve minutes crept by. Both the officers and enlisted heads in CIC, located against the starboard bulkhead just forward of the weapons locker, received a higher-than-usual number of visitors. Max used a one-key shortcut he had installed on his console to boost the compartment's air-refresh rate to dispel the distinct aroma of nervous sweat.

It was one thing for a man to be sweating from tension. But the smell of a few dozen doing so was definitely bad for morale.

The change in airflow was just starting to make a difference when Kasparov changed his posture and said a few words into his headset, then nodded. "Sir," he said, "we were just painted.

High-frequency tachyon radar, 12.29 centimeter band. Signal strength was 15.2 Hannums per square meter. Our estimate for this frequency is that the enemy can get a detectible return off the tender with anything more than about 12 Hannums. And because the Hannum scale for measuring the strength of modulated—"

"I know, Mr. Kasparov," Max said patiently. "I've sat in your chair. It's logarithmic. A reading of 15.2 Hannums significantly exceeds the detection threshold. The Krag have almost certainly detected the tender."

"Yes, sir." Kasparov turned his attention from his skipper to his headset, as indicated by a characteristic tilt of his head. He listened for a moment and clicked his MIC key for "yes," indicating that he understood what his back room had just told him. "Skipper, my back room is linked to the Sensors team on the tender, and the tender confirms both the paint and the signal intensity."

"Very well. Next comes the focus scan," Max said to everyone and no one.

Just over thirty seconds elapsed. "There it is, sir," Kasparov said. "Ultrahigh-frequency tachyon radar scan, multiple frequency, multiple source, very tight beams. I've got four frequencies and three sources so far . . . stand by . . ." He listened to his back room for a few seconds. "Make that *seven* frequencies from three sources. All continuous—the Krag are locked on and following the target. Signal strength is high enough that the enemy can identify the tender by type and maybe even by class. It's still far below the detection for the *Cumberland* so long as we remain in stealth mode. Signal strength is steady. They're locked in and tracking the tender. Do you want the rundown on the bands and sources?"

"Not necessary, Mr. Kasparov. Just be sure that the information is available on the right data channel so anyone who needs it can tie in."

Kasparov quickly turned to another display on his console and punched up data channel H, where the Sensors Back Room customarily transmitted information of that kind, confirming that anyone with a properly configured console could access the data. "It's on channel H, sir." Since time beyond reckoning, the navy assigned numbers to voice channels and letters to data channels.

Max looked at the chrono. "All right, people. We should be receiving an IFF interrogation in something less than two minutes."

One hundred and seven seconds later, Bartoli announced, "IFF transmission received. *Nicholas Appert* sending the response as per the plan. She's just identified herself as a captured Union tender proceeding to Krag Repair and Refit Base 446, which should cause them to allow us to proceed unhindered."

"Or if the Krag have changed the codes, she's just identified herself as a Union vessel attempting to penetrate Krag space using a captured IFF code," said Mr. Levy, "which should cause them to throw everything they have at us with the goal of blowing us to flaming atoms and capturing the tender."

"Have you always been such a sparkling fountain of optimism, Mr. Levy?" DeCosta asked.

"Absolutely, Mr. DeCosta," Levy responded to the XO. "I'm the youngest of five brothers, and I'm by far the most optimistic of the lot. You should hear my oldest brother, Moshe. Now *he*'s a real Bitching Bettie."

"Then may God save us from Moshe Levy," said Max. "Besides, if he's your oldest brother, he probably outranks me, right?"

"I'm afraid that's true, sir. He's a rear admiral with Special Projects in Norfolk. The shit he works on is so secret that our mother has to call him by a code name when she invites him home for dinner."

"Sir," Chin interrupted the banter, "receiving a signal from the Krag traffic control center for this area. Standard text protocol. They're authorizing the tender to proceed at present course and speed to one of their traffic-control points just inside the Sierra, then to reduce speed to 0.15 c and contact the control center for that point for instructions on entry into Krag space. The message provided the coordinates and frequency."

Sahin sighed heavily with relief. "So, it looks as though the Krag have been fooled by our masquerade."

Several men, including Max, turned expectantly to Mr. Levy, who shook his head and raised his hands defensively. "Why me? Why do all of you assume *I'm* going to be the one who says it? I was actually thinking that the skipper would tell him."

"Mr. Levy," Max said soothingly, "that kind of remark sounds so much better coming from you instead of me. I think you should have the honors."

"If you say so, sir." He adopted a melodramatic, almost lugubrious, voice appropriate for the narrator of a bad trid-vid drama: "Either the Krag have been fooled by wily Captain Robichaux's deception, or they know full well that the purportedly captured tender is actually under Union control and are luring the daring but tiny Union force deeper into Krag space, all the better to trap and destroy it. Bwahahaha." Then he added brightly, "There. How was that?"

"It will do, Mr. Levy," Max said. "But don't quit your day job. Mr. Bartoli, what's the enemy up to?"

"Nothing unusual so far, sir," said Bartoli. "There's no evidence of any change in the enemy's tactical dispositions or of any other activity consistent with detection of an incursion into their space. They are, however, tracking the tender very intently. In fact, they've just brought two more sensor beams to bear on her—I'm updating the scan information on data channel H right now.

That's pretty normal for them—they get as many sensor sweeps on her on as many frequencies and from as many sources as they can so that they can scope out the ship's configuration in high resolution to be sure it's not an escort carrier or something else that size masquerading as a tender."

"Thank you, Mr. Bartoli," Max said. "Mr. Bhattacharyya?"

"Nothing on my end either, sir," Bhattacharyya added. "Most of the Krag combat-vessel encrypts have changed from the ones we got from the data core, so we just have the signal characteristics to go on—we don't know in real time what the Krag are actually saying to each other anymore. But so far there's been no change in the volume, type, or sources of signal traffic of the kind we would expect to see if they had detected an enemy incursion."

"Very well. Let me know if there are any changes." That these officers would notify their commanding officer of any meaningful changes in the dispositions or transmissions of the enemy went without saying. Max said it anyway. Ship captains say a lot of things that go without saying, and go without saying a lot of things that most people would say. It's part of the job.

Another part of the job was enduring the intense stress of waiting for the enemy to react, or not react, to his moves. And not just enduring the stress, but enduring it right in front of men who had spent years watching officers in combat—men who were little more than an arm's length away. Close enough to see every drop of sweat. Countless skippers lost the confidence of their crews simply because they couldn't stand up to that kind of scrutiny.

Max bore up under that scrutiny as well as anyone. It wasn't that he wasn't anxious, because he certainly was, but that he had learned to manage that anxiety effectively, mainly by keeping himself busy. On this occasion he spent nearly an hour reviewing and approving the ship's maintenance and inspection logs for the past month. If there was any human activity guaranteed to have a tranquilizer-like effect, it was reviewing maintenance and inspection logs.

"Coming up on the traffic-control point," LeBlanc said. Max had already issued orders for this point in the mission, which the chief implemented with his usual skill. "Initiating compression field devolution. Speed is 959 c . . . 884 . . . 605 . . . 411 . . . 108 . . . 48 . . . 15 . . . 6 . . . 2 . . . field collapsing . . . ship is subluminal . . . engaging main sublight drive. Ship is on main sublight and stable on all three axes. Reducing speed to match the tender and taking up station keeping 2560 kilometers away from her at a relative bearing of one-zero-five mark zero-two-seven." Half a minute or so passed. "Speed is now 0.15 c."

"Tender is right where she's supposed to be, Skipper," added Bartoli. "No threats detected in our immediate vicinity."

Max took a quick look at the general status display on his console; all the lights were green, indicating that the major systems—propulsion, sensors, stealth, countermeasures, weapons—were all ready to answer his orders. He looked around at the men in CIC. It was for good reason that the ship's designers had laid out the compartment with every man at every station (save only the four men at Maneuvering and anyone seated on the Command Island) facing their commanding officer. How could a skipper lead his men if all he saw of them were the backs of their heads?

"Sir," Chin piped up, "the tender just signaled the Krag traffic-control center on the designated frequency and is awaiting routing instructions."

"Very well." Anderssen was playing his part according to plan.

When he observed that the CIC crew did not appear meaningfully less tense than before, Dr. Sahin did not have to ask for the explanation the men had come to expect him to need. By now his extensive researches in the ship's database and his rapidly expanding fund of experience were enough to tell him that, even though the transponder code that the *Nicholas Appert* sent in response to the Krag's "ping" hadn't provoked an obviously hostile response, there were any number of ways that the tender's most recent transmission might give the enemy a clue that something was amiss. The authentication codes might have changed. There might be a subtle error in how the message was structured or phrased or encrypted. The Krag equivalent of a comma might be in the wrong place. Bram was sure that there were other ways the message could be wrong. Maybe he could burrow into the database and find a few more.

Nothing made Bram forget his problems better than immersing himself in research, even if it was to find even more reasons he might be blown to flaming atoms sometime in the next twenty minutes. He got busy.

Bram had just finished a somewhat abstruse database section about a method the Krag used for making their messages more difficult to counterfeit by inserting carefully constructed time-coding errors in two of the five secondary authentication codes when Bartoli spoke up.

"Change in Krag tracking activity, sir. All the early-warning sensor stations are shifting their focus from the tender back into the Sierra. Right now there's nothing focused on her—just the standard area-wide traffic-control scanners the Krag use to keep everyone on the right routes so that none of their ships run into one another. Which would be a *terrible* pity."

Max chuckled. "I'm certain that any Krag ship collisions would fill you with great sadness, Mr. Bartoli. Would you send flowers to show your sympathy?"

"No, sir. A New Wisconsin gourmet cheese assortment," he replied.

"Laced with cyanide and 4-hydroxycoumarin," said Levy, "to enhance the flavor."

"Skipper, reply from the Krag traffic-control center. It looks like a standard set of traffic directions—they could almost have come from our own people. They direct the tender to a sublight low-priority traffic corridor to cross at .34 c from the Sierra into Krag-controlled space. Then, when she's about 300 million kilometers from the FEBA, they route her through a set of branching transit corridors, still at .34, until she hits one of their long-distance traffic routes. There, they put her into a slot in the traffic pattern and send her down the line at 875 c to the vicinity of Repair and Refit Base 446. After that she's picked up by the local traffic-control center in that sector. I've routed the message to Navigation."

"My back room is coordinating with my counterpart on the tender right now, Skipper," announced Ellison from Navigation. "We'll have the route plotted and fed to Maneuvering on both ships in just a few seconds." He returned his attention to his console, where he worked rapidly, making computations, pulling up data, and speaking quietly over his headset. "Course computed and routed to Maneuvering on both ships."

"Very well. Chin, signal the tender that she is clear to acknowledge the Krag order and proceed as they direct.

"Aye, sir." Pause. "Tender has acknowledged the order."

"Very well. LeBlanc, let's be their shadow."

"Shadowing the tender, aye," said LeBlanc.

Max listened to the reports that the tender was coming to the new course and speed that would put it into the Krag traffic corridor, and then the directions from LeBlanc to his men to bring the ship around to its new heading. Later he heard the veteran chief give instructions for the minute changes in course and speed necessary to keep the *Cumberland* in the correct position relative to the tender—with the tender between it and the source of the most powerful sensor transmissions painting the ships at that particular moment. Both ships were soon on course, traveling at 875 c along the designated traffic corridor leading to the Krag repair and refit base. Bartoli's contact reports soon showed that the *Cumberland* wasn't alone in the corridor. Rather, just as in a similar corridor in Union space, ships were lined up one after the other at a uniform distance, all traveling at the same speed, like ground cars following a vast highway in space. The only difference was that instead of the ships being the standard Union interval of 40 AU apart, they were 33.48 AU apart, a distance that came out to a nice even number of the units that the Krag used in place of the AU.

The exquisitely sensitive sensors on the *Cumberland* could detect five ships lined up ahead of it. It wasn't long before Krag traffic control began to slot ships in behind as well. The tender, shadowed by its tiny and virtually invisible escort, was just another boxcar in the light-year-long Krag train chugging down the tracks toward a sector deep in Krag space.

"Mr. Kasparov, Mr. Bhattacharyya, any evidence that the Krag are paying us any special attention?"

"No new contacts or anomalous readings, sir," Kasparov reported.

"And no unusual changes in Krag comm traffic or scan patterns," added Mr. Bhattacharyya from the Intel Station.

"Secure from Amber," Max ordered. "Set Condition Orange throughout the ship." Whereas Condition Amber, just one step below Condition Red or General Quarters, required that every man be on duty and at, or near, his battle station, Condition Orange allowed men to return to their normal watch schedule. As a result, two-thirds of the crew immediately left their stations, to eat, have a pint of "Bud" Schlitz's best lager, take a crap, goof off, or sleep. Most headed either for the galley or for their racks. Since the ship was now behind enemy lines, by unspoken agreement with his XO, Max left CIC while DeCosta remained behind. Max would relieve him in four hours so that one of the two was always in CIC keeping an eye on things. The men would get the rest they needed, but there would always be a senior officer in CIC with the experience to know whether the enemy was responding to the presence of an enemy moving ever deeper into his rear.

With each passing moment, not only was there more distance between the *Cumberland* and the relative safety of the Union lines, there were also more and more enemy ships that she would have to evade in order to escape. There was an old military maxim that Max could not get out of his mind: "When you are in the enemy's rear, he is also in yours."

Max headed immediately for his quarters, instructed the computer to wake him in three hours and fifty-five minutes, and stretched out on his rack, still in his Space Combat Uniform (SCU) complete with its oxygen-generator canister, pressure regulator, emergency radio, and zip-on pressure gloves and folding pressure helmet ready to serve as an emergency pressure suit. He was asleep within seconds.

After what seemed like only seconds, he was awake again, wondering what had roused him. Then he heard the Union Space Navy standard wake-up alarm: a chime followed by the purring, synthesized contralto of the computer voice managing, as always, somehow to be both intimately erotic and cybernetically cold, repeating, "It is time to wake up." The chime and the voice repeated themselves five seconds later, incrementally louder. Allowed to continue, the chime and the voice would continue to repeat, a little louder each time, up to the level at which the sound would bleed through the bulkhead. Then the computer would strobe the lights in the compartment and trigger a deafening Klaxon that would blare from right beside the sleeper's head. There were rumors that if the Klaxon went on for more than five minutes, the cabin sprinkler system would go off, showering the sleeper with cold water, but no one could ever stand the sound of the Klaxon long enough to test that particular bit of scuttlebutt.

Less than two minutes later, hair brushed and held in place by the stiffest hair gel known to human science (combs had no effect on the black wire that grew from Max's scalp; that same black wire laughed at ordinary hair products), face depilated, teeth microblasted, and SCU spritzed with both Wrinkl-Bustr and Evurfresssh, Max cycled through the armored CIC hatch.

"XO, report," he said in a reasonable approximation of alertness.

"Course and speed unchanged, no apparent change in enemy dispositions. No contacts within our defense perimeter. All stations still reporting secure at Condition Orange. All ship's systems reporting nominal. Last report from the tender was thirteen minutes ago. She's at Condition Orange, and all her systems are nominal. Change of watch is in forty-six minutes: White goes off duty, Red comes on."

"Very well. Officer of the Deck, I have CIC."

"Aye, sir," Bhattacharyya, who was performing that function for this watch, responded. "The skipper has CIC. Computer, log that the XO transferred CIC Con to the CO at zero seven hours, fourteen minutes."

"CIC Con to commanding officer transfer logged at zero seven hours, fourteen minutes," the computer announced.

Max looked at DeCosta and jerked his head subtly in the direction of the hatch. The XO nodded his understanding and made a beeline for his rack to inspect his eyelids for light leaks for four hours. His steps in that direction contained a noticeable lack of spring, notwithstanding that, as he usually did when the men were very tired, Max had sneaked the CIC gravity generators down to .85 G, a difference that was difficult to notice consciously, but that conveyed to the mind a subliminal sense of being less fatigued. As tired as these men looked, he thought about but discarded the idea of a further reduction to 0.75. The men would consciously notice the difference when he returned the settings to normal, and he didn't want that.

Now that men were back on their regular watch schedule and the compartment wasn't crammed with men at battle stations, CIC settled down into routine, or what passed for routine when each hour brought the *Cumberland* roughly a tenth of a light-year deeper into Krag space. The watch changed. There had been one change of watch when Max was sleeping. This was the second. These men had been off watch for eight hours, and Max noticed that they approximated living, breathing human beings much more closely than did the men who were at battle stations eight hours ago—with men that young and in such good physical condition, it didn't take much rest for them to bounce back. Another day or two of relative normalcy and these men would be ready for anything.

Max's four hours in the Big Chair had less than ten minutes left to run when Kasparov interrupted his review of a group of midshipmen's training progress reports. "Skipper," he said, "you might want to take a look at this."

"Whatcha got?"

"Sir, if you'll open channel D and tie one of your displays into it, you can see what I'm looking at."

Max did so and saw a line of icons representing the computer-inferred locations of nine Krag ships, each icon accompanied by a set of numbers representing the strength, nature, type, and time of the sensor contact from which the computer plotted the position. The brightness of the icons varied with the strength and recentness of the contact. The brighter icons were stronger and more recent, meaning that the crew should consider them as being more reliable. Two of the contacts, about halfway between the forward edge of the screen and the blue "You Are Here" dot in the center of the screen, were much dimmer than the others.

"As you know, sir, we deliberately set things up so that the Krag would slot us into a low-priority corridor because we believed that traffic-control sensor coverage would be spotty. My department has been looking for gaps in the coverage, and we think we've found one. We've been monitoring the returns we get off the ships in line with us, and if you look at the ones passing through this area," a segment of the corridor started blinking red, "you can see that the sensor strength is very low. Given the location of the Krag tracking stations, we are confident that those signal levels are low enough that the nearest station will have only intermittent contact with a ship moving through there. So, if the tender drops off their coverage, they're likely to attribute it to low signal strength, rather than to it changing course. And, Skipper, the segment is about 0.3 light-years long. We could pull out of the corridor right after we enter it, and it would be more than three hours before we would show up as missing."

"How confident are you of these conclusions, Mr. Kasparov?"

"Skipper, my department and I are very confident. We'll know for sure in two hours and eleven minutes when we get there. At that point we can measure the signal level directly. If the levels are higher than we expect them to be, we can abort the plan and make our move later."

"What about signal strength once we are out of the corridor? Do we have any way to plot a route to our patrol area while keeping the tender from being tracked?"

"Sir, based on the location of the stations and the signal strength we are measuring from them, I think we have a pretty good model of what the observability coefficients are going to be in that area of space. Once we leave that area, all we have is the captured Krag data to tell us the location of the tracking stations and their signal characteristics. We'll have a good idea of what route to follow, but we'll still need to go slowly and check signal levels against our predictions."

"Thank you, Mr. Kasparov," Max said. "Present that same information to the XO when he comes on watch in a few minutes. He has some tactical planning to do."

■

"I am pleased to report, Midshipman, that your injury is far less serious than one would conclude from appearances alone. While there were serious contusions and abrasions, as well as copious bleeding, there is no concussion, and no epidural or subdural hematoma. Neither is there injury to the brain." Dr. Sahin was scrutinizing a three-dimensional projection of Midshipman Hewlett's rather unremarkable skull and the remarkable brain encased therein. Nurse Church had already debrided and dressed the wound with his usual skill, leaving Hewlett with a large bandage on the back of his head, held in place by several orbits of standard naval-issue blue gauze wound around the boy's scalp, looking much like a rather bizarre and irregular blue garland. Hewlett sat on an examining table, attempting by means of his still-blurry vision to make sense of the slowly rotating image.

Sahin caught the boy squinting. "Don't worry, my good lad, your vision will return to normal in a few hours. You are simply experiencing the eminently reasonable objections of the delicate human brain to being shaken violently in its casing. I assure you there is no damage. You may experience some blurred vision, headache, and mild nausea over the next four to twelve hours . . . quite normal under the circumstances. I am going to release you to return to your quarters. If you experience any other symptoms, or a worsening of those you have now, report back here immediately. In any event report to me in twenty-four hours so that I can reexamine you. If by then you have improved as much as I expect, I will mark you fit for duty at that time. But for the next twenty-four hours, you are under medical restriction: rest in your quarters, meals where you normally take them, and quiet recreation, such as watching trid vids and playing trideo games.

"Or reading. I particularly recommend reading. In fact, I have prepared a list of readings I deem suitable for young midshipmen and have posted it in the ship's database. It includes offerings such as the immortal works of pre-starflight writers James Joyce, all three Brontë sisters, Leo Tolstoy, Kalki Krishnamurthy, Marcel Proust, and even wonderful contemporary writers like May Duvol of Kirkman II and Brenrach Bach of Romper VII. There are also several excellent volumes of contemporary variable meter verse . . ."

"Doctor," Church interrupted, noticing a pronounced droop in the midshipman's eyelids, which the nurse attributed equally to his injury and to profound lack of interest in the subject matter currently under discussion, "it might be better to cover these readings at a later time. Mr. Hewlett needs his rest."

"Indeed, nurse. Quite right. But before I release you, Hewlett, the ravenous informational demands of insatiable bureaucracy require that I collect from you a bit more information, given that your injury apparently resulted from accident rather than enemy action. I am correct, am I not, in my assumption that there are no Krag on board?"

"There are none, sir, at least that I've noticed," Hewlett replied in all seriousness.

"Excellent, young man. If there were, I would return your dirk to you and fetch my sidearm and blade. We would take them on together."

Hewlett smiled. "The rat-faced bastards wouldn't stand a chance."

"No doubt. Now that we have established that you were not injured in enemy action, exactly how did you come by this injury, Midshipman?"

"I misjudged my rebound in a game of Midshipman's Tag, sir. It's my own fault."

"Midshipman's Tag? I'm not familiar with it. It must be a singularly unusual game for you to have acquired an injury of that nature in the vicinity of your skull's lambdoid suture. Can you explain it to me?"

"I'm not sure I could do a good job of it," Hewlett said with some embarrassment. "If you want to know how the fusion reactor works or how the life-support system regulates atmospheric pressure, I can lay it out for you, but I'm not good at explaining the things that people do. Besides, I'm still learning the rules. But there's going to be a match in about four hours, sir, if you'd like to watch. It's going to be a good one, too."

"Match? You mean that such things are organized?"

"Of course, sir. It wouldn't work otherwise."

"I would very much like to see a match, Midshipman. Where are such things held?"

"In the main cargo hold," the midshipman answered in a voice that implied that only an idiot would ask such a question.

CHAPTER 9

01:57 Zulu Hours, 15 May 2315

"Max, you must trust me about this," Anderssen whispered. "Say and do nothing about the matter until it is decided."

"You know I trust you, Sig," Max replied. "But that's asking a lot."

"Indeed. Which is *exactly* why trust is required."

The skippers were walking down the corridors of the RSS *Makkah,* the Rashidian destroyer serving as the pennant vessel for Joint Operational Group Hotel Papa, and fell silent when they reached the hatch to which they were being led. Their XOs didn't hear a word of it, as they were following at a discreet distance, deeply involved in their own discussion: negotiating the barter of several freshly brewed barrels of the *Cumberland*'s ship's beer for a few hundred kilos of Parmesan and Romano cheese, a crate of pepperoni, and a Dixon-Sterling Industries "Micro-Pie" brand compact pizza oven.

Their guide and escort, a formidable-looking Rashidian spacer who had been carrying before him an equally formidable-looking curved sword and an even more formidable-looking submachine gun slung over his shoulder, ushered Max, Anderssen, DeCosta, and Maynard through the hatch. The *Makkah*'s Wardroom was half again the size of its counterpart on the *Cumberland*, but just as Spartan. A steward showed the Union officers to seats at the foot of the table and inquired whether they would like coffee or any other form of refreshment. All four men requested coffee, knowing that if the coffee were to be merely excellent, it would be subpar for the Rashidian Navy.

A moment later, and just as the coffee was being poured from a sterling silver pot into elegant, gold-rimmed china cups, another large and fearsome escort showed an adult male Pfelung, who massed 210 kilos if he massed an ounce, to a place at one side of the table where four chairs had been replaced with a long, low platform with a ramp on one end and the top contoured to fit a Pfelung body. The alien waddled on his four finlike limbs up the ramp onto the contoured area and plopped down, his eyes, mouth, and gills just higher than the edge of the table. He turned to the humans, pressed the ends of his forefins together, and blinked twice slowly, in the appropriate Pfelung greeting for the situation—recognition of the presence of other beings worthy of respect but to whom one has not been properly introduced.

The humans returned the greeting in kind by bringing the fingertips of their left and right hands together and blinking in the same manner. The formalities of the moment satisfied, the Pfelung turned away from the humans, produced some sort of pad computer from a satchel he wore around his neck, and began manipulating it using eight or nine of the twelve fingerlike appendages that surrounded his mouth. A moment later, likely in response to those manipulations, a two-meter-long and one-meter-high holographic projection of an adolescent Pfelung appeared over the center of the table. As befitted a being who was not physically present in the room, he made no sign that he saw or recognized anyone.

Max was on his second sip of coffee when four officers in the black and scarlet of the Rashidian equivalent of the Union Space Navy's dress blue uniform, in which Max and his party were clad, entered the compartment, bowed, and took seats. Following Rashidian naval protocol, the Union officers remained seated, acknowledging the bow by setting down their coffee cups and nodding. One of the newcomers, wearing the insignia of a full commander, sat at the head, while the other three took the seats nearest the table's head but on the side opposite the Pfelung. Without taking their orders, the steward served a beverage to the Pfelung that looked like muddy water, followed by coffee to the Rashidian officers, and then withdrew.

As soon as the door to the compartment closed, the commander stood, bowed to the Pfelung, then to Anderssen, then to Max, and began speaking. Max could not help but notice that he certainly looked the part of the captain of a rated warship during time of war. He was of only medium height, but his upright bearing, combined with his obvious pride and dignity, made him look taller. He was dark-skinned, even for a Rashidian, clean-shaven rather than wearing the thin, well-trimmed beard favored by most Rashidian officers, and had a strong but wiry build. Just from the way the other Rashidian officers looked at the commander, Max could tell that his subordinates held him in high regard.

Despite what he knew was about to happen, Max liked him immediately.

"Good day, gentlemen," he said. "Welcome to the *Makkah*. I extend to you the full hospitality of this vessel. Make known anything that you need, and if we have it, then it is yours. I am Commander Hajjam. I wish to introduce my executive officer, Lieutenant Commander Housseini." The man on Hajjam's right stood, bowed, and sat. "I am also honored to introduce to you Lieutenant Commander Shaath, commander of the Xebec *Boutouba*, and his executive officer, Lieutenant Riffi." Both men stood and nodded in turn.

Max stood and precisely followed the coaching he had received from Dr. Sahin. "I accept your welcome, extend thanks for your hospitality, and offer you the hospitality of my vessel at any time should you need or desire it. I am Lieutenant Commander Robichaux, commander of the *Cumberland*. I wish to introduce my executive officer, Lieutenant DeCosta." The XO rose, bowed, and sat. "I am also honored to introduce to you Reserve and Support Forces Lieutenant Commander, former Navy Captain, Anderssen, and his executive officer, Reserve and Support Forces Lieutenant (JG), former Navy Lieutenant, Maynard."

Hajjam spoke again. "It is also my honor to introduce to you Composite Force Leader Shamp-Sungnah 253, commander of the Pfelung Small Fighter Wing Carrier currently a part of this task force." He paused, appearing to be slightly embarrassed. "I'm afraid that the rendering of the vessel's name into Standard is far too cumbersome for the purposes of this introduction." Knowing the Pfelung as he did, Max suspected that rather than cumbersome, the name was too odd-sounding or absurd for the dignified commander to say out loud in a formal setting. "Allow me also to introduce Fighter Jaw Full of Sharp Teeth Flight Leader Brakmor-Ent 198, who is participating in this conference by vidlink."

Shamp-Sungnah uttered some bloops and blurps into his translator disk, which apparently was tied into the room's sound system, because the transducers mounted in the overhead and the bulkheads all spoke in a synthesized voice: "Your many courtesies are acknowledged and reciprocated. You may taste our mud at the time of your choosing, an event to which we look forward with great pleasure. May we now proceed, or does human social procedure require more formalities and verbal ritual? We would happily comply, if so."

So, he wants to fish or cut bait. Max cringed at the unspoken but still feeble joke. *He's not the only one.*

Commander Hajjam forced a smile. "No, leader, no more formalities are required. We may begin our business. To that end I direct your attention to the navigational plot of this sector, in which the blinking blue dot represents our target, and the blinking red dot represents our current position. To minimize the risk of detection as we approach our target, the tender will detach itself from the group and position itself . . ."

Hajjam's voice trailed off as the Pfelung commander showed rapidly increasing signs of distress, anger, or some other powerful emotion. He wriggled violently from side to side, cast his dinner-plate-size eyes back and forth between Hajjam and Max, and gave off a series of rapid, high-pitched, and apparently inarticulate sounds. "Apparently inarticulate" because the translator gave off one soft beep every second: the audible cue that it was receiving sounds that might be speech but that it was unable for one reason or another to render into Standard. After a few moments, the Pfelung became stock-still, bared its four rows (four rows on top and four rows on bottom) of small, needle-sharp teeth, and then quickly concealed them by closing its mouth. He then began to speak softly, slowly, and clearly. Although the words generated by the translator and given voice through the room's transducers were polite, there was something in the delivery that said that the velvet glove enclosed an iron fist.

"Translations between species are prone to error. My neurology is not evolved to distinguish one human from another. It is possible that I am mistaken. I do not wish to provoke an incident over a mistake. So, I must know that what I believe is true. Please answer these questions." He looked pointedly at Max. "Are you Robichaux?"

"Yes, I am," Max answered blandly.

The Pfelung looked directly at Hajjam. "Are you Hajjam?"

"I am," Hajjam said.

"Do you now claim—"

The cycling of the hatch cut off Shamp-Sungnah and the translator. Hajjam glared at the door. Clearly he had left instructions that no one was to enter. A man wearing Rashidian civilian dress came in, breezily, as though he were walking into his favorite restaurant. He wore a brown-and-tan flowing robe much like those worn by most men on Rashid, save that his garment was trimmed with gold braid. Over the wearer's left breast, Max could see the calligraphic representation of an Arabic letter woven into the fabric with gold thread. Although Max was accustomed to seeing him in substantially different attire, there was no mistaking the gentleman's identity.

"Commander," Max said to Hajjam in a severe voice, "do you allow just anyone to wander into critical strategic meetings whenever they please? I'm shocked that you allow this two-bit art dealer on your ship, much less into this meeting."

The other man ignored Max and spoke directly to Hajjam. "Commander, are you aware how dangerous—what a menace to the safety of everyone in this battle group—this man is?" He waved his hand in a vague but elegant gesture in Max's general direction. "He has destroyed a Royal Air Force STOL trainer and laid waste to the garden at the Ministry of Trade building in the capital. Rumor has it that he has even smuggled explosives on board another vessel hidden inside ham sandwiches. I warn you, he is well-known for guile, deception, and trickery."

Just as Hajjam was about to interpose himself between the two men to keep them from coming to blows, the man in the robes stepped up to Max and embraced him warmly. "Max, my brother," he said with genuine emotion, "it brings joy to my heart to see you."

"You too, Prince. I wasn't expecting to find you here."

"Indeed. One would not expect to find me away from the capital in these turbulent times, much less on a warship behind enemy lines. There has, however, been a highly unusual development requiring my personal attention. On some later date, this matter may even involve you, but it is not something that I feel at liberty to discuss at present."

"Of course, Your Majesty," Max replied.

"Your Majesty, you know this man?" Commander Hajjam interjected.

"Indeed, I do. In fact, he knew me as Ellington Wortham-Biggs, dealer in fine-art glass sculpture, before he had an inkling that I was Prince Khalid, King Khalil's older and far less martial brother, as well as holder of the high offices of Deputy Prime Minister, Foreign Minister, Minister of Intelligence, Minister of Defense, Master of the Rolls, Groom of the Second Floor Front, et cetera," answered the prince.

Max smiled at the Gilbert and Sullivan reference. He did not know that the prince was a fan, but apparently, the brilliant and always incredibly well-informed gentleman knew that Max was. Khalid continued, "But, please, Max, Commander, gentlemen, and guests, it was not my intention to interrupt these proceedings. I am not attending this meeting in any official capacity whatsoever. Rather, I ask that you consider me merely as an interested bystander. All I require is that a steward bring me some coffee, and I will be quite content."

Before anyone had the opportunity to call for coffee, a steward appeared with the referenced beverage and poured a cup. Prince Khalid seated himself in a chair that was one of a row set against the back wall of the Wardroom, removed from beside the table to make room for the Pfelung. He sat, calmly drinking his coffee, inscrutable.

Shamp-Sungnah had remained perfectly silent and perfectly still during this discussion. As soon as things settled down, he resumed speaking. "Commander Hajjam, I must be certain that I understand you correctly. Do you claim to be the commander of this task force?"

"Yes, I do," he answered.

The Pfelung made a sound like the rumble of thunder, which Max knew to be a vibration of his air bladder, an involuntary reflex used to frighten away predators. "You exceed your authority. Robichaux holds an intermediate certification in multiple-vessel command. You hold a basic certification. Under the terms of the Four Power Joint Forces Agreement, Robichaux is the proper commander. Further, Hornmeyer commands this theater under the agreement. His orders place Robichaux in command. Conclusions: you are not the commander. The reasoning is inescapable. The logic is watertight."

"Ridiculous," Hajjam responded. "I'm Robichaux's superior officer by a full rank. I also have greatly more experience than he. I have commanded warships for more than ten years, while Robichaux has had his own command for less than half a year. I am an experienced captain, and he is not. This is no place for our actions to be governed by a scrap of paper negotiated hundreds of light-years away by staff officers and bureaucrats who know nothing of real warfare and who are completely ignorant of conditions here and now. And with all respect to Admiral Hornmeyer, he is also a great distance from here and does not know our current situation. I am the senior officer in place, and I am intimately familiar with every detail.

"Further, Lieutenant Commander Robichaux, who is a very, very young man, has a reputation for implementing wild, rash, and reckless tactics, heedless of the risks. I am a sober, experienced, *mature* leader. So it is clear that I am entitled to make this decision and, accordingly, am claiming preference in command over this," he gestured toward Max, "this . . . this reckless *adolescent*. He would lead us to disaster. I will lead us to victory." He turned to the other Rashidian skipper, who took a long, slow breath and began speaking.

"The *Boutouba* is an important element of this group, and its participation is essential to the success of our mission," Lieutenant Commander Shaath said. "Be assured that we will not follow so young and inexperienced a commander into a major engagement. I have my ship and men to think about, and I will not sacrifice them based on an obscure clause of a mere working agreement negotiated by military commanders in the field. I was a diplomat before the deteriorating political situation in the galaxy induced me to join the navy, and I know that the legal status of the Joint Forces Agreement is questionable at best. The Kingdom and the Union are not allies, but are merely Associated Powers. This agreement is not a formal interpower convention. It is not a treaty. It has not been ratified by the Royal Counsel. No, we will not be bound by it. We will follow Commander Hajjam, or we will follow no one. It is only reasonable that our Union associates submit to the realities of this situation and consent to be commanded by Commander Hajjam, who is the better commander in any event."

Shaath turned to Anderssen. "Surely, you, Captain Anderssen, with your decades of service and history of many battles, understand the value of maturity and experience over youth and recklessness."

Anderssen nodded and took a sip of his coffee, letting the tension hang in the air, like smoke. He met the eyes of each being at the table in turn, as though he were measuring them. At length, he spoke. His voice was gentle, as though he were a wise old uncle serving as the voice of experience at a rancorous family meeting. "You are correct, Lieutenant Commander Shaath, that I know very well and profoundly appreciate the value of service and experience, perhaps more than anyone else at this table." He turned to the other Rashidian skipper. "Please make no mistake, Commander Hajjam, I respect greatly your experience and abilities and know very well what an asset you are to any fighting force fortunate enough to have you with them." Hajjam nodded his thanks.

"But," Anderssen continued, speaking more forcefully as he went, "this I know equally well. The experience that matters in a real battle is measured not in years on the command roster but in minutes of commanding a ship in actual combat. Further, in war, nothing speaks more loudly than victory. Lieutenant Commander Robichaux has a record of victories that . . ."

"I know something of these *victories*," Hajjam spat, earning looks of rapidly concealed anger from the other Rashidian officers for the rudeness of interrupting a respected senior officer. "Mere flukes, wild strokes of good fortune resulting from insane gambles that inexplicably paid off. Robichaux took insane chances, for which the consequences have not yet come due. I grant you that in the past, fate has tilted the scales to Robichaux's advantage. But, gentlemen, remember that while fate is a powerful ally, she is also a fickle one. She will withdraw her favor, the scales will balance, and the cosmos will inevitably collect its due from our reckless young officer. I will not let it take my ship in payment of this man's debt."

The Pfelung commander moved his forefins up and down slowly to indicate that he wished to have everyone's attention. "I have not served under Robichaux. But most of the fighters under my command have. They have complete confidence in him." He seemed about to say something more when the hologram of Brakmor-Ent interrupted.

"Human! Life in the dry air has dehydrated your brain if you believe we will follow you instead of Robichaux." The Rashidians recoiled in anger at the young Pfelung's provocative statement. Hajjam reflexively reached for his sword before willing his hands to rest on the table. Oblivious to this reaction, Brakmor-Ent continued. "My fighters and I swim the dark waters of space for one reason: to serve the Krag as a meal to the bottom-feeding worms. With Robichaux we have sent many Krag to be devoured by slithering creatures that feast on rotting flesh, and with him we know we can send many more to the same place. As for you, Hajjam, we have never fought beside you, but we know that you have little battle experience and even less in combat with the Krag. The worms that wait for what you send are few, lean, and hungry. We will not follow you. We will follow Robichaux. We have heard all we have to hear and said all we have to say about who shall be leader. We are now bored with the subject. Until we are ready to speak of how Robichaux will lead us in the fun of killing Krag with nuclear weapons, I am terminating the audio channel."

The transducers fell silent as the dolphinlike adolescent's hologram turned its tail to Hajjam and defecated.

"We Pfelung are a direct race. Tact is not one of our strengths. Our adolescents are even less tactful than our adults," the older Pfelung added. "For my young comrade's lack of tact, I apologize. But he also speaks truth, and for that I have no apology. The truth here is simple. Robichaux is the rightful commander. He is the proper commander. Therefore, we will follow no one else. When we discuss how Robichaux will lead us, I will listen. Until then, listening is pointless. I withdraw my organs of hearing."

He squinted for a moment, pulling his eardrums—pink disks in the middle of his gills, about the diameter of a hamburger, two on each side—completely inside his head and sealing the opening into which they vanished with a bony flap. Max suspected that the Pfelung were able to do this to protect their eardrums from being damaged in a fight or from loud sounds underwater.

Hajjam came to his feet. "This is outrageous. As the senior officer present, I'm giving you a direct order, Robichaux. Acknowledge my authority or face consequences that I do not believe you are prepared even to contemplate, much less experience. I have no compunction about placing you under arrest and confining you in the brig until you submit to my authority."

Max didn't budge. He didn't say a word. He didn't even blink.

"Then on your head be it, Robichaux." Hajjam keyed open an intercom circuit. "Marine detachment, send a four-man detail to the Wardroom."

"Belay that order!" Heads snapped around to face the source of those words at the back of the compartment where Prince Khalid had sat, sipping his coffee, almost forgotten.

"This absurd dispute has gone on quite long enough," the prince said quietly but in a manner that brooked no discussion. He was looking squarely at Hajjam. "Until now I have refrained from interposing myself into this *discussion*—to use the term charitably—because I had an apparently misplaced faith that the supposedly mature officers assembled here would find a way to resolve the matter at hand in an amicable and effective manner. It appears, however, that my faith was misplaced. Accordingly, it is my duty to settle the issue.

"I made something of a joke a few minutes ago when listing some of my offices in our government by also listing some of the positions held by Gilbert and Sullivan's fictitious Pooh-Bah character in the government of the town of Titipu. The offices of

Master of the Rolls and Groom of the Second Floor Front were Pooh-Bah's." He paused. "Minister of Defense, however, was mine. Because I detest the kind of meddling that is sometimes known as *micromanagement*, our field commanders almost never receive orders from me. Nevertheless, my authority over our armed forces is second only to that of the king, and I retain the authority to give orders on even the most inconsequential of subjects to even the lowest-ranking man in our service. I certainly have the authority to order you, Commander Hajjam, to take whatever action relative to this issue that I see fit.

"And because of the larger policy implications of this matter, particularly for our diplomatic relations with the Union, a matter that falls within my purview as Foreign Minister as well, I would have ample justification for exercising that authority in a definitive manner today," the prince said evenly. "You gentlemen certainly provided me with an excellent factual and logical basis for making such a decision. I listened with interest to your words, Commander Hajjam, and found myself in agreement with much of what you had to say. You *are* an experienced warship commander with a sterling record—of that there is no doubt. This fact stands in stark contrast with Lieutenant Commander Robichaux's dossier, which reveals him as comparatively inexperienced, very young, and possessing a record that is troubling in many respects. Of course, you hold the higher rank. Further, your command record is uniformly reflective of sobriety and responsibility, while Robichaux's is full of extreme risks and long shots.

"Undoubtedly, the string of victories enjoyed by Robichaux owes at least some of its existence to luck, good fortune, or whatever one chooses to call the reckoning of the pips when the cosmos casts its dice." The prince paused, took a sip from his coffee cup, and continued solemnly, "I have little doubt that you are correct: someday the cosmos will come calling and collect its due.

Seemingly, only a man who is similarly disposed to take enormous risks and to *bet on long shots* would place young Robichaux in command of the coming operation.

"And while *I* am most assuredly *not* such a man," the prince said, "the same cannot be said of Vice Admiral Louis G. Hornmeyer, the Supreme Commander of the Associated Power forces in this theater of operations. He bets on long shots with great frequency, and he usually wins. His record of success, in fact, is unequaled in this war. The admiral is generally accounted as an operational genius and is regarded by many as one of the greatest commanders in the history of interstellar warfare. One cannot attribute such a record merely to luck or to superiority in training and matériel.

"Our staff analysis of Admiral Hornmeyer's command technique suggests that part of his success lies in an almost uncanny genius for matching the right commander to the right assignment—for placing leaders in situations that harmonize with their unique set of strengths and weaknesses. In this case the admiral made a considered decision to place Robichaux in command in preference to Commander Hajjam. Admiral Hornmeyer is very well acquainted with Lieutenant Commander Robichaux's unusual *tactics and methodologies* and may have well counted on them in order to make this mission successful. These are, therefore, circumstances that weigh with particular gravity in favor of deferring to the admiral's judgment regarding who should command here.

"Further, and I do not wish to make too much a matter of this, even though I regard it as an issue of preeminent importance, there is the issue of the honor of the king. The king has on at least two separate occasions transmitted diplomatic communiqués to the appropriate Union representatives stating that the Kingdom will abide by the Four Power Joint Forces Agreement and pledging his best efforts to ensure that our commanders will abide by its terms, particularly those provisions relating to command and control of joint forces. Therefore, as a representative of the king and, indeed, as one empowered to speak for the king in these matters, I could never stand by and allow the king's honor to be sullied by violation of his solemn word.

"So, I could easily give the appropriate order and place Lieutenant Commander Robichaux at the head of this task force and would never be gainsaid by anyone whose opinion in the matter carries any weight. But the avoidance of criticism has never been the star by which I navigate, and such an act would be decidedly unsubtle. Indeed, as with most unsubtle acts, it would bring about a host of undesirable consequences. The commander's log of today's events would reflect that he assumed command of the task force only to be relieved on my order. My report to the king would have to reflect that the commander exceeded his authority and that I had to relieve him. There would, at the very least, be a formal inquiry into these events, which would very likely have the most regrettable effects upon the commander's career. Given that Commander Hajjam is, by all accounts, a highly capable and exceptionally promising officer—one almost certainly destined for higher commands—such an outcome would be most unfortunate."

He sighed with exaggerated regret. "And in the interest of brevity, I will eschew a lengthy description of the distinctly untoward diplomatic consequences for the relationship between the Kingdom and the Union should it become widely known that a Rashidian officer assumed command of joint forces in violation of the terms of a solemnly entered cooperation-of-forces agreement." His head shook, giving every impression of great sadness. One could almost hear him "tsk"ing. "'Tis a consummation greatly to be avoided."

The prince sat back in his chair and steepled his fingers. The pose would have looked relaxed in any other man, but Prince Khalid appeared to be anything but relaxed. He met the eyes of every man in the room, measuring their feelings, their thoughts, their wills. He saw an opening to get what he wanted and stepped calmly but directly into the breach. He touched the table in front of him, converting the surface into a terminal keyboard, and entered a short series of commands. The large display wall on one side of the compartment divided into three subdisplays, one of which contained a static table of Max's combat record: engagements, enemy vessels destroyed, enemy vessels taken, total tonnage taken or destroyed, cargo captured, and so on. The other two displays showed animated diagrams of some engagements in which the *Cumberland* had fought: the Battle of Pfelung, the Battle of Rashid VB, the battle in which the *Cumberland* escaped a Lehrer-Lobachevsky Hexagon and sliced through the upper layers of a star to lure another warship to its death, and others. The symbols on the displays, each of which represented real machines filled with real thinking beings, swooped and maneuvered in a ballet without music, telling in abstract how thousands of men and Krag desperately fought and bravely died. Commander Hajjam squinted hard at the wordless narrative, jaw clenching and unclenching, his agile and tactically adept mind rapidly processing everything he saw as he watched the battles play out in accelerated time, occasionally smiling with grudging approbation, shaking his head with stern disapproval, or raising his eyebrows with stark disbelief.

After a few minutes, the man Max continued to think of as Ellington Wortham-Biggs began to speak again. "Commander Hajjam has asserted command over this task force—that action has already been officially logged. As any navy man—Union, Rashidian, Romanovan, Texian, or Ghiftee—knows, logs are sacred writ. No one may change so much as a single letter of them once entered.

The Moving Finger writes; and, having writ,
Moves on: nor all your Piety nor Wit
Shall lure it back to cancel half a Line,
Nor all your Tears wash out a Word of it."

"English?" It was the first word Max had spoken in several minutes.

Khalid smiled ironically. "Perhaps." At Max's plain but quickly concealed irritation at being given an evasive answer, the prince continued, "It is a more complex issue than one would think. The quote is from *The Rubaiyat of Omar Khayyam*, which is styled as a translation into English by the British writer Edward Fitzgerald of a series of poems written circa 1100 CE. It is, however, a question of much debate as to how much of *Omar Khayyam* is actually Omar Khayyam and how much is Edward Fitzgerald. It is, notwithstanding the rancor of the academic disputation, a beautiful and profound work." He was about to say more on the subject, but stopped himself. "Alas, my good Robichaux, that is a discussion for another time.

"Back to the matter at hand. We must remember that an event in the past, no matter how immutable, can take on many different aspects, depending on the light cast upon it by the future. And the future, gentlemen, is ours to shape." He looked at the faces around the table and continued in an earnest, quiet voice.

"Indeed, we are shaping it now. Bearing in mind the highly unfortunate consequences I described a few moments ago, I ask that you consider a set of vastly different outcomes that will come to pass if we only nudge the future very slightly in a more favorable direction. Let us suppose that we explain what has already transpired by reminding the king and Admiral Hornmeyer—truthfully,

I might add—that Commander Hajjam's current security clearance does not give him access to Union after-action reports, leaving him to rely on second- and thirdhand reports of reports of the *Cumberland*'s recent engagements. Unfortunately for everyone concerned, those reports so exaggerated Lieutenant Commander Robichaux's aggressiveness and pugnaciousness that Commander Hajjam concluded that Robichaux was dangerously reckless to such an extent that putting him in command of the task force would lead to disaster. Accordingly, he sought to take command.

"Let us suppose further that all of the relevant logs and reports state with firm unanimity that Commander Hajjam—who, like all good officers, is perfectly willing to conform his theories to the evidence—reviewed with interest full and accurate reports of Robichaux's exploits as captain of the *Cumberland*. The logs would go on to say that review of those reports, combined with his personal impression of Lieutenant Commander Robichaux's mature and officer-like demeanor, persuaded the commander that he was in error. At that point he took the inevitable action, again clearly and unanimously described in the logs, of stepping aside in favor of Robichaux." He looked pointedly at Hajjam. "With apologies."

He stood and walked over to the two-meter-long viewport set in the port bulkhead of the compartment that Commander Hajjam had ordered be unshuttered, even though the ship was in enemy space. Because the prince had dimmed the lights to enable the commander to have a better view of the data on the displays, the stars were brilliantly visible—the Sagittarius Arm of the Milky Way galaxy and, beyond it, the lambent swath of the galactic core that, because there had been no reason to align the plane of the ship's decks with that of the galaxy, cut across the viewport at an acute diagonal. That way lay the Vaaach Sovereignty, the Sarthan Collegium, the Tri-Nin Matriarchy, and untold numbers of other races with whom humankind had not yet made contact. At more than 100,000 light-years across, the galaxy wasn't infinite, but it was mind-numbingly huge.

The prince resumed speaking, framed by the galactic vista behind him. "How much more felicitous would be the results of this course of events! Spacers of the Kingdom and of the Union, as well as those of the Pfelung, would fight side by side in the belief that the leaders of the task force are in harmony with one another. Commander Hajjam would make the best possible impression upon both subordinates and superiors—so concerned about his men and the mission that he was willing to stick his neck out when he felt their safety was threatened, yet so unselfish, reasonable, and open to persuasion that he graciously yielded in the face of contrary evidence. Interstellar cooperation is advanced, the Four Power Association is strengthened, and we cheerfully march forward together to kill the Krag in ever-greater numbers. All because Commander Hajjam stepped aside voluntarily rather than after having been ordered to do so."

The prince then turned to Hajjam. "So, Commander, what is your decision? You needn't make it immediately, you know." He glanced at the chrono on the bulkhead. "Anytime in the next sixty to ninety seconds would be quite sufficient." He turned to look out the viewport, sipping his coffee.

It didn't take ninety seconds. It didn't even take sixty. Whatever his occasional displays of ambition and stubbornness, Hajjam knew another aggressive and skillful combat leader when he saw one. He also knew that to persist in the course of action he had chosen would bring him in conflict with the prince and the king, which was always a bad idea. His always powerful pride was in conflict with his similarly powerful intellect. Intellect won. Barely.

He knew what he must do, but that knowledge didn't make it easy. Hajjam rose. He bowed first to the prince and then to Robichaux, after which he drew his sword and laid it on the table in front of Max. "My sword is at your disposal, sir. What is your command?"

Dr. Sahin had taught Max well. He rose, bowed to the prince and to Hajjam, and drew his own sword, placing it on top of Hajjam's with the blades crossing at right angles to one another. "I accept your sword, Commander, and have these three commands for you. First, that you shake my hand and know that you and I are fully reconciled as brothers who have disagreed but who are forever bound together by blood and honor." The two men shook hands warmly. "Second, that you serve as the group's deputy commander." Hajjam nodded his assent. Max picked up his sword and sheathed it. He then picked up Hajjam's sword, grasping the blade just below the handguard, and handed it to the commander hilt-first.

"And, third, that you receive your sword and bear it into battle against our enemies. May our blades shine together in victory!"

CHAPTER 10

6.85 Daytenths, Day 202, 18th Greening, Reign of the 11th Hegemon, 8th Dynasty, Post-Unification Era
(Union Calendar: 09:52 Zulu Hours, 15 May 2315)

Tap-tap. Tap-tap. The Warlike Commander of Military Operations for Sector 782-88585 heard two taps of a standard naval-issue steel tail-cap on the steel deck, a pause, and two more taps. The sound meant that a being of inferior rank—a category that included everyone within a radius of approximately forty-three light-years—was requesting his attention as required by ancient military protocol. After waiting for a pair of heartbeats, he slowly rotated the stool on which he was sitting to face the source of the sound: his Fleet Communications Officer, clearly bearing important news.

"Approach," he said, the squeaks and chitters of his speech uttered in the low-pitched monotone that signaled the degree of bored condescension appropriate to the disparity in their ranks. In response to the invitation, the officer stepped across the invisible but well-defined boundary that separated the portion of the Command Nest where officers and crew performed their duties from the portion reserved for the Warlike Commander, his private work or contemplations, and the privileged few invited into his august presence. He stopped just over a meter and a half from the commander and bowed until his wet, black nose pressed into a tiny indentation in the deck placed there for exactly that purpose. After a pause of three heartbeats, the commander dropped his own nose just slightly, acknowledging the display of submission and asserting his own dominance. The Communications Officer responded by smartly snapping to the appropriate posture of an inferior reporting to an officer of much higher rank: toes pointed out at forty-five-degree angles, knees slightly bent, palms forward, shoulders slightly hunched, eyes on the floor directly in front of the superior's feet. "Report," the commander ordered in the same bored monotone.

"Warlike Commander, we have just received a signal from Naval Materiel Transport 898-253."

The commander quickly pulled up the summary squib on that ship from the database. Naval Materiel Transport 898-253 was a captured Union fast tender, *Clarence Birdseye* class, currently traversing Sector 7-8-5 of his command's Outer Defense Perimeter on its way to Repair and Refit Base 446.

"And, pray tell, what does Transport 898-253 have to say that is of such tail-crimping importance?"

"Warlike Commander, the transport's commander reports that his vessel has been stalked by a Pfelung Reconnaissance Fighter for three daytenths. The captain of that vessel is of the opinion that the Recon Fighter would not have followed for that long unless it had summoned a force of Pfelung Combat Fighters and was guiding them to an intercept. He expects to be attacked at any moment and requests assistance."

The commander directed his attention to his neural interface, a splendid piece of his race's superior technology that tied his highly evolved brain directly to the main computer of his battlecruiser, and accessed the detailed record on the transport. Within less than a second, he knew that registry number belonged to a vessel listed as assigned to this theater of operations and that it had recently carried a load of missiles and replacement sensor arrays to Class Five Refit and Repair Laager 53 in Sector 553893, adjacent to the Forward Edge of Battle Area. The database contained no report of the ship departing the Laager and heading back toward the Core Systems, but given the exigencies of wartime, reports of that kind often lagged many days behind the event. Nothing was amiss. With the enormous attrition imposed on transports by enemy destroyers, such a vessel, even empty, was worthy of protection, notwithstanding that doing so would deprive the installation he commanded of most of its fighter defenses.

No matter. He had enough larger ships to repel anything the feeble humans and their ludicrous allies were likely to be able to throw at him.

"Dispatch the entire fighter squadron to rendezvous with the transport, but retain for our defense the fighter hand that is currently on combat-area patrol and the hand currently assigned as their reserve. The forty fighters comprising the other eight hands should be sufficient to fend off the one or two Pfelungian fighter hands typically assigned to a single recon vessel."

"As ordered, Warlike Commander. I will transmit the message immediately."

"See that you do." With an indolent wave of his left hand, the commander indicated that unless the Communications Officer had anything further, he should initiate the formalities that would end the interview. The young officer briefly touched his nose to the same spot on the floor as before and stood back up while the commander nodded his nose in two quick bobs, indicating the inferior's dismissal. He left.

Through the neural interface, the commander monitored the outgoing comm signals by which Fighter Control ordered the fighters to the transport's aid. After observing with satisfaction how quickly the fighters launched from their mobile hangar; formed into hands; grouped the hands into a large, tight formation; and burned toward the transport on afterfusers, he turned his attention to other matters. It never occurred to him to transmit a message to the fighters complimenting them on their performance. He was a busy being, and his cheek pouches were stuffed full of responsibilities.

So many responsibilities, in fact, that he had not noticed the passage of more than a daytenth when he once again heard his attention being requested. Turning toward the tapping sound with the same deliberate delay as before, he saw the same Communications Officer, this time in what was obviously a state of some distress. As much as he enjoyed the discomfiture of his subordinate, the commander was also concerned. What had happened?

"Approach." The appropriate rituals were completed. "Report."

"Warlike Commander, we have lost contact with the fighter squadron."

He bared his teeth and lowered his ears, an expression of condescending disbelief, the way a parent looks at a youngling lying about having his snout in the candied seed jar. "You mean you have lost contact with *elements of* the fighter squadron."

"With respects, Commander," the Communications Officer sputtered, forgetting the "Warlike," "that is not my intended meaning. We have lost contact with the entire squadron. The squadron commander's regular report is two hundred standard heartbeats overdue, and we have been unable to establish communications with either him or any of the hand leaders."

"Then try to open a channel with one of the nonleader fighters." The commander affected a tone of elaborate patience. "Try each of them individually. Put your entire section on it, and use every available transmitter instead of waiting for one communications operator to try all of the thirty-two remaining ships in sequence. Do I have to think of everything myself?" He clicked his incisors together in irritation, a holdover from his distant ancestors' instinct of biting anything that threatened them, akin to a human reflexively clenching a fist in anger. "I expect a report within one segment," he added, as though speaking to a youngling of roughly six greenings. "One segment. That's a tenth of a day-tenth. Don't be late."

"As ordered, Warlike Commander." The rituals of dismissal completed, the Communications Officer skittered away to do his commander's bidding, tail pressed defensively to his left side as he left, a reflex evolved to keep the tail from being bitten off.

"It is probably nothing," the commander said to himself. "Just some sort of communications system malfunction." Engineers were always tinkering and upgrading systems that worked perfectly well in the first place, occasionally with questionable reliability. "Wartime is not the time for experimentation," he muttered. "It is time to hold to that which is tried-and-true and proven." Still, something in the commander's nose wanted to twitch. Instinctively he sensed a cat nearby. A big one. He would take immediate precautions because, as the old saying went, "Better to dart into a hole a hundred times without need than to be eaten once without heed."

He used his neural interface to open a voice channel to his Fleet Operations Officer, who answered with reassuring promptness. "I am transmitting to you the projected coordinates of a rendezvous that was supposed to take place between the fighter squadron and a transport. Dispatch Destroyers 43-5325 and 43-6872 to that location. Their orders are to conduct a remote reconnaissance, observation protocol five, and report the results directly to me. Specifically remind the captains that protocol five requires that they avoid any engagement and that delivery of complete and accurate tactical information is their only priority. No matter how tempting the target, they are not, repeat NOT, to engage. If the enemy engages them, they are to evade, escape, and report. Is that clear?"

"Perfectly clear, Warlike Commander. I will transmit the orders immediately."

"And further direct the captains that I want progress reports from each of them—not just the senior of the two—every thousand standard heartbeats. Tell them that if any report is so much as two heartbeats late, I will have their tails in my soup." Unlike many officers of his rank, the commander had never actually dined on an errant subordinate's tail, but the destroyer captains did not need to know that. After all, there was a recipe for Miscreant Tail Soup in the database, and it was reputed to be quite delicious.

"I will include that in the orders. Is there anything further, Warlike Commander?"

"Nothing further. Proceed." He closed the circuit with a mental command.

The commander was pleased to observe that, within a hundred heartbeats, the pair of destroyers was accelerating hard in the direction in which the fighters had disappeared. Naturally he communicated this pleasure to no one, but returned to the daunting task of completing the setup of the installation under his command, one critical to the conduct of the current war.

He was pleased with his role in his race's great holy war against the humans. The Hegemonic Naval Forces of the Sovereign and Supreme Viceroys of Creation, known to humans as the "Krag" (a ludicrous name that was simply a mangled rendition of the sound his species made at the beginning of each communication to attract the attention of the listener) had recently defeated their secondary enemy, the Thark. Two massive strike forces that had been assembled in the heart of the Hegemony to be used on that front had been retasked and were now just inside the space controlled by the Hegemony, poised to attack the humans. Soon they would be joined by hundreds of ships that had been fighting the Thark and that were at that very moment streaming across more than 2000 light-years of space from that theater of operations to this one.

Because the shortest route between the two battlefronts stretched through a thinly settled and resource-poor region more than eight hundred light-years from the Hegemony's core worlds, the Central Command Nexus had decided not to provide the vessels making the transit with resupply beyond that necessary to get them from one battle zone to the other. Accordingly, they arrived depleted of fuel, food, and munitions, as well as, in many cases, requiring substantial repair and refit.

The commander's installation, given the simple name "Naval Field Readiness Station #252" (a much more impressive title in the Krag language) was one of two created to fill that need, 251 previous stations having been created at other times during this and previous wars, then dismantled when no longer needed. Located at the L4 Lagrange point in the orbit of a gas giant planet, the installation consisted of a large repair and refurbishment station, a battle station, an enormous fuel dump, and an equally enormous cargo transfer hub. Plus, 5000 standard linear units from the rest of the facility, there were two vast cargo supply and munitions dumps, each of which consisted of literally millions of cargo containers orbiting a low-power artificial gravity source in a ring that was as thick as a small continent, the diameter of a small moon, and too large to be destroyed easily.

These dumps were the facility's most valuable asset. Each neatly orbiting ring of containers contained war matériel equal to roughly a fifth of the Hegemony's total industrial output for an entire year. In preparation for a decisive push against the humans, the Krag had been accumulating these supplies since the sixth year of the war. They contained no single item that was difficult to obtain or unique. But in terms of quantity and ready availability, what these dumps contained was irreplaceable.

The commander's facility would service roughly half of the forces being transferred, those destined to be sent into battle against Admiral Hornmeyer's Task Force, with the half going into battle against Admiral Middleton's forces routed to Naval Field Readiness Station #253, roughly 350 light-years rimward.

The commander focused on the next issue requiring his attention. It was just the kind of matter at which he excelled: unsnarling a nasty bit of confusion over the traffic patterns and docking priority for three hands of deuterium heavy tankers, whose cargoes would soon refuel carriers and battleships and cruisers headed to battle with the humans. Fifteen tankers, comprising nearly all of a hundredday's deuterium production of three major separation facilities, were now lined up, waiting to have their bulky tanks detached by tugs and attached to one of the facility's four bulk pumping stations, where their contents would be used to fill the bunkers of warships headed for the front.

He affixed his electronic signature to another order. He cringed inwardly every time he used his name: "Spits Out Bitter Roots." He hated it, even though it was much shorter and more euphonious in his own language than in Standard. Scarcely a day-tenth passed in which he didn't wish he could leave his litter name behind and earn, by a decisive victory over a force of equal or greater strength, a name of triumph like "Victoriously Attacked when His Executive Officer Begged Him to Retreat" or "Surprised and Destroyed Many Cruisers Near a Neutron Star." Perhaps then he could eradicate the shame he and his littermates carried because his officer father perished and went to the Desiccators still bearing the name "Urinates When Startled."

The Commander solved the tanker problem with a series of bitingly sarcastic communications to the tanker captains instructing them in the proper interval and relative positions to maintain while in a holding pattern, thereby addressing almost by accident the real underlying problem: confusion between the captains regarding which of the three sets of navigation rules that might apply was appropriate under the present circumstances. The Commander then proceeded to issue minutely detailed instructions on how to rectify a series of errors in the placement of early-warning sensors. The arrangement in place at that moment would work perfectly, but still deviated from the established protocol and must, therefore, be corrected.

In the middle of that painstaking exercise, an attention signal directed through his neural interface broke his concentration. Because, under naval custom, only the most urgent matters came in that manner instead of through the ancient rituals of reporting, he opened the channel with no small measure of alarm.

"This is the Commander. You may speak."

"Warlike Commander, this is Communications."

"Proceed."

"We have been unsuccessful in contacting the fighters. We tried to raise each fighter individually, making three separate attempts, fifty heartbeats apart, on each fighter's primary, secondary, tertiary, and emergency frequencies. Further, it is with extreme regret that I report that contact reports from both Destroyers are one hundred standard heartbeats overdue. We are attempting to contact both ships, but without any success so far."

Cat. The Commander definitely smelled a very large cat. He knew about large cats. On his species' homeworld, there were cats the size of Earth buffalo capable of killing any animal on the planet. The evolutionary pressure created by the predations of such creatures was one of the reasons his race became bipedal, and then developed high intelligence, toolmaking, and weaponry. It wasn't until they invented high-powered repeating rifles that his people had any effective defense against these huge, ravening animals other than cowering behind high walls and thick, barred doors when they were known to be on the prowl. To this very day, a loaded rifle was part of any mature male's civilian attire—these days more a symbol of his adulthood and readiness to deal with danger than a weapon for his actual defense.

"Very well. Continue your efforts to contact all the missing vessels and report any positive results to me promptly. Commander out." He used his interface to open another voice channel.

"Fleet Operations."

"Operations, this is the commander. Order the entire command to Alert Condition Two. Launch the reserve fighter hand and order them to their standard picket positions. As soon as that is accomplished, have the combat area patrol fighters refueled in flight and pull them back to the Inner Defense Perimeter. Make sure all fighters are carrying a full combat load of antiship ordnance."

"Immediately, Warlike Commander."

The commander closed the circuit and stepped briskly from the Commander's Retreat to the Commander's Battle Niche. The computer detected his presence and activated the appropriate displays. He turned to the Systems Controller, a senior noncommissioned officer. "Bring all maneuvering and combat systems to full readiness." As his vigilant second-in-command, working from the Auxiliary Command Nest located in a distant part of the ship, had been closely monitoring the communications regarding the fighters and the destroyers, the key systems were already preenergized and ready to be called into action. In fewer than a hundred heartbeats, a series of octagons in the lower right corner of his display changed from red, to orange, to green, to blue, and finally to violet, indicating that the systems in question were ready. "Running Officer, take us to the ninth prepared defense position. High-Acceleration Profile."

"As ordered, Warlike Commander," the Running Officer replied. He slipped his hands into the interface gloves that allowed him to maneuver the ship. Two taps of his left foot converted the left glove into a controller for the maneuvering thrusters. Four tiny motions of his hand caused four short puffs from the huge vessel's thrusters to push it away from its moorings. When he had sufficient clearance, another tap changed the left glove into a controller for the main sublight drive, which he activated at a low setting, while his right hand manipulated a virtual trackball, manifesting in the nondigital realm by means of a three-dimensional projection in front of him and through tactile feedback pressure actuators in the glove. He rolled the ball, roughly the apparent size of a grapefruit (for which there was a counterpart on his world, visually almost identical but considerably less tart) that appeared to float in the air in front of him. Its digitally stabilized and smoothed movements directed by his gloved hand, he used it to steer the vessel through a gradual turn that pointed its bow in the direction of Prepared Defense Position Nine. Once he aligned the ship's bow with the destination, he ran the drive up to its rated maximum. The commander was clearly in a hurry. There were only two higher drive settings—what someone in the Union Space Navy would call "Flank" and "Emergency."

"Vessel is under way, Warlike Commander."

"Report acknowledged," the commander said blandly, privately noting the Running Officer's skill without acknowledging it. "Communications, signal the other vessels of the defense detachment to rendezvous with us at the ninth prepared defense position. Order each ship to depart as soon as it is able. They are not to wait to travel in company. Have each of them individually acknowledge the order and their understanding of the need for immediate departure."

"Immediately, Warlike Commander."

The commander used his neural interface to monitor the transmissions. He attached electronic flags to them, telling the Communications Officer to dispense with the standard formality of verbally notifying him when the responses arrived. It never occurred to him that the verbal announcement audible to everyone in the Command Nest was of benefit to the other officers not privileged to have a neural interface implanted in their skull, which was everyone except himself, the Executive Officer, and the Operations Officer. It was not his habit to consider what others needed to know and how they would come to know it, even though this kind of information, if announced verbally, would help everyone in the Command Nest maintain their situational awareness.

A few moments later, the acknowledgments arrived. Shortly thereafter, the first ship set out. "Communications, signal the Sector Commander. Inform him that we have likely lost the bulk of our fighter squadron and two of our destroyers to enemy action. Request that they be replaced immediately. Mark the message Urgent."

"As you wish, Warlike Commander," responded the Communications Officer.

He twitched his whiskers, four quick back-and-forth motions: his people's equivalent of a smile. Yes, the humans had managed to carry away a few seeds from his winter hoard. They had lured his fighter squadron into some kind of trap and somehow destroyed it, and then managed to do the same to two destroyers. No matter. They would be replaced within days.

Whatever success it had enjoyed against those light forces, the enemy lurking beyond the range of the commander's sensors would have a harder time dealing with a Type 34 heavy battlecruiser, two light cruisers, and a destroyer, particularly when those vessels were operating in cooperation with a medium battle station. He opened a channel.

"Communications, this is the commander. Alert the battle station at the ninth prepared defensive position to our impending arrival. Instruct the commander to go to Alert Condition Two, Rules of Engagement Orange. Remind him that under Orange Rules, he is to take any and all measures consistent with the safety of his command. If he finds himself under actual or imminent attack, he is to fire on the enemy without awaiting authorization from me. Obtain an acknowledgment of the signal, and have him acknowledge his understanding of that point specifically."

"Immediately, Warlike Commander." He began to implement the order and stopped short. "Warlike Commander," the Communications Officer announced with joy in his voice, "we just received a communication from Destroyer 43-5325." He paused for a moment. "Authenticating." Pause, a few heartbeats. "Sender identification code is valid, and the encryption is correct for today's date. Referring it to your interface now."

"Very well. Do not forget to signal the battle station as I ordered."

"Understood. It will be done immediately."

"See that it is," he said haughtily. The commander accessed the incoming message.

FROM: EATS SMALL SEEDS FIRST, OFFICER GRADE 14, COMMANDER, DESTROYER 43-5325

TO: SPITS OUT BITTER ROOTS, OFFICER GRADE 23, COMMANDER, FORCES AND AREAS AS CODED

DATE/TIME: AS CODED

THIS FORCE AMBUSHED BY MIXED FORCE OF PFELUNG FIGHTERS AND VARIOUS OTHER ENEMY VESSEL TYPES. DESTROYER 43-5325 SUSTAINED MODERATE DAMAGE. DESTROYER 43-6872 REGRETTABLY LOST WITH ALL HANDS TO ENEMY ACTION. ENEMY RECEIVED ONLY MINOR DAMAGE, DATA FILE TO FOLLOW. ENEMY FORCE LINGERED IN BATTLE AREA TO RESCUE FIGHTER CASUALTIES BUT IS EXPECTED TO PURSUE AT ANY MOMENT. NEITHER SPOOR NOR SCENT OF TRANSPORT DETECTED: PRESUMED TO BE DESTROYED BY ENEMY BEFORE OUR ARRIVAL. HAVE LOCATED AND AM IN COMPANY WITH INSTALLATION FIGHTER SQUADRON, CONSISTING OF ELEVEN OF THE ORIGINAL FORTY SHIPS. OTHERS LOST TO ENEMY ACTION. I HAVE ASSUMED TEMPORARY COMMAND OF REMAINING FIGHTERS AND AM RETURNING WITH THEM TO BASE. MESSAGE ENDS.

"Communications, are the sender's coordinates, course, and speed encoded in the message?"

"Affirmative, Warlike Commander."

"Have the tactical section calculate the destroyer's current position and transmit a tight-beam transponder interrogation pulse toward those coordinates. In fact, send two pulses. I want to make sure he is able to provide two correct responses to two different challenges."

"Immediately, Warlike Commander." Twenty or so heartbeats passed. "Valid transponder codes received. The signal characteristics are within acceptable parameters." Pause. "But, sir, there are some subtle but detectible variations from baseline norms in the electronic characteristics of the destroyer's signal."

"Could the variations be explained by damage to the sending vessel?"

"It is possible, Warlike Commander." His tone said, "possible, but unlikely."

Such subtleties were lost on the warlike commander. His tactical brilliance was such that he did not need to listen attentively to the nuances of communications from subordinates. "It must be damage then," the commander said dismissively. "In order to send a communication with a valid identification code as well as the correct encryption, and then to provide correct responses to two distinct transponder interrogations, the enemy would have had to capture one of our warship data cores intact, an event as unlikely as my giving birth in the next ten heartbeats to a litter of kittens."

Around the Command Nest, practically every set of ears perked up and wiggled slightly in amusement. Everyone knew the elaborate precautions that prevented such an event from taking place, including the system that reset every data bit in the memory core to zero at the press of a button or if a "dead switch" was not pressed every three hundred standard heartbeats. If for some inexplicable reason, those expedients failed, there was always a hybrid electromagnetic pulse–conventional explosive charge in the center of the memory core that would blow it to useless fragments and scramble every data bit at the turn of a key. The commander knew in the marrow of his being that not a single readable bit of a Hegemony warship memory core had ever been captured by any enemy and that none ever would.

"Communications, have we received the data file mentioned in the transmission?"

"We are receiving it now, Warlike Commander."

"As soon as it is received, transfer it directly to the primary database."

"As you wish, Warlike Commander." A few heartbeats later, after the ship's computer indicated that the file transfer was complete, the Communications Officer keyed in the commands that decompressed the file and copied it from the impressively firewalled and quarantined database used as a temporary holding place for incoming files and moved it into the ship's main database. As the file was coming in, the computer had scanned it for malicious code, line by line. Ordinarily, once the file was loaded, the Communications Officer would also direct the computer to perform an additional check. While keeping it sequestered from the ship's operating system, the computer would decompress the file, recompile it into the format in which the main database would store it, scan the file in its final form, and then subject the data to being used in several thousand simulated operating modes to determine whether any part of it posed a hazard in its new form. But since the file had been received directly from another warship rather than from a networked computer or a fixed installation, the file posed no conceivable risk to the ship, and in accordance with standard procedure, the Communications Officer omitted this step.

And at first, the reconstituted file behaved as would any other after-action report, sitting inert in the subdirectory of the database created to store reports of that kind. But after just over three thousand standard heartbeats, a period suspiciously coinciding with an interval known to the Hegemony's primary enemies as an "hour," a portion of the recompiled code quietly awakened, organized itself into an autonomous and executable bit of programming, found its way into an obscure bit of the ship's operating system, and then erased all traces of its previous existence. Over the next several minutes, the code busily spawned hundreds of copies that stealthily insinuated themselves into some of the more poorly protected software used by the battlecruiser to interpret sensor data and to manage various interfaces throughout the ship. Once rewritten, the now-malicious code distributed itself through the other ships commanded by the warlike commander as part of the standard fleet-wide data synchronization process.

Meanwhile, the calculated location of the destroyer and the fighters appeared in the 3D tactical projection. The commander quickly determined that the force was unlikely to be able to reach the limited protection of the installation's fighter cover and defensive outposts before the humans caught up with them. Standard tactical doctrine dictated that, under these circumstances, he concentrate his forces at the ninth prepared defensive position rather than divide them.

Like any sensible being, the commander always acted in accordance with doctrine.

"Communications, direct the destroyer and fighters to rendezvous with us and continue to make what repairs can be made. I want that destroyer as battle-ready as possible when the enemy arrives, which I expect to be very soon. Inform the captain that he is to remain in command of both his vessel and the fighters, that they are designated as the reserve combat force, and that he is to position his force one hundred thousand standard linear units to our rear. I may need them to harass the fleeing enemy once we break its formation."

The officer acknowledged his orders and moved swiftly to carry them out. On the tactical display, the commander watched as the other ships of his detachment left their moorings or patrol patterns for the rendezvous. The seeds were coming together quite nicely.

"Warlike Commander," said the Sensor Officer.

"Proceed."

"Distant mass detection, bearing eight-three-six break five-five-three. Preliminary indications are that the contact or contacts are at constant bearing, range decreasing. Bearing is consistent with calculated bearing of our destroyers and fighters."

"Communications, interrogate their transponders—the destroyer and all of the fighters. Two separate challenges to each, separated by fifteen standard heartbeats."

"As you order." The Communications Officer did as he was instructed. "New challenges sent and correct responses received." This time he did not mention anything about anomalies in the transmitter characteristics, even though they were present.

The commander should have been reassured. He was not. Something was making his tail curl. "Sensors, actively scan the destroyer, high-intensity, high-resolution. Paint it for as long as you need in order to be able to tell me without doubt that this is our ship."

"As you order, Warlike Commander." Nearly a hundred heartbeats passed. "Warlike Commander, the scans show one Type 43 destroyer, with mild to moderate damage."

"Are the scans of sufficient resolution to detect the internal structure, the power-flow patterns, the electromagnetic fields, the mass distribution, and other signature characteristics?"

"Affirmative, Warlike Commander. They are. Those characteristics match expected parameters in all respects."

The commander's tail, which had acquired an involuntary, nervous twitch, stopped its spasmodic movements. He had to be very careful not to rely on a general sensor profile for a positive identification. Some Union vessels had a sophisticated ability to mimic the sensor profile of friendly ships. Not only that; some of those ships were particularly deadly. He had just received an intelligence report that one such type, the *Khyber* class destroyers, not only had that capability, but tended to be under the command of the most aggressive and gifted young Union commanders and were being refit with a chin-mounted rotary missile launcher that allowed them to launch ten missiles in quick succession, in addition to the two in the fixed forward-mounted tubes. He very much wanted to keep that set of incisors away from his neck veins.

He could relax, though. No matter how effective the emulation emitters, it would be impossible to mimic a ship at that level of detail and fidelity without comprehensive intelligence of the kind he knew the humans did not possess. And because the Hegemony's fighters used a mixture of deuterium and tritium in their reactors, their higher energy output made them easily distinguishable from Union, Pfelung, or other enemy fighters, which used the more-abundant deuterium only. There was no way that an enemy fighter could pass itself off as Krag so long as the Krag sensors and the computers interpreting their output were in working order.

The destroyer and fighters arrived at their designated position and began to array themselves into one of the standard formations for tactical reserve forces. There was every indication from sensors that the destroyer's crew was busy implementing field repairs, as were the pilots of several of the fighters. Those vessels had evidently received more damage than he initially thought. For that reason and because they had recently been defeated in battle, the commander was even more strongly resolved to hold them in reserve. He expected to be able to destroy the enemy easily with the other forces under his command.

"Warlike Commander, there is an unidentified mass detection from Early-Warning Picket Buoy 22," the Sensors Officer announced. "Transferring readings to your board and to the Tactical Section."

"Understood. As soon as we get a detection from one of the other buoys, be sure to triangulate, and provide me with a set of rough coordinates," the commander ordered, essentially telling the Sensors Officer to follow the procedure that the tracking protocols dictated that he follow in any case.

"As you wish, Warlike Commander." The commander was oblivious to the resentful clicks of the young officer's teeth as he answered. Within a few moments, Early-Warning Buoy 37 also made a detection, allowing the contact to be localized and tracked.

"Identification challenge sent three times," the Communications Officer announced. "No response to challenge, and no return transponder pulse received."

"Classify contacts as hostile," the commander ordered.

"Enemy vessels are on direct course for this position," the Tactical Officer said. "Initial indications are that the enemy force is composed of one larger vessel and two smaller ones. Range is still too great to identify by type. The enemy force should be within weapons range in approximately one-half of a daytenth."

Weapons range. The enemy was already within range of weapons that the Hegemony had in its arsenal. But as a purely defensive command located far behind the front lines, the force the commander controlled had not been issued any of the new Type 965 long-range, superluminal missiles (Union reporting name: "Ridgeback"), which were in short supply throughout the theater. The force was armed with the older Type 961's (Union reporting name: "Foxhound"). The commander would have to hold his fire until the enemy was close enough to smell.

No matter. The enemy was coming right to him.

Spits Out Bitter Roots looked to the arrangement of his forces, which were arrayed in a plane perpendicular to the path of the approaching enemy force. Viewed from the enemy's perspective, the battle station was in the center, anchoring the defenses. In a line along what one could arbitrarily call the bottom of the formation, the center of which was 1000 standard linear units from the battle station and spaced 1000 standard linear units apart, were one of the light cruisers, the destroyer, and the second light cruiser. "Above" the battle station, separated from it by 1000 units, was the battlecruiser. In that way, a vessel attempting to go "under" would encounter both light cruisers and the destroyer, one going "over" would encounter the battlecruiser (equal in firepower to all three of the other ships), and one going around either "side" would encounter the battlecruiser and one or the other of the light cruisers. And if the enemy came straight in, he would face the fire of all. The ships and the battle station were able to provide supporting fire to each other and could direct overlapping fire against most plausible enemy-approach vectors.

"We have derived preliminary identifications of the enemy vessels, Warlike Commander," the Tactical Officer said. "The large vessel is a Type 2 Pfelung escort carrier. One of the smaller vessels is a Rashidian destroyer, Type 5, and the other is a class of vessel unique to them, known as a Zebec, roughly the size of a small destroyer but faster, less heavily armored, and armed differently—no pulse-cannon but a larger supply of missiles fired from a battery of nine missile tubes." The commander smiled. His force possessed five times the firepower of the attackers, perhaps more. This would be an easy victory.

The three enemy vessels approached the prepared defensive position as the Hegemony ships waited for them. Just outside of extreme missile range, the escort carrier disgorged nineteen fighters of a standard thirty-ship contingent. The commander surmised that the other eleven perished in battle with his own fighter squadron or the two destroyers. The carrier removed itself to a safe distance while the fighters formed into two groups of seven and one group of five. The groups, in turn, arranged themselves in a triangle, with the smaller group forming the apex and the two larger groups forming the base. The two Rashidian ships then fell in behind the fighters, and the whole formation began to accelerate toward the defenders.

"Enemy force is now within missile range, Warlike Commander," the Tactical Officer advised.

"Understood. Weapons, hold your fire," the commander ordered. "We will wait until they reach optimum range." If the warlike commander launched his missiles too soon, the enemy would have ample time to track and engage the weapons with its point-defense systems. Too close, and the weapons would not have time to accelerate to full attack speed.

"Holding fire," the Weapons Officer responded. Just outside optimum range, the formation turned to travel parallel to the plane of the Krag formation, moving toward the "top." The commander saw through the enemy ruse immediately. Obviously, the attackers believed that he would be reluctant to remove his ship from the cover of the battle station's protective fire. They were assuming that he would not move to engage them until he could be joined by the ships on the other side of the battle station. He would prove himself far braver than they believed.

"Running Officer, shape course to intercept the attacking formation, ahead flank. Fleet Operations, order the other ships in the formation to rendezvous with us as soon as they are able."

Shortly after receiving acknowledgments of his orders, the commander heard his ship accelerating and felt it pivot underneath his feet. Immediately after he committed his ship to an intercept course, the Pfelung fighters kicked in their afterfusers and began to accelerate much more rapidly, leaving the remaining enemy ships behind. The fighters were headed for the vulnerable tankers and fuel stores that his force was supposed to be defending, and there was no way the commander could catch them. He had, however, planned for that contingency.

"Operations, order the reserve fighter-combat force to intercept and engage the enemy fighters. Notify the combat-area patrol fighters that reserve combat force is being deployed against the enemy. When the combat-area patrol reaches the enemy, the reserve force should already have engaged them. Direct the patrol to hold their fire until they positively identify the enemy fighters. I want to be certain that we have no friendly-fire casualties in this engagement." He was going to earn his name of triumph today, and he wanted nothing to mar his achievement.

Operations gave the appropriate orders. The Pfelung fighter formation and the reserve force of his own fighters that had just returned from battle were on an intercept course with one another and would meet several hundred heartbeats before the combat-area patrol fighters joined the fight. That combination of the two fighter elements would be more than sufficient to pin down the Pfelung fighters as well as the Rashidian destroyer and Xebec, preventing them from destroying the vital facilities of Naval Field Readiness Station #252 until Spits Out Bitter Roots could get his larger ships into position to destroy them.

A blinking alert on his console notified him that his first officer wished to communicate by voice. He opened the channel. "Speak," he said, with no small amount of impatience.

"Warlike Commander," the first officer proceeded with a great deal of trepidation, "I wished only to remind you that we have no reliable intelligence on the capabilities and tactics of Pfelung fighters. Either no vessel of the Hegemony has ever encountered these vessels in combat, or no vessel that encountered them survived long enough to make a report of the engagement. We know very little about the Pfelung, their technology, their ways of warfare, their physiology, their culture, or anything else. A certain degree of caution would, therefore, be warranted in engaging them."

"We will discern the enemy's capabilities when we engage him. I'm not some trembling, pink runt of the litter to be frightened with fables of the Night Owl or the Black Cat. We will proceed as I have directed. If you think caution is warranted, I suggest you be particularly watchful and develop contingency plans to implement if the enemy shows himself to have capabilities we have not suspected." The commander closed the circuit with no small measure of irritation.

Irritation turned to satisfaction, however, as the commander watched his plan begin to come together. In just a few seconds, the fighters of the reserve force would engage the Pfelung fighters, forcing them to abandon their end-run attack in order to defend themselves. He used the neural interface to direct the tactical display to show the optimum firing range for the reserve force's Type 961 missiles. A yellowish-brown sphere appeared around the fighter formation, which appeared as a dot at the present scale.

In a few heartbeats, the enemy fighters—another dot—entered the sphere. He eagerly awaited the satisfaction of watching the Type 961 missiles blot the enemy from the display. And yet, the reserve fighters did not fire.

He waited. And waited. After a hundred heartbeats or so, his ears swiveled down and forward in an expression of extreme irritation as he opened a voice link. "Communications, signal the commander of the reserve force and ask why his formation has not fired on the enemy."

Half-listening to the inferior officer's acknowledgment of his order, the commander turned his attention back to the tactical display. He increased the scale so that he could see the icons representing individual ships in each formation. Now the formations were near enough to one another to use their projectile weapons, but they still did not fire.

"Warlike Commander, no response from the fighter commander," the Communications Officer said.

"Keep trying. Attempt to contact the hand leaders and the individual fighters if unsuccessful."

Something is seriously wrong.

Just as that thought formed and took root in his mind, the commander watched with incomprehension as the fighters did something wholly unexpected. The reserve group turned away from the Pfelung fighters and braked to allow the enemy formation to close. Much to the commander's surprise, the enemy did not fire, either. Instead, the enemy formation and the reserve-fighter formation merged. The new formation accelerated rapidly as the fighters of the reserve formation fell out of their attack-hand formation and joined with the Pfelung fighters in an apparently random swirling, darting, weaving movement that reminded the commander of a school of fish.

There was only one explanation for what he was seeing: somehow the enemy had managed to install a keyhole, a kind of limited back door that allowed them to transmit a specific instruction or limited set of instructions to the battlecruiser's computer. In this case someone was instructing the computer to display as friendly fighters a group of vessels that the raw sensor data would undoubtedly show to be hostile. There was a procedure for restoring the sensor-interpretation software from a protected backup file, but doing so required that the computers running the software be shut down and restarted, something that the commander was loath to do in the middle of a battle, particularly when he was confident about what the restored systems would show.

He watched as the swirling enemy-fighter formation accelerated at a rate that no known fighter could match, easily evading the combat-area patrol. There was only one hope for delaying the fighters long enough for the battlecruiser and other ships to catch them. "Fleet operations, advise all forces in the vicinity that all fighters in the area other than those attached to this facility are to be classified as hostile, notwithstanding sensor readings to the contrary. Direct destroyer 43-5325 to intercept and engage the fighters now crossing grid 133-454. Instruct the vessel's commander that he is to delay the fighters until relieved by other forces and to do so at all costs. To that end he is to consider his vessel and crew to be expendable."

Before the order could be acknowledged, the destroyer went into motion. It wasn't long, however, before it became apparent that the destroyer wasn't on an intercept course with the fighters but was headed directly toward the formation of tankers to which tugs had just finished attaching a maximum load of filled modular fuel tanks. It took the commander only a few seconds to derive an explanation for this apparently impossible development—destroyer 43-5325 had to be a Union *Khyber* class destroyer that had somehow come into possession of detailed operational data for the Hegemony's Type 43 destroyer in order to emulate it with sufficient accuracy to fool a detailed scan.

As the Union ship's acceleration curve bent into a range impossible for a Type 43 to attain, it dropped the pretense of being part of the Hegemony's navy, engaged its stealth systems, and disappeared from the battlecruiser's scans. At the same time, the Rashidian vessels veered away from their previous courses. A diversionary force, they would not engage the commander's warships. He watched as they engaged their compression drives and left the area at high lightspeed multiples.

He ordered his own vessels to change course toward the tankers that were still at the edge of the fuel dump, but knew his actions were in vain. He watched with increasing frustration as the Pfelung fighters spread out and worked their way through the huge field of thousands of modular fuel tanks, vaporizing them with some kind of directed energy weapon. The *Khyber* class destroyer, still not showing on sensors, nonetheless made its presence known by using its pulse-cannon to obliterate the facility's three large main fuel storage tanks, the cargo transfer hub, and the repair/refurbishment station. The tankers, observing the danger, powered up their drives and attempted to escape. The enemy destroyer, however, caught them easily and blew them to atoms in fewer than a hundred heartbeats.

As a parting gift, the humans' destroyer fired two extremely large, fast missiles, each aimed at the gravity generator for one of the cargo dumps. The commander smiled. A single warhead, even the 3.15-million explosive-yield unit (1.5 megaton) warhead on the Union's Raven missile would do little more than destroy the gravity generator and something like a quarter to a third of the supplies that orbited it. Tugs would simply chase down the remainder as they slowly drifted out of formation, and the commander would very shortly be back in the business of provisioning the Hegemony's warships.

The two missile warheads detonated within a heartbeat of each other. The commander was shocked at their brilliance. He had never seen a 3.15-million unit warhead detonate before, but he had seen smaller weapons. He expected something two or three times as bright as the other detonations he had witnessed, while this one was vastly brighter, so bright in fact that the automatic polarizers had stopped down the transparency of the viewport by several steps. He pulled up a yield analysis of the explosions.

The commander's tail hit the floor in shock and despair. The Union destroyer had not fired two Ravens. It had fired two Condors. The preliminary analysis was that the enemy warheads had a yield of more than 180 million explosive yield units. He quickly used the computer to confirm what his mental estimate had already told him: that a yield of anything more than 155 million units or so would destroy virtually all of the dump and propel any surviving cargo containers into a set of high-speed trajectories spreading radially away from the center of the explosion, where they would almost certainly never be located, much less caught and recovered.

The commander had presided over one of the greatest strategic disasters since the Hegemony had first reached out for the stars. Instead of a name of triumph, the commander was certain that he had today earned a name of disgrace. Henceforth, he would be known as something like "Allowed Enemy to Destroy Critical Materiel" or "Watched Humans Blow Up Supplies."

His shame would cling to him for the rest of his life and to his descendants for generations.

The enemy fighters then veered away from what was left of the Hegemony installation and headed back to their mini-carrier, with the Union destroyer in their wake. The commander noticed that his tail was lying limp on the deck, a sign of almost inconsolable grief and dejection. As he willed the wayward appendage into a more appropriate posture, he told himself that he would not need to worry about his tail for much longer, as the theater commander, Officer Grade 37 Rammed Enemy Battlecruiser, would almost certainly cook it into his soup.

"Warlike Commander, transmission in the clear from the enemy destroyer," the Communications Officer said.

"Display it."

The warlike commander didn't have to wait the twenty or thirty heartbeats it took for the computer to generate a translation. While incompatible vocal and hearing organs meant that virtually no members of his race could understand any human spoken language and no member could speak it, the commander was well educated and fluent in written Standard. He had no difficulty understanding the text that appeared on his display, except that he needed the computer to provide the meaning of the mysterious term "y'all."

TO COMMANDER HEGEMONY FORCES IN THIS AREA FROM COMMANDER UNION FORCE, I HOPE YOU ENJOYED

THIS LITTLE GIFT FROM TASK FORCE 88C, THE ROYAL RASHIDIAN SPACE NAVY, THE 16TH ELEMENT OF THE 332ND FIGHTER GROUP, PFELUNGIAN SPACE DEFENSE FORCE, AND THE USS CUMBERLAND, UNION SPACE NAVY. WE APPRECIATE YOUR WARM HOSPITALITY AND ENJOYED OUR VISIT SO MUCH THAT WE WILL SOON BE PAYING VISITS ON MANY OF YOUR FRIENDS AND NEIGHBORS. Y'ALL HAVE A NICE DAY. BEST REGARDS, LCDR MAXIME TINDALL ROBICHAUX, UNION SPACE NAVY. MESSAGE ENDS.

A hundred or so heartbeats later, just long enough for this additional humiliation to sink in, a warning on his display alerted him that a routine internal radiated-frequency scan routine had spotted a series of anomalous signals being transmitted to all of the neural interface modules implanted in his brain and those of some of the senior officers on board. Out of an abundance of caution, he ordered the computer to disable all of the neural interfaces. For reasons the commander did not understand, the computer refused to accept this order. He immediately transmitted a similar shutdown order to the officer charged with computer-interface issues and then entered an order directing the computer to determine the nature and likely effect of the signals.

As the computer was working on that request, the commander, along with the other officers with neural interfaces, felt a sharp pain in their heads, excruciating at first and rapidly escalating to a level beyond unbearable. The commander and the rest fell to the deck screaming, blood pouring from their noses and ears.

Before any medical assistance could reach the commander, he was dead.

CHAPTER 11

04:27 Zulu Hours, 16 May 2315

"Skipper, signal by lights from the RRS *Makkah*," Chin said. "The Rashidian vessels, the *Nicholas Appert*, and the Pfelungian mini-carrier request leave to part company." The *Cumberland* had completed filling her fuel tanks and transferring from the tender all of the provisions and matériel that she could cram into her holds only a few moments before. Under Admiral Hornmeyer's orders, at this point Max had to relinquish the tender for the support of other operations.

"Reply *Permission granted and Godspeed.*" A look of uncertainty crossed Max's face. "Belay that." He turned to Bram, who, as often happened, was sharing the seat at the commodore's station with Clouseau. At the moment the doctor was giving the cat, who clearly was in no danger of malnutrition, a small brownish cube from an aluminized Mylar packet labeled: *Union Space Navy Field Ration (FRFD-6-F), Feline Personnel Only, Supplemental Discretionary Ration ("Treat"), Nuggets, Fish with Shrimp Flavor (8). Note: IT IS RECOMMENDED THAT NO FELINE BE FED MORE THAN FOUR (4) NUGGETS PER DAY OR OBESITY*

MAY RESULT. Sahin had long ago gotten over his bemusement at the notation "Feline Personnel Only." As for the note regarding "obesity" that "may result" from too many cat treats, Clouseau was far beyond the point at which such a warning had any preventive value.

"Doctor," Max asked, "is it appropriate to say *Godspeed* to a Muslim? Or a ship full of Muslims? I wouldn't want to give offense to an outstanding officer such as Commander Hajjar, particularly over so small a matter as a farewell wish."

The doctor discreetly slipped the shiny packet of cat treats back into his pocket, hoping that none of the midshipmen had seen him violating his own lectures to them about overfeeding the cat. He contemplated the issue for a moment and used his console to pose two quick queries to the ship's database. Sahin was a deliberate man and rarely spoke without due consideration, particularly on matters that bore on his faith. "I can assure you that no offense would be taken by any reasonable follower of *Islam*," he said. "As I have just learned, *Godspeed* is a survival from the Middle English expression *God spede*, which meant *May God grant you success.* It is a perfectly devout wish. We Muslims even say it ourselves when speaking Standard, as there is no equivalent and equally economical expression in Arabic, Turkish, or Persian."

"But what about saying *God* instead of *Allah*?"

"A reasonable question, Captain. Ordinarily we Muslims do not take lightly the substitution of *God* for *Allah*. But here we are dealing with a linguistically specific idiom, which Commander Hajjar will certainly recognize as being well meant. Besides, I'm certain that he would recognize—as do most Muslims—that when you refer to *God,* you are invoking the name of He Whom we call *Allah.* After all, your faith and ours both recognize that there is only one God, the God of Abraham."

"Thank you, Doctor. You can be a very handy—if somewhat overly loquacious—man to have around. Chin, transmit by blinker *Permission granted. Godspeed and good hunting.*"

Chin acknowledged the order and busied himself at his console to send the message. "Response from the *Makkah,*" he said a few moments later. "*May Allah send his angels to guard and watch over you.*"

"Very well. Acknowledge the message."

As Chin acknowledged the order, Max looked at Bram, tilting his head expectantly.

"In most circles that would be regarded as an exceptionally kind benediction to give to someone outside our faith," Bram said, knowing what information Max wanted without being asked.

"Sir," Chin said as soon as the doctor stopped speaking, "message by lights from the Pfelung mini-carrier."

By unspoken agreement everyone on board the *Cumberland* referred to the vessel in question as *the Pfelung mini-carrier* rather than by its name in Pfelungian, which—as far as Max knew—no human could pronounce, or by the translation of that name into Standard, which he had recently learned was *Bearer of Tiny but Ferocious Hatchlings Hungry to Attack and Eat the Entrails of All Evil Predators.* Everyone on the *Cumberland* assumed that the name was much shorter and sounded a lot better in Pfelungian; otherwise they would entirely lose their faith in the bureau that named the ship—the Intermediate-Grade Naval Administrative Command for the Assignment to Warships of Names That Are Suitably Bellicose Yet Still Appropriately Dignified.

"Let's have it, Chin."

"I think I'd better give it to you on Commandcom," he said, suppressing a snicker.

"Very well." Max instructed his console to access the Commandcom data channel, the one reserved for communications intended for the ship's CO.

TO ROBICHAUX FROM BRAKMOR-ENT 198. THANK YOU FOR THE FUN OF SNEAKING UP BEHIND THE KRAG AND STICKING NUCLEAR WEAPONS UP THEIR CLOACA. WE LOOK FORWARD TO THE HONOR OF SWIMMING WITH YOU AGAIN AND WISH YOU GOOD FORTUNE IN FEEDING MORE KRAG TO THE FOUL BOTTOM-MUD DWELLING SCAVENGER FISH AND SLIMY WORMS. MAY WE TOGETHER RIP OUT THE ENTRAILS OF THE LAST LIVING KRAG AND FLOAT GILL TO GILL AS WE WATCH IT THRASH IN PAIN BLEED AND DIE. MESSAGE ENDS.

"Mr. Chin, acknowledge the message and tell Brakmor-Ent that a reply is forthcoming." Max began typing.

"Wow," Levi said, "I'm glad the Pfelung aren't pissed off at *us*."

"No argument from me, but there is such a thing as carrying hate too far," DeCosta added from his place at the XO's station.

Max stopped typing. "True, XO, but I'm not sure that anyone's carrying anything too far here. Given that the Krag came within half a millimeter of wiping out the Pfelung as a species, I can't say I blame them." Max turned to the Weapons Officer. "Mr. Levy, any chance of your people forgiving Hitler?"

"Sir, as you are aware, that slimy little nutcase motherfucker blew his brains out 370 years ago. So, not yet," he responded. "Check back in another thousand."

"Probably not even then. Hell," Max said quietly to DeCosta and Sahin, "*I* haven't forgiven him, and it wasn't my relatives the sick, evil bastard was having herded into the gas chambers and shoveled into the ovens."

Max resumed typing for a few moments. "Okay, Chin. Send this by lights to the Pfelung."

TO BRAKMOR-ENT 198 FROM ROBICHAUX. OUR PLEASURE. IT IS ALWAYS AN HONOR TO SWIM WITH YOU. YOUR COURAGE AND SKILL ARE AN EXAMPLE TO ALL WHO FIGHT AGAINST THE KRAG TO PRESERVE THEIR FREEDOM AND THE SURVIVAL OF THEIR SPECIES. MAY YOUR ATTACK TEETH FIND THE SOFT WHITE BELLIES OF YOUR ENEMIES. I HOPE THAT WE ARE IN THE SAME WATERS AGAIN BEFORE TOO MANY TIDES HAVE EBBED. MESSAGE ENDS.

"Message sent and acknowledged, Skipper," Chin said a few moments later.

"All vessels are engaging their sublight drives," Bartoli reported. "Now running them up to FULL and shaping course for this system's Bravo jump point."

"Very well. It's time for us to make our exit as well," Max said. "Maneuvering, may I safely assume that you've received the coordinates of the waypoints worked out by Messrs. DeCosta, Ellison, and Bhattacharyya to put us in place to intercept Admiral Birch?"

"Yes, sir, you may," LeBlanc answered in kind. If the form of the skipper's question deviated from standard naval phraseology, custom on the *Cumberland* established since Max took command dictated that so should the answer.

"Outstanding. Then set course for our first waypoint. Keep it very stealthy: make your speed 137 c. Let's go see if we can catch us a legendary Krag admiral."

When LeBlanc had acknowledged the order and set about implementing it, DeCosta gazed at the icons in the 3D tactical display that represented the Rashidian and Pfelung ships as well as the tender. "I wonder where they're going," he said.

"Hmpf. So do they," Max said. "All they have right now are orders for the next two or three jumps, with no knowledge of their final destination. After that they'll get their rendezvous orders by means of Hornmeyer's new BBC-French Resistance embedded message technique: they'll just monitor a different civilian entertainment broadcast for two or three different commercials for specific products, use the skipper's voiceprint as the key to perform a decrypt on one of the metaspacial subcarrier signals, and watch as the computer pops out a set of detailed mission orders. It's brilliant—Hornmeyer retains the flexibility of being able to give new orders to forces behind the lines without the enemy even knowing a coded message is being sent, much less what it says. And even if the Krag knew that the messages were in the broadcasts somewhere, there isn't enough computing power in the whole Hegemony to perform an iterative decrypt on every minute of every commercial on every channel in time to be militarily relevant.

"He infiltrated Commander Hajjam's group and two or three tenders—I didn't ask which, and Hajjam didn't tell me—in Krag space five months ago more than a hundred light-years from here. I suspect that he slipped some other forces in as well, probably a few other destroyers like us, and he's been sending them where he thinks they can do the most damage ever since."

Max turned forward. "Mr. LeBlanc, estimated time to the first waypoint?"

"Nine hours, fourteen minutes, sir."

"Very well."

■

00:43 Zulu Hours, 18 May 2315

"I was greatly exasperated by the regrettable but obvious necessity of eschewing our planned attack on the admiral's convoy," Bram said between bites as he devoured a white bean and lamb dish, the name of which Max could never manage to remember but which even his Cajun nose could not help but conclude smelled delicious. "And given that your nature is considerably more bellicose than mine, I'm sure that your level of frustration is quite high at this particular juncture."

"I'm not as unhappy as you might think," Max answered as he wolfed down a chicken-fried steak roughly the size of a hatch cover. "It was while we were shadowing that convoy that we picked up ship-to-ship chatter indicating that the admiral would be more vulnerable to attack at our next destination. Of course, I would much rather have already achieved our objective than have it still lie before us. Not only is a bird in the hand worth two in the bush, but Admiral Birch's convoy is leading us deeper into Krag space, which, as I'm sure you understand, increases the danger to us and complicates an already difficult fuel and consumables situation. Nevertheless, I'm pretty confident that we are going to be able to get the bird in the bush in one of these systems he's about to visit.

"The admiral inspects a base or meets with a local commander or whatever he does, and then his convoy takes him at sublight to the system's jump point. We get a shot at him when he's going to or from the jump point, or when he's crossing from one jump point to another in one of the systems between stops on his schedule. If we can't get at him at one of these attack opportunities, we'll just run ahead on compression drive to the next system or the one after that. That's one of the upsides of having his itinerary—we know where he's going. So, since he's got to travel in system at sublight, we can always get ahead of him."

"Then I will allow my exasperation to abate somewhat, conditionally at least, provided we are able to blow that other bird to flaming atoms. I find that I derive more pleasure than perhaps I should from watching the destruction of our enemies on the displays. But what of our earlier concern that the laurel-laden rodent admiral is not embarked on this convoy and that it is nothing more than bait for an elaborate trap?"

"I'm really not worried anymore about the convoy being a trap," Max said, "at least in the conventional sense of the word. Having a whole library of old Krag encrypts makes it easier to break the new ones, which has helped Batty, Bales, and the gang in Crypto break the encrypt this convoy is using. We monitored enough of the rat-faces' comms in these last few systems to know that the real Admiral Birch actually arrived at those systems when the convoy arrived, left when the convoy left, and has been communicating with his headquarters as well as systems on his itinerary from the VIP transport in the convoy. My gut tells me that Birch is in that convoy, which explains why it has that new multiship sensor signature-suppression system, probably bolted onto that huge tanker they've got. It's making it far more difficult to find the convoy, resolve the sensor contact into individual ships, and ID the ships. If we didn't have the itinerary, we'd really be screwed. Anyway, Ensign Bhattacharyya's analysis of the SIGINT to and from the convoy says that Birch is on that convoy. I ask you, do you ever remember my gut and Batty's intel analysis to be wrong about the same thing at the same time?"

"I can't say that I have," Bram said. "But if he is actually on or in or with that convoy and if it is as lightly protected as I understand it to be, isn't the admiral quite dangerously exposed to attack? Why would the Krag risk so valuable a military asset?"

"I don't know, Bram. There are only three things I can think of. One, Batty and I are both totally, unprecedentedly wrong about the admiral's location. Two, Admiral Birch is protected from attack in some way that I am not aware of. Or three, the Krag for some reason are supremely confident that we won't attack the convoy—maybe they think it's too deep in their space, or we have no hope of finding it, or we have no idea that the admiral is even out here in the first place."

"I may not know much about such things, but none of those possibilities strikes me as being at all likely." Bram noticed that, once again, Max was looking at his plate of lamb and beans with a look of perplexity on his face—a look that he seemed to be going to great lengths to hide. So he added, "Etli Kuru Fasulye."

"What?"

"Etli Kuru Fasulye," he said, this time more slowly. "That's what the dish is called. I provided my mother's recipe for it to the virtuoso old francophones in the galley, and they prepare it splendidly. I had expected their efforts to be less than inspiring given that these fellows are not used to cooking with lamb or white beans, but they seem to have adapted in a most admirable fashion. One of them told me that it was quite natural that this particular mess staff should make it well because, with all the onions and garlic and pepper, although it's a Turkish dish, it's practically Cajun food."

Max smiled at the compliments of the Turkish/Arabian/European-descended doctor for the *Cumberland*'s largely Cajun/Southern United States–descended mess staff, all the while taking healthy bites of his own cornbread and green beans. The two men were having a late dinner in Max's day cabin. The failed stalking of the convoy under discussion was the reason for the lateness of the dinner, although the meal tasted none the worse for having been held and reheated.

"Another reason I'm not particularly put out," Max said as he began to make inroads on his peach cobbler, "is that there was practically nothing to fault about the crew's performance in the attack. Sensors picked up and identified the target nearly at the theoretical maximum range for the equipment we've got, Tactical assessed the enemy's disposition of forces and lined us up for a textbook attack, Stealth kept us undetected the whole time, and Weapons had everything ready to vaporize the rat-faces. Finally, the Tactical Section and the XO jointly came to the conclusion—with which I agreed totally, by the way—that the unexpected arrival of that fighter squadron from the escort carrier that happened to be going through the system at the same time meant that there was no way to pull off the attack without unacceptable risk. Even Midshipman Park didn't miss a beat when you asked him if you could perhaps have jasmine-scented green tea instead of coffee."

Max shook his head at the borderline sacrilege of any hot beverage other than coffee, or in rare cases, hot chocolate, being consumed on the Command Island of a Union Space Navy warship. Little did he know that Bram had gotten the idea from Ensign Bhattacharyya, who had not only consumed the same beverage while on watch in the Big Chair on at least one occasion, but had spilled the same beverage on the XO's station when the ship lurched due to an accident in Engineering.

"The only fault I have for anyone's performance during the entire operation," Max continued, "is the extent to which the Casualty Station was unprepared to receive wounded personnel because the Chief Medical Officer was in CIC drinking jasmine-scented green tea."

When Bram sat bolt upright in his chair, opening his mouth prepared to launch a stream of indignant words, Max smiled broadly and shook his finger gently in his friend's direction. "Gotcha," he said gently. "You are way too touchy about some things."

Bram deflated slightly and responded with a rueful nod. "As I am very well aware, my friend. It is a personality trait that has not served me well. I do tend to be something of a hothead and respond too quickly with cutting invective of inappropriate strength when I perceive a slight."

"Really? I hadn't noticed." Max's smile grew broader. He had, of course, noticed many times and had been the target of the referenced *cutting invective of inappropriate strength* more times than he cared to count. "You are in good company, my friend," answered Max. "I have my own share of personality traits that do not serve me well."

"I would be interested to hear them." Bram could, of course, have supplied a list without any prompting, but he was truly interested in learning what the skipper's introspection had told him about his own weaknesses.

"Well, the one I'm worried about right now is go fever."

"I'm afraid I've never heard of that one. Is it a communicable disease from Go IV or Geaux C II?"

"No, it's a fever only in the figurative sense. People get it worst when they get frustrated by delays or failures. It's a Jurassic Space term. When those old NASA hands would have trouble getting one of their balky chemical rockets to work, go fever was the urge to launch or "go" even when things were not quite optimal. It was a big deal because even the smallest technical glitches would often cause the most spectacularly violent explosions. Anyway, I'm worried that, having had to let this convoy pass, I'll be too eager to get the next one."

"I can certainly agree that to do so would be a natural, and perhaps even a nearly universal, human psychological trait," Bram said. "Although I cannot recall that tendency ever having been identified in the literature or being given a specific term."

"It may not be in the psychological literature, but there's a lot of evidence of it in the navy, especially in the flight recorders of warships destroyed by enemy action. Skippers who get go fever commit to attacks on which they should pass."

"I am no judge of tactics, at least the naval kind, but your crew and your superiors seem to be fairly well pleased with your tactical judgment, so I am not particularly concerned with it." He took a sip of the splendid Four Planet coffee served with the meal. "Speaking of tactics, I saw something interesting recently."

With a tilt of his head, Max invited Bram to elaborate.

"I recently watched a game of Midshipman's Tag. I think I gained some insight into how you naval warrior types teach your tiny acolytes how to think and fight in space. I could see clear correspondences between things I saw those lads do in the air in that room to things I have seen you do in space during engagements with our rodent adversaries."

"You're right, of course. The sport started with midshipmen having fun, essentially chasing one another around in cargo holds with the gravity generators turned off, but it has evolved into a powerful training tool." Max paused, considering for a moment. "I'm surprised you took the time. But then, I expect that you treated a mid who was injured in a match, and his description of how he got hurt piqued your well-known curiosity."

"I do not believe my curiosity is at all *well-known*, except by present company. You are, nevertheless, accurate in your hypothesis about why I came to view a match. As I said, it was a most instructive experience. I am glad to have yielded to my *well-known curiosity*."

"I like to watch matches whenever I can. It gives me an insight into the mids' tactical skills, their temperaments, and their character. Who'd you see play?"

"I don't quite know how to tell you. I have no idea how these teams are identified—didn't catch a name like *Eagles, Wildcats, Wolverines,* or *Tigers.* But I can tell you that the captain of the winning team was a young gentleman whom I have treated repeatedly for xeroderma in the vicinity of the medial olecranon process—"

"What's that?" Max interrupted with uncharacteristic abruptness.

"Not to worry, Max," Bram answered soothingly. "It's only a patch of flaky, dry skin over the lad's right elbow. I assure you that if any of the young gentlemen were to present with a serious medical condition, I would notify you as soon as practicable."

"Okay. And thanks for the reassurance." He paused, struggling briefly with the unaccustomed act of turning this particular emotion into words. When he resumed speaking, his tone was almost confidential. "I worry about them, you know. I worry about them a lot. I know I was a mid myself and that some would regard me as a success. But I've never been totally comfortable with the idea of having *children* on board a warship and taking them into combat. They're only boys—adventurous, bright, resourceful, incredibly brave boys, I will grant you, but still only boys. The image of little Midshipman Park, dirk in hand, facing a Krag assault warrior is the stuff of nightmares."

"It seems that, although our dreams are very different, our nightmares are woven from similar cloth. I worry as well. Since I have come on board, we haven't had any serious casualties in the Midshipmen's Berth, but I regard with considerable anxiety the prospect of performing emergency trauma surgery on young men who are still sopranos and contraltos in the ship's choir."

"But, Bram, this ship doesn't have a choir."

"Then I have nothing to worry about. You comfort me greatly, brother." He paused for another sip of his coffee. "Perhaps you should consider starting one. I would enjoy the diversion. But we have wandered far afield from the topic I introduced a few moments ago—the tag game I recently saw the midshipmen play."

"Right. Who did you see play?"

"The captain of the winning team was Midshipman Kakou."

"Oh! You saw *that* game." Max's excitement practically levitated him out of his chair. Cobbler forgotten, he even set his fork down so he could gesture with both hands. "I hear that was a match for the books. Kakou's last attack was supposed to have been incredible. Players will be copying that one for years and will probably name it after him. I wish I had been there. What audacity! One-on-one, diving down from the ceiling right at Huang's head." Max was using his hands to depict the movements of the players. "Then, when Huang went lateral, Kakou was perfectly set up for a firing pass." He pantomimed throwing. "He just tagged Huang hard as he went past. The beauty of it is that Huang couldn't throw because he was too busy trying to evade, so Kakou had him dead to rights. Bang. Bang. It was all over."

"You sound as though you played."

Max actually blushed. "Yes, I did," he said. "At least until I was a mid second class."

"Why not play once you were promoted to mid one?

"I was . . . uh . . ." His voice trailed off. "Well, I suppose I shouldn't be embarrassed about it this many years later. I was scarcely more than a hatch hanger at the time. Okay, here it is. I was banned from the game. For life."

"What could you have conceivably done to get yourself banned? Did you deliberately injure another player?"

"Actually, that's allowed as long as there is no deliberate bodily contact—you can get some of those boxes moving pretty fast if you know what you're doing. But, no. It wasn't anything I did to another player."

"Then what?"

"I was banned for *unfairly manipulating the conditions of play.*" Prompted by Bram's stupefied stare, Max continued, "There are all sorts of rules about the size, mass, and capacity of those tanks the players wear on their backs that hold the nitrogen gas used to push them around in zero G. But the rules were absolutely silent about the tanks' composition. So I had my team make their own tanks out of an alloy that was doped with trace amounts of gold, silver, and tantalum to resonate slightly with the tiny inverse gravitational field in the hold that has to be put out to null the graviton leakage into the compartment from the rest of the ship. A smart player could exploit the variances in strength and orientation of the residual to get a tiny push or pull or nudge in the right direction—not enough to be obvious, but enough to obtain a subtle advantage. Using that nudge took a lot of skill—we couldn't even practice it in any kind of obvious way—but we learned how to make it work for us. We'll never know if we won any matches because of it, but it made us feel like we had an edge, and that extra confidence was almost certainly the margin of victory more than once."

"How did you get caught?"

"After we won the championship for our whole theater of operations, video of the match was widely distributed through the fleet. Two old friends were watching the match over a drink, and together they noticed something strange about my team's movements—we went places we wouldn't go unless we were trying to exploit slight gravity wells or rises, subtly sped up or slowed down faster than we should, turned sharper, that sort of thing. I thought that we were very careful and were totally nonobvious, but we couldn't fool those guys. Anyway, they jointly sent a fleet signal to our skipper, saying that he shouldn't tear our team's equipment apart or subject the video to computer analysis looking for cheating. Instead, he should *just ask Robichaux.*

"Well, Captain Komarov, a noble man of the highest honor if ever there was one, called me to his day cabin, told me to sit down, and without any preamble asked me, on my honor as a Union Space Navy midshipman and a member of the crew of the USS *Adelaide*, if in that match or any other, we had *in any way altered the graviton response coefficient of the players and/or their equipment.*"

"And you admitted what you did?"

"Of course. After I answered his question in the affirmative, he asked me what we did, and I told him in complete detail," Max said, trying not to sound offended and not entirely succeeding. "It was a matter of honor. Besides, I didn't consider what we did to be cheating. It was entirely consistent with the rules. Other players had modified their equipment to obtain some advantage before and weren't penalized, although a rule change usually resulted after the fact."

Max fortified himself with a few bites of his now-room-temperature cobbler before continuing. "So, I never even seriously considered the possibility of not being entirely truthful to Captain Komarov. If you knew the late captain, you probably wouldn't have asked that question." Bram shook his head. "I thought not. In any event, he was quite an imposing figure, and one did not lie to him. About anything. Ever. And, of course, if you lie on your honor and get caught, you're finished in the navy. To bring this dreary tale to a conclusion, once he sent me back to my duties, Komarov replied to the joint signal explaining what had happened. After that, the men who sent it went out of their way to see that I was banned from the sport for life."

"In light of what you told me," Bram said carefully, "that hardly seems the most appropriate outcome in terms of determining whether there was an infraction of the rules and applying the proper consequences, particularly as the rules did not prohibit your actions."

"That's what you would think, but the fellows who did it told me privately that they knew the outcome was unfair to me as an application of the rules, but they wanted to teach me a lesson that I would never forget: *always treat your naval brothers as fairly as you are able.* I hated having to give up my championship ring, deal with being known throughout the fleet—at least for a while—as a cheater, and not be able to compete anymore. But it was a good lesson. And I have never forgotten it."

"And just who were these *gentlemen* who did this to you? Have I heard of them?"

"Probably so. At the time, they were known as Rear Admiral Middleton and Commodore Hornmeyer."

"That sheds a little light on a few things. I'm beginning to think that your relationships with these gentlemen are more complex than I had suspected."

Max took a thoughtful sip from a glass containing a few swallows of liquid the color of strong tea. This liquid, however, rather than having been hastily brewed on board the ship formerly reviled as the *Cumberland* Gap, had been lovingly distilled very near the actual Cumberland Gap on Earth, in the misty, tree-cloaked mountains of Kentucky.

"You have no idea."

CHAPTER 12

09:55 Zulu Hours, 20 May 2315

"Aspect change on Hotel two, at least thirty degrees negative X and somewhere between five and fifteen degrees positive Y, plus I'm reading braking thrusters consistent with deceleration," Bartoli announced. "It looks like a course change consistent with a zigzag . . . Now there goes Hotel three, similar change." He paused a moment. "Same thing with Hotel four. Insufficient data for a heading just yet. Target motion analysis in progress. I should have the new heading for you in about five minutes. No sign that they've detected us, though. Their course changes appear to be at random or pseudorandom intervals; the shortest leg they've run was one hour, fifty-three minutes, twenty-two seconds, and the longest, three hours, four minutes, fifty-eight seconds." He listened to his back room for a moment, called up a different set of displays, and scrutinized them for about a quarter of a minute. "Yes, sir, definite zigzag—a two-axis change in course plus decel, followed by a steady heading."

"Very well," Max said. "Maintain current status."

"Why the change in tactics, Skipper?" DeCosta asked quietly.

"You mean from constant helming like they did in the last system to three-axis zigzag?"

"Right. Sure, making course alterations in X and Y and varying their speed makes deriving a firing solution more difficult, but it's harder by an order of magnitude if they are *constantly* changing course and speed. If there was any chance of being ambushed, you bet I'd be constant helming rather than following a simple zigzag. And that's with just any old plain vanilla convoy, not with someone as important as Admiral Birch. I mentally put myself in the position of transporting Admiral Hornmeyer, and I would absolutely adopt the squirreliest, twisty-turnyest, constantly changing course you ever saw."

"So would I," Max said. "You can bet on it. But I might be singing a different tune if I were trying to maneuver one of those huge deuterium tankers. Those things are a forged Michiganium bitch to steer." He saw the executive's eyebrows raise ever so slightly, so he explained. "I know. You're thinking that you helm a big tanker just like you do any other cargo ship: you just enter the course and speed parameters, and the computer steers the ship. But when you're talking about one of those huge honking one- or two-million-ton modular tankers, it takes unbelievable quantities of fuel to turn those commands entered from the helm console into actual delta V. Plus, those things don't have gimbaled drive nozzles or ducted exhaust that let you use your main sublight to maneuver when you're under way, so these ships make all their course changes with maneuvering thrusters, which really aren't designed to be used to make constant course changes for days at a time. We've captured a few of those ships and wound up having to replace the maneuvering thrusters almost immediately, because the Krag don't build them to take the kind of use we put them to."

"So, you don't think it's anything sinister like making it easier for us to track the convoy to lure us into a trap, because it kind of feels like one," said DeCosta with evident relief.

"Probably not. But don't stop trusting your hunches. Remember Rule 12 from Commodore Middleton's book?"

"I'm afraid not. I never learned the rules by number," DeCosta replied with obvious embarrassment.

"You should learn the numbers. Makes for good shorthand talk, as in: *Sir, aren't you forgetting Rule 7?* and so on. Rule 12 states as follows." Max quoted as though he were reciting Holy Scripture, which as far as he was concerned, he was: "*Anything that feels like a trap probably is. But don't forget Rule 13.*"

"Which is?"

Max shook his head and "tsk"ed in mock disapproval. "You've got a lot of studying to do, XO, in your copious free time, of course. Rule 13: *While it is usually best to evade the traps by the enemy, it is sometimes necessary to walk into them.*"

The *Cumberland* had spent most of the last day and a half station-keeping relative to Steigenberger V A, a geologically active moon, which, as its name indicated, was the first moon of the fifth planet in the Steigenberger system. The planet, Steigenberger V, was a gas giant 2.2 times the mass of Jupiter, possessing a powerful gravitational field that continually stretched and compressed its nearmost satellite, heating the moon's interior and keeping its crust and upper mantle in a constant state of furious volcanism such that the tiny world had a surface comprised mostly of molten rock. The destroyer had been using the moon's heat to mask its own, allowing it to remain stealthy while radiating its accumulated thermal energy into space, so long as the ship maintained a position directly between the convoy and the moon. In that way, the Krag infrared detectors (which, the Union now knew, had poor angular resolution) would not spot the comparatively hot ship silhouetted against the cold of space, but would detect only the searing magma of the planet's surface behind.

As the convoy approached the point along its course closest to the moon, a distance of just over 4 AU, the *Cumberland* had engaged its stealth systems, slipped away from the gas giant and its moon, and was now quietly creeping into the convoy's path, where it would lie in wait to pounce on the enemy.

"I've got enough data points for a rough course and speed, sir," Bartoli said. "Our target motion analysis is giving us one-two-zero mark two-four-zero and a speed of .5 c—that's with a margin of error of plus or minus 5 degrees on each axis and plus or minus .07 c in speed. They're moving into a position where the probe we launched yesterday will be able to give us good cross bearings like we planned, so we'll be able to generate a precise solution a lot faster. I'll have something a lot better for you in another ten or fifteen minutes."

"Is the new heading consistent with their base course?"

"Affirmative, Skipper. It's a plausible zigzag around a base course toward their expected destination, the battle station at the second planet's L5."

"Very well. Mr. Kasparov, do we have a Posident on those ships yet?"

"Negative, Skipper. We have the confirmed flag traffic that Batty's intercepted and decrypted from the last system showing that Admiral Birch was definitely in one of those ships. But we didn't get close enough last time to get enough data for an ID on the ships themselves or to figure out which one the admiral is on. Given our rate of closure, though, I expect we'll have enough data for a good ID within the next hour or less."

"Thank you, Lieutenant. Mr. Bhattacharyya, do we have any results from your work on the transponder codes?"

"No answer yet, sir, but I expect something soon," he answered from the Intel Console. Even before the doctor could ask, Max jerked his head in Sahin's direction. The young intelligence officer continued, addressing his remarks to the doctor, "With the captured Krag data, we were able to cobble together a version of one of the enemy's IFF interrogation signals close enough to trick the ships in the convoy into sending a response."

"What good is that going to do? I thought transponder responses to IFF interrogations were too heavily encrypted for us to be able to get anything from them," the doctor said, setting his coffee mug down. Several highly astonished heads containing deeply surprised minds swiveled rapidly in Sahin's direction. He pretended not to notice, all the while smiling the beatific smile of a man who knows that others have underestimated him.

"Well, Doctor, that's not entirely true." Sahin tilted his head as an invitation for him to continue. "The transponder codes *are* highly encrypted, and the encryption changes each time the transponder receives an IFF signal, so all of the keys we captured have expired. But the captured data core does give us a huge library of expired keys, allowing us to know what the parameters are, which cuts the number of permutations down from something like 4.5 x 10^{45} to 7.2 x 10^{28}. That first number is impossible for any computer to plow through in less than a year, but Mrs. Denny can get through the second—"

"Excuse me," the doctor interrupted. "Mrs. Denny?"

"It's customary for the crew to give a woman's name to the ship's computer. Our crew didn't come up with this one until a few weeks ago," DeCosta said. In response to Sahin's look of total incomprehension, the XO continued, "Mrs. Denny is the heroine of Vera B. Scott's series of Mrs. Denny murder mysteries. You know, from the thirties and forties of the last century . . . *Murder in an Airlock*, *Murder in Zero G*, *Murder at the Ringview Resort*,

The Hideous Tachyo-Graviton Murders . . . she must have written forty or fifty of them."

"Mrs. Denny was the smartest woman that Bales could think of," Bhattacharyya said, "besides his mother, who had some Welsh name that not even I could pronounce. Anyway, without compromising her ability to tend to other business, Mrs. Denny can make it all the way through 7.2 x 10^{28} permutations in about fifty hours, meaning that on average she can crack a transponder code in about a day. That's not fast enough to tell us anything during an engagement, but within a few hours from now we should be able to ID those ships right down to the registry numbers."

"Thank you for that *outstanding* explanation, Mr. Bhattacharyya," Sahin said.

The ensign acknowledged the thanks with a nod, smiling at the joke that Max showed no sign of noticing.

Midshipman Hewlett, who had drawn CIC duty for this watch, took advantage of the lull to put on another pot of coffee and refill a dozen or so mugs of a dozen or so watch standers who wanted to fortify themselves for what they expected to be the action to come.

"I've got a better plot for you on that convoy," Bartoli said. Max raised his eyebrows as a signal for the tactical officer to proceed. "We've derived a firm course of one-one-seven mark two-four-two. Speed is .52. We haven't gotten solid IDs, but we're starting to be able to tease out the separate mass and other characteristics of the individual ships, rather than just getting one blur of data." He made a few entries from his console that caused three "Hotel" icons and associated labels showing range, bearing, heading, and speed, plus a distance scale, to appear in one of the secondary tactical displays on the Command Island. "As you can see, we believe them to be in a line ahead formation with an interval of approximately 7900 kilometers. Hotel two, which is on point, is shaping up as an intermediate-size vessel, something in the 75,000-ton range. Hotel three, next in line, looks like a small vessel, something around 6500 tons. Hotel four, tail-end Charlie, is very large, at least a million tons, maybe even a million and a half."

"Thank you, Mr. Bartoli," Max said. "I know you just said you don't have solid IDs yet, but I'm sure you have some pretty reasonable conjecture about what these vessels are, based on their mass, their mission, the convoy intervals, and so on."

"Well, yes, sir, I reckon I do." Several men in CIC smiled at Bartoli's idiomatic Southern *reckon*. "My best guess is that Hotel three is one of those armed freighters that the Krag have been favoring lately for their convoys through low- to moderate-threat zones, maybe a *Fragmenter* or *Frostbite* class. And, sir, that would not be good news at all. Those guys have excellent sensors: not only up to warship standards but as good as most Krag escort types have got. Plus, while they've got typically weak freighter hulls and nothing like a warship's deflector power, their pulse-cannon batteries and missile capabilities are equivalent to what we've got."

"They can dish it out, but they can't take it," Max commented.

"Exactly, sir. Next, Hotel four would likely be the admiral's transport, probably one of their military VIP transport vessels—informally we call them 'admirals' yachts.' Because near the FEBA, VIPs are usually on board warships, we've never gotten good scans of any of the current generation of that type, and the captured Krag computer core had little more on them than vessel recognition data—so we've assigned class reporting names but don't have any useful intel about their speed, maneuverability, armament, defenses, or resistance to damage. In the past, in general, admirals' yachts have been reasonably fast, with no offensive capability to speak of. I could give you a few guesses as to which class we're looking at, but I don't see the point because the name wouldn't convey any kind of meaningful information."

"Makes sense to me," DeCosta said quietly to Max.

"I concur, XO," Max said loudly enough for the whole CIC to hear. It never hurt for the men to see the skipper backing the XO. "Tell me about the third ship."

"Skipper, the immense target at the end has got to be a tanker, likely a *Tangerine, Tannhauser, Tangipahoa,* or related class. Not that the class really matters for this type. Modular tanker. There's basically one overall design, even for most of the alien races we know."

Convergent evolution had brought several diverse cultures to build almost identical tankers for the same reason every known technological culture had invented the pump-action shotgun and Velcro: it worked. Forward, there was a command, control, and habitation module containing the control stations, sensors, computer core, crew quarters, and galley. Then came a long metal spine, to which the modular fuel tanks were easily attached or removed and also containing control cables, life-support conduits, power and comm lines, and an access tunnel. This led to a reactor and engineering module for the fusion reactors, the fission auxiliary reactor, power distribution, engineering control stations, and the hold containing consumables for the crew and ship's systems. Finally, there was the main sublight drive module, with the thrust chambers, the plasma accelerator annuli, and the exhaust nozzles.

"Very well, Mr. Bartoli," Max said. "What does this new course do to our intercept solution?"

"The solution is still good, Skipper. Unless they stay on this leg far longer than they have on any other, or unless they make some other radical deviation from what we expect, this change still puts them well within the predicted zone. Our current heading will put us directly along their mean course two hours and fourteen minutes from now, with the targets coming into attack position one hour and twenty-seven minutes after that."

"Very well," Max said. "Mr. DeCosta, please see that everyone on watch has food brought to them over the next two hours and that the rest of the men cycle through the mess during that time. We'll be going to General Quarters in two hours and twenty minutes."

The time passed quickly. Two hours and twenty-two minutes later, Mr. DeCosta had seen that the men had eaten, and the chiefs had seen that all of the men under their charge were at their stations, ready for action. All compartments were at their full airtight integrity, the missile tubes were loaded, and all systems were ready to respond to Max's orders. The Main Tactical Display, as well as variously configured tactical displays on other consoles located throughout CIC, reflected the knowledge gained over the past few hours—mainly the class identifications and precise masses of the three ships—and that information, along with bearing, speed, range, and heading, appeared near the icon representing each vessel.

The *Cumberland* was at station keeping, her stealth systems fully engaged, like a leopard hiding in the underbrush, waiting to spring on its prey. Max expected the convoy to make another course change shortly before reaching the destroyer's position, at which point the destroyer would slip into silent motion, needing only to cross a comparatively short distance to make the intercept at an angle of roughly sixty degrees from dead ahead. Intercepting the convoy immediately after a course change made it less likely that the enemy would change course during the destroyer's approach, throwing off its intercept and targeting solutions and possibly even resulting in detection.

Indeed, less than twenty minutes after the destroyer went to General Quarters, the convoy zigged. Bartoli, of course, immediately reported the course change. Only a few minutes later, he had more information—the laws of geometry dictate that when using measured changes in bearing to deduce a moving object's course and speed, decreasing range to the target results in increasing precision. "Skipper, I've got a firm course plot on the convoy. New heading is one-four-one mark two-one-one. They have accelerated slightly to .57 c, which is pretty fast for this kind of convoy—I suppose they think that it will prevent any interception." Most of the men chuckled to themselves. The *Cumberland* was built for speed, and from any reasonable starting position could intercept a convoy at .57 c, or for that matter, at .75 c.

"Anything further on the convoy's makeup or capabilities?" Max asked.

"Negative, sir. As you know, Hotel two has turned out to be a *Frostbite* class armed freighter, Hotel three is a *Treadmill* class VIP transport, and Hotel four is a *Tanzanite* class tanker. You've got what we know about each class on your enemy capabilities display, which isn't very much." Bartoli sighed. He liked having more data. "We've had no new signal intercepts or other data to shed light on the situation. There's no data to contradict our earlier conclusion that Admiral Birch is on the *Treadmill*."

"Thank you, Mr. Bartoli. Maybe Admiral Birch is on the *Treadmill* because he needs to lose a few pounds." When that feeble joke died, Max continued, "Maneuvering, give us course and speed for our planned intercept."

"Aye, sir," replied LeBlanc, "course and speed for planned intercept. New course is zero-seven-nine mark one-five-three, speed .13 c. ETA at the IP in forty-seven minutes." Under Chief LeBlanc's direction, the three young spacers at the Maneuvering stations put the ship into motion and pointed it toward the IP or Initial Point, from which the Cumberland would begin its rendezvous with the enemy.

Max busied himself paging through status reports—both human- and machine-generated—from various stations around the ship. As usual he discovered a few instances in which the computer was reporting results with which the designated human had not dealt correctly. These instances, much to Max's satisfaction, were fewer and less severe with each passing week, usually involving a subtle issue that only an old space dog would spot. Max was able to address them all with a few short conversations over the voice channels. When that was done, Max paid a quick visit to the head, washed his face, peeled off his SCU and undergarment to hit the sweatiest spots with some absorbent powder, zipped back up, and returned to CIC.

He was just in time to hear LeBlanc announce, "IP in three minutes."

At that moment the hatch cycled. Without turning his head, Max called out, "Welcome to CIC, Doctor. Things are about to heat up, so I'd advise sitting in your usual place and securing your station harness. Lately you've been pretty lax about clipping on, and I don't want my Chief Medical Officer bouncing all over CIC in case we lose artificial gravity or inertial compensators." The newcomer was, indeed, Dr. Sahin, with the ship's cat at his heels. Max had noticed Clouseau shadowing Bram with increasing frequency and wondered whether the cat slept in the doctor's quarters. "I see you brought your friend."

"If you are referring to this morbidly obese feline," the doctor replied as he took his accustomed seat at the Commodore's Station, "he is most certainly not my friend. As I have told you repeatedly, I am not in the least bit fond of cats, and I particularly dislike this egregiously rotund specimen." As soon as Sahin sat down, Clouseau leaped into the seat beside him. The doctor was stroking the cat's well-tended sable fur even as he uttered the protestations about not liking cats. Max could hear quiet laughter from around the compartment.

Smiling, Max turned to DeCosta. "XO?"

"All stations report ready to execute the attack in all respects. We've got Talons in tubes one and two, targeted on Hotel three and ready for firing in all respects, save that the missile doors are closed." DeCosta would have the missile doors open as well if doing so didn't greatly compromise stealth. "We've got an Egg Scrambler in tube three, ready for firing in all respects, missile door closed. Pulse-cannons are at PREFIRE. I've conferred with Chief Engineer Brown: he told me something about being *ready to answer bells*. I looked it up and saw . . ."

"I know what it means, Lieutenant. I'm the one who taught him the expression back when we served together on the *Emeka Moro*. Very good, XO. Now, let's see if we can bag ourselves a Krag admiral."

"IP in thirty seconds," said LeBlanc.

"Mr. Bartoli," Max said, "any change in enemy dispositions?"

"Negative, sir. No change."

"Very well."

"IP in fifteen seconds," LeBlanc announced.

"Remember, gentlemen," Max said, "you are to execute the attack plan without further orders when we reach the IP."

Around CIC, heads nodded. Almost as one, practically every man, Max included, wiped sweaty palms on the leg of his SCU.

"Initial Point," LeBlanc said, half again as loud as he intended. "Executing."

The *Cumberland* turned hard, directly toward the VIP transport, and kicked its main sublight drive up to Emergency. DeCosta and Bartoli had simulated the attack dozens of times using several different techniques and had come to a surprising conclusion. Tactical orthodoxy held that the highest probability of success was for the attacking destroyer to approach the target stealthily, launch its missiles when detected, and then accelerate away while the missiles found and destroyed their quarry. The simulations predicted that this kind of attack would fail over 80 percent of the time. The excellent sensors on the freighter would detect the *Cumberland* at a range of more than 75,000 kilometers; the reasonably good and overlapping missile defenses provided by the freighter and the tanker would be able to defeat any missiles fired by the destroyer unless it waited to fire until it closed to within a few thousand kilometers of the transport, while all three ships would be able to keep the Union vessel under fire as it closed to launch its missiles. The *Cumberland*'s best chances, it turned out, came from making a stealthy approach to a range of about 200,000 kilometers, then accelerating rapidly toward a firing point about 2500 kilometers "below" the target, and continuing in a straight line to accelerate away from the convoy, engage compression drive, and escape. In that way the time during which the destroyer was vulnerable to enemy weapons fire was kept to a minimum. She would be moving at a high enough speed to make her hard to hit, while the ship's high speed also meant that—even though she would be detected at greater range—the enemy would actually have less warning time.

At least that's what the simulations said.

In perfect conformity to the plan, the destroyer accelerated hard toward its prey. With its drive radiating practically enough light and heat to allow anyone a million kilometers away to read a newspaper and roast marshmallows, any effort at stealth would have been futile. Accordingly, the ship's stealth systems were shut down, and she had extended her thermal fins to allow her to radiate her stored heat into space.

"They've spotted us, sir," Bartoli reported. "Hotel two is turning to bring her weapons to bear on us. Hotel four is powering up its amidships pulse-cannon batteries. And, sir," he added with evident surprise, "Hotel three is staying put, right between the other two ships. There's no evidence of her throttling up her main sublight. I have no idea why she isn't running, Skipper."

"Maybe the admiral believes the other two ships provide adequate protection," Max said absently. He was focused on the attack, not on dissecting the reasons his target was doing just what he wanted it to do.

DeCosta shook his head. "I don't know, sir . . ."

"New contact, designating as Hotel five!" Kasparov interrupted. "Tachyon Radar, Tango Band, high intensity, three pulses. Bearing is NOT consistent with other targets. The source is 485 kilometers from Hotel three and appears to be moving toward us." In his excitement, he forgot to read off the bearing to the contact. Everyone who needed to know could see it on his console anyway.

Oh, shit.

"Yankee search, ten-degree spread around bearing to Hotel five." Max tried to sound calm. "Weapons, pull the Egg Scrambler from tube three and reload with a Talon. Countermeasures, anything you can do to confuse Hotel five would be appreciated. Maneuvering, evasive, your discretion."

"Already on it, Skipper," a very busy Sauvé answered. The others acknowledged their orders. The ship changed course radically, veering away from its course toward the transport.

"Getting returns on the Yankee search now, Skipper," Bartoli said. "Bearing and range changing rapidly as both ships maneuver, displaying on the tactical summary screen." Max punched that screen up on his console. "They know we've scanned them, sir. They just dropped their stealth . . . Preliminary ID is *Denarius* class destroyer, sir."

Bartoli totally failed in what Max hoped was an earnest effort to keep the "oh, shit" tone out of his voice. Max didn't blame him.

Denarius was such a new class that N2 wasn't even sure it was in operational deployment yet. Faster, more powerful, and more maneuverable than the *Cumberland*, the class also boasted better stealth and even a reasonably effective sensor emulation. The scuttlebutt was that *Denarius* was the Krag answer to the *Khyber* class. "She's trying to get a missile lock," Bartoli finished.

"Sauvé," Max said, "if we stop evading, how long can you keep Mighty Mouse back there from getting a missile lock?"

"As long as the range is at least 5500 kilometers, I can keep shedding lock for three, maybe four minutes," he answered. "No more than that, though."

"Good enough. Maneuvering, put us alongside the tanker."

"How close do you want us?" LeBlanc asked once he had brought about the course change.

"Like a flea in their fur, Mr. LeBlanc. Between the deuterium tanks."

"Aye, sir," said the chief before muttering, "*Couillon*."

"Sir?" DeCosta said.

"The chief thinks that I'm either crazy or a fool. *Couillon* can mean either," said Max.

"I was asking about the tactic, not the word, Skipper."

"It puts us under the guns, XO," Max said.

With the *Cumberland* making a beeline for the tanker, the *Denarius* class destroyer came around to an intercept course, accelerating for all she was worth and gaining, particularly as before long, the Union ship was decelerating in order to pull alongside the tanker rather than crash into it at an impressive fraction of the speed of light.

"Sir," Bartoli said, "Hotel five has brought his pulse-cannon to Prefire—I guess he's decided he's gotten tired of trying to get a missile lock."

"Mr. LeBlanc, be sure to keep us directly between Hotel five and Hotel four. I want him to be afraid that any pulse-cannon shots that miss us might hit the tanker."

"I'll try, Skipper," said the chief.

The two ships began a serpentine dance, with the Krag destroyer trying to catch the Union ship while also attempting to get far enough away from an alignment with the other two ships so that it could safely fire its pulse-cannon—a task that became progressively more difficult as the *Cumberland* got closer to the tanker. In the end, the immutable laws of geometry combined with the dazzling skill of Chief LeBlanc prevented Hotel five from getting off a shot.

Hotel four, on the other hand, got off several, pounding the Union vessel with hit after hit from its low-powered but wickedly accurate point-defense systems, until the *Cumberland* got so close that the weapons could not traverse far enough to bear on their target. A few seconds later, deft coordination between maneuvering thrusters under LeBlanc's control and the grappling field under the direction of Mr. Levy pushed, nudged, and pulled the ship into the gap between the third and fourth ring of the tanks, so that the ship was resting on one of the Krag vessel's tank support members that encircled its central spine like the rings in an old-fashioned hoopskirt.

"Now, no matter what angle they shoot from, they can't fire without risking hitting the tanks and severely damaging the tanker," Max said.

"That looks like a tight squeeze," Sahin said.

"That's no step for a stepper," LeBlanc replied. "That gap's nearly 10.4 meters wide, and we've got a beam of right at 9.5 meters. That's forty-five centimeters on each side."

Sahin looked down at his forearm, knowing that the distance from his elbow to the tip of his middle finger, known in the ancient world as the cubit, was almost exactly forty-five centimeters. "Of course. All the room in the world."

"Skipper," DeCosta said, "how much time does this buy us? What are they going to do next?"

"Well, XO, not very much time at all, but it's going to be enough. What the Krag do next, as soon as they think of it, is jettison the tanks on either side of us. That will let that *Denarius* get right in beside us, and since we're a stationary target, they can hit us at close range with one of those particle beams they use for point-defense. They keep shooting until it burrows through the deflectors and cuts through the hull right into the fusion reactor. Then it's *au revoir, Cumberland.* But that's not going to happen. I'm not ready to bid this shiny new ship *adieu* just yet.

"Mr. Levy, I need you to set the missiles in tubes one and two for close-range targeting. Tube one is to be fired at the fuel tank on our portside, tube two at the one on our starboard. Program the warheads for minimum yield, post-contact detonation. Program the missile in tube three for firing along generated bearing, delayed homing. I'll tell you just before firing how to set the timing. I want all three missiles ready to fire right after Mr. LeBlanc puts us into motion."

As Levy was repeating those orders, a low thud echoed through the ship—the sound of pyrotechnics, transmitted through the members of the Krag ship and then through hull contact into the *Cumberland*. "Sounds like they're jettisoning one of the tanks," Max said. A second thud. "That sounds like the tank on the other side. It'll take a little while before the tanks drift far enough away for Hotel five to get into position. Now, Mr. LeBlanc, you know what I'm going to want, right?"

"Babatundé Hop?"

"Exactly."

Propelled by the pyrotechnics that severed them from the tanker and by small onboard thrusters, the two enormous deuterium tanks moved lazily away from the tanker. The enemy destroyer positioned itself to port of the *Cumberland* on the other side of one of the tanks, ready to slip into place as soon as there was room. As soon as the tank had moved so as to completely block the *Denarius* from being in line of sight with the Union vessel, Max said, “Mr. LeBlanc, *now.*”

Chief LeBlanc touched a flashing key on his console, initiating a set of programmed maneuvers that collectively constituted the Babatundé Hop. First, the forward maneuvering thrusters fired, pushing the ship's bow away from the tanker. As soon as the bow was pointed directly away from the center of the enemy vessel, the main sublight engine fired, rapidly throttling up to Emergency. The powerful plasma exhaust from the *Cumberland*'s drive cut through the tanker's long spine almost instantly and shredded the deuterium tanks on the opposite side. “Mr. Levy, fire tubes one and two.”

The missiles shot from their tubes and flew past the deuterium tanks, then turned back toward them. Each easily penetrated the relatively thin skin of the tank at which it was targeted. Within a microsecond of entering the tanks, the warheads detonated, their five-kiloton explosive yield sufficient to turn the tanks into shrapnel and the deuterium inside into a cloud of incandescent, ionized gas. Even though the fuel could not burn in the vacuum of space, heated by the nuclear warheads, it was sufficiently destructive to make short work of most of the surviving parts of the tanker as well as to prevent Hotel five's sensors from being able to track the *Cumberland* as it made its escape.

Rapidly accelerating away from the holocaust that now surrounded the whirling, disintegrating remnants of the enemy tanker, the *Cumberland* said its farewell to the convoy by firing the Talon loaded in tube three at the VIP transport, which was now pulling away from the tanker to make its escape. Without the missile-defense umbrella provided by the other two ships and its own sensors confused by the glowing, highly energized deuterium scattered by the two thermonuclear explosions, the transport was an easy target for the Talon, ending the small vessel's existence in a sudden flash of brilliant light.

CHAPTER 13

04:43 Zulu Hours, 22 May 2315

"Report," Max said to Bartoli, who was holding down the Big Chair for that watch.

"Probe two, the one we parked at this system's Bravo jump point, just picked up a burst of Cherenkov-Heaviside radiation consistent with multiple ships jumping into the system. The probe's sensors don't have the resolution ours do, and the effects front hasn't reached us, but preliminary typing is one bulk ammunition carrier, one VIP transport, and one tanker. We're still in a parking orbit around the primary at the fifth planet's L4 point. The mines we emplaced are still fully stealthed and report themselves to be fully operational. All stations report set at Condition Orange, all systems are nominal, and we went into full stealth as per your standing order as soon as we got the notification from the probe. Change of watch is in one hour and fifty-four minutes. And the Tactical Section is officially pissed that we did not kill the admiral."

In the manner of Cato the Elder's *ceterum censeo Carthaginem esse delendam*, Bartoli had been ending all of his reports with that particular expression of displeasure at Admiral Birch's apparent survival. Max could not dispute the sentiment. When Bhattacharyya had finally cracked the transponder codes, it was clear that the second convoy was made up of a different set of ships than the first. Apparently Admiral Birch's convoy had taken a more indirect set of jumps from one stop to another, while a decoy convoy, designed to entrap and destroy the *Cumberland*, had proceeded on the direct route.

Max had been concerned that the attack on the decoy convoy might have caused Admiral Birch to cancel his plans. Fortunately, several signal intercepts indicated that the admiral's next stop was eagerly awaiting his arrival on schedule. Accordingly, it appeared that the *Cumberland* was going to get another shot at the elusive leader.

"Very well." Bartoli and Max went through the rituals of the formal transfer of the con to the latter. Max settled into the Big Chair and waited for Bartoli to take his station at Tactical. "Mr. Bartoli, how long until our little rat pack reaches us?"

"As you recall, sir, the L4 is within 0.6 AU of the direct line between the Bravo and Charlie jump points. The Krag ships will be at their closest approach in three hours and nine minutes, assuming that they maintain the same acceleration profile."

"Thank you. Mr. LeBlanc, nudge us out to a position 72.7 percent of the way between our current position and the rat path, but offset us perpendicular to the lubber line by 1.218 million kilometers in any direction of your choosing."

"More odd numbers, sir?" the XO asked.

"Yes, Mr. DeCosta, always odd numbers. And I checked to make sure that they were odd in Krag measurements, as well."

LeBlanc and his acolytes at the maneuvering stations "nudged" the *Cumberland* into motion, and the deadly ship crept, unseen and nearly unseeable, like a black leopard in the darkest jungle, into the path of her prey.

Through his feet Max felt a change in the amplitude and the frequency of the CIC deck-plate vibrations, telling him that the fusion reactor's output had stepped up to supply additional plasma to give motion to the ship. He always drew comfort from that feeling. Like anyone long on board the fleet's smaller fighting ships—patrol vessels, corvettes, destroyers, and frigates—Max didn't like sitting in one place, and "sitting" included traveling in any kind of known path, like a synchronous orbit or at a Lagrangian point like L4 or L5.

After drinking in the comfort of the deck-plate vibrations for a few minutes, Max looked pointedly at the Tactical Station, but Bartoli—perhaps feeling his skipper's eyes—failed to look up. Instead, he kept his head down, seemingly immersed in the displays on his console and occupied by conversations with his back room. Lacking the laser vision he had so often wished was issued to skippers of rated warships, Max said, with affected breeziness, "Mr. Bartoli, things are getting a bit dull here at the command stations, so any scraps of trifling news about the enemy's dispositions that you might see fit to toss in our direction would be entirely welcome." Max glanced over at DeCosta and enjoyed seeing how hard DeCosta was working not to smile.

"Sorry, sir, I was just trying to figure something out, but I'm not having any luck. Here's what I've got. First, types. One large fleet tanker, *Tangerine* class. One bulk freighter, munitions subtype, *Frycook* class—much better weapons than the *Frostbite* the decoy convoy had, but the sensors aren't nearly as good. One VIP transport, probably a *Trapdoor* class. Currently the convoy is in line ahead formation, arranged just like the decoy convoy—freighter, transport, tanker. There's no sign of a stealthy destroyer hanging out with the formation like the last convoy, but then again, we had no sign of that other destroyer, either. They are maintaining an interval of about 355 kilometers. I'm not reading any fighters, drones, or anything else sneaky protecting their flanks. Also, sir, they're keeping a straight lubber line between the jump points. No zigzag, drunkard's walk, Spee's Spiral, Coffey's Canter, or anything else. Maybe they think we were destroyed in that conflagration two days ago."

"They're certainly acting very confident," DeCosta said, his voice sounding anything but. "Sir," DeCosta said at a much lower volume, "if I were these guys, I'd be expecting us to hit them again. The rat-faces would have to be dimmer than a Y class star not to suspect that the admiral is at risk here."

"True, XO. But we just picked up a flurry of traffic three sectors over that I suspect stems from the activities of our good friend Commander Hajjam and his group, who, I have a strong hunch, are presently working with another of our good friends, Commander Kim Yong-Soo on the *Broadsword*. Our not-so-good friends—the ones with the overbite, pink ears, and tails—may be shifting what they've got in that direction to deal with that threat. And for all we know, they may be thinking that we are all part of a single force, rather than a bunch of destroyers aided by a force that shifts from one to the other."

"Which would be a classic Hornmeyer tactic, because once the Krag have located the larger force, they won't perceive any threat from the other destroyers," DeCosta said, the scheme finally dawning on him. "You're right. That does sound like a page from old Hit 'em Hard's playbook."

"I'd pay real money to get a good look at *that* book," said Max.

"Man, oh, man, so would I," DeCosta answered. "I'd also like to see what kind of destruction Hajjam and Sue are inflicting on the local rodent population."

"Definitely. That's a scrap I'd pay cash to see." Max paused as a smirk wrote itself across his face. "I bet there's some kickin' and a gougin' in the mud and the blood and the beer."

"Beer, sir?"

"Yes, XO, beer. Check out the section in Commander Kim's Biosum on his nickname, and you'll get it."

"If you say so, sir."

As the Krag convoy approached, Max got his ship and its complement ready for the encounter. Each man was given an opportunity to go to the mess or Wardroom, as appropriate, for a hot meal. Max had the weapons crews pull the Talon missiles in tubes one and two, as well as the Egg Scrambler in tube three, check all their systems, and reload them. He also had engineering crews recheck the launch coils in all three tubes and every step in the chain of systems used to fire the pulse-cannons.

During this process something kept nagging at him. Finally Max put his finger on it. "Mr. Bartoli, back when you gave me your first type and formation report on the Krag convoy, you said that you were trying to figure something out but weren't having any luck. Would you kindly fill me in on what you were trying to figure out and whether you have had any luck doing so?"

"Well, sir," said Bartoli, "I'm ashamed to admit that I keep coming up with a minor mass discrepancy on the tanker. No matter what estimation technique I use, the tanker we've got has a lower mass than calculations predict."

This made Max and DeCosta both sit bolt upright. Neither liked surprises. "How much lower?" DeCosta managed to say before Max could.

"Somewhere between 5 and 10 percent, depending on the predictive model I use, my estimates for the amount of fuel the tanker has in its own propellant tanks, stores in its hold, et cetera, and how heavy their deuterium is."

"How heavy?" DeCosta asked. "I thought all deuterium was the same density."

"It is, XO," said Max. "If we're talking about pure deuterium—or all deuterium of the same purity. You know from your greenie days that deuterium is denser than standard hydrogen and that our deuterium is standardized at 95.4 percent deuterium, 1.2 percent tritium, and 3.4 percent regular hydrogen and impurities. Our fusion reactors won't run, or at least not run very well, on anything lower than 94 percent or so; therefore, we refine to 95+ percent in order to have a bit of a safety margin in case one batch comes in low for whatever reason. Of course, the richer the mixture, the more efficiently the reactors run, so higher is better. The Krag reactors are a bit more *impurity-tolerant*, which I translate as *technologically advanced*, than ours. They run fine on a mix as low as 90 percent deuterium or so. And because richer is better, any given batch of fuel will run somewhere between 91 percent and 98 percent, so there are variations in the density of their fuel."

Max turned back to Bartoli. "And there's no hypothesis you can come up with that explains this difference?"

"None."

"What if they're not fully loaded?"

"Skipper, our probes have given us good visuals of the tanker from all sides, and there's a full-size tank in every bracket."

"Then she must be hauling some empty tanks."

"Sir, there is no report of any fleet tanker on an outbound run ever carrying any empty tanks."

Max looked at Ensign Bhattacharyya at Intel for confirmation. "Affirmative, sir. Bartoli asked me to double-check his research on that subject. I have, and it is confirmed. Over the course of the war, there have been 338 observations of Krag fleet tankers where there is good data on the tank loadout and the ship's overall mass. On none of those occasions is there sufficient mismatch between the number of tanks and the mass to suggest that any of the tanks was empty."

"On top of that, sir," Bartoli added, "if I put in the mass data for an empty tank, I come up light. If I had to guess, one of the tanks is filled with something other than deuterium."

"Well, then," said Max, "that's got to be it. Maybe they've hollowed out one tank and used it for passenger transport space or to haul bulk cargo or spare parts. Three hundred and thirty-eight observations of the hundreds of thousands of tanker runs that have had to have taken place over the course of the war is hardly a sample size I'd want to draw any serious conclusions from. They've got to have something in that tank other than deuterium—that's got to be it."

"Yes, sir," Bartoli said. "That's got to be it."

Somehow, neither felt entirely reassured.

■

"Casualty Station, Nurse Church here." Church's gravelly voice came from the transducer on Max's console. As Max was about to start speaking, he heard another voice in the background that he instantly recognized as that of Dr. Sahin.

"Nurse," Sahin said, with definite shrillness, "if you are not *too* busy, Able Spacer Second Class Hoffman, his torn medial collateral ligament, and not the least of all, I, would be eternally grateful if you would return to the procedures table. And on your way, would you do me the favor of shooing that infernal cat into the next compartment. You know regulations explicitly prohibit the presence of the ship's cat within 1.5 meters of any sterile field."

Max knew that Church could see on the source identification display above the transducer indicating that the call was from CIC and could almost hear him shrugging helplessly. Max decided to rescue him. "Doctor, this is the skipper."

"I have already recognized your voice, sir." The doctor's voice leaped into the auditory foreground as the computer automatically activated an audio pickup over the procedures table. "Is there anything I can do for you that doesn't interfere too meaningfully with my efforts to repair a serious knee injury incurred by a spacer who doesn't have enough sense to get out of the way when a loudly beeping forklift in the cargo hold is backing toward him?"

"Sorry, Bones," the man could be heard to murmur in the background. "Had my head up my ass."

"Indeed you did, Spacer," said the doctor. "Now stop speaking and lie still. We'll be done in a few minutes."

"Not a thing, Doctor," said Max. "I merely wanted to advise you that our attack on the convoy is about to begin. You usually like to be in CIC when such things transpire."

"And I'm sorry to have to eschew an opportunity to view yet more Krag being destroyed yet one more time by you and yet more thermonuclear explosions, but I don't think that doing so would be fair to young Hoffman here as I repair yet another of his injuries sustained yet again due to his inattention to his surroundings. One of these days, young man, you're going to break something that I cannot fix, and our skipper here is going to have to send an *I'm sorry for your loss* commgram to your gray-haired grandmother on Ben-Shieber V."

"I concur wholeheartedly, Doctor," Max said, leaving open whether he concurred with Bram's decision to stay with his patient or with his admonition to Hoffman. "Give my regards to your patient. Thank you, Nurse Church. CIC out." He closed the circuit.

Max looked around CIC and noticed the men smiling at Sahin's comments. Once again he wondered whether the comic relief Bram provided was incidental or intentional or some combination of both. "Now that we've settled that weighty issue, XO, status?"

"Sir, we are keeping station with the convoy on her left flank at a distance of 25,818 kilometers—rate of advance 0.24 c, heading three-two-eight mark one-zero-one. We are fully stealthed, and there is no sign of detection. All stations report manned and ready at Condition Yellow. Weapons loadout: Talon in tube one, Talon in tube two. Drives on both weapons are enabled, warheads armed, safeties disengaged, tubes energized, outer doors are closed. Both weapons are targeted on the VIP transport. Tube three is loaded with a Talon as well and is ready for firing in all respects, save that the outer door is closed. That weapon is not targeted at this time. All three warheads are set for maximum yield. All systems report as nominal. The crew has been fed, and all of the junior mids have been told to go take a leak."

"Seriously, XO? Someone made them go?"

"Absolutely, Skipper. Chief Tanaka and I discussed it after the last attack and agreed that it would be a good idea before we went into combat. It wouldn't do for someone to make a puddle in the middle of an engagement."

"I suppose not. All right, then," Max said. "The weapons are ready, the ship is locked down, and the hatch hangers have all piddled. I suppose that now we can do battle with the evil rodents intent on the extermination of the human race. Mr. Tufeld, set Condition Red throughout the ship."

"Aye, sir. Condition Red." Tufeld keyed the Klaxon and opened MC1. His arresting voice filled the ship. "General Quarters, General Quarters. Set Condition Red throughout the ship. Close all airtight doors and secure all pressure bulkheads. All hands to action stations: ship versus ship."

Less than a minute later, a time consumed mainly by fulfilling the requirement that he get confirmations of the "secure" lights from every action station, Tufeld announced, "All decks and stations report secure at Condition Red. All hands at action stations."

"Very well, Tufeld," Max said. "Mr. LeBlanc, let's execute our closure maneuver."

"Closure maneuver, aye." LeBlanc had his men carry out the maneuver planned by Max, DeCosta, and Bartoli to bring the *Cumberland* into position to attack the convoy. For once, it was nothing particularly tricky or elaborate, given the poor sensor suites on the convoy vessels. The ship, which had been traveling beside the convoy, angled its course a fraction of a degree toward the convoy and inched up its speed. The change brought the destroyer closer to the convoy without a change in bearing. An observer on the convoy, assuming he could see the *Cumberland* at all, would see it hanging in the same position in the viewport but growing gradually nearer.

"No sign of detection," Bartoli announced after a few minutes.

"Enemy sensor emissions are well below any reasonable estimate of their detection thresholds," Kasparov added.

"I'm confirming that, sir," Nelson said from the Stealth console. "My systems' internal sensors are detecting almost no energy being reflected in the direction of the enemy, and even less being emitted on our own systems."

"Outstanding. We don't want these guys to know we're here until after they're dead." A few heads turned at that peculiar turn of phrase, but not many and not much. By now these men were used to hearing things like that from their skipper.

"Sir," Bartoli said after ten more minutes had passed, "we'll be at point victor in one minute."

"Very well. Officer of the Deck, this is a nuclear weapons launch order. I intend to launch the Talon missile in tube one and the Talon missile in tube two at the VIP transport."

"Nuclear weapons launch order acknowledged and logged. Confirming missile programming. Input and confirmed. Missiles in tubes one and two are ready to launch in all respects, save only that missile outer doors are closed." Levy was able to accomplish all of these steps because for this watch, perhaps by no coincidence, he was Officer of the Deck as well as serving in his normal billet of Weapons Officer.

"Very well. Open missile doors on all tubes."

Levy hit the key for each of the three tubes, watched the status lights change, and then checked the video feed from the inside of each tube. "Outer missile doors open on tubes one, two, and three. Visual feed confirms that all three doors are open and all tubes unobstructed."

"Very well."

"Skipper," Bartoli said, "we're at point victor."

"Very well. Maneuvering, execute maneuver as planned—unmask tubes one and two. Main sublight to Full. Weapons, fire tubes one and two as soon as we get within 2500 kilometers of the target. I don't want the point-defense systems from that tanker swatting those missiles down. Fire three as soon as the first missile detonates."

Both men acknowledged their orders. Under LeBlanc's direction, the ship turned so that the bow faced the enemy formation and then accelerated toward it. Within a few seconds, the Krag on board the convoy ships were aware of the destroyer's approach, as evidenced by the powering up of their point-defense systems.

"Mr. Levy, after we destroy the admiral's ship, I don't want to hang around longer than we have to waiting for missile tubes to be reloaded. Let's bring pulse-cannons one, two, and three to PREFIRE so that we can take out the tanker and then the freighter immediately after we destroy the transport."

"Aye, sir," Levy acknowledged. "Pulse-cannons one, two, and three to PREFIRE." A few seconds later: "Tubes one, two, and three at PREFIRE."

"Very well. Bring all three tubes to READY."

"Aye, sir. Pulse-cannons one, two, and three to READY." Three lights changed from orange to green on Levy's pulse-cannon status screen. "Pulse-cannons one, two, and three now at ready. No targets yet designated."

"Lock all three on the tanker."

"Sir," Bartoli said uncertainly, "the tanker has initiated a left roll. Otherwise, neither she nor the ammo carrier are doing anything. No evasive, no weapons, nothing. If we hadn't already escaped our enemy trap for this mission, I might be getting nervous."

So would I. But I want to get that damn admiral.

Max pulled up a few displays on his console, trying to figure out what was going on. He found no satisfactory answers.

This is damn peculiar.

"Kasparov," Max said with what he hoped wasn't too much alarm, "I want a high-magnification visual on the deuterium tanks on that tanker that are facing us. Pronto."

"Understood." Kasparov spoke rapidly into his headset. The visual-scanner man in the Sensors Back Room was on the ball, because it wasn't five seconds before Kasparov answered, "Up. Channel U."

Max, DeCosta, Kasparov, Bartoli, and a few others tied their displays into that channel and were rewarded by a close-up view of a deuterium tank slowly rolling to face the destroyer. When Max looked closely, he could see that the seams between one of the side sections of the tank, forming about an eighth of the long cylinder that made up all of the tank except for the domes on each end, were darker and more distinct than the others. Looking even closer he could see tiny bumps on that section.

Shit. It's a Q-ship.

Max found himself on his feet, the rush of adrenalin too great for him to remain sitting. "Weapons, set all three pulse-cannons for minimum acceleration on the coils. Target all three cannons on that deuterium tank. Immediately upon firing, fire tubes one and two, same target." He didn't wait for an acknowledgment. "Maneuvering, as soon as those weapons are fired, execute evasive Sierra Hotel. Deflectors, be ready to surge. Alerts, notify all hands: prepare to receive fire."

While those orders were being acknowledged, Max leaned over and whispered to DeCosta, "XO, I need you, Mori, the doctor, and Nurse Church in the captured assault shuttle. Save a seat for me, but if I tell you to go, you go, no questions asked." In response to the executive officer's questioning look, Max said, "Listen, Ed, no time to explain. Just do it."

DeCosta nodded and dashed out of CIC.

It took less than five seconds for Levy to fire the pulse-cannons, sending three balls of highly energetic plasma toward the deuterium tank. They were traveling at only about 1500 meters per second because, if fired at their normal velocity from so close to the target, the hole in the deflectors through which the weapons had been fired would not have time to close before they detonated. Two seconds later, the Talon missiles left their tubes.

At the same moment, powerful pyrotechnics detonated around the deuterium tank seam that had so alarmed Max, severing that section from the rest of the tank. A third of a second later, the innocuous-looking bumps on the section revealed themselves to be tiny rocket engines that pulled the section away from what was left of the tank.

Exposing a *Parable* class particle-beam cannon. The kind of particle-beam cannon that one mounted on a good-size moon or small planet because it was too big to put on a ship—that is, unless you put it and its huge power supply in one of the gigantic deuterium tanks that the Krag stuck on the side of one of their even more enormous tankers. The weapon was powerful enough to punch through the strongest deflectors and armor. Two or three hits could obliterate a battleship.

The monster weapon had already accumulated a charge and was ready. As soon as the tank panel was clear, the huge Krag weapon's targeting scanners locked on, the beam tunnel aligning with the *Cumberland*, and the weapon fired its deadly beam for what was supposed to be three Krag standard heartbeats, which was close enough to three seconds as to make no difference.

But after the beam had fired for only four-hundredths of a second, the pulse-cannon bolts fired a moment before by the Union ship struck the tanker's suddenly much stronger deflectors. Although the pulse-cannon bolts did not penetrate the deflectors, the electromagnetic pulse created by the detonation of the *Cumberland*'s pulse-cannon bolts scrambled the Krag weapon's aiming systems, causing the firing mechanism to shut down as a safety precaution to prevent unintended damage from an unaimed shot.

Although four-hundredths of a second was all the time that the Krag weapon was striking the *Cumberland,* four-hundredths of a second was more than enough. The beam, about two and a half meters across, punched right through the destroyer's deflectors and the hull, main engineering, the main cargo bay, main fire control, the galley, a row of crew quarters, auxiliary fire control, the main computer core, and then out through the hull right behind the main sensor array.

Before the men on board the *Cumberland* had time to take a breath, the missiles they had recently fired struck back. The 150 kilotons of energy unleashed by each of the two fusion warheads carried by the Talon missiles pushed through the Krag deflectors weakened by the pulse-cannon bolts of a few seconds before, obliterating the false tank and tanker in a swirling orgy of fusing hydrogen, made all the more violent when the destruction reached the tanker's five gigantic fusion reactors. The explosion was so catastrophic that it showered debris at tens of thousands of feet per second in every direction, including a 2632-kilogram piece of reactor shielding that tore through the VIP transport, nicking the fusion reactor containment vessel, causing a jet of fusion plasma to escape and obliterating the ship. Anyone on the VIP transport was certainly dead. Another fragment struck the main sublight drive of the ammunition carrier, temporarily knocking it off-line.

"Two hull breaches," Ardoin announced from Damage Control 1, "frames two and eight, azimuths unknown due to internal sensor failures. Integrity failures and unspecified internal damage to twelve compartments, including main engineering, main fire control, and auxiliary fire control. Complete list displayed on your emergency display. Compartments open to space at this time. Remaining compartments intact. Ship has retained airtight integrity and is not, repeat, NOT venting atmosphere. Fusion reactor just scrammed, propulsion by maneuvering thrusters only, power being supplied by the Rickover. Negative fire control on any weapons at this time. Negative function on all deflectors. Negative function on any forward sensors at this time. Lateral arrays functioning at one-quarter resolution due to computer limitations. Attitude control is functional on all three axes. There's a lot more, sir, but it would take me all week to list. It's on everyone's board."

"Thank you, Ardoin," Max said. "Order all litter bearers to search for wounded and to carry Cat III or IV to the assault shuttle. Cat I and II wounded will have to make their own way with the rest of us. Category V . . . well, they know what to do with Category V." The last group were those who would die even with treatment. They would be given painkillers and allowed to meet their ends where they were.

Max punched open a channel, knowing whose voice he would hear.

"This is Engineering. What's left of it, at any rate."

"Wernher, what's your status?"

"We're dead in space, that's what, and no prospect of that changing without a trip to the yard. The fusion reactor itself is intact, you understand, but all of the computers and high-energy transfer conduits used to route power generated by the reactor to run the graviton generators that compress and contain the hydrogen are totally gone. There's just a big hole where the main components used to be. I've got the spares, but there's no place to put them and nothing with which to connect them—I can't get the mains up no matter what I do."

"I suppose that the graviton generators can't be powered by the Rickover?"

"It's pence to pounds. The Rickover's total power output is only 2 or 3 percent of what it takes to run them. That's how we start the reactor, by running power from the Rickover into the accumulators for several minutes, but that's just enough to start the reactor and run it and the main sublight for fifteen, maybe twenty, seconds."

Max sighed heavily. "But you can start the reactor and run it for that long with what you've got now?"

"Affirmative, sir. It'll take a few minor reroutes. Give me three or four minutes."

"Get started, Wernher. I think I'm going to need that fifteen seconds from the sublight. Bartoli, any idea what our friends out there are doing?"

"Sensors are not nearly up to snuff, sir, but here's the best I've got. The admiral's transport is toast: a piece of debris from the tanker ruptured her hull and hit the fusion reactor. Nothing left but plasma and tiny pieces. The tanker is gone, too. We got her reactor. The freighter is intact. It's looking like she took a hit from some debris in her aft section. Her main sublight is out and her main power is down, but we're getting power readings indicating that she's putting her fusion reactor through a restart. She'll be up and running in ten or fifteen minutes, maybe a bit longer. And when she is . . ."

"She turns, comes back toward us, gets within pulse-cannon range, and blows us to flaming atoms, and there's nothing we can do about it," Max said.

"Aye, sir," Bartoli said solemnly. "Nothing that I can think of, at any rate."

Well, there is one *thing.*

Max punched a circuit open. "Wernher, don't stop what you're doing; just listen."

"I fairly relish the opportunity to multitask, sir."

The bloody-minded Englishman jokes in the face of almost certain death. Good man.

"Ignore the next announcement, good fellow, you and your lads. Keep doing what you're doing until it's done, and then you can go. Can I count on you to do that?"

"Aye, sir. *England expects that every man will do his duty.*"

"Damn straight." He closed the circuit.

"You too, Levy. I need you with me rather than obeying the announcement. We've got a little mission of our own." Max ignored the look on Levy's face that fairly cried out, "What announcement?"

Max turned to Chin. "I need to speak to Chief Tanaka, this second."

The fastest way to do that was to signal his percom, which Chin did. It took three seconds. "You got him, Skipper."

Max opened the circuit. "Chief, this is the skipper. I'm going to ask you to do something for me even though I'm sure you would do it in any event. Take care of the squeakers."

"Aye, sir. With my very life."

"That's what I wanted to hear. Out."

Back to Chin. "Mr. Chin, send CODE VERMILION to all Union vessels in this sector. That's CODE VERMILION. Get a confirmation that they received it from at least two ships. Then you're released."

"Released, sir?"

"You'll see." Max turned to Tufeld. The grizzled, senior noncom met his eyes soberly. Max could see him bracing for what he knew Max was about to say. Max said it. Two words, like death.

"Abandon ship."

Max's voice left him for a moment, and he felt a sudden tightness in his chest. And then, a cold emptiness, as though his heart had been ripped out of his body and the void filled with ice. *Another abandonment.* "Condition Violet, Tufeld. Repeating the order, all hands abandon ship."

Tufeld nodded gravely, punched up MC1, drew a breath, and said what no one with his job ever wanted to say. "Abandon ship. This is a Condition Violet order. Repeat, all hands, all decks, abandon ship. This is not a drill, repeat, this is not a drill. All hands, all decks, abandon ship." Tufeld paused for a second, looked at the skipper to see if there was anything further. Max shook his head slowly. "Final announcement, all hands, abandon ship." Long pause. "That is all." He closed the circuit with finality, shut down his console, and stepped back.

Max looked around CIC and made a circling motion over his head, followed by a distinct gesture toward the hatch. Max hit the hatch cycle override, causing the CIC hatch to open and stay open. Everyone but Levy strode out of the compartment, briskly but calmly.

Max stepped over to Levy's console and gave the young weapons officer a few quick instructions. He then returned to his own console, slipped his finger into a small notch on the back, and popped off one of the rear panels. He let the panel fall to the deck, where it clattered jarringly in the sudden quiet. Behind the panel was a numeric keypad, a thumbprint scanner, and an old-fashioned key-operated mechanical lock. Max put his thumb on the scanner and entered an eight-digit code. He then reached around his neck and removed a chain, on which were his titanium dog tags, a backup to the q-chip buried in his thigh, and a key that hung from the chain on a small metal loop. He pulled at the key, breaking the loop, and inserted the key in the lock, giving it a sharp turn ninety degrees to the right. A red light above the keypad blinked three times. Max put the chain back around his neck and pressed sharply down on the head of the key with his thumb, breaking it off just inside the lock. The key wasn't coming out absent special tools and a locksmith. Then he allowed himself a quick look around the compartment. A moment ago he thought that he was about to kill his ship, but he was wrong.

Without men to give her life, the *Cumberland* was already dead.

Their absence brought the memory of his crew to him, suddenly and vividly.

God, I'm proud of these men.

Suddenly he allowed himself a flicker of a smile as he took a few steps over to the Operations console, quickly called up a control interface, and punched in two commands.

He took a deep breath, stood up straight, and pulled his shoulders back. He had come on board this ship with his head held high, and by God, he was going to leave the same way.

"Levy, you about done?"

"Closing out the sequence now, Skipper. There. The deed is done."

"Then let's get to the assault shuttle and see if we can save our asses to fight another day."

"I'm all in favor of that, sir."

Without a backward glance, Max strode out of CIC with Levy at his heels. The two men jogged through the empty corridors, feeling jolt after jolt under their feet as escape pods launched. They reached the hangar deck in under two minutes and jumped into the crowded assault shuttle. Max noted that Dr. Sahin was sitting in one of the seats near the front. He turned to DeCosta. "XO, status of the evacuation."

"Of the 182 souls on board at the beginning of watch, twenty-five are confirmed dead, leaving 157 to be evacuated. All 157 are now confirmed on board escape pods, which are confirmed as launched; the *Clover* microfreighter, which launched three minutes ago; or this shuttle. I might add that the compliment on board the shuttle includes one enormous, overweight black feline."

"Outstanding. Mr. Mori, get us out of here. Take up a position 1348 kilometers away from the destroyer's present position." Max couldn't bring himself to say *Cumberland*. "Directly away from the freighter. XO, signal the pods and the microfreighter to form up around us, standard evac formation."

Mori keyed the controls that opened the bay in which the assault shuttle was stored and nudged the drive to take it out. Out of habit, he keyed the commands to close the bay doors behind him, knowing that it didn't matter.

"Captain," the doctor said hesitantly, "I hate to say anything, but in a few minutes when that ammunition ship carrier freighter vessel ship out there gets its drive running, isn't it going to come over here and blast this shuttle and all those little escape pots to tiny bits?"

Escape pots?

"It would, Doctor, if we did nothing, which is not the plan. We'll do something. In fact, this is as good a time as any to start doing something." Max turned to Levy. "Ensign, you know what I need."

"Aye, sir." Levy got up from his seat and went to one of the equipment bays, retrieving an ordinary-looking carry-and-stow box, which he handed to Max. Max opened the box and pulled out another box, this one apparently some kind of piece of equipment wrapped in translucent plastic. He pulled out his utility knife, cut the plastic open, and removed the box, revealing some sort of rudimentary control panel.

"Mr. Mori, kindly bring the ship around so that the destroyer and the enemy are visible in the forward window."

As the destroyer came into view through the window, DeCosta took in a quick breath. A few of the men who had been looking in the right direction nudged their neighbors and pointed. A low murmur of approval ran through the shuttle.

Max turned to Sahin before the latter could ask. "There's no need to be inconspicuous now. So I turned on all her running lights and illuminated her battle stars and her 'E' for 'Excellence,' which the admiral awarded. I want her to go down with her colors flying."

Max heard a few murmurs of "damn straight" and "you're goddamn right."

With a courteous gesture, Max indicated to DeCosta that he needed to sit in the copilot's seat, which the XO promptly yielded. Max sat down and hit a few keys, causing the panel to light up. He hit a few more keys and got a green light to blink three times.

"What is that?" Sahin asked while standing over Max's shoulder.

"Remote control for the ship," Max answered.

"That's insane," Sahin blurted. "If the ship can be controlled remotely, what's to keep an enemy from doing it?"

"It doesn't work unless the receiver unit is first manually enabled with a physical key, a thumbprint, and a security code input from CIC or Main Engineering, the most securely guarded compartments on the ship."

"Oh. Never mind. Proceed."

"Thank you." Max adopted a formal but quiet tone, almost as though he were uttering a solemn benediction. Although his voice was low, Max knew that he could be heard throughout the shuttle. "The Union Space Ship *Cumberland*, Registry Number DPA-0004, has one last duty to perform for her crew and her country."

Max manipulated some controls and squinted at a tiny display at the top of the unit. "I'm having the computer reorient the ship so that it is pointed at the enemy, which it is doing. There. That's done. Now I'm keying the restart sequence for the fusion reactor. A cold start would take about five minutes, but since the British have brought the start sequence right up to the final initiation, we will need less than a minute."

Everyone in the assault shuttle sat still and silent while the time passed. Except Clouseau, who pranced up to the copilot's station and laid down with his legs in the air and his head resting on Max's foot. His purring could be heard through most of the shuttle. What could have been a very, very long minute passed more easily.

"Okay, reactor's running. Now let's kick in the drive."

The destroyer's main sublight drive came online. The damaged systems were able to provide only about 8 percent thrust, but it was enough. Aided by small corrections from computer guidance, the *Cumberland* gradually accelerated straight toward the Krag vessel. The Krag, seeing their doom coming, tried to evade on maneuvering thrusters. The destroyer's computer compensated easily for the feeble acceleration thus imparted. Less than a minute and a half after Max had put the *Cumberland* into motion, it rammed the Krag freighter at a relatively sedate 1959 kilometers per hour.

Bram was disappointed at the collision, as he was expecting something more spectacular. He could see that the enemy ship was damaged, but that its cargo—which was likely a real cargo of real munitions bound for the real front—was mostly intact. Just as he was about to point out this fact to Max, he saw Levy's lips moving. It took him a second to figure out what the young man was saying. He was counting. In Hebrew. Backward.

"*Shalosh. Schtayim. Achat.* Now."

At that moment the cabin of the shuttle was flooded with a blue-white glare that seemed to come from every direction—from the bulkheads, the seats, the control panels, and most powerfully, through the window. Levy had manually overridden the safety protocols inside two Talon missiles, the ones that prevented the warheads from detonating unless the missiles were actually launched, and programmed them to detonate six seconds after the destroyer hit the enemy ship. Two warheads, each packing 150 kilotons, went off simultaneously. The fireball completely encompassed the freighter. One moment it existed. The next, it did not.

The glare of the thermonuclear explosion slowly dimmed. In less than a minute, it was gone, leaving only the blackness of space and its scattering of distant stars.

There was no trace of the *Cumberland.*

The silence in the shuttle was deadly.

"She was a good ship," Finnegan said from the back of the shuttle. His voice was low, but it still carried.

"Aye," murmured many voices, like the call and response of a liturgy.

"It was only near the end that we were worthy of her," said Sanders.

"Aye," they said again.

"She died to save us all," said Greenlee.

"Aye," was the response.

The men fell silent. This silence, however, was not deadly. The men were silent, not because they were too downhearted to speak. It was simply that there was nothing else to say.

Dr. Sahin, who had left his former seat to position himself in a squatting position between Mori and Max, looked up at his skipper. "Max," he said softly, "our ship is gone, and we're dozens of light-years behind enemy lines with practically the whole Krag navy between us and Union space. Presumably, as is your wont, you have some convoluted, improbably dangerous, and laughably unorthodox plan to extricate us from this precarious predicament and allow us to fight another day to save the Union from defeat at the hands of its implacable enemies."

"I'm afraid not," Max said. "In fact, I don't know what I'm going to do." Max had been looking out the window. Now he turned to meet Bram's eyes. "But I can tell you absolutely that there's one thing we're *not* going to do, my friend."

"What, my friend, is that?"

"Give up. This crew and I are never giving up."

He looked back at the stars.

"Never."

GLOSSARY AND GUIDE TO ABBREVIATIONS

Excerpted from *The USS Cumberland Midshipmen's Introduction to Naval Terminology and to Expressions Used by Ship's Senior Officers*, Ship's database article by Menachem Levy, ENSN USN, April 2315.

4-hydroxycoumarin: A class of organic compounds, many of which are powerful vitamin K antagonists, some of which are used as anticoagulant medications. One chemical in this class, warfarin, is used not only as a pharmaceutical but also as a primary ingredient in rat and mouse poison.

Alphacen: Alpha Centauri, as viewed from Earth, the brightest star in the constellation Centaurus (the Centaur), a trinary star system and the star system nearest to the Sol System. Primary Star, Alpha Centauri A, a type G2V main sequence star.

AU: Astronomical Unit. A unit of length or distance, defined as the mean distance between Earth and the Sun, most commonly used in measuring distances on an interplanetary rather than an interstellar scale because it yields manageable numbers for such distances. For example, Mercury is about .35 AU from the Sun, while Neptune is about 30 AU from the sun. One AU is equal to 149,597,870.7 kilometers or 92,955,807.3 miles.

back room: *See* SSR.

battlecruiser: A large, powerful warship carrying offensive weaponry of the size and power of a battleship, but intermediate in size between cruisers and battleships. Typically massing between 40,000 and 60,000 tons, battlecruisers possess shielding, armor, speed, maneuverability, and defensive capabilities more equivalent to those of a cruiser than a battleship. Naval officers are split on the utility of this type, with some believing that, with the killing power of a battleship and the speed of a cruiser, it offers the best of both; others believing that its large guns make it as tempting a target for the enemy as a battleship, but lacking in the armor, shielding, and point-defense capabilities of a battleship to defend itself, thereby combining the worst of both. A battlecruiser is generally under the command of a full captain.

battleship: The largest and most powerful type of weapons platform ship (carriers are larger and, with their fighter groups, arguably more powerful, but do not mount heavy offensive weapons). Typically massing 60,000 tons and up, battleships mount large batteries of the most powerful offensive weapons carried on starships and are equipped with the heaviest armor and defensive shielding. The firepower and toughness of a battleship rival those of a battle station. While capable of fairly high sublight speeds, they are very difficult to maneuver. In addition, their enormous bulk means that under compression drive, they are limited to fairly low c multiples. Accordingly, battleships cross interstellar space almost exclusively by jumping. A battleship is typically under the command of a full captain or a commodore.

battle star: An award conferred by a fleet or task force commander upon a vessel that has comported itself honorably in direct combat with the enemy. In the days of the Saltwater Navy, vessels displayed their battle stars on the hull or superstructure, where other vessels could see them. Union warships display their battle stars by the use of colored running lights on their hull, arranged in the shape of a star and illuminated when they are not stealthed. Battle stars come in three grades: bronze (orange lights), silver (white lights), and gold (yellow lights). The battle star is a permanent award displayed by the vessel as long as it remains in service. Not to be confused with a battlestar, which is an archaic name for a former type that was essentially a cross between a battlecruiser and an escort carrier, mounting heavy pulse-cannon and missiles while also carrying fighters. This type fell into disfavor because of the difficulty in conducting fighter operations while firing guns and missiles through the fighter formations.

bearing: The position of an object relative to another object, measured as degrees of angle on a horizontal and a vertical plane with the two numbers separated by a slash, which is pronounced as "mark" when giving a bearing out loud. The zero reference in both planes is the geometric center of the Milky Way galaxy. Hence, a Sensor officer will say that a contact is at bearing two-three-seven mark zero-four-five. Also, a sphere, usually made of some hard metal alloy, used in conjunction with several similar spheres to provide lubrication between a rotating shaft and its housing (ball bearings).

boarding cutlass: A sword made of high-tensile-strength steel, in fashion similar to the United States Navy's Model 1917 Cutlass. It is 63.5 centimeters long (25 inches) and weighs approximately 935 grams (33 ounces), slightly curved, and primarily regarded as a slashing weapon, but can be used as a thrusting weapon as well. Carried by naval personnel for close order battle in confined quarters on a ship, particularly in locations where gunfire might puncture pipes or pressure vessels, releasing toxic or radioactive substances, or might cause the venting of atmosphere into space. A boarding cutlass and a sidearm of his choice (either an M-1911 or an M-62) is issued to a midshipman when he is promoted to Midshipman First Class.

Boudreaux and Thibodeaux: The more common name for the Etienne V. Boudreaux and John G. Thibodeaux Advanced Aerospace Group of Nouvelle Acadiana, S.A., a specialty spacecraft design and construction firm known for developing and building cutting-edge warships for the Union Space Navy. Approximately 15 percent of current Union warship designs come from the virtual drafting tables and shipyards of Boudreaux and Thibodeaux. B & T is the only design firm in the Union with authority from the Admiralty—for the duration of the present war—to spend naval funds to undertake new warship designs on its own initiative up through the preliminary design phase, as no design from the firm has ever failed to be accepted by the navy, at least for construction of a prototype.

Bravo: The second letter of the Union Forces Radio Alphabet (*see*); a colloquial name for Epsilon Indi III (*see*).

BuDes (*pronounced* "Bew dess"): Bureau of Design. The naval office responsible for designing warships and warship power plants. Its most important component offices are: OfSpaF (pronounced "off spaf"), Office of Space Frames, which is responsible for designing the hulls and the interior support structure that gives them strength and rigidity; OfPropSys (pronounced "off prop sis"), Office of Propulsion Systems, which is responsible for designing the engines and drives; OfHab (pronounced "off hab"), Office of Habitability, which is responsible for designing the interiors of the ships, including location and arrangements of compartments and furnishings; and OfSupSys ("pronounced "off soup sys") Office of Support Systems, which is responsible for designing the life support, plumbing, and similar systems necessary for sustaining life in space. Weapons, sensors, navigation systems, communications systems, and building of the ships after they are designed are all supervised by separate bureaus.

BuPers (*pronounced* "bew perz"): Bureau of Personnel. The naval department responsible for managing naval personnel assignments, recruiting, and similar matters.

butterbars: The dress uniform insignia of a naval ensign, consisting of a single brass bar, so-called because the brass is yellow like butter; term may also refer by extension to any naval ensign.

c: The speed of light in a vacuum, commonly stated as "lightspeed," 299,792,458 meters per second or 186,282 miles per second. Unless a warship is traveling very slowly (in which case, its velocity is given as meters per second), its speed is generally given as a fraction or multiple of c, e.g., .25 c for one quarter of lightspeed or 325 c for 325 times lightspeed. In common usage, sometimes only the number is given. Hence, a tactical officer might inform his captain that a "bogie is approaching at point 25," or an engineer might advise that the ship "should not exceed 250."

***Ca c'est bon* (Cajun French):** That's good. Equivalent to *C'est bon* in Parisian French.

Cajun: A person descended from the French-speaking Roman Catholic residents of Nova Scotia (which they called Acadia) who were exiled by the British at the end of the French and Indian War because of concerns regarding their loyalty to the British crown and who settled in what was then the French territory of Louisiana. Most Cajuns spoke their own version of French well into the twentieth century and maintain a distinctive culture to this day. On Earth, Cajuns mostly reside in the parishes of South-Central and Southwest Louisiana, centered on Lafayette. The largest population of twenty-fourth-century Cajuns, however, may be found on planet Nouvelle Acadiana (Hyukutaki-Matshushita IV), colonized by a mostly Cajun expedition in the early twenty-second century. Cajuns are often referred to by each other and by their friends as "Coonasses." The word *Cajun* is a worn-down form of "Acadian."

carrier: A large vessel designed to launch, retrieve, arm, fuel, and service fighters and other smaller ships. Large fleet and command carriers can carry as many as two hundred fighters, while smaller escort and attack carriers as few as thirty. Carriers range in size from 40,000 to 1,000,000 tons. As of January through March 2315, there were rumors that the navy was currently constructing a new class of carriers massing 2,000,000 tons, with one being built at the Luna Fleet Yards, one being built at Alphacen, and two at 40 Eridani A. These vessels are supposedly to be known as the *Churchill* Class.

***C'est pas rien* (Cajun French):** It's nothing, think nothing of it. Equivalent to *De rien* in Parisian French.

***C'est tout* (Cajun French):** That is all.

***Chara* (Hebrew):** Shit.

Cherenkov-Heaviside radiation: The burst of radiation emitted as an object emerges from a jump (*see*). So-named for its two components: Cherenkov radiation, which is the radiation emitted when a charged particle passes through a dielectric medium at a speed higher than the normal speed for the propagation of light in that medium; and Heaviside radiation, the radiation emitted when a particle traveling faster than the speed of light in a spacial regime in which that can occur (e.g., in n-space) is decelerated to subluminal velocities in our own spacial regime.

Chief of the Boat: The senior noncommissioned officer on board any naval vessel. He is considered a department head and is the liaison between the captain and the noncommissioned ranks. Sometimes referred to as COB (pronounced "cob") and informally known as the "Goat."

CIC: Combat Information Center. The compartment on a warship from which the ship's operations are controlled, analogous to the "bridge" on an old seagoing vessel before the functions of that space were split between the Bridge and CIC with the introduction of radar to combat ships in the years leading up to World War II.

CIG: Change in grade. Promotion or demotion. Official orders will never state that a person is "promoted to commander." Rather, they will say that the person is "CIG to commander." A CIG order always states the date, hour, and minute the CIG becomes effective, so that there is no question of the relative seniority (and, therefore, who gives orders to whom) of two officers of the same grade.

Clarke orbit: Synchronous or stationary orbit. An orbit in which the orbiting body remains stationary relative to a point on the surface of the orbited body on the latter's equator, also defined as an equatorial orbit in which the orbital period is equal to the rotational period of the orbited body. Known as a "Clarke orbit" because the concept was first described in detail by British science and science fiction author Arthur C. Clarke in a 1945 article published in *Wireless World* magazine.

class: A production series of warships of highly similar or identical design, designated by the name of the first ship of the series. Accordingly, if a series of heavy cruisers is produced from the same design, and the first ship of that design to be produced is the USS *Faget* (pronounced "fah zhay"), then the vessels of that class are known as *Faget* class cruisers. Vessels of the same class are usually named after the same thing. For example, *Faget* class cruisers are all named after influential designers of aircraft, launch vehicles, and space vessels. Hence, the class contains the *Faget, Wright, Bleriot, Langley, Kelly Johnson, Von Braun, Korolev, Caldwell Johnson, Northrup*, etc.

class (Krag vessels): The Krag apparently have a class system similar to that of the Union, producing warships of similar design in series. Because Krag vessel names are, however, unknown, difficult to pronounce, or impossible to remember, the navy uses a system of "Reporting Names" for Krag vessel classes. Essentially, when a new class of Krag vessel is identified, a name is assigned to that class by Naval Intelligence. Class names generally start with the same letter or group of letters as the name of the vessel type, with the exception of battlecruisers, the class names of which begin with "Bar" to distinguish them from battleships. In this way a ship's type can immediately be determined from its class name, even if the name is not familiar. Examples of class names for each major warship type follow:

Battleships: Batwing, Battalion, Battleaxe, Baton
Battlecruisers: Barnacle, Barnyard, Barrister, Barsoom, Barmaid
Carrier: Carousel, Carnivore, Carpetbagger, Cardigan
Cruiser: Crusader, Crucible, Crustacean, Crumpet, Crayfish
Frigate: Freelancer, Frogleg, Frycook, Frigid
Destroyer: Deckhand, Delver, Dervish, Debris, Deputy
Corvette: Corpuscle, Cormorant, Cornhusker, Corsican, Cordwood

Cobra's Nest: A developmental group at Boudreaux and Thibodeaux (*see*) devoted to designing particularly innovative high-performance warships for the Union Space Navy. Among others, the group was responsible for designing the *Drake* class battleship, the *Boudica* class cruiser, the *Battleaxe* and *Khyber* class destroyers, and the "Night" type intelligence, reconnaissance, and surveillance vessels (*Nighthawk, Nightshade,* and *Nightwind* classes). The idea of having such a group, as well as the name, were inspired by Lockheed's "Skunk Works." Noteworthy Cobra's Nest designers over the years include John "T-John" Thibodeaux, Polycarp Phillipe Pecoe II ("Number Two"), Clyde "True Blue" LeBleu, and Harvey "Humble Harv" Robichaux.

Comet: Colloquial term for the Warship Qualification Badge, a medal, shaped like a comet with a curved tail, indicating that the wearer has passed either a Warship Crew Qualification Examination or a Warship Officer Qualification Examination. The decoration shows that the recipient can competently operate every crew or officer station on the ship, perform basic damage control, engage in close order battle with sidearm and boarding cutlass, use a pulse rifle, and fight hand-to-hand. The Comet was created in the early days of space combat to be the equivalent of the "Dolphins" from the United States Submarine Forces.

compression drive: One of the two known technologies that allow ships to travel faster than lightspeed (the other being the jump drive). The compression drive permits violation of Einsteinian physics by selectively compressing and expanding the fabric of the space-time continuum. The drive creates a bubble of distorted space-time around the vessel with a diameter approximately thirty-four times the length of the ship. This bubble, in turn, contains a smaller bubble of undistorted space-time just large enough to enclose the ship itself. The density of space-time is compressed along the ship's planned line of travel and expanded behind it (hence, the term "compression drive," which was thought to sound better than "expansion drive" or, heaven forbid, "warp drive"), creating a propulsive force that moves the ship forward faster than the speed of light as viewed from the perspective of a distant observer. This superluminal motion does not violate Einsteinian physics because the ship is stationary relative to the fabric of space-time inside the bubble and, therefore, from the point of view of an observer located there, does not exceed the speed of light. Because the volume of distorted space rises as a geometric function as ship size goes up under the familiar $V = \pi r^2$ formula multiplied by 34 (pi times half the length of the ship squared times 34), even a small increase in the ship's dimensions results in a substantial increase in the energy required to propel it through compressed space. Accordingly, until the recent acquisition of field synchronization algorithms from the Sarthan, only smaller ship types could move at high speeds or for any appreciable distance using compression drive, which means, in turn, that major fleet operations and planetary conquests require the taking and holding of jump points so that carriers, battleships, tankers, and other larger or slower vessels can be brought into the system.

compression shear: A dangerous phenomenon caused by a compression drive experiencing poor speed regulation, a common occurrence at speeds of less than about 80 c. Compression shear occurs when radical fluctuations in the degree of space-time distortion caused by a poorly regulated drive exert variable and rapidly fluctuating force against the "bubble" of normal space-time surrounding the ship. As the small undistorted bubble around the ship must exist in precise equilibrium with the larger zone of differentially compressed and expanded space that surrounds the smaller one, sharp variations or "shear" along the boundary rupture the bubble and destroy the ship.

Core Systems: The fifty star systems located near the astrographic center of the Union, which, while constituting only about 10 percent by number of the Union's inhabited worlds, are home to 42 percent of its population and 67 percent of its heavy industrial capacity.

cruiser: A large, heavily armed, and heavily armored vessel providing an excellent mix of firepower, armor, speed, and endurance. Cruisers are highly powerful and flexible warships that can operate as component parts of large task forces or as the center of small task forces of their own. Cruisers are capable of delivering heavy doses of sustained weapons fire against warships, orbital installations, and surface targets, and can operate without support for more than a year. Most cruiser types mass between 25,000 and 40,000 metric tons and are often loosely divided into the subtypes of light, medium, and heavy. A heavy cruiser is only slightly smaller and less powerful than the smaller classes of battlecruiser.

DC: Damage Control. The set of duties and techniques associated with limiting and repairing damage to a ship sustained in space, particularly battle damage. The term is also used to refer to the CIC station used to display damage to the ship and coordinate the efforts of Damage Control parties as well as to the person who mans that station.

delta V: Change in velocity. Delta is the physics/aerospace symbol for "change," and V is the symbol for velocity (velocity technically being both speed and direction). Space-vehicle maneuvers are typically measured in terms of the delta V necessary to carry them out, as that number immediately tells a pilot whether he has enough fuel and thruster power to complete the maneuver.

destroyer: The most numerous type of rated ship in the navy, destroyers are comparatively small vessels (as measured against cruisers, battleships, and carriers) optimized for speed, maneuverability, and firepower. Known as the "workhorses of the navy," destroyers typically mass in the 16,000- to 20,000-ton range. They are not heavily armored and are not capable of carrying enough stores, fuel, and munitions to operate for long periods of time without resupply, but carry pulse-cannons equal in power (though usually fewer of them) to those carried by most frigates. Destroyers are typically operated as escorts to larger vessels as part of a fleet or task force. When a destroyer encounters a ship of greater force, it is supposed to either call upon a heavier vessel with which it is operating or, if none is available, rely on its maneuverability and speed to evade and run away (ELEVES or "elude, evade, and escape"). The CO of a destroyer is typically a commander, although ships in the smaller destroyer classes sometimes have an unusually able lieutenant commander as a skipper.

deuterium-separation plant: A facility for producing deuterium fuel for fusion reactors. Such plants function by separating naturally occurring deuterium oxide, also known as heavy water, from ordinary water, taking advantage of the two substances' differing densities through the use of a series of high-speed centrifuges. Once heavy water of suitable concentration (more than 95 percent) is obtained, the deuterium is then broken down by electrical hydrolysis into elemental oxygen and deuterium. Such facilities tend to be located on water-covered moons similar to Europa in the Sol System because they provide a large supply of relatively high-deuterium water, a shallow gravity well, and some kind of large hard surface (either ice or rock) on which to construct the facility.

***droga, merda, porra* (Brazilian Portuguese):** Bummer, shit, fuck. An exclamation of shock and dismay.

***dummkopf* (German):** Stupid. In German, though, the term *dummkopf* can be used as an appellation in a way that "stupid," which is primarily an adjective, is rarely used in Standard. Accordingly, in some ways, the term may equate better with the Standard nouns "idiot" or "moron."

Dusang: The standard unit for measuring the interaction between a stated surface area and a tachyon-based scan.

"E" for "Excellence": An award, conferred upon a vessel by a task-force commander or higher authority, for conspicuous excellence or achievement in any area of endeavor. The award is displayed by illuminating running lights arranged in the shape of a large letter "E" when the vessel is not stealthed. The award is typically made for some demonstration of outstanding proficiency by the vessel and is authorized to be displayed for a limited number of days, usually sixty.

EM: Electromagnetic. Usually short for the term "electromagnetic radiation," meaning visible light, radio waves, ultraviolet, infrared, and similar forms of energy forming a part of the familiar electromagnetic spectrum. Often used to distinguish sensors that detect EM radiation from those that detect other phenomena, such as gravitational effects or neutrinos.

EMCON: Emissions Control. A security and deception measure in which a warship not only operates under what twenty-first-century readers would call "radio silence" but also without navigation beacons, active sensor beams, and any other emissions that could be used to track the ship.

***Emeka Moro*:** Union Space Navy frigate, *Edward Jenner* class, Registry Number FLE 2372, commissioned 8 December 2295. Currently (as of 20 February 2315) undergoing extensive repairs and refit at James Lovell Station to repair damage sustained in battle against a Krag *Barsoom* class battlecruiser on 11 November 2314. For the person, *see* Moro, Emeka.

enlisted ratings: The ranks of enlisted men in the Union Space Navy are listed below, in order of increasing rank. Within each rank, not separately listed here, are three classes—third, second, and first. So within the ranks of able spacer, one can rise through the ranks of able spacer third class, able spacer second class, and able spacer first class.

recruit
ordinary
able
petty officer
chief petty officer

Epsilon Indi: As viewed from Earth, the fifth brightest star in the Constellation Indus (the Indian). A main sequence star, class K, orbited by two brown dwarf stars and seven planets, located approximately twelve light years from Earth. The name is also used to refer to the third planet of this system, Epsilon Indi III (sometimes referred to as "Bravo" for the letter "B" as it was the second Earth colony outside the Sol system, coming after "Alpha" or Alpha Centauri), which is the home of the Clara Barton Military Hospital, the largest and most advanced hospital for military casualties in the Union. The term "Indians" for residents of that world is regarded as a slur and should be avoided by persons who do not want to start a fight with one of that world's notoriously pugnacious inhabitants.

FEBA: Forward Edge of Battle Area. The "front line," or in three-dimensional space, a plane or other two-dimensional surface, marking the boundary between space controlled by friendly forces and space controlled by enemy forces. Alternately, the surface marking the forwardmost friendly forces. Sometimes referred to as FLOF or Forward Line of Own Forces (from Forward Line of Own Troops in pre-starflight Earth ground combat).

frame: A vertical cross section of a warship, numbered from bow to stern for the purpose of describing the location of damage to the ship's structure or to large areas. A destroyer might have as few as eight frames, while a carrier has hundreds.

frigate: A type of warship with a slightly higher displacement range than destroyers (frigates typically mass between 18,000 and 26,000 metric tons; note, the largest classes of destroyer are heavier than the smallest classes of frigate), but usually somewhat slower and less maneuverable, more heavily armored and armed (particularly in the matter of the number of missile tubes—most destroyers have only two forward firing missile tubes, while most frigates have at least four and many have six or eight), and carrying a larger supply of consumables and weapons reloads to give them significantly higher endurance on station without resupply. Frigates are most commonly used in detached service. Frigates are typically skippered by a full commander. While frigates in saltwater navies are typically smaller than destroyers, they are larger in the Union Space Navy because the type was introduced into service after destroyers, and because "frigate" was the most reasonable saltwater navy term available and there was no appropriately "naval-sounding" name for a vessel type intermediate in size between destroyers and battlecruisers.

FTL: Faster than light. Superluminal.

Gates: The traditional naval nickname for a respected and highly able Computer and Information Systems Officer. The name is taken from that of William "Bill" Gates (born 28 October 1955; died 23 August 2077), the founder of the Microsoft Corporation and one of the architects of "the Personal Computer Revolution." The term was first applied to computer officers upon the formation of the UESF (*see*) in 2034.

***genau* (German):** Exactly, precisely. Often used to express agreement.

Goat: Informal name for the Chief of the Boat (*see*).

***Gott im Himmel* (German):** God in heaven! An exclamation of shock and dismay.

Greenie: Colloquial term for a recruit spacer. So called because the working uniform for that grade is light green in color.

Gynophage: An extremely virulent genetically engineered viral disease launched by the Krag against the Union in 2295. The disease organism is highly infectious to all humans, but a gene sequence unique to the human "Y" chromosome prevents disease symptoms from manifesting in all but a tiny fraction of males, thereby keeping infected males contagious but asymptomatic. It is 99+ percent fatal to human females. It is believed that, left to itself, the disease would have killed all but a few of the human females in the galaxy and resulted in the virtual extinction of the human race. It was disseminated by thousands of stealthed compression-drive drones launched by the Krag in the early days of the war, each of which launched thousands of submunitions that exploded in the atmosphere of human-inhabited planets. The disease functions in a manner similar to Ebola, by breaking down the tissues of the internal organs, but kills much more rapidly. Once the disease begins to manifest, the subject is dead within minutes. The disease is currently treated/prevented by the Moro Treatment, a combination vaccine and antibody devised by a team led by the brilliant Dr. Emeka Moro (*see*).

hopping the wort: The process of adding hops (the female flowers of the hop plant) to the boiled grain product that will be fermented into beer (wort), one of the stages in the art of beer making that most calls for skill on the part of the brewmaster.

Hotel: Union Forces Voicecom Alphabet (*see*) designator for the letter "H." Sensors and Tactical designation for a hostile contact or target.

hottie Scotty: A particularly industrious or capable member of the Engineering crew, sometimes used disparagingly regarding a person who, for the moment, is the favorite of the Chief Engineer for reasons unconnected with merit (*see* Scotty).

hypergolic: Two substances that, when combined, will ignite and combust without need of an ignition source—a term used in the navy primarily to describe fuels for missiles and thrusters. Rocket motors employing hypergolic fuels are mechanically simpler and inherently more reliable than those that do not because no ignition source need be provided in the design. On the other hand, hypergolic fuels provide a lower specific impulse (essentially the amount of thrust developed per unit of fuel and oxidizer) than cryogenic fuel/oxidizer combinations such as hydrogen/oxygen.

IDSSC: Interstellar Data Systems Standardization Convention (pronounced "id sick"). An informal agreement among the major computer and data systems manufacturers of the Union, most human worlds, and several alien races providing for standardization of data formats, transfer protocols, design of cables and connectors, and other matters to allow interchangeability and transferability of data and computer equipment from one star system to another. Because of IDSSC, a Pfelung printer can be attached to a computer made on Alphacen, and used to print a document written and saved to a data chip on Ghifta Prime.

IFF: Identification Friend or Foe. A general descriptive term for any system that allows vessels to identify each other as being friendly or hostile, usually involving an exchange of coded electronic transmissions.

inertial compensator: The system on a space vessel that negates the inertial effect of acceleration on the crew and vessel contents (known as "G forces"), enabling the ship to accelerate, turn, and decelerate rapidly without killing the crew and ripping the fixtures from the deck.

jump: The process by which a space vessel uses its jump drive (*see*) to transition from one point in normal space to a distant point in normal space by transitioning for one Planck interval through n space.

jump drive: One of the two systems that allows a space vessel to cross interstellar distances in less time than it would take to travel at sublight speed (the other being compression drive, *see*). The jump drive transfers the vessel in a single Planck interval from one point in space, known as a jump point, to another jump point in a nearby star system and never less than 3.4 nor more than 12.7 light-years away. Jump points are generally located between 20 to 30 AU from a star and almost always lie at least forty-five degrees away from the star's equator. For some unknown reason, systems either have no jump points, three, or a multiple of three (most commonly three), usually located several dozen AU from each other. Jumping is always more energy efficient and much faster than traversing the same distance with compression drive. However, it is almost impossible to jump into an enemy-held system, because the enemy will almost always have weapons trained and ranged on the jump points, and the process of jumping requires that the jumping ship power down all sublight drives, weapons, shielding, and point-defense systems, making it virtually helpless when emerging from a jump. Accordingly, in order to take a system, it is usually necessary to send in ships from a system within ten light-years or so under compression drive and take the jump points, thereby allowing heavier ships, troop carriers, and supply vessels to jump in.

Jurassic Space: The period, technology, or practices associated with human space exploration, particularly manned or crewed space exploration, before humanity acquired the technology to explore interstellar space by defeating the Ning-Braha at the Battle of Luna (circa 1960 to July 2034).

***Khyber* class:** A class of destroyer, the first of which, the USS *Khyber*, was commissioned on 24 April 2311, making these vessels a "new" class in 2315. The Khybers are exceptionally fast and maneuverable, even for destroyers. The thrust-to-mass ratio of these ships is in the same range as those of many fighter designs; accordingly, it is said that they handle more like large fighters than escort vessels. They are equipped with pulse-cannon as powerful as those on many capital ships (although they have only three of these and a smaller rear-firing unit, whereas a capital ship might have a dozen or more). Ships in this class are extremely stealthy, possess a sophisticated ability to mimic the electronic and drive emissions of other ships, and have a highly effective sensor suite. They are also equipped with SWACS (*see*). The trade-offs made to optimize these characteristics include highly spartan crew accommodations (spartan even for a destroyer), a radically reduced number of reloads for her missile tubes (twenty Talons and five Ravens versus a typical destroyer loadout of sixty and twelve), a small crew making for a heavy workload for all personnel, modest fuel capacity, and a reduced cargo hold. Unsupported endurance is rated at seventy-five days (as compared to 180 days for most destroyers), but in practice, it is somewhat shorter. It is believed that the class was designed to make quick, stealthy raids into enemy space and destroy his supply lines and means of communication, thereby disrupting his logistics and command/control/communications. Mass: 16,200 metric tons. Top sublight speed: .963 c. Compression drive: 1575 c cruise, 2120 c emergency. Weapons: three forward-firing Krupp-BAE Mark XXXIV pulse-cannon, 150-gigawatt rating; one rear-firing Krupp-BAE Mark XXII pulse-cannon (colloquially known as the "Stinger"), seventy-five-gigawatt rating. Two forward- and one rear-firing missile tubes. Standard missile loadout of twenty Talon (*see*) and five Raven (*see*) antiship missiles. Ships in this class are named after historically significant mountain passes and ocean straits. Length: 97 meters; beam: 9.5 meters. Commissioned ships in this class as of 21 January 2315 are: *Khyber*, *Gibraltar*, *Messina*, *Cumberland*, *Hormuz*, and *Khardung La*. The projected size of the class is eighty-five ships.

Known Space: That portion of the Milky Way galaxy explored by humans or of which humans have reasonably reliable information from alien races, mostly consisting of a portion of the Orion-Cygnus galactic arm centered on the Sol System.

Kuiper (*rhymes with* "piper") Belt: A belt of bodies, made mainly of frozen volatiles such as water ice, methane, and ammonia, found in the outer regions of many star systems. In the Sol System, it begins about 30 AU from the Sun (the orbit of Neptune) and extends out to approximately 50 AU. Kuiper belts typically contain several planet-size objects, known as *Plutinos*—a name taken from Pluto, a Kuiper belt object discovered in 1930 and classified as a planet for more than seventy years. Kuiper belts are tactically important mainly because the large number of massive icy objects provides a good place to hide a warship's mass and heat signatures.

lubber: A person unfamiliar with space and not possessing the skills and knowledge associated with service on a space vessel. From the old Saltwater Navy term "landlubber," which is, itself, of obscure origin.

lubber line: A space vessel course consisting of a straight line through space from the point of origin to the destination.

Mark One Eyeball: Naval slang for the human eye without any artificial aid of any kind. Called "Mark One" because it is the original unimproved model (often, naval systems are numbered Mark I, Mark II, Mark III, and so on as new versions are introduced).

M-62: Model 2162 pistol. One of the two sidearms approved for use by Union Space Navy personnel (the other being the M-1911), the M-62 is a ten-millimeter, semiautomatic, magazine-fed handgun. It was introduced to naval use in 2062 during the First Interstellar War, when the Glock polymer-framed weapons then issued were found to become brittle, to warp, and even to sometimes melt in the temperature extremes of space combat, requiring that the navy issue an all-metal handgun to supplement the M-1911. The resulting weapon, designed by the Beretta-Browning Arms Corporation, was based superficially on the venerable Browning Hi-Power design modified to fire the larger cartridge (the older weapon was originally designed for the 9 mm cartridge but was also manufactured for the .40 S&W round).and constructed with modern alloys and coatings. It has a fourteen-round magazine.

M-72: Model 2072 close order battle shotgun. The Winchester-Mossberg Arms Company Model 2072 is a semiautomatic twelve-gauge shotgun designed for close order battle against boarding parties or for use by boarders. It has a "sawed-off" thirteen-inch barrel and is fed from a ten-round box magazine rather than the traditional tube magazine so that it can have a short barrel for use in close quarters while retaining high magazine capacity. The most common load fired in this weapon is a high-velocity 00 buckshot shell that propels ten .33 caliber (8.322 mm) hard cast lead balls at a muzzle velocity of approximately 350 meters per second. The weapon is also capable of firing various slug, slug-sabot, dart-penetrator, and exploding rounds. It is of steel, aluminum alloy, and composite construction (no polymer parts) and is equipped with fixed military aperture sights.

M-88: Model 2288 pulse rifle. The Colt-Ruger Naval Arms Corporation Model 2288 is a 7.62 x 51 millimeter, select fire, magazine-fed battle rifle issued to navy personnel for boarding actions, ship defense, and ground combat, similar in form and function to the M-14 battle rifle issued by the United States of America in the mid-twentieth century, but containing an improved internal mechanism and made significantly lighter through the use of aluminum and composite materials (5.56 mm rounds were found to lack sufficient penetrating power to reliably kill Krag wearing combat gear). It is also the standard-issue personal weapon of the Union Space Marine Corps. The rifle is fed from a thirty-five-round box magazine and is of all metal/composite construction (no polymer parts). The naval version has standard military aperture sights adjustable for range only (not windage), while the marine version is equipped with a detachable optical aiming device that operates either as a red-dot reflex sight or a low-light-capable zoom telescopic sight. Muzzle climb and recoil in full-auto mode are nearly eliminated by a miniature, power-cell-driven, inertial compensator unit in the stock. The weapon has four firing modes: semiauto, three-shot burst, six-shot burst, and full-auto. It is called a "pulse rifle" because, coaxially mounted below the rifle barrel, is a launcher from which can be fired the MMD ("Make My Day") pulse grenade, a 35-millimeter self-propelled short-range projectile containing a shaped-charge-equipped pulse slug capable of penetrating the armor on a Krag fighting suit at a range of fifty meters and then exploding, killing the occupant. The MMD is also effective against lightly armored ground vehicles.

M-92: Model 2292 shotgun. The Remington Model 2292 shotgun is a double-barreled (over and under), short-barreled (what was formerly referred to as a "sawed-off"), twenty-gauge shotgun. The stock of this weapon is shorter than on other Union Space Navy shoulder-fired weapons, and the weapon is equipped with lightweight, impact-resistant furniture. The M-92 is specifically designed to be carried by smaller personnel, such as midshipmen, so that these personnel can be provided with a highly deadly yet simple, lightweight, and easy-to-shoulder firearm. Loads available for the M-92 are 00 buckshot, 0 buckshot, Foster rifled slug, and a penetrating-exploding round designed to defeat a Krag armored pressure suit. The weapon is also known to be issued to and carried by "ancient mariners," older mess personnel whose arthritis and bursitis make the recoil of other shoulder weapons difficult to tolerate.

M-1911: Model 1911 pistol. One of the two sidearms approved for use by Union Space Navy (the other being the M-62), the M-1911 is an 11.48 millimeter (sometimes referred to by the archaic designation ".45 caliber") semiautomatic, magazine-fed handgun invented by perhaps the most brilliant firearms designer in Known Space, John Moses Browning, who was active in the United States of America on Earth in the late nineteenth and early twentieth centuries. The M-1911 was the official sidearm of the armed forces of the United States during World War I, World War II, the Korean conflict, and the Vietnam conflict. It has remained in use by certain units in the United States armed forces, later by at least some units and personnel in the armed forces of United Nations of North America, United Earth, the Terran and Colonial Treaty Organization, the Earth and Colonial Confederation, and the Terran Union. The current version is only slightly different in form and mechanical arrangement from the Model 1911 A1 used by American Forces in World War II. The changes include an ambidextrous thumb safety, lightweight alloy frame (the original frame was made of ordinance steel), extended beaver tail, three-dot luminous/fiber-optic sights and a laser sight, bushingless barrel, and twelve-round magazine. As is the case with all of the current weapons based on older designs, the weapon currently issued bears little resemblance to the older weapon metallurgically, as it is constructed from alloys that are lighter, stronger, and with vastly lower friction coefficients than those available to the gunsmiths of the twentieth century, and as a result, the current weapon is 25 percent lighter than that carried in World War II, is virtually immune to corrosion, and can be fired almost indefinitely without cleaning. This weapon design continues to be used more than four hundred years after its introduction because it is powerful, accurate, well balanced, and easy to shoot. It is effective against humans and most aliens against whom humans have fought (it is especially effective against Krag), and offers an excellent combination of high stopping power with low muzzle flash and reasonable recoil.

midrats: Short for midnight rations, food made available beginning at about midnight until the mess crew begin to clear for breakfast, consisting usually of dinner leftovers, sandwich makings, snacks, cookies, and other simple but sustaining foods. As men on a naval vessel work around the clock, midrats are designed to carry them through the long hours between dinner and breakfast, during which many of them will be awake and on duty.

midshipman: A boy between the ages of eight and seventeen taken on board ship both to perform certain limited duties and to be trained to serve in the enlisted or officer ranks. Commonly referred to as mids.

midshipman trainer: A senior noncommissioned officer, typically the second-most-senior chief petty officer on the ship, in charge of the training, housing, discipline, and welfare of all midshipmen on board. Also known as Mother Goose.

MMD: *see* M-88.

***mon cher amis* (Cajun French):** My dear friend or friends (often used ironically to describe an enemy or adversary). Similar to *notre cher amis*, meaning "our dear friend(s)."

moquequa: A Brazilian stew, traditionally made in a large unglazed clay pot, consisting of saltwater fish, coconut milk, garlic, onions, coriander, and other ingredients.

Moro, Emeka: Physician and medical researcher born in Mombasa, Kenya, Earth, on 15 April 2241. Winner of the Nobel Prize for Medicine in 2295. Perhaps the foremost expert in human infectious diseases in the galaxy, Dr. Moro headed the effort to devise a treatment or preventive for the Gynophage (*see*), an effort that involved more than a million physicians and researchers on more than four hundred planets, at its peak consuming 43 percent of the interstellar communications bandwidth and 15 percent of the computing capacity available to the human race, and costing more than 300 trillion credits. When the research's early work began to indicate that neither a vaccine nor an antibody-based treatment would be more than 25 percent effective, it was Dr. Moro who personally had the insight of combining a vaccine with a set of broad-spectrum antibodies synthesized not only to match the current disease organism, but the nine most probable mutations of its external protein coat, thereby creating a vaccine that prevents infection in those who are not infected, and prevents manifestation of the disease in those who are infected but asymptomatic. It is believed that the vaccine also provides some protection to asymptomatic individuals. Dr. Moro is literally the most honored human of the last thousand years, being the namesake for one inhabited planet, two colonies on inhabited moons, five medical schools, dozens of hospitals, and hundreds of schools. For decades "Emeka" was the most popular male given name in Human Space. Dr. Moro currently lives with his spouse, famous molecular biologist Dr. James Warington, in London. For the ship, *see* Emeka Moro.

Mother Goose: The semiofficial title for the midshipman trainer (*see*).

N2: Naval Intelligence Staff, the equivalent of G2 in the old Army General Staff system.

***Nevi'im* (Hebrew):** The second main division of the *Tanakh* (Hebrew Bible), coming after the *Torah* (Teachings or the Law) and the *Ketuvim* (Writings). The *Nevi'im* consists of the books (as divided in the Hebrew Bible) of Joshua, Judges, Samuel, Kings, Isaiah, Jeremiah, Ezekiel, Hosea, Joel, Amos, Obadiah, Jonah, Micah, Nahum, Habakkuk, Zephaniah, Haggai, Zechariah, and Malachi. It includes the story of David and Goliath, which can be found in the book of Samuel.

Ning-Braha Expedition (2037): The first interstellar military operation undertaken by the human race. In January 2033, the Ning-Braha deployed forces to Luna (the Earth's moon) and began to construct bases there as part of their lead-up to an attack with the objective of conquering Earth and enslaving humankind. Human astronomers detected the aliens' activities on the lunar surface on 14 January 2033, resulting in the dispatching by the United Nations of three separate diplomatic expeditions in March 2033 to establish a dialogue with the aliens. The Ning-Braha destroyed all three vessels before they got within 10,000 kilometers of Luna. On 25 March 2033, high-resolution imaging of the lunar surface showed that the aliens were constructing an enormous mass driver, apparently for the purpose of bombarding Earth. Upon collapse of the now-discredited UN, the United States and Canada, the European Union, and the China-Japan Alliance signed the Earth Space Forces Convention of 2033, forming the United Earth Space Forces (UESF, *see*). On 16 July 2034, seven Orion-type gunships launched from Earth and managed to destroy the Ning-Braha forces. A follow-up expedition obtained several Ning-Braha computer cores and starship debris, allowing Earth experts to determine the location of the Ning-Braha homeworld; develop graviton-containment fusion, the jump drive, and many other advanced technologies; as well as determine that the Ning-Braha would likely continue to send expeditions to the Sol System until Earth was conquered. Accordingly, after a crash naval construction program, the UESF launched a 162-ship armada, known as the Ning-Braha Expedition, in 2037. The UESF was victorious in the resulting First Interstellar War. At the end of the war, under the Ieyoub-Duke-Thompson Treaty, the Ning-Braha ceded all conquered worlds back to their native inhabitants, disbanded their navy, abandoned all colonies outside of a six-light-year radius of their homeworld, and were confined in perpetuity to a six-light-year radius quarantine zone that is maintained and guarded by the Union Space Navy to this day.

***nique á rats (les)* (Cajun French):** Nests of rats.

officer rank abbreviations: GADM—Grand Admiral (five stars)
FADM—Fleet Admiral (four stars)
VADM—Vice Admiral (three stars)
RADM—Rear Admiral (two stars)
CMRE—Commodore (one star)
CAPT—Captain
CMDR—Commander
LCDR—Lieutenant Commander
LT—Lieutenant
LTJG—Lieutenant Junior Grade
ENSN—Ensign

One MC (*also written* 1MC): One Main Circuit, the primary voice channel on a naval vessel, allowing a properly authorized speaker to be heard over every audio transducer in the ship. The term dates back to the Saltwater Navy.

PC-4: Patrol Craft, Type 4. A sublight-only high-speed patrol and light attack craft used for system and planetary defense as well as for light intrasystem escort duties. Length: 72 meters. Beam: 5 meters. Crew: two officers, ten enlisted. Armament: 1 75-gigawatt pulse-cannon, six Raytheon-Hughes Talon (*see*) ship-to-ship missiles. Top speed: .97c.

pennant: In a multivessel group commanded by an officer below the rank of commodore, the vessel from which the group is commanded and in which the overall commander of the group is stationed.

percom: A wrist-carried communication, computing, and control device worn by all naval personnel when on duty.

Posident: POSitive IDENTification.

pulse-cannon: A ship-mounted weapon that fires a pulse of plasma diverted from the ship's main fusion reactor and accelerated to between .85 and .95 c by magnetic coils. The plasma is held in a concentrated "bolt" by a magnetic field generated by a compact, liquid helium-cooled, fusion cell–powered emitter unit inserted in the bolt just as it is about to leave the cannon tube. When the emitter stops generating the field—either because it has consumed its coolant and is vaporized by the plasma, the timer turns the emitter off at a set range, or the bolt strikes a target thus destroying the emitter—the bolt loses cohesion and expands explosively. Pulse-cannon are rated based on the power output of their coil assemblies, which determines how much plasma can be fired in a given pulse; the explosive power of a pulse-cannon bolt, measured in kilotons, is roughly 1/300 of the power rating in gigawatts. Accordingly, a maximum-power bolt from a pulse-cannon with a 150-gigawatt rating will be approximately 0.5 kilotons. If the firing ship is traveling at a high fraction of lightspeed, the speed of the plasma pulse can exceed .99 c.

quantum orbital manipulation: An advanced materials technology that allows the reconfiguration of atomic electron shells, thereby permitting the combination of elements that would not otherwise be able to form compounds, as well as arrangement of the molecules created thereby into pseudo-polymeric matrices to form materials far stronger and more dense than possible through conventional chemical and metallurgical processes.

Raven: A large antiship missile carried by Union warships. Much larger than the Talon (*see*) and with a higher top speed, the Raven accelerates more slowly, is less nimble, and is more vulnerable to point-defense systems and countermeasures than the Talon due to its larger size. Manufactured by Gould-Martin-Marietta Naval Aerospace Corporation, the Raven finds its target with both passive and active multimodal sensor homing and then inflicts its damage with a 1.5-megaton fixed-yield fusion warhead powerful enough to destroy all but the largest enemy vessels and to cripple any known enemy ship. Ravens are equipped with an innovative system known as Cooperative Interactive Logic Mode (CILM—pronounced "Kill 'em"). When more than one Raven is launched against the same target, CILM causes the missiles to communicate with one another and attack the target jointly, closing on the enemy from multiple vectors to render defense more difficult and exploding at the same instant to inflict the most damage.

***regardez donc* (Cajun French):** An expression of awe and amazement, roughly equivalent to an extremely emphatic "wow." Literally translates as "look at that."

registry numbers: The unique identification number assigned to each warship, consisting of its three-letter class code followed by a number.

Richthofens: Fancy maneuvers. From Baron Manfred von Richthofen, better known as the "Red Baron," the famous World War I German fighter pilot.

Robinson, Will: (*see* Will Robinson).

RRS: Royal Rashidian Ship. Used to identify a Rashidian naval vessel, much as USS (Union Space Ship) precedes the name of a Union naval vessel.

Saltwater Navy: A navy comprised of oceangoing ships as opposed to one comprised of ships that travel in space. In the Union Space Navy, the term is particularly used to refer to the navies on Earth, the officers and traditions of which formed much of the basis for the United Earth Spaces Forces in 2034 (the navies of the United States, Canada, Great Britain, and Japan were particularly important).

scones: Small, single-serving cakes, usually lightly sweet and baked in flat pans, traditionally a part of English Tea refreshment, often served with cucumber finger sandwiches. Believed to have originated in Scotland. Likely an acquired taste, like cucumber finger sandwiches.

Scotty: The traditional nickname for a warship's chief of engineering, irrespective of the national origin of his ancestors. The nickname is believed to have originated with the *Star Trek* franchise, as "Scotty" was the nickname of Lieutenant Commander Montgomery Scott, the chief engineer of the fictitious USS *Enterprise.* As the character became incorporated into spacer lore, it was said that Scotty could repair a fusion reactor with nothing but duct tape and a lady's hairpin, drank Scotch like it was weak green tea, and defied hostile aliens with icy ultimatums articulated in a rich Highland burr.

SDMF: Self-Destruct Mechanism, Fusion. A fusion munition carried on all Union warships prior to the Battle of Han VII for the purpose of destroying the vessel as a last resort to prevent it from falling into enemy hands.

Senate: Generally and historically, this term refers to the upper chamber of a bicameral legislature of either a state of the United States of America or of the United States of America itself. In current usage this term refers to the Union Senate, also called the "New Senate" (although this usage is becoming less common), one of the two bodies of the Union Parliament (the other being the Union Assembly). The Senate consists of five members each chosen by the Congress of each of the Estates: The People (the "Voters"), Agriculture (the "Farmers"), Manufacturing (the "Makers"), Shipping and Transportation (the "Movers"), Academia and Science (the "Thinkers"), Extractive Industries (the "Miners"), the Information Media (the "Reporters"), Retail and Consumer Sales (the "Storekeepers"), Lending, Deposits, and Investments (the "Bankers"), Architecture, Construction, and Civil Engineering (the "Builders"), Public Employees (the "Governors"), the Armed Forces (the "Warriors"), Health Care (the "Doctors"), Attorneys, Brokers, Accountants, and similar professionals (the "Lawyers"), and Publishing, Cinematic and Broadcast Tridvid, and Trideo Game Design and Sales (the "Entertainers"). The New Senate, with representation based on the Estates, replaced the Old Senate, with membership consisting of two members from each Major World or Inhabited System, after the Revolt of the Estates, in which the Estates determined that a government in which representation was based on population and locality failed to reflect the economic communities that had arisen in Human Space and that such a government tended to impose unfair burdens on some estates in favor of others. Accordingly, all changes in taxation and declarations of war, as well as significant changes in the Union budget, require the unanimous concurrence of each Estate represented in the Senate.

SEUR: Safety and Equipment Utilization Regulations (the acronym is pronounced "sewer"). Regulations promulgated by the navy governing the appropriate use parameters for virtually every imaginable vessel, device, system, or piece of equipment issued by the navy.

simhead: A person who spends inordinate time or energy playing military and other simulation games, particularly such a person who obtains simulation software by illegal means.

six: Shorthand for "six o'clock position," or directly astern.

SOP: Standard Operating Procedure.

Sparks: The traditional nickname for a warship communications officer.

squeaker: A particularly young or puny midshipman. Also squeekie, deck dodger, panel puppy, and hatch hanger (the last for their habit of standing in the hatches while holding the rim, thereby blocking the way).

SSR: Staff Support Room. One of several compartments located in the general vicinity of the CIC, containing between three and twenty-four men whose duty it is to provide support to one CIC department each by performing detailed monitoring and analysis of the sensors or equipment for which that department is responsible at a level impossible for one or two people assigned that function in CIC.

Standard: The official language of the Union; Standard also serves as the official language or a widely used second language on virtually every non-Union human world. Standard is derived mostly from English, which was the most widely spoken second language on Earth and was the language of international science, commerce, shipping, and aviation in 2034, when the first human space forces were formed.

SVR: Space Vehicle Registry. Usually used to refer to the database containing registry information for every space vehicle known to the Union, including information for vehicles of friendly powers who share registry information with the Union Space Vehicle Registration Bureau. The Union Space Navy maintains the classified SVR database containing the registry information for all naval vehicles, as well as the ones on file with the Registration Bureau.

SWACS: Space Warning and Control System. An integrated sensor, computer, and command/communications/control suite placed on various warships to provide an exceptionally high level of sensor coverage and detail and to coordinate the defense against attacking vessels.

synchrotron radiation: Radiation emitted as a result of the acceleration of super-relativistic charged particles through a magnetic field.

Talon: The primary antiship missile carried by Union warships. Manufactured by Raytheon-Hughes Space Combat Systems, the Talon is an extremely fast, stealthy, and agile missile, with both passive and active multimodal sensor homing and a 5–150-kiloton variable-yield fusion warhead. The Talon is designed to elude and penetrate enemy countermeasures and point-defense systems, use its onboard artificial intelligence and high-resolution active sensors to find a "soft spot" on the enemy ship, and then detonate its warhead in a location designed to inflict the most damage. One Talon is capable of obliterating ships up to frigate size and of putting ships up to heavy-cruiser size out of commission. Against most targets with functioning point-defense systems, the Talon is a better choice than the heavier Raven (*see*). Beginning in February 2315, Talons were equipped with Cooperative Interactive Logic Mode, a technology adopted from the Raven (*see*).

Terran Union: The common name for the Union of Earth and Terran Settled Worlds, a federal constitutional republic consisting of Earth and (as of January 2315) 518 of the total 611 worlds known to be settled by human beings. Often simply referred to as the "Union." Formed in 2155 upon the collapse of the Earth and Colonial Confederation (commonly referred to as the "Earth Confederation" or simply the "Confederation"), resulting from the Revolt of the Estates, which began in 2154. The territorial space controlled by the Union has a shape roughly like that of a watermelon 2500 light-years long and 800 light-years wide, aligned lengthwise through the Orion-Cygnus Arm of the Milky Way galaxy. Population, approximately 205 billion. With the exception of the Krag Hegemony, the Union is the most populous and largest political entity in Known Space, as well as the most economically successful.

TF: Task Force. A group of warships assembled for a particular mission or "task." Distinguished from a "fleet" in that a fleet is a permanent or very long-lived formation usually assigned to a particular system or region of space, while a task force is assembled for a limited period of time and then disbanded. Task forces are generally designated by letters of the alphabet, e.g., Task Force TD or Tango Delta. Units may be spun off from a task force; these are usually designated by the name of the task force followed by a color or a number, e.g., Task Force Bravo Victor Seven or Task Force Galaxy Foxtrot Green.

Type: When applied to warships, this term refers to the general category and function of the vessel, as opposed to class, which refers to a specific design or production run of vessels within a type. The most common types of warship are, in decreasing order of size: carrier, battleship, battlecruiser, cruiser, frigate, destroyer, corvette, and patrol vessel. There are, of course, other types of naval vessels that are not categorized as warships, including tanker, tender, tug, hospital ship, troop carrier, landing ship, cargo vessel, etc.

UESF: United Earth Space Forces. The international military arm formed in 2034 by the United States, Canada, the European Union, and the China-Japan Alliance to retake the Earth's moon from the Ning-Braha who had occupied it, presumably as a prelude to a planned invasion of Earth. The UESF drew its personnel primarily from the navies and air forces of the founding powers and drew its command structure, regulations, traditions, and other institutional foundations mainly from their saltwater navies. Nevertheless, the UESF is a joint force that regards itself as the successor to all of the armed forces of all of the nations of the Earth. The Ning-Braha technology captured by the UESF in this campaign was the catalyst for mankind's colonization of the stars. The UESF is the direct institutional ancestor of the Union Space Navy.

***unge kamerater*:** (Norwegian) Young comrades.

Union: *see* Terran Union.

Union Forces Voicecom Alphabet (or UFVA): Because letters of the alphabet as normally spoken can be easily confused over the voice channels (for example, *B* and *D* sound very much alike), military and police forces have long used standardized sets of words to stand for the letters of the alphabet with which the words begin. The UFVA is used universally by all Union Naval, System Guard, marine, and other forces, as well as by civilian space vessels and Space Traffic Controllers in Union Space and by most non-Union human worlds. The UFVA is derived, in turn, from the alphabetic system introduced by the North Atlantic Treaty Organization on Earth in the 1950s. Only a few letters have been changed: *Golf* to *Galaxy* (the game of golf having become extinct centuries ago), *November* to *Nebula* (the month being associated with some of the bloodiest and least decisive battles of the First Interstellar War), *Quebec* to *Quarter* (the official pronunciation, "kay beck," leading many civilian operators to believe that the designator stood for *K* rather than *Q*), and *Yankee* to *Yardarm* (the association of "Yankee" with the United States of America was deemed to be inappropriate in an alphabet used on an interplanetary basis). The alphabet is as follows:

Alfa (not "Alpha" because some will mispronounce the "ph")
Bravo
Charlie
Delta
Echo
Foxtrot
Galaxy
Hotel
India
Juliett
Kilo (pronounced "kee low")
Lima (pronounced "lee ma")
Mike
Nebula
Oscar
Papa
Quarter
Sierra
Tango
Uniform
Victor
Whiskey
X-Ray
Yardarm
Zulu

URSF: Union Reserve and Support Forces. A space service allied with and under the control of the navy, but under the direct command of its own admiral-director, who holds the joint rank of vice admiral URSF and USN. The navy's tankers, supply vessels, hospital ships, tenders, waste-transport vessels, harbor tugs, and fleet tugs, as well as the personnel who man them, are all part of the URSF. The same is true of remote R & R stations, supply depots, fuel dumps, deuterium-processing plants, and similar facilities. Most of the senior officers in the URSF are former naval officers who are either too old or too badly injured for frontline service but who are still able to go to space.

von Braun, Werner: Born: 23 March 1912; died: 16 June 1977. German-American rocket engineer best known for leading the development of the German A-4 rocket (commonly known as the V-2), humanity's first operational ballistic missile and the first man-made object to reach outer space, as well as for leading the team that developed for the United States the Saturn series of space-launch vehicles. This series included the Saturn V, which propelled the Apollo spacecraft to the Earth's moon in a series of memorable missions extending from December 1968 (*Apollo 8*) to December 1972 (*Apollo 17*).

watch: The period of time that a member of the crew who is designated as a watch stander mans his assigned watch station. Also, the designation of the section of the crew to which the watch stander belongs. On Union warships, there are three watches, usually known as blue, gold, and white. They stand watch on the following schedule:

first watch: 2000–0000 (1 blue) (2 gold) (3 white)
middle watch: 0000–0400 (1 gold) (2 white) (3 blue)
morning watch: 0400–0800 (1 white) (2 blue) (3 gold)
forenoon watch: 0800–1200 (1 blue) (2 gold) (3 white)

afternoon watch: 1200–1600 (1 gold) (2 white) (3 blue)
first dog watch: 1600–1800 (1 white) (2 blue) (3 gold)
second dog watch: 1800–2000 (1 blue) (2 gold) (3 white)

The captain and the XO do not stand a watch. Rather, all officers other than the CO, XO, and CMO serve as "Officer of the Deck," serving as the officer in charge of minute-to-minute operations in CIC when neither the CO nor the XO is in CIC. Officers of the Deck stand watch for eight-hour shifts on a rotating basis.

Will Robinson: The traditional naval nickname given to the youngest or the smallest of the squeakers or new junior midshipmen in service at any given time on board a warship. The name is taken from the name of a character in the 1960s television series *Lost in Space.*

wort: The liquid obtained when malt is cracked and steeped in hot water. Hops and yeast are added to the wort, then fermented to make beer.

XO: Executive Officer. The second-in-command of any warship.

Yankee search: Active sensor sweep, i.e., a sweep in which the ship broadcasts sensor beams and detects the reflections from objects in the vicinity, as opposed to the normal sensor mode, which is passive detection of emissions from contacts. A Yankee search omni is a sweep in all directions around the ship, as opposed to a Yankee search down a particular bearing or bearings or of a given zone. The term dates back to Saltwater Navy submarines, but is otherwise of obscure origin.

Z: (when appended to a time notation) Zulu time. Standard Union Coordinated Time. So that all USN vessels can conduct coordinated operations, they all operate on Zulu Time, which is, for all intents and purposes, the same as Greenwich Mean

Time—mean solar time as measured from the prime meridian in Greenwich, England, on Earth in the Sol System. When any other time system is used in any naval communication (such as the Standard time of a planet on which operations are taking place or local time at some place on a planet), that fact is specifically noted.

ACKNOWLEDGMENTS

I owe the same debts and hold the same gratitude for this book as for the first two in this series, "with interest," given that they have enjoyed some modest success with the reading public.

Mrs. Mildred Hobbs, whose inspired teaching I recognized in this section of my last novel, has since passed away. I hope that if she turns her attention to these books, she doesn't find too much that cries too loudly for her skillfully used red pen.

The contributions of conceptual editor Michael Shohl are particularly important in this book as compared to the two that went before. I am thankful for his skill, creativity, hard work, and professionalism in bringing this book to print. The delivery of this baby was particularly difficult, and he was a good set of hands to have in the delivery room.

I am also thankful to Jason Kirk at 47North, who lined up and coordinated the efforts of copy editors, the cover artist, book designer, and all the other professionals whose efforts need to be brought forth between the delivery of a copyedit-ready manuscript and publication. As a former Law Review editor, I know the hard work that goes into a publication after the author is done with it. I have seen the final product in the form of the last two books and know that my message would not go nearly as far or be received nearly as well were they not delivered by such a well-spoken messenger.

Finally, as always, I convey my deepest thanks to my ever-patient wife, Kathleen. Her creative contributions to this series are too numerous to count or articulate and go far beyond being the motivating force that called them into being at the beginning. Further, her acceptance of my uncounted eccentricities and the other traits of character and personality that make living and working with me so very challenging are not only an astonishing achievement in personal forbearance, but are a debt I can never repay. All of which does not even begin to touch her other gifts of kindness, generosity, and wisdom. For this and for everything else she does, I offer these feeble but heartfelt words of thanks.

ABOUT THE AUTHOR

Kathleen Honsinger 2013

H. Paul Honsinger is a retired attorney with lifelong interests in space exploration, military history, firearms, and international relations. He was born and raised in Lake Charles, Louisiana, and is a graduate of Lake Charles High School, the University of Michigan in Ann Arbor, and Louisiana State University Law School in Baton Rouge. Honsinger has practiced law with major firms on the Gulf Coast and in Phoenix, Arizona, and most recently had his own law office in Lake Havasu City, Arizona. He has also taught debate, worked as a car salesman, and counseled teenagers. He is a cancer survivor, having been in remission from advanced-stage Hodgkin's lymphoma since January 1997. He currently lives in rural Mohave County, Arizona, with his beloved wife, Kathleen (who is also known as fantasy/romance author Laura Jo Phillips), stepson, and two highly eccentric cats—all the while cheering on his daughter, who is a first-year college music student.

This is his third novel.

Keep up-to-date on the future exploits of Max Robichaux and Ibrahim Sahin by following Paul's blog at http://hpaulhonsinger.com.

You can also follow Paul on Facebook at https://www.facebook.com/honsingerscifi and on Twitter at @HPaulHonsinger.

Readers can contact the author at honsingermilitaryscifi@gmail.com.